IF THE DRESS FITS

A CRICKET CROSBY CAPER BOOK 2

LIZ TALLEY

Copyright © 2022 by Liz Talley

All rights reserved.

No part of this book may be reproduced in any form or by any electronic or mechanical means, including information storage and retrieval systems, without written permission from the author, except for the use of brief quotations in a book review.

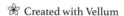 Created with Vellum

For every person who isn't afraid to leave behind the old and grab hold of the new

HELLO, AGAIN!

Dear Reader:

I have no intention of writing a follow up to *Deconstructed*. My publisher was only interested in stand alone books, and so I moved on to other ideas for books I wanted to write. But I kept getting emails, reviews, and requests clamoring for more Cricket and Ruby! Then my mind did what writer minds do - it started down the "what if" path that leads to a new book.

So here she is! Another misadventure with the most fashionable of gals! I hope you enjoy! You pretty much made this happen!

Liz

1

Cricket

I WAS REPLAYING the YouTube video for repairing a sink for the twelfth time when the sound of someone calling my name scared the bejeezus out of me, causing me to conk my head on the trap and drop the big wrench thing on my thumb.

"Oww!" I yelled, immediately sticking the appendage in my mouth—which was gross considering attempting to replace a pipe was nasty business.

"What in the world are you doin' down there?" Marguerite, aka my mother dearest, asked.

She must have bent over, too ladylike to shout the question, though I could see only the toes of the Roger Vivier everyday pumps she preferred.

I wriggled out from under the sink in the kitchen of Printemps, my upscale antiques store, and rubbed my head while drying my damaged digit on my shirt. Which took true talent. "Knock next time, why don't cha?"

"I did knock. Three times," my visitor said imperiously, tidy as usual in her pressed slacks, silk blouse, and painted-on eyebrows. This was my mother. A true Southern monarch. And I was her royal subject. Full stop.

"Well, I didn't hear you." I sat up, grateful that the pain from the lumps and bumps was already fading. Since it was my mother, muscle memory kicked in and I brushed a self-conscious hand over the flannel work shirt that, come to think of it, was making me sweat in a rather unladylike fashion. I peeled it off, lifting my hair off my neck. "I was trying to fix the little spray nozzle tube thing, but then I saw there was another drip from the main pipe. It's really damp and smells horrible. So—"

"Good heavens, Cricket, call a plumber. Look at your nails—they are a wreck. And you're wallowing around on the floor like a... a..." Marguerite made that face, the one your mama makes when you cut bangs or paint your toenails turquoise. Or maybe that was just *my* mama.

"A what?" I prompted.

"Never mind." Marguerite squinched her eyes the way she did when I tried on bathing suits for her one time. Trust me, *one* time had been plenty. "However, your bosom is hanging out for all the world to see."

"Or just you. No one else is here. Well, Ruby's upstairs." I looked down at my tank. So the girls were sorta spotlighted by the tight Lycra tank and the expensive bra that salesperson at Lily Ann's Lingerie had proclaimed did *all the work you need to get the good jewelry*. Not that I was interested in getting jewelry. At least not until I was officially a free woman. "I called Larry. He's backed up and can't get here until next week. Then I found this video and thought I would try myself, but I obviously lack that particular skill set. I mean, I had to google what a channel lock was."

I tried to rise gracefully from the worn linoleum floor but failed, which meant my tank top bobbed with the motion. But I wasn't covering up no matter how much my mama made that face because it was September and the coolish front that had blown through North Louisiana that morning had already dissipated like a toot in the wind.

I don't, as a rule, wear flannel unless it's cute pajamas or something, but Ruby's stud muffin cousin Griff had lent me the shirt in the spring when I rode on the back of his motorcycle after one of our Blue Moon Sting Posse meetings—the BMSP were a ragtag bunch committed to helping me catch my husband and his dirtbag accomplice who were swindling my friends and neighbors.

The Blue Moon Posse's meetups had tapered off with summer busyness and the start of high school for my just-turned-fourteen-year-old daughter Julia Kate. I missed my interesting friends and couldn't wait until Juke, my assistant Ruby's cousin (who just happened to be a professional private investigator), found out that I had followed through with my vow to get my own private investigator's license. Only a few more weeks and I would be able to assist Juke in cases when he needed extra help. After all, I had proved to be dang good at catching dirtbags. I'd be the perfect part-time private eye.

"Cricket, I know you prize your new identity as an almost-single woman, and I know you're a competent businesswoman—"

"Wait! Was that a compliment?" I faked astonishment.

Marguerite narrowed her eyes and looked around at the messy kitchen of my Shreveport antiques store, housed in a historic home nestled among boutiques and bakeries scattered down Line Avenue. "My point is that you cannot allow your ego to overshadow common sense. I will call Larry and remind him who employed his mother for over thirty years and who still sends him a tin of nuts every Christmas. Loyalty means something. Or used to."

"Mama, do you know how hard it is to get some of those parts these days? He's working through a ten-page list of customers." I dusted off my knees and wished immediately that it was a regular business day for the store and not Monday, the only weekday we were closed. I tilted my head, listening, and sure enough, the hum of Ruby's sewing machine continued. My assistant spent most Mondays upstairs working on her line of clothing while I puttered around downstairs. "It's fine. Do not be the person who thinks the world owes you. Larry will get to me when he can. Besides, I'm not sure a tin of nuts gets as much as you think these days."

Marguerite sniffed, shook her head (without a single strand of hair moving), and shrugged a thin shoulder. "I suppose you're right. Throwing my weight around would be... I can't think of the word."

"Douchey?"

My mother's eyes flashed. "Don't be common."

"Well, Mama, I find that I rather like common." I gave her an impudent smile and pulled a chair from beneath the Shaker set with the chipped insert. I moved a few catalogs out of the way along with a ginger jar that had a crack marring the cloisonné. "Would you like a cup of tea?"

"No. I would *like* a martini, but it's not an appropriate hour, so I'll have exactly nothing." Marguerite frowned. "And what's wrong with nuts? I like a good nut tin at Christmas."

I suppressed a smile. I really shouldn't irritate my mother, but it was such fun, especially since she'd lightened up. Okay, not exactly lightened, but the woman had cracked a joke or two and stopped wearing her bra to bed.

Marguerite moved purposefully toward the chair. "I don't need refreshments. I merely came by to tell you that I talked to Coraline about Ruby this morning."

Frogs jumped in my belly. I had been waiting for months for my mother to broach the subject of Ruby's dress designs with her younger sister who worked as the global creative director for *Vogue*. Ruby had surprised us all with a talent for taking apart damaged couture and redesigning the pieces into something marvelous. She had been steadily working toward a collection but needed to break out of Shreveport. My mother's sister was the ticket, but Marguerite had declared that she had to pick the right time to ask—my aunt didn't dawdle with anything less than fabulous. So my mother had kept me waiting on approaching Coraline, probably because she had a love/hate relationship with her sister that mostly had to do with the fact they were polar opposites in every way. "And...?"

"She has invited Ruby to New York City."

My heart thumped. "What does that mean? Like, for good?"

Marguerite settled herself into the proffered chair, shrugging a shoulder again. "I think it's more for a 'get to know you' visit and to take a peek at a few pieces of Deconstructed. So Ruby will need to wear her most fabulous designs."

Whew, it wasn't for good. But then I immediately felt horrible for thinking that way. Ruby deserved a shot at kicking booty in the fashion world. She belonged in New York City, making her dreams come true. "Well, that's something. I think Aunt Coraline will like Ruby. Maybe help her a little?"

"Perhaps. As you know, I think Ruby is highly talented. That's why I invested in Deconstructed. And even Nancy is inviting some of her influential Dallas friends to the event next month. But I can't do what Cora can. New York Fashion Week is in a few weeks, so it's a bit last minute, but Cora must fly to Paris for some marketing something or other right afterward and then is spending a few weeks in Italy. It's now or wait until spring."

I plopped down across from her. "But we wanted Aunt Coraline to come *here*. Ruby's fashion show is in late October. She doesn't have time to go to New York City."

"*Who* doesn't have time to go to New York City?" Ruby asked from the kitchen doorway.

"You, dear girl." Marguerite glanced down at her perfectly polished nails with a little smile. "My sister Coraline has issued an invitation to Fashion Week. She'll be hosting you and me at the shows and events. In a few weeks' time."

Ruby stopped. She had a plastic storage container in her hand, no doubt full of her gran's low-carb Weight Watchers fare. I had been sharing recipes with Ruby's grandmother on the Shreveport-Bossier WW Crushing It page, and she often sent the leftovers to Ruby since her son Jimbo fussed about all the "rabbit food" in the house. My once somewhat shy assistant looked like a different person these days. Ruby's hair was longer —a riot of curls—and she wore her own designs. Today was a pair of black satin pants, a tank with light pink beading, and a tribal-looking print blazer. No one else but Ruby could have pulled off the look.

But then my mother's words registered. "Wait, *you* and Ruby?"

Marguerite's mouth twitched into something that could have been a triumphant smile. "Well, darling, you're taking those classes, though I have no clue why. Besides, I've not visited my baby sister in ages. Now that we're free to move about the country, I'll be the perfect chaperone for Ruby."

Ruby blinked a few times. "I can't—I mean, how can I leave? I have class, and I'm barely going to finish the pieces I need for the iSpy show as it is."

"It will be a long weekend, dear girl. Not a cruise on the

Queen Mary. We can fly up on a Thursday and return on a Monday." Marguerite looked at her nails again and then at Ruby. "This *is* your career, correct?"

Fighting words. Line drawn. Gauntlet thrown.

Ruby glanced at me.

I made the "it's your call" face.

Then she twisted her lips, thoughts no doubt galloping a mile a nanosecond. "Well, yeah, but did you say *fly*?"

My mother considered that. Her pause told me a good deal. "Are you afraid of flying?"

"I don't know. I've never flown anywhere." Ruby set the container in front of me and pressed her fingers to the table, a true sign of being unsettled.

"Well, flying is simple. Not as simple as it used to be, of course. Back when I was a young woman, flying was more glamorous. You wore pretty clothes, and they gave you actual food on the airplane. It was like going to dinner in the skies. Now people wear their pajamas. Disgraceful if you ask me, but no one does because if they did, I would require people wear proper attire."

"And she's a riot at parties," I quipped.

Ruby smiled. "So no pajamas on the plane?"

"Good heavens no," Marguerite said.

"Do you want to go?" I asked Ruby, half hoping her answer would be no. Which was wrong of me. And part of it was because I had to stay home. Who wanted to miss out on New York City and Fashion Week? All those parties, delicious food, and celebrity stalking—eh—spotting. And I would be stuck here, learning about dumb laws and databases. For some reason, completing the course to be a private investigator sounded more fun than it was. When I had taken *The Gumshoe's Guide to Private Investigations* to class to show my instructor the inspiration for getting my license, he'd chuckled and suggested maybe I was glamorizing being a private investigator. But he had never worn a wig and kissed a hunky tow truck driver while spying on a mark either. Catching cheaters could be sorta fun.

Ruby swallowed and glanced out the window where the leaves of the pecan tree fluttered in the afternoon breeze. "I don't know. Yes. Maybe."

"Of course you're going." Marguerite looked at Ruby like she had suggested wearing white after Labor Day. "This will be your introduction into high fashion, and Cora is the right person to do it. We can stay with her and her lady friend. They have a lovely place on the Upper East Side."

"Mama, Jill is Auntie Coraline's wife. You don't have to call her a *lady friend*." I gave her a look because we'd had this conversation before. Marguerite is old-fashioned with a capital O— which is why she and her younger sister barely tolerate one another at times. Coraline was born progressive, creative, and ready to run from the South before she even walked.

Marguerite squared her shoulders, a steeling of herself. "I am aware. I went to their wedding. So anyway, you will adore Cora and her *wife*, Jill. They're such good hostesses. A piece about a dinner party they gave was even in the *New Yorker*."

Ruby looked at me, and I shrugged. My mama was trying, bless her. I smiled. "You should go, Ruby. When opportunity knocks, you answer the door. And Mama will be on her best behavior. Just don't take her back to the sex store."

"Cricket!" my mother yelped, slamming a hand on the table. "You know very well that I didn't realize it was a place that sold inappropriate items. The advert said it was a poetry reading."

"*Lysistrata's Delights* didn't give it away?" I tried not to laugh. *Tried* was the key word.

Ruby's brown eyes danced. "Wait, what?"

"*Lysistrata* is an ancient Greek play, for heaven's sake," my mother said imperiously, turning a delicious shade of shrimp. But I was unable to relay the story about Mama thinking she was going to a literary reading and ending up in a sex store in Chelsea because a knock sounded at the back door.

"Jeez... we need people to come to the front door and buy things." I laughed as I went to the door.

And there stood my favorite tow truck driver in all his rugged, grumpy glory. I hadn't seen Griffin Moon in a few weeks, though we had played Words with Friends just last night, and I have to say my heart did a little disco dancing because he *was* rather dishy. "Well, hey there, stranger."

His gaze dipped, and I remembered that I was in dishabille, as my mother would call it. Maybe that bra *was* earning its ridiculous price.

"Hey there, Cricket. Is Ruby working? She's not answering her phone."

I opened the door wider to display Ruby, who stood next to my mother. Griff hesitated when he saw Marguerite—she'd sent him some beard oil she found on sale at TJ Maxx. Giving him that from my mother had been a little awkward. Griff might or might not now be afraid of her. Or perhaps he didn't like beard oil.

"Mrs. Quinney." Griff nodded his big head her way before fixing those stormy gray-blue eyes on Ruby. "You gotta minute, coz?"

Ruby opened the microwave and popped in the Tupperware. "Sure. And I didn't answer my phone because I'm working."

I wanted to know why he was here, but I couldn't out and out stand there and snoop, so I closed the door after her. Wasn't my business. But I wanted it to be. Which was silly because Griff and I weren't anything other than friends. That's why we played that game together. Duh.

"Hmm," my mother said from behind me. I might or might not have been trying to catch a glimpse of Griff from between the kitchen curtains.

I spun around. "What?"

She lifted her perfect eyebrows. "You know that he's not the guy for you."

"Who said I want him to be?"

"Your body language. I remember when you were this way over Clayton Barr. You mooned about, wearing short skirts and bright lipstick. Wrote his name all over your nice planner. That's why I took you to Dr. Porter for birth control."

"I never slept with Clayton. And I'm not sleeping with Griff. I'm sleeping with no one. I'm technically still married. At least until next week." My divorce from my ex-banker husband, Scott, would be finalized in just a week, and the money the ass had stolen from our savings and retirement would be restored from the frozen offshore accounts within the next few months. The financial stuff had been a tangle, but my cooperation with the federal authorities in the arrest of Scott and the brains behind the Ponzi scheme, Donner Walker, had greased a few wheels, and the feds had managed to get a federal judge to review the case sooner rather than later. My husband had done some singing and had managed to make a deal with the government for time served along with probation for his role in feeding clients to Donner Walker and accepting bribes in exchange for his testimony. Scott was recently out of jail and working an insurance job part-time for a friend who felt sorry for him. I was allowing supervised visits for Julia Kate's sake. Personally, I would be happy to never see him again, but my daughter needed her father, even if he was a rat fink.

And me? Finally, after months of therapy, uncertainty, and, yeah, a bit of grieving over what I had lost, a blank slate stretched before me.

What would I do? Who would I be?

Something exciting and scary had lingered in those questions for a while. But I had come up with a solution for my emptying nest and next level—moonlighting as a private investigator. I was talented at sussing out injustices, and if I could help women like me catch their husbands or locate the person who'd swindled their elderly grandmother, well, that would be very satisfying.

My mother sighed. "I can't say I'm sad to see your marriage over, but I *am* sorry your husband ended up being such an ass. Scott always bothered me with his slickness and oozy charm, but then again, I couldn't really rely on my own instincts. I stayed married to your father for fifteen years, after all."

I never knew Scott raised questions in my mother. She'd always been, well, not nice to him, but accepting as she could be. Which meant she let him have one of her accounts at his bank and let him carve the turkey at Thanksgiving.

Ruby came back inside, and Griff followed. They both looked worried.

"What's wrong?" I asked before I could stop myself.

Ruby looked at Griff. He sucked in a breath. "Juke's missing."

Alarm curled in me. "What? Missing for how long?"

"Not long. A few days. Not that concerning except... it could mean that he's backsliding." Ruby looked disheartened. She'd championed her cousin's recovery.

"He's been staying sober, but yesterday would have been his and Loralee's thirtieth wedding anniversary. He said he was coming by my mom's for Jimbo's birthday dinner but didn't show. Not answering the phone. His truck isn't at his office. No one has seen or heard from him." Griff delivered this with stoicism, but I could tell he was bothered by not being able to locate Juke.

"Have you reported it to the authorities?" my mother asked.

"No, ma'am. Not yet. I figure he went off on a bender. That's what he usually does."

"Maybe I could help," I said, thinking about all I had learned at the private investigation course on tracking down missing persons.

"Nothing much to do. I'm going to go comb the bars close to his house and office. Maybe try some of his old stomping grounds." Griff looked out the kitchen window.

I followed his gaze. The Harley sat parked by my grandmother's red convertible. Yes, I had taken to driving the vintage roadster more. That shiny red car reminded me that I was alive. Riding on Griff's motorcycle had given me the same feeling—crackling with energy and appreciative that I got to wrap my arms around those abs.

"I'll go with you to look for him. If we don't find him, we can call the police and make a report," I said.

"You don't have to do that." Griff looked surprised and maybe a little pleased. I was probably imagining that last thing. "I'm sure you're busy."

"Just trying to repair a leak that I can't really repair." I gestured to the open cabinet door and the channel locks and screwdriver littering the bottom along with various cleaning bottles I had shoved to the side. Griff's flannel shirt hung on the open door, and he noticed it.

"Oh, that's your shirt, by the way. I've been meaning to return it. Uh, I brought it here to give to Ruby to return to you."

So Ruby knew I had been wearing the flannel upon occasion, and I hope she wouldn't say so. I was already embarrassed that I had been holding on to it like some besotted teenager. I mean, I wasn't really into Griff, though I sometimes let my mind wander back to the day he'd kissed me at the lakeside bar on our stakeout. Oh sure, the kiss had been initiated by me so my husband wouldn't realize I was sitting on a stool wearing a brunette wig, motorcycle boots, and fake tattoos. But Griff wasn't the kind of guy to receive. He gave back. And that giving had curled my toes and made me shave my legs every three days since just in case.

But I wasn't sleeping with Griff. Or any man. At least not until I was officially divorced, and probably not then. Dating wasn't on my radar.

But still, I shaved those legs.

"It's old. You can keep it if you want," he said, moving toward the sink. "What's the problem here?"

"Oh, just a slow leak. I have a plumber coming next week." I glanced over at Ruby, who stood next to my mother. They were both watching Griff and me like spectators at the US Open, a little slack-mouthed and very into the play that was on the court, or rather the kitchen.

"Did you turn the water off?" Griff dropped to a knee and peered inside the cavern of mildew and chemical cleaners. No plumber's crack for him, though his T-shirt rode up a little to reveal a tanned lower back. I sorta wished for plumber's crack because Griff's would probably be spectacular.

"Of course I did." I had learned to do that after the great toilet flood of 2016. "But what about Juke?"

"I'll just take a quick peek. Probably needs a new seal, which we can pick up while we're out. Grab your stuff while I double-check the issue."

My "stuff" consisted of my cute crossbody bag. But on second thought, a swipe of lip gloss wouldn't hurt. I ran my fingers through my hair, shaking it out, and huffed a little puff of air to check my breath.

"So I'm going to eat my lunch upstairs and call around about Juke. He's probably holed up somewhere," Ruby said, looking at the microwave. "Thanks for going with Griff. *So* nice of you, Cricket."

Okay, so she might have raised her eyebrows and made a face that said "I see you, girl." Griff couldn't see her, thank the

Lord, so I made a straight line of my mouth and shook my head, letting her know it wasn't like that.

Her side-eye's meaning was clear: *I know what I know.*

My mother stood. "I'm off to brunch with friends, and then I must go by Atkin's Nursery to pick up the African violets they repotted for me. Some of us have things to do other than chase around after a man who may not wish to be found. Some people enjoy privacy for their grief," she said pointedly. And disapprovingly—though I knew she liked Griff; she'd bought him beard oil. Though come to think of it, that could have been an unspoken commentary on his grooming habits.

"Or not. Some people need their friends and family to care enough to check on them so they don't do something stupid," I said.

"Which is why I keep tabs on you, dear," my mother said.

Well, tou-effin'-ché.

"Just so you know, a shipment didn't come today, and Julia Kate is going home with a friend after volleyball practice. That's why I'm free to help Griff this afternoon. And since I almost have my PI license, my investigative skills might come in handy." I tried for smooth, nonchalant, just a chick doing a friend a favor.

"What's this about a PI license?" Griff said from under the sink, then backed out, muscles all bulging. Not that I noticed. In a matter of seconds, he twisted a metal piece and removed the curved pipe I'd been working to get out for a good twenty minutes.

"I'm about to finish a course that will give me my private investigator's license. Well, eventually."

"Why are you doing that?" He inspected the pipe. "I thought you were joking. You run an antiques store."

"I know. It will be more of a side gig," I explained.

"You're going to be an antiques-dealing snoop?" He looked amused.

I didn't like being a joke.

Lots of people had hobbies. They took ballroom dancing, tae kwon do, painting lessons, or charcuterie board classes (yes, that's a thing now), so what was so wrong with exploring my natural gift?

And it *was* a gift. I had single-handedly brought my husband and his scheming friend's Ponzi scheme tumbling down. And I had managed to get all the money Scott had swiped from our joint accounts back. Okay, not single-handedly. Ruby, Juke, and Griff had all helped. And the money wasn't back in the accounts yet, but it would be. I felt deep in my gut that I could be instrumental in helping other women like me. Women whom others had failed. Was getting my private investigator's license sort of a weird side gig? Some might say. But I liked helping other people, and if Juke had a part-time gal on his staff of one, he'd have a more successful business.

Truth was, being a single mom with an antiques store that barely squeaked over the line into the black overwhelmed me. Scott had been fired by the bank, but he had family money, so he could still pay child support. And sure, I had money. But I didn't want to rely on generational wealth to pay my bills. I wanted to be of use. I liked the way I had felt being part of the Blue Moon Sting Posse. And I had liked that version of myself. Conspiring, conniving, and daring suited me.

"Yeah." I set my hands on my hips, determined. "I'm going to be an antiques-store-owning part-time private investigator. And I'm going to kick ass at it."

Griff gave me a good hard look before nodding his head. "That's the spirit, Sunshine. Oh, and you definitely need a new seal."

2

Ruby

I climbed the stairs to the upper floor of Printemps and tried not to smile at the thought of my boss lusting after my cousin Griff. Cricket might not have come to terms with it yet, but she *so* had a serious case of the hots for him.

Understandable. Griff had a track record of being emotionally constipated but fantastically good-looking. Which meant he was crack to any woman with functioning ovaries. The sweetest thing was that Cricket also intrigued him. Well, sort of sweet. They went together like anchovies and sugar cookies, so I couldn't see it truly working out. But it was fun to watch them tango around the attraction. And that's what they were doing—step-ball-changing around the inevitable.

My phone buzzed in my pocket, and I pulled it out to find my not-quite-boyfriend Dak calling.

"Hey, shouldn't you be at rehab?" I checked the time. He'd

recently had surgery on his knee to clean up some scar tissue from a prior surgery. Being an all-American catcher had had repercussions.

"Rescheduled." Dak sounded like he was in a tunnel. "I'm in the elevator, annoyed that they didn't call me before I hauled myself up here. Thought I could at least pick up lunch and come see you."

It wasn't a good time to entertain Dak—I was behind on the chartreuse leopard Lanvin jacket I was transforming into a bustier. The metallic thread woven throughout wasn't the easiest to keep from fraying. I had lucked up and found the beauty at a local thrift shop, and the rip on the arm hadn't dissuaded me from paying the somewhat hefty price tag. The store owner knew couture and that an item of that quality in Shreveport was rare. But if I could get it to come out the way I envisioned, it would be a statement piece for the collection.

Collection. That idea totally boggled my mind. I was creating a collection! Me. Ruby Balthazar, also known by my family as Ruby Roo and by the state as former prisoner 56551 at Long Pines. That last moniker is why I had been sitting at the sewing machine when I wasn't working, going to class, or eating tacos at Dak's house. I was sewing myself into a second chance, one that could erase the stupid mistakes I'd made in my past, with a new sustainable, renewable couture-fashioning business. I had only been up and running for the past two months, mostly online to showcase what I was doing: pulling apart vintage couture and remaking it into new high fashion. The pieces were one of a kind, but I had some couture prototypes that I would like to make ready-to-wear when the time was right.

I pinched myself, almost yelping at my own strength. "Um, well, it may be a working lunch for me. I'm so behind where I wanted to be by this time, and now Cricket's mom wants me to go to New York City with her in a few weeks."

"New York?" He paused for a moment. I heard someone talking in the elevator and then a ding. "You're going to New York City with Cricket's mom? The one who handwrote that skin care routine out for you? The one who told you that eating corn and potatoes would make you fat? The one who thinks shorts are disgraceful? That woman?"

I suppressed a laugh. "One and the same. And for what it's worth, that routine totally works. My skin is so soft. Never knew Ponds was that good. But, yes, New York City. Mrs. Quinney's sister is a fashion editor or something at *Vogue* and scored us tickets for Fashion Week."

"And you're actually going?"

A flash of annoyance hit. "I would be stupid not to."

"Oh, I just thought you were happy here. You know, with the show and website and the buzz and stuff." Unspoken was the implied "and me."

I *was* happy with Dak. After so many years apart with fast-moving water under our shaky bridge, we had found safe ground. But that didn't mean I was okay with abandoning opportunity. Going to runway events with a high-up at *Vogue* was almost scary in how big the opportunity was. Maybe too big for me.

Stop thinking that way.

I shook my negative thoughts off.

"This isn't about not being happy, Dak. It's about picking up what someone like Cricket and her family is dropping down. I want to succeed in this new venture. I think I can do this." I forced the bravery into my words because I wanted that to be true. After so many years of feeling not good enough, I had finally arrived at a place where I was comfortable in my skin. No, more than that. I believed I was exactly where I belonged, doing exactly what I was born to do. And any time I doubted myself, I gave myself a pep talk or listened to Cricket rave about my outfits. I wasn't going to give up because it got hard.

When I was growing up, sitting at the sewing machine was mostly monotonous—sewing hems for neighbors who paid my gran hatpin money, patching up torn coveralls for my papaw, and making pillows for the Sunday school craft fair never thrilled me. But those chores taught me how to sew a straight line, make pleats, and rip out my mistakes without damaging the fabric. Later, as I got better on the machine, I could make play clothes for the kids down the street, figuring out when I could abandon the paper patterns and add my own modifications. My gran taught me how to tat, crochet, knit, and embroider, which came in handy when I went all *Pretty in Pink* and made the prom dress I wore to the only prom I ever went to—Dak's senior prom.

That was before we broke up and he went off to play baseball at college and I stayed home to live up to my family name as a "sometimes" criminal.

But that was then, and this was now.

I was no longer that Ruby, and Dak and I had found our way back to each other.

"I know you can do this, Ruby. I believe in you. I guess I just feel protective. I've been out in that world and it's—"

"My turn to learn on my own, okay? I don't need your protection, Dak. Just your support."

A pause on the phone made my stomach tilt south. I didn't need Dak to go all patriarchal on me. Southern guys had those tendencies.

"You have my support. And I will try to not protect you, though you know it's against my nature. I care about you, but you're right. You have to live your life and take the chances you want to take. I will stand behind you," he said.

"Or beside me." I rallied, relieved that he had seen what he was doing without me having to spell it out.

"Yeah. Absolutely. Now what do you want to eat?"

"Surprise me." I slid into my chair. "Oh, by the way, have you seen Juke lately? Griff said he can't get in touch with him. His van hasn't been at the office for days, and he's not answering his phone."

"No. But now that I think on it, I remember Shirley saying something about him not coming down for coffee. He usually works on Saturdays and files paperwork on Sundays, so we see him at some point."

I chewed my lip, then asked, "And it's just coffee, right? He's not been asking for anything stronger?"

Dak owned a sports bar below Juke's private investigation firm. The bar was super popular with the working crowd and über-fanatic LSU fans. Dak had been a popular player for the LSU Tigers, which meant if he hadn't owned a bar and all, he would never have to buy his own drinks in this state. As it was, people came to drink at The Bullpen and talk about the good ol' days with their favorite son. Juke had been a regular before he'd gone back to AA.

"Nope, and if he were, he wouldn't drink at my place."

"That's what Griff was thinking. He's going out to all Juke's old stomping grounds. His and Loralee's anniversary was a few days ago. I hope Juke kept it together." I tried not to sound worried, but I was. Juke had started drinking heavily after his wife's death, which had resulted in being dismissed from his job as a detective with the South Lafourche Sheriff's Department down on the bayou. He'd returned to his birthplace to set up a private investigations firm, but his demons had followed. Still, after busting Cricket's husband and his thieving partner last spring, Juke had been faithfully going to AA and cleaning himself up. His efforts had resulted in steady business, more

interaction with the fam, and even an onlin[e]
uncle Jimbo's urging. Juke had been doing g[ood]

"Let me know if you want me to call [...]" jarring me out of my thoughts.

"Nah, let's wait. No sense in making wa[ves]. See ya in a bit." I clicked the phone off be[fore] that awkward pause where most couples said "love ya, babe." We weren't there yet, mostly because neither one of us wanted to be casual about that sort of statement. The only man I had ever loved outside of my daddy (and that was a stretch some days) was Dakota Roberts. Maybe that love had never gone away, but something still held me back. I knew what that something was, but I wasn't going to give it a name or acknowledge it because I wanted to be stronger than I was.

Looking down at the scattered elements of several dresses, I tried to focus on completing what I needed for the show. My process wasn't certain yet—I often hopped from one piece to the next as inspiration hit and initial infatuation with another piece waned. Obsessed with the notion of creative, fresh, and still wearable, I had ripped and torn myself into a time crunch. I needed help, but Gran had arthritis so bad she couldn't handle the finish work that took so much time, and with every nickel and dime accounted for, I couldn't afford to pay what most seamstresses would demand. Maybe if I didn't have to work at Printemps as much, I could spend the time doing the tedious beading.

Time was a dragon, and my neck was warm.

"Ruby," Cricket called up from the bottom of the stairs.

She probably needed help with something. Irritation blanketed me, but I tucked it away, Cricket was the supporter of my dreams, the signer of the paychecks, and, well, also my only friend at the moment. I went out to the banister and looked over. "Yeah?"

thinking about hiring someone to help us out."

Was she reading my mind?

"And I got an application from someone who named you as a reference."

"What? Someone named *me* as a reference?" I grappled with that. Lord, I didn't know many people. And most of them I wouldn't hire to babysit a rock. "Who?"

"I can't remember the name. But I'm off to help Griff find your uncle. Just wanted you to know. I mean, I think it will help you to, you know, focus more on your collection. Bye!"

"Bye," I called as the back door slammed shut.

Who in the hell would have put me down as a reference? I couldn't imagine. Instead of worrying about it, I sat down and started taking out the tucks I'd put into the miniskirt I'd created out of a swath of a vintage Diane von Fürstenberg wrap dress in a geometrical print. The tiny red and pink prisms would go well with the sheer silk blush blouse with the oversized pockets. Now I just needed to get the tiny tucks to lie so that the short skirt swished when the model walked. Which reminded me to text my co-worker Jade about a few of her friends who'd volunteer to model. I needed to match the last few pieces to the models so I could showcase all sizes in the show.

The event was scheduled in just six weeks—the end of October—as part of Shreveport's iSpy Fashion Festival. After a long hot summer of everyone staying inside soaking in the air-conditioning, almost every event in the fall had an outside component. There was the annual Red River Revel arts festival, the exciting Louisiana Film Prize, and the Louisiana State Fair which drew big numbers around the Ark-La-Tex, but there had been nothing for the fashion-forward who used scissors and thread to create art. This year after a few days of workshops and booths that included hat making, shoe designs, some home goods, the Junior League would host a cocktail party and style show with four curated designers with local ties. I was one of the four.

The event had garnered a nice response since a few Instagrammers with local connections had agreed to take part. One was a designer who lived in Portland and was coming home to showcase some of her lingerie line—she had drawn the biggest buzz since she had nearly a million followers on her social. Also showcasing his work was an East Texas athleisure designer who had a few rappers wearing his label. He too had a big following for his merchandise and music. The other participant was a local seamstress who'd created a children's line full of smocked dresses and Southern traditions. She'd pulled big with the Junior League crowd who bought her designs for their little darlings. And then there was me, the unknown, the multipurposer of vintage throwaways, the upcycling convict.

That last thought caused me to snort a laugh.

Maybe that could be my thing. My imagination ran wild at the thought of a television host saying, "Our next nominee for most interesting person of the year went from making license plates to creating high fashion for celebrities. She once traded cigarettes for a needle and thread and wrote long prison letters to the designers who inspired her. Give a big welcome to the woman behind the massively popular brand Deconstructed. Ruby Balthazar!"

Yep, that's me. A real rags-to-riches story. Well, at least I was in my mind.

I rethreaded the bobbin on the old machine my gran had given me and eyed the fabric I'd found in a bin at the back of a drapery shop in Fort Worth. It was pretty thick and could work nicely as a vest. I wanted a pantsuit in the collection—a sort of feminine power suit with wide lapels. This fabric would look nice against the black wool I had slotted for the suit, and it would lie nicely. Then I could line the jacket with a matching houndstooth silk that allowed for a cut away. Lengthen the jacket to soften the lines, maybe—

My phone blipped a text message.

I picked it up.

Hey, bitch. This Resa.

My heart dropped. Theresa Smalls had been my only friend at Long Pines Women's Correctional, and while I was glad to see that she was out, I wasn't sure I wanted to, well, hook up with her again. I was done with my past, and Resa was *so* my past.

You out? I typed.

Stayin' with my aunt over off Clyde Fant. Been out a week. Crazy.

I struggled to figure out how to respond to someone from Long Pines popping up in my life. But Resa had been so good to me at a point where I needed some milk of human kindness. Prison wasn't sleepaway camp. Though I had screwed up a lot as a teen, doing stupid things like getting caught selling weed and driving a car full of stolen crap my good-for-nothin' friends had swiped, I never planned to be sleeping on a cot behind bars. My uncle Ed Earl had been the cause of me getting sent away—well, that and my family loyalty—and I had served almost two years of a possession and distribution charge for the meth my stupid uncle had hidden in meat intended for Hunters for the Hungry —frozen meat I had delivered and been caught with. When I got to Long Pines, I had been scared shitless and stupid as a stump. My fellow inmates fastened bibs around their necks and prepared to have me for dinner.

Resa had put an end to that with one leg sweep in the showers.

I owed her the same courtesy on the outside. Not the leg sweep. The goodwill.

It can be hard. Let's meet up. I'll treat you to dinner.

Little bubbles appeared. Then disappeared. Then appeared

again. Maybe Resa felt the way I felt—not so sure that reviving our friendship was a good idea.

That's cool. When?

You tell me. I got a lot going on, but I will make it happen.

Tomorrow?

I sifted through my mental calendar. I opened Printemps in the morning. Class in the afternoon. Parole officer meeting at four. I wasn't supposed to associate with other felons, so I needed to find a work-around for Resa. Lieutenant Dwyer was pretty cool, and I belonged to a local group called Spring! that assisted women just out of prison. The past summer I had graduated to counseling those who needed reentry help. The program functioned similarly to AA, with a leader, a sponsor, and biweekly meetings that you were required to attend. I would position my dinner with Resa as a recruitment for the program, which would frankly be good for my old friend—the program's success rate at helping women restart their lives was impressive. Still, I hadn't worked with very many former inmates who knew me and my past. It made my belly wriggly.

How about 5:30?

Cool. Can we go to Casa Cruz? I'm dying for the salsa.

Perfect. Need me to pick you up?

Nah. I gotta bus pass.

I set the phone down with a sigh. I was still working on myself—I had lots o' baggage—but I wasn't trying to handle everything by myself. Part of becoming who I wanted to be meant addressing the mistakes of my past. My bad decisions had seasoned me, allowed me to see where I didn't want to be. I couldn't lop off the people of my past the way I cut away excess fabric. That was why I stuck with Spring! There I could do work on myself and help others. I hoped I could get Resa involved in the program. The director was terrific at helping people transition back into the real world.

Before I returned to my work, I shot off a text to Juke, hoping that he was not drinking but out fishing or something. We all dealt with the hurts in our life in different ways, some healthier than others.

Call me. Everyone is worried about you.

No response. But I didn't expect one.

This is so not cool.

3

Cricket

THERE'S something about the wind in your hair and your arms around a hot guy five years your junior that makes a woman feel like a girl again. Griff was warm and solid, something to wrap myself around. Okay, I pretty much had to curl around him so I wouldn't end up on the pavement. But the slight danger of riding on the back of a Harley along with the way his tight stomach felt against my hands made me feel alive.

And I needed that after the year I'd had.

All that had happened paired with a new sense of purpose had me flipped upside down, but the challenges had made me stronger, happier, and more at home in my own skin. This new Cricket didn't worry about propriety or the way her mother would freak out at her clinging to a huge, tatted-up tow truck driver zooming down North Market.

We probably should have taken my car, but Griff had once

told me that since he spent a lot of time in his giant tow truck, he loved to take his bike out when he could and I was okay with hopping on the back of his Harley and jetting around town.

I mean, obviously.

Griff jabbed his finger toward a run-down bar that skirted Grimmett Drive, an industrial road parallel to North Market, which was the busy highway where his tow truck yard occupied an entire block. A quarter of a mile from Blue Moon Towing was Dak's bar, and above that was Juke's private investigation firm, North Star Investigations. The area was a mixture of fast-food restaurants, pawnshops, and oil field supply stores. Grimmett Drive held more industrial businesses interspersed with neighborhood pubs for the after-work blue-collar crowd. Griff motored into the cracked parking lot of one such bar called Jellyroll's.

Maybe they liked jazz music here?

Or a good pastry?

Griff unbuckled his helmet. "I would say stay here since it won't take long, but it's a rough crowd on Monday lunch hour. No one's happy on Mondays around here. Come on."

I shimmied my leg down to the cement and swung my other leg over, tripping a little, bumping into Griff. He caught me, and it was nothing like a romance movie where we looked into each other's eyes… tilted our heads… leaned in, music swelling in the—

Nope.

Griff just righted me firmly with two hands on my shoulders and then spun off toward the tinted glass door with the bar's name flaking off.

Yeah. I had no clue where I stood with him. I guess I was just a friend and nothing more. Which was fine because I was still technically and legally married to Scott. And even if I wasn't married to my dirtbag husband, I wasn't sure Griff would be the sort of guy I could date. *If* he was even interested, which, judging by the way he acted (mixed signals much?), was iffy. We were very different. I served on charitable committees and wore cardigans. He frequented honkytonks and drank domestic beer straight from the bottle. Still, there was that whole yin-and-yang thing, right? Or maybe we'd get too mixed up in each other and end up a blob of gray?

Probably the blob of gray.

"You comin'?" He turned back, looking all delicious in Dickies work pants and a tight T-shirt. His hair was longish and messy from being under the helmet, but his beard looked—

"Hey, did you use that beard oil my mom bought you?" I asked, taking off my helmet and attempting a Farrah Fawcett flip that only sent my dark blond hair right into my mouth. I spit it out and tucked the helmet under my arm, trying to look cool. And probably failing, but hey, my boobs looked great in that tank.

Griff stroked his neatly trimmed beard. "Well, it was there on my counter."

"It looks good. Very soft."

"So I've been told." He pulled open the bar door.

Wait. What the hell did that mean? But then I knew. Some hussy had been stroking his beard. A beard *my mother* had made softer and shinier. Betrayal burned in my gut. I narrowed my eyes and followed behind him. I might or might not have shimmied my breasts higher in my bra before entering the bar just for spite.

The place was a single large room, the dimness penetrated by lighted-up beer signs and a glow behind the bar. There was a pool table, and the air smelled of old cigarette smoke, stale beer, and desperation.

Four patrons sat at the galvanized steel bar.

None of them was Juke.

"How's it goin', Jelly?" Griff called to a very large black man wearing an apron.

"Griff, my man." The giant held out a hand, slapped it against Griff's, and then gave a big, gap-toothed smile. His gaze found me, and he lifted his eyebrows. "Y'all wanna table? I got some wings that will make you drop to your knees and praise God that he made chickens."

Griff's smile flashed against his smooth silky beard of betrayal. "Nah, we're just checking to see if you've seen Juke around."

"Ain't seen him, man. He's off the juice." Jelly eyed the other guys nursing their beers. "Y'all seen Juke?"

Masculine noises that amounted to "negatory" emerged, but they all eyed me and my newly lifted boobs in my "doin' work for me" bra. That's what I got for being spiteful. I hunched my shoulders a little.

Griff handed Jelly a twenty and ten. "Thanks. Buy these fellas a round on me."

Then Griff turned and walked off, leaving me standing there like a bozo. I smiled and lifted a hand. "Well, you gentlemen have a good afternoon."

"You can stay here if you want, blondie. I won't ignore you." One of the guys patted the stool next to him and leered at me.

I curled a hand around the strap of my crossbody and started stepping backward because he looked like a rough customer and possibly a little drunk. Griff should not have bought these guys drinks. They'd had enough. It wasn't even eleven o'clock, for heaven's sake.

I felt Griff behind me, like a train coming fast through a tunnel. "You want to lose the rest of the teeth in your mouth, Frank? 'Cause it looks like you only have about five left."

Frank blanched.

I mean, I would too. Griff was like that guy from *Yellowstone* who broke people's faces at the slightest offense. Yummy and violent—two things I must have really liked deep down on that primal level that worked to ensure progeny. My ovaries probably popped an egg loose right that second.

Frank held up a hand. "Sorry, Griff. Just messin'."

"Well, unless you'd like your parts rearranged, keep your invitations to yourself and your eyes off her." Griff took my elbow and started toward the door.

I wrenched it away, slightly irritated at his presumption that I couldn't tell Frank to lump it on my own and slightly pleased at his violent intervention. Though I would not say so to him.

"I don't need you to do things like that. I'm perfectly capable of handling guys coming on to me," I said, stomping behind him into the daylight.

"Sure you are, Sunshine." He shoved his helmet back on his head and strapped up. "Look, you may not like it, but that doesn't mean I'm going to watch some shithead insult you... and me."

"How is that insulting you? We're not together."

"But he didn't know that, and he implied I don't take care of my women." Griff patted the seat. "Come on."

I stood there with one hand on my hip, glaring at him.

Griff lifted a gorgeous, misogynist shoulder. "Unless you wanted to suck face with Frank? But I'm warning you, he hasn't been to a dentist since Jimmy Fallon took over the *Tonight Show*."

He might have smirked. I wasn't sure because I had jerked my chin away and stared off in my "pissed off and not dealing with you" posture that had worked on Scott at least half the time in our marriage. "I'm calling an Uber. You go ahead and look for Juke on your own."

"Hell, Cricket. Don't do this. I was protecting your honor." He sounded like he believed it. More like he was protecting his reputation as a ladies' man. Well, I wasn't going to be part of his macho bull crap, not when I wasn't even sure he thought of me as a woman. Okay, he checked me out sometimes and had been pretty good at making me forget that the pretend kiss at the Channel Marker back in the spring wasn't just a ruse. Truth be told, I *had* forgotten all about being a good Christian woman who wore a wedding band during that kiss. He'd turned me into a mewling jezebel, ready to climb him like a tree.

Which had been both shocking and stimulating.

But my weirdo libido when Griff came around didn't blind me to the fact that I wasn't going back to being a woman men stepped over or shoved aside as a nuisance or fluff. I had spent too many years taking a back seat in my own life, and I wasn't about to climb onto that motorcycle like a good little girl just 'cause he thought it best.

I pulled my sunglasses out of my purse and crammed them on my face. Then I slid my phone out and hit the Uber app. "No longer interested. Do you want to put this helmet in your little storage thing, or should I take it back with me and give it to Ruby?"

"Stop being difficult."

And that was it in the nutshell. I had never been difficult. I cheerfully went along with whatever anyone wanted, donning my gosh darn game face, and never ruffling feathers. That was why people had never taken me seriously. Candy-coated Cricket with her fluffy blond hair and tasteful clothing. She could be counted on to pick up the monogrammed napkins, bring the good wine, and buy a table at the silent auction. She never drank too much, talked too loudly, or embarrassed the family name. Until last spring... when I'd tossed out my reputation as good ol' Cricket for cunning, petty-assed Cricket.

I liked the latter version way better.

"I live to be difficult now, Griff. Really, I do. So you can crank up your hog and drive yourself right on out of here. I can take care of toothless Frank and myself. Hold on a sec..." I held up a finger as I growled at the phone. No Ubers? Ridiculous. I clicked on Lyft. Grr. Nothing there either. I clicked over to Safari and looked for cabs. I clicked on the first company that came up. "Do you know what this address is?"

Griff had been glaring at me. Which wasn't so unusual. He only smiled every other month or so and had met his quota moments ago with Jellyroll. "Just come on, Cricket."

"No. I'm not getting on your bike. I'm mad. You treated me like I was stupid and couldn't handle a simple situation." I glanced around and found a street sign. We were on the corner of Grimmett Drive and Aero.

"Fine. Overreact." Griff's bike roared to life, and he kicked away from the cracked concrete, steering his dumb motorcycle out of the parking lot. Momentarily, I felt a lump in my stomach because I had sort of thought he might fight a little harder to get me to go with him. But I dashed that disappointment away as I dialed the number to the cab company. My gaze followed Griff's form as he wheeled onto Grimmett Drive and gunned the bike loudly.

He was angry.

Well, so was I.

Overreact? He was lucky I was nice enough to keep his spare helmet tucked under my arm and not throw it at his ginormous head.

"'Lo?"

"Hi, I'm on the corner of Grimmett Drive and Aero. Can you send a cab? Quickly?"

The dude said he was the driver and only five minutes away, so I hung up and posted up next to the door, trying to look like I was doing something on my phone. But I was practicing some surveillance techniques by noting my area (dangerous) and escape routes (left or right) and potential hazards (eight potholes that could swallow a cab whole.) The noise of Griff's bike had faded, but then it came back. I slid my eyes under my sunglasses to the right to see Griff pull into the abandoned gas station across the street from Jellyroll's. He sat there, idling and looking all pissy.

Something slightly warm flooded my chest.

He might be a grump ass, but he *was* a gentleman.

Sorta.

A green cab seesawed up to the corner. And I do mean seesawed. The suspension on the twenty-plus-year-old cab was shot, and it looked like it was dancing, but I was a beggar and so couldn't be too choosy.

The window rolled down to reveal a wizened black man with a friendly smile. He wore a newsboy hat and had an unlit cigarillo clenched between his teeth. "You my fare?"

"I am." I shoved my phone into my purse, walked over, and climbed inside the surprisingly pristine cab.

"Where to, sugar?" he asked as I clicked my seat belt into place.

"400 Chester, right off Line Avenue by the old Shreveport Orpheus Theater." I slammed the door closed and peered out at Griff who still eyeballed me from across the street. I rolled down the window and gave a little wave that I hope portrayed that I was fine so he could leave. A thought kernel blistered up, and I wondered if I had been a little overreactive. My feelings had been hurt at the thought of some faceless bimbo stroking Griff's beard. Okay, so maybe she wasn't a bimbo. Maybe she was a perfectly nice person, and I was just jealous as a hound and had let an inappropriate feeling guide my behavior. Or maybe I was thinking too damn hard about everything. Still, Griff had been heavy-handed, treating me like I was helpless.

And I did not want to be helpless.

That desire had been established six months ago, and he'd had a front-row seat and should know better. Which is why I was taking this leap into a new career. Well, part-time career. I wasn't helpless. I was help*ful*. And I was going to prove to everyone that I could be a hard-boiled detective. Or at the very least, parboiled.

Pulling my crossbody bag into my lap, I withdrew my phone and stared at it, wondering if I should say I was sorry for acting dramatic, but then an envelope caught my eye and distracted me. I pulled it out.

"Sir, do you think you can make a quick stop on the way? I'll pay extra."

"Sure thang. I'll just keep the meter runnin'," the cab driver said.

"Right up here off North Market is the Bullpen. Can you pull in there?"

"You wantin' a drink?" He sounded surprised.

"No. I need to run something upstairs." I pressed my fingers against a wrinkle in the envelope. I had been carrying around a form that Juke needed to close my case for over a month, and I had added my résumé to the paperclipped form along with a letter requesting he consider me as an apprentice investigator. In order to get my license, I needed hours under a professional investigator. Juke had always thought I was joking about getting my license and going to work for him.

But I wasn't.

Juke wasn't at his office, but since I was essentially driving right by it, I could leave it for him. And maybe he would be there. Who knew?

The cab driver pulled into the lot which held only a few cars. Dak didn't open until two p.m., and so the ones parked around back were likely his employees. Juke's old van was nowhere in sight, and I felt a pang of regret for not continuing to help Griff search for the older PI. I hoped that Juke was okay. Surely, he was.

"Meter's running, sugar." The driver shifted into park. The cab bounced like a hip-hop concert, and I felt slightly nauseated.

"Be right back." I climbed out, planting my feet on the newly paved parking lot before going around to the rusted metal steps that led up to North Star Investigations. I had pulled on new suede booties that morning, and they made a merry little clacking as I ascended. When I reached the landing, I stood wondering how I was going to leave the envelope when there was no mail slot. How did Juke get his mail?

Probably the post office a few streets over.

Feeling a little foolish, I decided to knock.

No answer. Of course.

I shrugged a shoulder and tried the door handle just in case.

It was locked. Of course.

Glancing up, I noted there was no overhang to protect the envelope from the elements. Dang it. Why hadn't I already mailed it like a normal person? Of course I knew why. I had hoped to hand it to Juke because that felt more in touch with who I was—someone who gave a more personal effort.

I squatted down and studied the crack under the door. If I could get the right angle, the envelope should slide it under the door. There was shag carpet that could impede it, but surely the carpet was worn down at the threshold. That stuff was likely thirty years old. I tried to push the envelope through, but it caught on the metal and crumpled.

"Dang it," I said out loud, pulling the envelope back out and trying to smooth it. "Ugh."

Standing, I started back down the stairs. But then something niggled on the back of my neck, the same sort of feeling one got when something bad was about to happen. A single window, fuzzed over with age, was positioned right next to the door. Ugly curtains hung against the cloudy glass, but there was a three-inch gap in the middle. I pressed my face against the dirty surface and squinted, trying to see inside.

I could make out the lumpy couch and a desk that was—yep—piled high with folders. Leopards didn't change their spots, after all. Juke wasn't the neatest of dudes, but if he would let me work for him, I could get those files neatly labeled and into a system that would make them easier to find. I envisioned color tabs, a new system for past clients, active cases, and maybe...

Pressing harder, I studied the floor beside the desk.

Socks.

On feet.

On a body.

I reared back, my heart galloping, my ears ringing with shock.

Oh. My. God.

I fumbled for my phone, dropping it on the metal grate. Thankfully, it didn't fall through the cracks. With shaking hands, I picked it up and managed to dial 911.

"911, what's your emergency?"

"Oh my God, I think my friend is dead. I can see his feet through the window. I can't believe this. I can see his body." I sucked in breaths, trying to make the words without hyperventilating.

Juke was dead.

Or gravely injured.

"Ma'am, ma'am, can you tell me your location please? Are you in a safe place?" the man on the phone asked.

I looked around. Was I in a safe place? Probably not. "I'm in front of his office. It's on North Market. It's called North Star Investigations, above the Bullpen—uh, that's a bar. The door's locked. I can't get in, so you need to bring something, like a tool or something. I don't know the address."

"I'm sending someone. Please make sure you are in a safe location, okay? Deep breaths, okay?" He sounded like a doctor. Calm. The opposite of me.

I wasn't sure I could get down the stairs because my legs were shaking and I was freaking out. Palms sweating, breath shallow, and my head was a little swimmy. I tried to take deep breaths and not collapse into a heap on the landing. "Okay. Just send someone. I'll stay here and wait."

The 911 operator asked some more questions, and I tried to answer them as I sank down onto the top step. And then it struck me.

Ruby.

How in the hell was I going to tell Ruby that her cousin was dead?

I couldn't. Then there was Griff. He wasn't far away. He could get here fast. Maybe faster than 911. I picked up my phone and tapped on his name.

"Yeah," he said by way of greeting, not sounding the least bit friendly.

"Griff, it's me. I-I think, well, I think Juke might be dead in his office."

4

Cricket

I HEARD the roar of Griff's motorcycle below just as sirens sounded faintly in the distance. People were coming to help. I wasn't alone.

Please don't let Juke be dead... and just when I was going to go to work for him.

Then I realized how selfish that last thought was. What was wrong with me, thinking about myself at a time like this?

My heart beat hard in my chest, and I had already had to put my head between my legs twice so I wouldn't hyperventilate. That was after I had tried to kick the window in so I could unlock the door. Now my foot throbbed. The plexiglass window was stronger than it looked. Kicking in doors always looked so easy in the movies, but in reality, not so much.

"Cricket!" Griff shouted as he pounded up the metal stairs two at a time.

I stood, legs still shaking, foot bruised. I still held my phone because the 911 guy told me to remain on the line, but there was nothing left to say to him. Only wait until the fire department arrived to bash in the door. But Griff was here now, and I was certain he could do what I couldn't. Maybe what even the firefighters couldn't do. "I tried to kick out the window, but it's so high and I—"

Griff reached the top step, moved me aside, and cranked back his leg. The plexiglass popped with the impact of his big boot, and I yelped even though I knew it was coming. He continued kicking the crap out of the split plastic as I clung to the metal rail behind me, hoping that we weren't too late.

"Ma'am? Ma'am? What is going on?" the 911 operator shouted. Of course it didn't sound like a shout because the phone was in my hand away from my ear, but I heard him anyway.

I lifted the phone. "The cavalry has arrived."

"What cavalry?" the 911 operator asked.

"The Griffin Moon kind." I winced when the plastic scratched the underside of Griff's arm as he strained toward the lock through the busted window.

The sirens grew louder, whining shrieks that echoed the fear inside me. Griff managed to twist the lock, so I helpfully reached over and opened the door.

Griff moved me back so he could go in first. No doubt it was to protect me from what lay inside the office, but I didn't like being cast aside. I dogged his heels as he entered Juke's office, the door slamming against the rail behind us.

Beyond the desk I could see Juke's legs. He wore a pair of black dress socks, and his brown Hushpuppy loafers were neatly paired under the desk. Which seemed weird.

Griff bounded toward the desk, knocking a few papers off, and then stopped.

I slammed into his back because I was watching Juke's feet and not where I was going. Sure enough, Juke lay there, arms crossed, eyes closed. He looked like a man in a casket except he was lying on a yoga mat.

Griff stuck out his foot and tapped Juke's leg.

Juke's eyes flew open, and he sat up. "What the—"

"Oh God," I yipped, rearing backward and nearly falling because that's pretty much my level of grace.

Juke pulled wireless earbuds from his ears, blinking at us framed against the light in the open door. "What the hell are you two doing? My window! What the fu—"

"What the hell are *we* doing? What the hell are *you* doing?" Griff yelled, and I could tell he'd been scared to death by Juke's still body lying on the floor of the office. Griff's back trembled beneath my hand. Oh yeah. I still had a hand on his back. I retracted it, tucking it behind my own.

"I was *meditating*." Juke looked like a baby bird who'd just hatched out of his shell, all wide-eyed, hair sticking in every direction, still blinking. "Wait, are those sirens?"

Yeah, the firefighters and EMTs had arrived by the sound of boots coming up the metal stairs. "Uh, we may have thought you were dead."

"Dead?" Juke looked at me, making a horrified face just at the first responder charged into the dimness. I could see other rescuers behind him carrying a stretcher.

"Someone call for help?" The paramedic asked, reshouldering a bag that I assumed had medical supplies inside.

"We did, but it was a false alarm. Juke isn't dead." Griff gestured to Juke who struggled to his feet.

"Damn right I ain't dead."

"You *looked* dead," I said, not one to be left out of the drama I had caused.

"I was in Savasana and a deep meditation." Juke jabbed a finger toward the entrance. "Y'all broke my window, damn it."

"You haven't answered your phone in days. No one could get in touch with you. How were we supposed to know that you were in sava... sauce anah... whatever?" Griff folded his arms over his broad chest, looking like he was having none of Juke's surliness over the broken window.

"I got invited last minute on a weekend retreat and didn't have my phone. I texted Ma on Thursday before I left. We got back last night, and I came here to sleep rather than drive all the way out to the lake. I parked my van in your yard because of the thefts around here."

The EMT put up a hand to the others who had crowded in behind him, peeping around the doorframe like a clutch of baby chicks. "Looks like a false alarm."

There was some grumbling, and a few of the first responders went back down the steps if the sound of their boots was any indication. A guy with an official-looking hat shoved past them. I could see all this because Griff had busted that window up good.

"Ah, Jesus." Griff rubbed a hand over his face. "Your mother didn't tell me that when I called her looking for you. And I didn't see your van out there."

"She don't check her texts sometimes."

The EMT left, and the official-looking guy—who appeared to be a fire captain—flipped on the lights and considered the busted window. "So I'm assuming you didn't need us to break down a door and check for a dead body?"

Juke rubbed a hand over his face. He and Griff were definitely related and really good at showing how annoyed they were. "I can't believe y'all thought I was dead."

Griff looked at me. I shrugged and addressed the fire captain. "He sure seemed dead through the window."

Juke glanced down at his yoga mat. "I've been using an app to guide my meditation. It was cranked up pretty good. I didn't mean to scare anyone."

"What kind of earbuds are you using that you can't hear someone breaking your window? I may need some of those. My bunkmate snores so bad the people next to the station called the police." The fire captain waved back some new guys coming up the metal stairs. Then he moved toward Juke, who looked a bit silly in gym shorts and black dress socks.

I felt pretty silly myself. The adrenaline that had flash flooded my body drained away, and I lowered myself onto Juke's rather beat-up couch (which was miraculous, considering I wouldn't even let my dog Pippa sit on that thing.) Maybe Ruby could sew him a couch cover. Or we could burn the travesty of a sofa and get him a new one. "I'm sorry."

Griff set his big paw on my shoulder, and I forgot I was supposed to be mad at him. "You didn't know, and you were only trying to help. I mean, he looked pretty dead when I first saw him too."

"You're just trying to make me feel better."

"Yeah." Griff sank down beside me. The couch cushions were so beat up that I listed toward him, knocking into his shoulder. I threw out a hand, and it landed on his warm, firm thigh. Very firm. And I left it there for a moment before I snatched it back and tried not to look like I had enjoyed it. Why did that fire captain have to turn on the lights anyway? Now Griff could see my cheeks turning pink.

Griffin Moon knew what he did to me and, damn him, seemed to enjoy the mess out of it. But I refused to look at him because that would be acknowledging my attraction and I didn't want him to know that I knew that he knew that I was attracted to him. I was stubborn that way.

We heard a thump, thump, thump, and in the open door,

Dak appeared and waved a crutch toward Juke. "I see he's still alive."

"You sound disappointed," Juke said.

"You're not the best tenant." Dak made a face at the yoga mat. "What? You were working out?"

"Meditation." Juke shrugged.

"Since when do you do that?"

"Since I gave up getting trashed every night. I belong to a group of guys who practice meditation and prayer. We did a retreat this weekend over at Caddo Lake State Park. It was a weekend of silence and contemplation, which sort of, you know, restores me and helps me center myself. I really like it. Got back late and I stayed here. I slept late and began my day with a deep meditation."

"He looked dead," I said rather unhelpfully.

"I'm sorry about the window, Dak. I'll get it replaced." Juke indicated the scattered plexiglass on the old shag carpet. An ugly curtain fluttered slightly as if drawing attention to the sad state of things. "And I'm sorry you had to come out, Captain, but I appreciate the consideration."

"No worries," the fire captain said, accepting a clipboard from another firefighter, who slipped in and slipped out quick as spit. "Just need to fill this out and have you sign it."

Dak thumped over to us. "Meditation? Centering himself? Are you sure this is your cousin, G?"

Griff narrowed his eyes. "Well, if anyone would have told me a year ago that Juke would be meditating on a yoga mat, I would have punched them in the throat for being utterly ridiculous."

I mouthed *utterly* because it seemed so not a Griff word. Dak saw me and suppressed a laugh.

"I know," Griff continued. "But I guess everyone has to change or try new things."

"Exactly," I said. It was the perfect opportunity to mention the whole reason I had come to Juke's office to begin with. Well, sort of. My initial intent had been to find Juke, which I'd done in spectacular fashion. The second was to deliver my résumé. "Which is why I am here in the first place."

Juke had scrawled some stuff on the clipboard, and the fire captain lifted his hand in farewell as he left, shutting the door a little too adamantly. The curtain did its unhelpful thing again, waving to remind everyone that the window was broken. Juke frowned and walked over to where we sat—Dak had sunk into a beat-up captain's chair that had probably once been part of an unfortunate dining set. Juke looked at me. "So thanks for trying to save my life, Cricket. I appreciate it."

"You're welcome." I tried to sound like I hadn't just created a lot of drama. Just a chick trying to save a friend. Nothing to see here, folks.

"So yoga is your new thing?" Dak grinned. "No judgment. I did a lot of yoga when I was in rehab before."

"Aren't you in rehab now?" Juke asked, perching on the edge of the wobbly chair. "Because I can bring a guest once a month."

"Uh, yeah, maybe." Dak lost the grin, as if he wished he'd kept his mouth shut.

Sensing a need for a shift in the conversation, I leaped up and retrieved my now very crumpled envelope which I had dropped at some point during the false death. As I lifted it, I noted it had also been stepped on by Griff's big boot. "I had a reason for coming by. Um, other than trying to find you. And, uh, save your life."

I walked over and handed Juke the envelope. He studied his name printed neatly on the nice vellum stationary.

"It's my résumé," I said.

"Résumé? For what?"

"For part-time employment, silly man," I said with a smile and a shake of my head. "I told you I was going to take the course."

Griff seemed amused, but Juke appeared to be horrified, which made my stomach feel a little wriggly. Juke glanced up at me. "You took the PI course?"

"Taking. But in a few weeks, I'll be finished. Then I can be an extra set of eyes for you. You know, like when you need someone to help with a big case."

"You want to work for me?"

Juke seemed a bit thick-headed. Wasn't that what I had just said?

"Just part-time. I have the antiques store, of course, and I'm helping Ruby a little with her new business, though my mother is sort of taking over that." I wasn't resentful of her taking an interest in Ruby. Okay, maybe a little tweaked that Mama had taken very little interest in anything I had done in my entire life. It was like when I quit taking dance lessons back in the sixth grade, she'd written me off. I didn't like to feel insecure about my mother. I was very happy that she'd tossed her pillbox hat into the ring regarding Ruby's venture. And a good deal of capital. Marguerite had faith in Ruby, and I would not be jealous about that.

Would. Not.

"So just so I'm clear—you aren't selling your store or anything? You're just wanting to help me?"

Poor Juke *so* wasn't on my wavelength.

Yet.

"Exactly. I mean, now that you're on the road to success—you're sober, and I've been referring a lot of people to you—you're sure to need a little assistance from time to time. And you have to admit I was pretty good at catching Scott and busting up a Ponzi scheme. I'm a natural."

"A natural at what is the question," Griff deadpanned.

"What do you mean by that?" I remembered that I was mad at him for his shenanigans at Jellyroll's bar. Treating me like I was an annoying little sister and then getting miffed when that guy with no teeth invited me for a drink... Ugh, whatever was between Griff and me was as clear as swamp water.

Griff's humor fled because he seemed to remember that we weren't exactly pleased with one another about an hour ago.

Juke stared at the envelope in his hand before lifting the flap. The room was a morgue—no one moving—well, other than Juke. He unfolded my résumé, and his lips moved as he read it over.

I was rather proud of my résumé. I'd had to look up my college GPA, but it was respectable enough to earn cum laude honors. And surely my leadership skills were easily recognizable. Back in college, I had been the Kappa Delta house manager, philanthropy chair, and a Kappa Alpha sweetheart. Currently I chaired PTA committees, served on my church's local missions board, and chaired the Shreve Memorial Library's annual book bonanza book sale. I also belonged to the Dogwood Garden Club, the Cotillion Club, the South Highlands Business Owners Association, and various other organizations. And as soon as I passed my licensure exam for private investigations, I would join their society. Maybe even chair something for them. Surely they did luncheons and conferences. I was brilliant at silent auctions.

"You were a Demoiselle debutante? How is that relevant to being a private investigator?"

"I was. In 1997. Well, we wore gloves and everything." I had loved the long gloves... that would not leave fingerprints. Point in my favor. "And please tell me who other than a debutante can pull off wearing that much white in the middle of winter? I was so pale, but way better off than poor Deidre Ballenger, who had an unfortunate tanning-bed disaster that turned her the color of orange sherbet. Look, just so you know, debutantes are a very resourceful bunch."

Juke looked at Griff and Dak like he really didn't know what to say. He held my résumé like it could possibly detonate. I guess I should have thought of that, like the old Max Smart shows. Now that would have made an impression. "Fine, I know that y'all think I'm silly at times. And I am. But I'm also smart, responsible, and get the job done. You don't need another you, Juke. You need a me."

Dak pursed his lips. "She's right. You know a lot of dirt bags who are obvious, Juke. Cricket knows a lot who aren't so transparent. Besides, she's a female, and—no offense, Cricket—a little, uh, innocent and apt to not be taken seriously. Which means she's perfect for undercover work. Some of the best spies are women, women who others don't think are savvy enough to put two and two together."

"Four," I said.

Juke smiled at that, refolding the résumé and sliding it back into the envelope. "I'll consider it, Cricket. You have been very good to me, giving me a second chance on your case and referring people to my business."

"He even paid his rent on time this month," Dak said.

Juke made a face. "I did last month too."

I guess I had expected him to be more excited. But it was a step in his business that he might not be ready to make. "Okay then. I'm still taking classes, so I'm not ready yet. But I will be in a few weeks. I guess I should go now. I'm sorry about everything."

"You were trying to help me," Juke said.

"Yep. See you guys later." I pulled my keys from my pocket and made my way down the flaking metal stairs, feeling weird.

The adrenaline had gone to be replaced by a sort of void. I knew Juke had some doubts about me, but I had thought my record on the Scott and Donner thing would sway him. I had done a good job nailing my husband and his creep of a partner. Of course Scott had squealed and wasn't the originator of the scheme. He'd just taken bribes to steer fat cat victims Donner's way, including my own mother, which I had pretty much raked him over the coals for. Scott was sorry, but I wasn't sure it was about getting caught or true regret over his actions. After all, if I hadn't overheard some stupid gossip and gotten suspicious, my husband would be sipping mai tais on a Cayman beach with the fickle Stephanie, formerly of country-club tennis fame, now only God knew where. Someone said she'd jumped off a federal court judge's boat onto some trust-fund millionaire's yacht. The woman was resourceful, I'd give her that.

The fire trucks and EMT vehicles were gone, leaving Griff's bike, Dak's truck, and a few other nondescript cars that likely belonged to customers at the Bullpen. My cab was gone, and the motorcycle helmet sat on the curb. I sighed and picked it up, then sank to the curb—and discovered real quick that the pavement was hotter than Satan's butt crack. I tapped on the Uber app and requested a pickup. Jeez, Louisiana didn't play from May to October. I would kill for the cool breeze we'd had that morning. Right then it was plain scorching.

Where the heck was fall?

I was watching the screen where the little Uber car turned this way and that in its effort to get to North Market Street when a loud noise nearly scared the devil out of me.

"Shit!" I slammed my hand down and spun around.

Griffin had dumped something into the metal trash bin beneath the stairs. "Did you just use a bad word, Mrs. Crosby, lily-white debutante?"

"Debutantes cuss. Debutantes do a lot of improper things."

"Oh, I bet they do," he said in a salacious manner that I begrudgingly sort of liked.

He tromped over, picked up his helmet, and sank down beside me, a little too close. Griff was a large, threatening guy, but I knew that he was more than some brute. For one thing, he had a tender heart somewhere under all that bluster and brawn, rescuing cats, making sure they were fixed and fed before letting them roam the tow yard. For another, he'd been nice enough to help me with the whole Scott-cheating-and-taking-bribes thing when he had not a single stake in that game. I had thought Griff had done it because he liked me, and I guess he did... a little. But since our not quite flirtation months ago, he'd held back, and today the mixed messages he'd sent had become annoying. So I didn't want him right next to me. I scooted a few feet away.

"Are you okay?"

"Of course I am," I said a bit pettily.

"About earlier—"

"No need to apologize." I waved my hand.

"I wasn't. I... why would *I* apologize?"

I sucked in a deep breath and exhaled it noisily. "For being a Neanderthal. For grabbing my elbow and trying to steer me out the door. For thinking you know what is best for me. For being all the patriarchal things that women hate and want to smash to death."

"So you *wanted* me to leave you there with Jerry?" He looked grumpy. Very grumpy.

"No. But I didn't need you to intervene."

"Okay, note taken. Don't treat Cricket like a lady. Treat her like she's one of the guys."

"I didn't say that. I like being treated like a lady. I just don't want you to treat me like I'm stupid. Or ineffective. I've been treated like that my whole life, and I'm more than a pair of tits and heels." I was getting more and more worked up even as I knew I wasn't doing any good. Sweat ran down my temples, Griff was now looking at my boobs, and I had used a word I hated —*tits*—immediately becoming a vulgar version of myself. This is what Griff did to me. He stirred me into being common.

The image of my mother popped into my head followed quickly by the words I had uttered that morning. *Well, Mother, I find I rather like common.*

Might as well put salt on those words I was eating.

"I've never thought you were just a pair of tits and heels. You know that. But I will say, Cricket..." He positioned his body more toward me, bringing that delicious scent of mountain air and saltiness that sent a little alert to my girl parts. Damn that Griffin Moon alert system. His gaze leveled to mine, and I couldn't look away at the intensity in the stormy depths. Heavens, he was something dark, magnetic, and yummy, all right. My breathing hitched a little. "You have an amazing pair of tits and legs. And if that makes me a chauvinist pig to notice those spectacular parts of you, then... oink."

A black Chevy SUV pulled into the lot. Uber to the rescue.

I hopped up and gave the driver a wave, trying to pretend that Griff hadn't just oinked at me in a way that was, well, almost enough to make me do something crazy like kiss the daylights out of him. But I resisted. And just before I climbed into the waiting car, I spun around and gave him a comical lascivious look. "Well, so you know, I like your tits too."

Then I slid into the air-conditioned splendor of the Uber and shut the door.

The driver, who had an unfortunate perm, looked back at me. "Did you just tell that dude you liked his tits?"

And despite all that had happened that afternoon, which

included a full spectrum of emotions, I managed a laugh. "Yeah, I sorta did."

"Well, honey, he looks like he has a lot to offer, but them ain't one."

I caught a glimpse of Griff moving toward his Harley in the rearview mirror. "Yeah, you aren't blind."

5

Ruby

A WEEK LATER...

Visiting New York City was something I had always wanted to do but had never really planned for, so as I stood looking at the wild-graphic-patterned hard-shell suitcase that had seemed a bold choice when I was standing on the aisle at Marshall's, my stomach felt two pounds heavier.

"You think it's all going to fit?" Dak slid a hand at my elbow which he knew was my trigger erogenous zone. The man never played fair.

I leaned back into his shoulder. "It will have to. It's the only suitcase I have."

"I can loan you one of mine." He dropped a kiss against my head and placed a hand on my bottom. See? Nothing fair in that either.

I turned and wrapped my arms around him. "I'm so excited, but I also don't want to go. Is that weird?"

"No. Manhattan is totally unknown to you and overwhelming, and you have a hunk of burning love here... who is perfectly happy to lock you in his lair and turn you into his personal sex bunny."

"Sex bunny?" I smiled.

"Personally, my favorite kind of rabbit." Dak cracked a grin that went straight to my heart.

Yeah, that was the thing—my heart. I knew I loved Dak, but there was something that held me back from saying I love you. An anvil of doom swayed above my head and felt primed to drop. I wasn't supposed to be this happy. Wasn't supposed to be on the verge of something so good, wrapped in the arms of the guy I had always wanted. Not Ruby Balthazar, high school dropout, convicted drug offender, daughter of "those" people.

But here I stood, prepping to go to NYC Fashion Week, nestled beneath the chin of one Dakota Roberts—the dream of too many girls to even name.

"You think I can do this?" I laid my cheek against that sweet spot over his heart.

"Of course you can," he said, giving me a squeeze and sounding so confident that my spirits lifted. "Now tell me about this friend of yours that you've hired."

"Resa?" I pulled out of his embrace and went over to the chest of drawers I had chalk painted and given new hardware. The light pink looked fabulous against the navy accent wall. "She was my closest friend in Long Pines. She's having trouble finding a job that isn't frying chicken—not that that isn't a good job—but I need some help finishing some pieces, and she's good with a needle and thread. At Long Pines we worked in a program that made quilts for domestic violence victims, an irony 'cause most of the women who were behind bars were abused themselves at some time or another."

"But you weren't?"

Dak's statement sounded more like a question.

"I wasn't. I was always loved. My bad choices stemmed from other things—things I couldn't control like immaturity, and, well, that last thing I got busted for wasn't on me. But Ed Earl made good on that. Well, as good as he could." The blood money my uncle had insisted I take had seeded the website and supplies for Deconstructed. I still had to build more of a platform in order to aspire to bigger things. I had started an Instagram page for that very reason, but I was far from collecting enough interest to launch me much farther than the city limit sign of Shreveport. The upcoming show was my shot.

And perhaps New York Fashion Week could help.

If I managed to select the right pieces to wear. I still had another week until we flew out.

"So this Resa is okay to have around?"

"Yeah, I got her into Spring! and I got approval from both parole officers. Connecting to good influences is key to preventing recidivism."

I had been surprised at how easily Resa and I had slipped into our old routine. I had arrived at Casa Cruz first, which worked well because it enabled me to tell the waiter that I would be paying the bill. Cricket had done this for me a few times, which had struck me as strange. I had never gone out to eat with someone without automatically splitting the bill, but she'd picked up the ticket like it was no big deal. I realized afterward that her generosity was part of who she was, and I wanted to be the same. I wasn't in any sort of position to treat people often, but I was in a helluva lot better one than Resa. When my friend arrived, I noted she didn't look as weary as I had when I got home from Long Pines.

"Hey," Resa exclaimed, giving me a huge hug. "I'm so happy to see you!"

"You too! You look pretty good."

"Surprised?"

I had forgotten how endearing her smile was. She had a crooked tooth and light brown eyes that could go from happy to dangerous in mere seconds. A bit mercurial but fiercely loyal, Resa had given me an anchor during many storms. The least I could to was buy her lunch and pitch joining Spring! to her.

"A little."

"Ah, my little gemstone! Always telling the truth." Resa plopped down and picked up a menu. "God, I missed chips and salsa. I might eat just that by itself. Oh, and a margarita. That's the upside to having no ride and taking the bus. And so you know the reason I look good—I moved from the sewing center to the garden. Got me some Vitamin D and definition in these arms. Picking up bags of manure and shoveling the stuff onto tomato plants makes for kick-ass toning."

"You should get the Burrito Bandito. It's the best thing on the menu. And then I want to hear the scoop. Tell me about Long Pines and then what you're planning on for your future."

"I'm planning on staying out of that hell hole is what I'm planning." Resa scooped up a chip as the waiter put the basket in the center of the table. "And my first step is a job. Which according to my parole officer is the biggest step. Why don't people want to hire ex-cons?"

"Because they have a history of stealing?" I grinned. "Or maybe it's the getting caught part that's the barrier. There are plenty of people stealing and lying every day. They just don't get caught."

"Right? But I'm done with that. Done with Groot and his whole bullshit. Steering clear of everything that took me where I was. I'm not going back. I want more for myself."

I glanced at the menu and decided on fish tacos and then looked up at Resa. "So two things. One, I might have a job for you."

"At your store? Cause I went in there a few days ago and told the lady that I wanted to apply if they had something. I wasn't sure about telling you 'cause I wanted to see if you and me, well, you know..."

Resa looked anxious, lowering her eyes and focusing on the chips that she was steadily inhaling. Couldn't blame her—the food was crap at Long Pines. "So that was you? You told her I could be your reference?"

"Well, she hired you when you got out, so I thought she might be one of those do-gooders who wanted to help people make a new start." Resa still wasn't meeting my gaze. I understood. It's always hard to ask for a hand up.

"Well, Cricket *is* a do-gooder, though I'm not sure she would have hired me if she'd known about my past. Thing is I think she *is* looking for someone to help part-time at the shop. But I'm looking for someone too."

At this she met my eyes. "You?"

"I started a business. Ed Earl finally—"

"That son of a bitch." Resa's eyes went from uncertain to homicidal in less than a second. "Don't tell me you have anything to do with him."

"He's made restitution. Gave me eighty thousand to start the business and an apology."

Resa made a scoffing noise. "Lunch money compared to what he owes you. You did his time... though I still don't know why."

I *had* done my uncle's time, and on some days, I myself didn't know why. On the surface, I didn't want Gran to get in trouble. Ed Earl had used her to hide his meth distribution operation, tangling her into a web she had no knowledge of. Then he had used me to transport the meth. When I got busted at the Hunters for the Hungry office, I had refused to talk until I had an attorney—something all Balthazars learned before they could crawl. My attorney, ridiculous as he was, couldn't get me off without me making a deal. I could have ratted out my family and sent Ed Earl to prison for a long time, and maybe part of that deal with the DA might have kept Gran out of it. But I didn't. Without my mom or dad in my life and Gran oblivious to Ed Earl's dealing, I felt adrift. And maybe part of me believed that I deserved what I got. After all, I had sabotaged all the good in my life and had made some questionable decisions, like a snowball ricocheting down a mountain, picking up more and more of what weighed me down but unable to stop myself. So I went to prison and served just under two years for possession with intent to distribute.

I held so much shame in my hands it was a wonder I could use them for sewing.

Deconstructed was my salvation, my second chance, and I wasn't going to squander the opportunity I had been gifted. "Yeah, he owed me. And I'm working on myself. My past is under the bridge, and I'm not interested in doubling back. I have a green pasture ahead somewhere, but first there be mountains to climb."

"Yes, girl, talk pirate to me." She laughed, stopping when the waiter came by the table to take our orders. Resa took my advice and got the Burrito Bandito and a large margarita. I rarely drank alcohol, unless it was good wine, so I went with water.

"So what is this about your business? It ain't like meat processing or frozen transport or anything?" Resa laughed.

I couldn't not chuckle at that. "No. You know how I love to sew."

"And are so good at it. My aunt wears the shawl you embroidered her all the time. So did you open a shop doing alterations or something?"

"Not exactly. I'm taking apart vintage couture that has been compromised in some way. I use the good parts to make a new garment. You'd be surprised at how many vintage pieces exist in the South and how many are tossed aside because of rust stains or mildew. Anyway, I am designing a line that will be showcased in an upcoming fashion festival. I'm hoping it will be a launching pad for a new career for me. I'm going to New York Fashion Week with Cricket's mom next Wednesday."

"New York? Girl... that's so lit."

"Yeah, but I'm nervous. The biggest cities I've been to are New Orleans and Dallas. And this is Fashion Week. There will be cocktail parties and all these famous designers running around." And just like that, a bowling ball materialized in my stomach.

"But isn't that the point?"

She had me there. It *was* the point. I knew from the many self-help podcasts I listened to and the therapist I started seeing after I got out that to grow, we had to be uncomfortable. New York would be like a rectal exam. At my core I was an introvert, and from what I had seen on TV shows and movies, Manhattan was like a drunken uncle at the karaoke mic. Then there was my psyche and tendency to feel not good enough. When faced with designers who had attended Parson's or other design schools, I would be a lost thimble, unnoticed and insignificant. I was going to need a lot of inner cheerleading, and my pom-poms, aka, Cricket would not be there to yell give me an R-U-B-Y!

"You're absolutely right. That's the point. Anyway, getting back to that first thing I wanted to discuss with you, how would you feel about helping me in my studio? I need someone to do finish work, and you're darned handy with a needle."

Resa smiled. "Abso-freaking-lutely. The bitches back together again? Yes, ma'am."

"Is that what we were?"

"We were the Stitchin' Bitches. Did you forget the name of our prison club?"

I chuckled and made room on the table as the waiter arrived with our "don't touch; they're so hot" plates. "And I think Cricket is looking for some extra help since I'm going to be gone a lot this fall. I can give you a recommendation for working there. And that leads me to the second thing I wanted to ask you. There's this program called Spring!, and I think it would help you accomplish what you're hoping to. It's aims to reduce recidivism."

"What's that? I hear everyone sayin' it all the time but..."

"Not going back to the joint."

Resa laughed, propped her chin on her hands, and batted her eyes. "Tell me more."

By the end of the dinner, I had hired Resa and made a plan to pick her up for the next meeting of Spring!

"I'm proud of you," Dak said, pulling me back to the reality of prepping for New York City. "You've changed a lot from the girl who went looking for trouble to the one keeping others out of trouble. And that's just the gravy on the biscuit of what you're doing with your life. You're going to rock Manhattan."

"No, I'm not rocking anything. This is merely an exploratory mission to meet Cricket's aunt and maybe get her interested in me and what I'm doing. I mean, she could think my designs are too passé."

"What's that?"

"I'm not exactly sure. Cricket said that it's a term for not so hot. I'm still learning to speak like she does."

"Why do you need to?" Dak plopped down on my bed and

hugged the ridiculous duck pillow my dad had given me when I was eight years old. "I like you just the way you are."

I walked over and sank into his lap. Dak tossed the pillow, curled his arms around me, and pulled me close. I laid my head on his shoulder, allowing the warmth of this man to seep inside me, give me the confidence I lacked. "Thank you. I don't mean to be so needy. I really don't."

"I like that you need me. You're so damn independent that it feels good to give you something you need."

Was I really that independent? I suppose to most people I looked tough, but on the inside, I was often like a gelatin salad, unstable and full of weird things. I could slide off a plate at any moment. But on the outside, I was talented at looking unaffected. Cool, even. Maybe it was a skill I had learned early at the feet of my parents who'd done plenty to make me wary of revealing my emotions. My mother had been particularly good at exploiting every emotion I felt so she could manipulate me into whatever she wanted. She was also good at ignoring me. Something gave when a child was manipulated and ignored for alternating swaths of time. That giving for me was a defensive wrecking ball of a woman who had stood in handcuffs in front of a judge. So much for independence.

"You give me plenty, Dak Roberts. I'm so lucky to have found you again."

"I wasn't hiding."

I stood and, for the second time, refolded the pajamas I had bought at Target. It seemed wrong to take an old Buc-ee's T-shirt to a chic Upper East Side apartment owned by a lesbian power couple (according to the *Manhattan Ladies Quarterly*. Yeah, I did research.)

Trying to shift the convo away from where it was heading, I said, "I think Cricket might be a little jealous that I'm going away with her mother. Truthfully, I feel sort of crappy about it. She tries so hard to get Marguerite invested in her life. That lady's just a tough nut."

"Well, Cricket will have her hands full here with trying to get Juke to take her on. Especially after the Incident of the Corpse Pose," Dak cracked. He'd decided to put Nancy Drew-ish sounding titles to Cricket's misadventures. He also called the Scott takedown last spring the Case of the Cheating Dickhead. Vulgar but still funny.

Of course that whole spying and snooping period had given Cricket the idea that she'd missed her calling as an investigator. She wanted the tutelage of an experienced PI, and Juke was her mark. She was adamant that she could go work for the handful of other PIs in Shreveport, but she knew Juke. It didn't seem to faze her that Juke was now avoiding her.

"Poor ol' Juke is looking around every corner for sure." I opened a drawer and pulled out a camisole. I didn't know how chilly it would be on my trip. On that thought, I grabbed a scarf off the hanger in my closet and folded it. "I tried to tell her that his business was too small potatoes to hire another person, but she actually said she didn't need to get paid, just use her God-given gifts."

Dak grinned even bigger. "Come over here and let me do a little investigation work of my own."

My heart did a little squeezy thing. "Make it snappy. I'm due at Gran's for dinner. Haven't seen her in over a week and she's fit to be tied." I dropped the camisole and sashayed toward Dak.

"Can't be too quick. I'm a thorough investigator," he said, scooping me up and tossing me onto the bed.

I definitely preferred this kind of investigation.

∽

My gran quickly slid the ceramic pot under the counter when I came in the back door, like a dieter hiding her cookies.

"I saw that," I said by way of greeting.

Gran made a face. "You can't make good cornbread without a cast-iron skillet and bacon drippings. I ain't never delivering bad cornbread to the table, sugar."

"How many points is bacon grease?" I asked, knowing that she was on Weight Watchers and watching her point intake. I shrugged off my jacket and hung it on the back of the chair where I had always sat. Even as a child, it was my spot, claimed fiercely each time one of my boy cousins plopped down in it. I had once cut my chin defending my spot.

"Don't you worry about it." Gran pulled a cast-iron skillet from the oven, then returned to her mixing bowl. The cornbread batter sizzled as she poured it into the hot pan, and the comforting scent of home wrapped round me. Gran lifted the lid of the dutch oven and swirled a spoon through some purple-hull peas, releasing another aroma from my childhood into the air. "Got a good scald on these."

"You always do."

Gran nodded her head and tugged on the bottom of her workout shirt. "Dinner will be ready in about an hour or so. Until then, let's have a cuppa and a chat. I wanna hear all about that crazy Cricket and the firemen last week. Land sakes."

"She was pretty embarrassed, but when you see a man lying still and not answering, you assume the worst." I settled myself at the table as Gran put the kettle on the burner. A fierce overeater, Gran had learned that sipping tea before she ate dinner kept her from going overboard. Ever since her health scare almost six months ago, she'd lost almost twenty-five pounds, started taking water aerobics classes at the YMCA, and modified her tried-and-true down-home recipes. Well, mostly. My uncle Jimbo complained about missing chicken-fried steak, but even he had reaped the benefits, dropping some much-needed weight. He now looked only five months pregnant rather than nine.

"I bet Juke was fit to be tied. All those firemen storming up the stairs and busting in."

"Griff did the busting in. He kicked down the window. Juke is more upset about that." I picked a tea bag from the assortment on the lazy Susan and plopped it into a chipped cup that Gran had bought in Dollywood. Herbal caffeine-free for me. "Cricket had gone off with Griff to look for Juke but somehow ended up there on her own. I think she and Griff got pissed at each other."

My gran gave me the look.

"Sorry, PO'd at each other," I amended, falling into line on the no-cussin' rule proudly displayed on the kitchen wall. Gran had raised a lot of boys and loved a lot of Jesus. "I don't know what is going on there. I can't figure out if they are into each other or not."

"They don't seem to be a likely couple, do they? She's so prissy and proud, and he's—well, he's Griffin. Always been difficult, grumpy, and apt to skip out on festivities and such. He's a good-looking rascal, sure, but he ain't the going-along sort." Gran poured the water from the kettle over our tea bags, returned it to the stove, and flopped down into the chair with a sigh. "Now I want to hear about how your sewing is going. Tell me what you're working on."

We spent a few happy minutes talking about my issues with the darts on the jacquard jacket and the color of thread I should use on a lapel portion. Then I told her about New York City and how Cricket's aunt was going to—fingers crossed—help me.

"That woman has a gay sister? Well, knock me over with a feather. I ain't seen anyone as straight as that woman. She's got a poker up her backside and her nose so far in the air she should carry an umbrella so she don't drown every time a rain comes.

You know what Cricket told me?" Gran leaned forward, blue eyes glittering with amusement. "She sleeps in her brassiere."

"Gran."

"All I'm saying is that you're gonna have your hands full trying to mind your p's and q's with ol' Marguerite."

"Yeah, but it's fine. She's committed to helping me, and that feels good."

My gran thought about that. "And you're taking the help, which feels good to me. You've gone too long without letting people in. I get it. You had to watch your back in the joint, but that way of livin' made you as puckered up as a butthole."

I gave *her* the look.

"Sorry." Her cheeks pinked adorably. "I sometimes forget and your Pawpaw's words just pop out. He was a good man but a man, you know."

I smiled because that was pretty much with all men. They couldn't seem to stop an occasional scratch, fart, or crude comparison. DNA probably. "Well, my time at Long Pines taught me a lot about life—tend to yourself, help others when it makes sense, and trust no one."

"That's not how life is. That's how prison life is, and you ain't there no more. Never should've been. But I ain't rucking that up again. I will say that the key to life is loving one another. When you love on people, you learn that accepting help ain't so bad. We're all like a bunch of potted plants needing a bit of water, and you can't always do that for yourself. We are made to give and receive, and it's the receiving part you forget. So I'm happy you're letting Drill Sergeant Marguerite Quinney invest a little in you."

She was right—I didn't like accepting help. When Ed Earl gave me the check that had seeded my new venture, I had sat on it for weeks, not certain I wanted to take his help. I damn sure hadn't wanted to accept Dak's help the day my car wouldn't start.

But that had led to a new start with him. And Ed Earl had given me the ability to pursue my dreams. Now both Cricket and Marguerite were helping me with contacts in the fashion industry. If I hadn't let them help me, where would I be? "I'm working on it, Gran, and I'm getting better at it."

Gran smiled. "That's my girl. Now let's talk about New York City. That's a big place."

"Where dreams go to die," I cracked.

"Or soar." Gran jabbed a turquoise-painted finger down on the scarred table. "That's what we're talking about, sugar. Your thoughts become your actions. We don't need no negative Nancying going on."

Jimbo bumbled in, wearing a pair of coveralls stained with grease. "Afternoon, my people. Where's the coffee?"

"We're having *tea*," I said.

He made a face. "A man don't drink tea. Unless it's sweet and iced."

I made a face at Gran, and she ignored her youngest son. "I always wanted to go to that Rainbow Room. They always made it sound so glamorous in movies. And the Empire State Building. Oh, I loved *An Affair to Remember*, the thought of meeting at the top and—"

"Who's goin' up there?" Jimbo asked sounding horrified as he rifled through the cabinet. He withdrew a package of Community coffee.

"Our Roo is going to Fashion Week in New York City so all them people up there can discover what true talent is." Gran folded her arms over her shrinking stomach.

Jimbo snorted. "Hell, New York City ain't got nothin' but crime, rats, and liberals."

My uncle delivered that platitude like someone approaching a pile of horse hockey. He wasn't the most enlightened of creatures.

"Oh, for heaven's sake, they won't eat you. You're full of preservatives." I rolled my eyes.

"Who? The rats?" Uncle Jimbo died laughing. My gran's lips twitched.

I retrained my gaze on my grandmother, taking a page from her book and ignoring Jimbo. "I don't know how much time I will have for sightseeing. Cricket says her aunt goes to a ton of shows and parties. But I will try to get to the Empire State Building and take some pictures for you. And you know, you and I could go to New York City one day. Just a girls' trip to take a bite outta the apple."

"I'm too old for New York City." My grandmother waved a poo-pooing hand. "Take that young gentleman of yours."

"He's already been there." Jimbo slammed around the kitchen, sloshing water from the coffeepot onto the counter. "Went all over when he was playing ball. Bet he hated it. But whatever, 'cause he's settling down. Saw him comin' out of Mitchell's Jewelry yesterday. Might be *really* settling down. With our little Roo."

My stomach contracted at his words.

A jewelry store?

Surely Dak wasn't visiting the jewelry store for an engagement ring. That would be too soon, too fast, too much. I didn't want a diamond, not right now when my whole world felt so uncertain yet blooming with a possibility. Jimbo had to be mistaken in his presumption. "No way. Dak was probably running an errand for his mother. We're not even close to that sort of thing. And don't call me Roo."

Gran reached over and squeezed my hand. "Don't get your panties in a wad over what Jimbo's saying. Dak knows that you're not ready for commitment."

"Well, I'm not."

"I'll marry him." Jimbo scooped out a measure into the

coffee maker basket. "He has a sick house on the lake and good tickets for LSU games."

"Spoken like a true Louisianian." Sarcasm might have been all drippy on my words. I didn't mind a little drippiness. What I did mind was a red box and a big diamond. Not ready for that by a country mile.

My cell phone vibrated in my pocket, tearing me away from thoughts of rings. I pulled it out. Cricket. "Hey, what's up?"

"You gotta come help me," she yell-whispered, the sound of a whimper in the background.

I glanced out the window at the dying day. I didn't want to move from this table and my gran's TLC. "Where are you? And is that a dog I'm hearing?"

"Yes, and I'm not exactly sure what street I'm on, but my van is stuck."

"Where?"

"All I know is that it's not the best part of town. There are a bunch of run-down houses and a pit bull on a chain, poor thing. I mean, he would attack me if not for the chain and all, but I still feel bad for him. Anyway, I need some help. Uh, with my van. Pretty please. I'll pay you overtime."

I sighed. "You don't have to pay me to help you. We're friends, remember? Drop a pin, and I'll see if I can get in touch with Griff so we can get you out."

"No," she squeaked. "I think we can do it by ourselves. But we might need a rope or something. It's stuck pretty good."

Irritation nudged aside the unsettled feelings I had over Dak and upcoming trips. I had planned on a nice dinner with Gran before going home and watching *The Bachelor*. Marguerite and I texted each other during the episodes, though I was not allowed to say so to anyone on penalty of death. Cricket's mother loved a little camp, which is why she low-key loved my designs. On one level, Marguerite was Queen of England with her matriarchal shoes and firm jawline; on the other, she thrilled at a little lowness. Cricket had once told me that she got her daring from her grandmother, a woman who had worked with sex-trafficking victims back in the day, but I knew that Cricket couldn't see beyond her blinders when it came to her mother. At any rate, I would have to run to her rescue overtime or not. That's what friends did for one another.

But I was calling Griff.

"I'll be right there. And why are you in this area again?"

"Well, I am on a case. Nothing official of course. Just helping out a neighbor whose little dog was stolen right out of her side yard. She's been frantic, and I told her I would help. Um, I will tell you more later. Oh wait. Snap. Someone's coming." Cricket trailed off, and I heard her talking to someone, saying she was okay, and a friend was on the way. She sounded super stressed out. Then the call ended, making my heart gallop a little bit.

I glanced at the screen, making sure she'd sent the pin, and pushed my chair back as a ding sounded. I frowned at the pinned location. Rough territory for sure. "Gotta go, Gran. Cricket got her van stuck over in the Creighton Bluff area."

"You ain't going over there by yourself. Jimbo, go with Ruby to help Cricket."

"He doesn't have to come with me. I'm going to stop by the tow yard and see if Griff can send a truck."

"Good thought." Jimbo lifted the lid on the peas and picked up the tasting spoon.

"Drop it," Gran said, jabbing a finger his way. "And yeah, you better call Griffin for that job."

I sighed and dialed my cousin's number, wondering if this was going to be standard procedure in the coming months when Cricket obtained her private investigation certification and tried to go to work for Juke.

Griff answer with a gruff "Yeah?"

"Cricket's stuck in Creighton Bluff, and I need to borrow a tow truck."

I couldn't repeat the word he uttered in polite company. Or even impolite company. I just grabbed my light jacket off the back of the chair and waved goodbye to Gran.

"Call me and let me know you're safe," she called back.

6

Cricket

Gunning one's minivan on a slick road after an afternoon storm wasn't smart private detective maneuvering. It wasn't even everyday smart person maneuvering. I had fishtailed after pealing out and ended up stuck on a high embankment two houses down from someone who could be very dangerous.

The French bulldog I had just recovered sat beside me, drooling all over my upholstery, but that wasn't the worst part of it. He was covered in mud from sliding beneath the fence of the dognapper's house.

Yes, dognapper.

Louis, aka, Louie, aka Mr. Pooper Pants, had been stolen from the side yard of my across-the-street neighbor, Mrs. Ava Easley. The eighty-two-year-old former attorney was dotty for her Frenchie. And plain, well, dotty in her old age. Once upon a time, she'd been a fierce civil rights attorney, blazing paths and kicking ass, but these days she struggled with her memory, and since I had done years of tennis clinic with her daughter Eileen, I checked on Mrs. Ava regularly. She let Louie out at the same time every morning, but three days ago, he'd not come in from the patio courtyard where he took his daily constitutionals. Mrs. Ava's next-door neighbor Mr. Shively had reported seeing a pickup truck pulling away from the curb. French bulldogs were often a dog of choice for people who participated in dastardly deeds such as taking people's prized pups. Mr. Shively had not managed to get the license plate because the cameras in his driveway didn't show the rear of the truck. But I knew the truck was red and it had a bumper sticker with a local radio station on it. Oh, and it was a Ford.

Mrs. Ava had called the theft in to the police, and I had gone over at lunchtime to settle her down with a calming cup of tea. Because Eileen worked at the DA's office (which Mrs. Ava fondly called the Death Star,) she'd made a special request, and the police department was sending someone over to take Ava's statement. When I answered Mrs. Ava's door, I was taken aback at how handsome the detective was. Who knew the Shreveport Police Department had six-foot blond hotties hiding behind their detective desks?

"Hi," I said opening the door and waving him inside. "I'm Cricket, Mrs. Ava's neighbor. I told Eileen that I would come help her mother since the poor woman is totally freaked out by Louie being taken."

The detective blinked. "Is that the name of the missing person?"

"Missing person? Well, not exactly. Well, I guess to Mrs. Ava he's like a baby," I amended, leading the way toward the living room.

"I already have a call in to the FBI. I was told that this was a critical missing." He sounded confused, looking at the shadow box collection of thimbles centered on the wall—a leftover of the 1980s that Mrs. Ava refused to part with.

"Well, it's critical to Mrs. Ava, but I don't think we need to call the FBI," I said, noting that Mrs. Ava had finally stopped crying. Her teacup was trembling, however, spilling Earl Grey onto her crocheted shawl that I had draped across her lap. "Do they do that for dogs?"

The handsome detective with a perfect little dimple on his chin, a la Cary Grant, stopped in the center of the white carpet and put his hands on his hips. "You telling me this is about someone stealing a *dog*?"

"Oh, Louie, my precious angel," Mrs. Ava moaned, stifling a sob.

I shot Mr. Hot Copper a fierce look and sank down beside Mrs. Ava, curling an arm around her. "It's okay. This *nice* gentleman is here from the police department to help you get Louie back."

The detective, as handsome as he was, looked perturbed at his mission being about a dog and not a child. He pulled out his phone, held up a finger, and stepped into Mrs. Ava's kitchen. He put his phone to his ear, and I had to presume he was calling off the FBI for the critically missing person. His low voice was indistinguishable under the yard guy blowing off Mr. Shively's patio next door.

Mrs. Ava's frail little bird arms trembled as she set the cup on the saucer, sloshing tea onto the floor. I would have to get the carpet cleaner. White carpet was the devil.

The detective returned, and his face was schooled into a more compliant expression. "Okay, had to call it in. Sorry about that. I'm Detective Wesley McNally, and I'm here to take down the details of the personal property theft."

Those last words were uttered with a little derision. Obviously, Wesley thought he'd caught a career-making case with a kidnapping. I watched enough *Law and Order* and *Major Crimes* to understand that a dognapping was peanuts and a little disappointing. And now as a professional—okay, sorta professional—private investigator, I understood that some cases would be more exciting than others. Wesley wasn't pumped about finding a dog.

"Mrs. Ava, tell Mr. McNally what happened to Louie."

Mrs. Ava clasped her hands, sat up straighter, and pulled herself together, so to speak. "I rose as I always do at eight thirty a.m. I slept just fine last night. But Louie had gotten up earlier than normal, yapping at the courtyard door to go outside for his constitutional. Usually he sleeps in, but Eileen was here last night and fed him some yogurt. He really doesn't tolerate dairy very well. I told Eileen not to give him any, but she never listens. Does what she wants. Always has. My late husband... I can't remember his name at the moment... used to say—"

"Ma'am, let's stick to the facts." Detective McNally glanced at his cell phone.

"What facts?" Mrs. Ava looked at me. "Who is this man? Did I have a doctor's appointment today?"

I shot Wesley McNally another look. Interrupting Mrs. Ava only confused her. "It's fine, Mrs. Ava. We're talking about Louie and this morning."

"Oh yes. Someone took my Louie! Right out of my courtyard! Oh, the world these days. Taking people's babies!"

Wesley McNally was trying to look professional, but I could see he was struggling. Perhaps he wasn't a man of patience.

I patted her hand. "Yes, so tell him what you know."

"Well, I let him out and went to use the Keurig coffee maker that makes one cup at a time. Eileen gave it to me for Christmas this year. No, maybe it was last year. My memory is not so good anymore. I do love the—"

"Ahem." Detective McNally cleared his throat. "And Louie...?"

"Yes, well, he went out to do his business, you see. And I went to make my coffee. That was about five minutes. Perhaps seven. Louie is a very efficient dog, so he doesn't dawdle in the morning because he wants his treat. There it is," she said, flinging out a hand, gesturing to the milk bone treat still sitting on the granite counter.

"Aren't you going to take notes?" I asked Detective McNally.

He touched his temple. "I have an incredible memory."

That wasn't how I would have done it, but I wasn't a detective with the Shreveport Police Department. Well, yet. I mean, I could do it if I wanted, but I knew I would look terrible in those uniforms. And who would run the antiques store? Investigation was a moonlighting gig for me.

"Well, he didn't come inside. So I went around the patio, calling him. He wasn't there." Mrs. Ava sounded so sad that my heart squeezed. Louie really was her everything.

"You checked the perimeter?" Detective McNally glanced toward the french doors that led to the courtyard.

"Indeed I did. No digging or anything. But the gate was slightly ajar and not latched. So I pushed it open to the side yard. He wasn't there. Mr. Shively was watering his begonias. He is very fussy about his begonias, you see, but he hadn't seen Louie. What he had seen was a red truck pulling away from the curb, just there." She pointed toward the open french doors. Through the opening, one could see a small courtyard with petunias somewhat withered from the hot summer and beyond, the street.

"And this truck did not belong to one of your neighbors?" Detective McNally asked.

"Heavens no. Mr. Shively drives a Cadillac. He's fussy about it too. Always out there polishing on it and such. No, this was more like a laborer's truck. We get those around here. Lots of lazy people who don't do their own lawn care. Now when I was able, I liked to mow my own grass. I had an adorable red lawn tractor that I could sit on and drive. I even ran the Weed Eater. There is no better satisfaction than trimming one's own yard just so. I even cut little patterns the way they do on the ball field. Do you cut your own yard, young man?"

I looked at Detective McNally who looked a little dazed. "Ma'am?"

"Do you cut your own yard? What sort of a mower do you have?"

"Uh, uh." He looked at me as if asking for help.

I complied. "Mrs. Ava, I'm sure that's not important right now. We need to be quick in finding Louie."

Her eyes welled up. "Oh, my dear boy. I hope they aren't unkind to him. He's such a sensitive fellow."

"I mow my own yard. I have a John Deere," the detective said.

Hiding my smile, I presented Mrs. Ava her tea. "Here, have a sip."

"I think I got the gist of it all." Detective McNally rose from the blue-mist satin brocade chair. I adored that fabric. "I will check with the guard and see if I can locate this truck and question the driver."

"And arrest him!" Mrs. Ava said quite dramatically.

"If that person is the person who stole your pet." Detective McNally glanced my way and gave a curt nod. "I have what I need."

I rose and followed him into the foyer, wincing when his shoulder almost caught the nice reproduction of an orchid sitting on the ornate table just to the left of the door. I wanted to tell him that I already asked the gate guard but maybe the police could have access to the log without a warrant. I wasn't exactly sure and couldn't remember discussing that in my class. "Thank you for coming. When should we hear from you?"

Detective McNally turned and put his hand inside his breast pocket, withdrawing a business card. "I hate to say don't call us, we'll call you, but that's pretty much the truth. I wish the SPD had the time and resources to update you on cases such as this. We don't. I would recommend going on local lost-and-found pet groups on places like Facebook. Often this online alternative to neighborhood watch can help locate missing animals quickly. I would also recommend checking with the animal shelter. They have a three-day stray hold."

"But Louie isn't missing. We think someone stole him." I tried to sound conversational and not accusatory. I understood the whole honey-and-fly thing very well.

"Yes, well, that can't be proven at this time. The gate was open. Let's hope Mr. Louie has merely wandered off and will show back up in time for some kibble." He put his hand on the doorknob. "If there is anything more I can do, call me."

He handed me his card, and I took it.

Then he did something very unexpected. He cocked his head and narrowed his eyes. "Is your name really Cricket?"

"It's a nickname. Who in the world would name their child Cricket?" I smiled even though I felt a little perturbed at him. He'd blown off this whole missing-dog thing. In one way, I understood—Shreveport's murder rate was on the rise and the number of officers on the decline. I wasn't great at math, but I could figure that one out. Louie wasn't going to get a lot of attention.

"So are you the Cricket married to the guy who was involved in the Ponzi scheme? The one who helped nail him?"

"I *was* married to him. Monday our divorce will be finalized. And as for nailing him?" I held up my hands playfully. "You got me, officer."

So that came out a bit flirtier than I intended, and I felt a little shift in the air. That kind of shift when a dude suddenly noticed how full a woman's lips were (thanks, hydro plump lip lover gloss) and how a T-shirt dress might hug some curves (thanks, Southern Maid donuts) and how my ring was noticeably missing (thanks, slimeball ex-husband).

He delivered a devastating smile, the kind that made a girl feel a flutter. "Do I now?"

I gave a throaty laugh like I did this sort of thing all day long. "Well, only if you want."

Oh my God. Who was I?

Wesley McNally, no doubt one of Shreveport Police Department's finest, tapped his card. "Call me and we'll see about who gets who."

And just like that, I became the Cricket I had never thought I could be. I had just flirted my way into getting gotten by a fairly hot police detective. Question was... did I want to be gotten? An image of Griffin Moon popped into my head. I had thought I wanted to get gotten by him, but for some reason, whatever we'd had between us now sat on a shelf. It was at the point that I needed to take us off the shelf or maybe find a new display.

Or none of the above.

I could be totally reasonable and work on myself, not worrying about men at all. Follow the recommendations in *Divorce for Dummies* and *How to be a Single Lady in a Hooking Up World*. Experts always advise the recently released to work on themselves, take vitamins, do yoga, and go on girls' trips. I was down with that, but to be honest, I had felt alone even when I was married. Monday I would sign the papers ending our marriage, and that part of my life would be over. A tiny part of me was sad, but the other part of me was ready to move forward in life.

I longed for change... and maybe a date or two. I slid Detective Wesley McNally's card into my back pocket and went to check on Mrs. Ava.

"Cricket, Eileen mentioned to me that you're a detective now. Maybe you can find Louie." Mrs. Ava's eyes were no longer misty. She looked determined. Probably the same way she did when she was grilling witnesses.

Why had I told Eileen I had just completed my private investigator's course? "Well, I'm fresh off the course. Not really licensed yet. I have to do my hours under a trained private investigator. But I'm going to do what I can to help you."

"I want to hire you. What's your rate?"

I didn't have a rate. Frankly, I was still waiting on Juke to give me a call. I had sent a very polite, professional email as a follow-up to my résumé. Maybe he was still miffed I had called 911 when I thought he was dead. Maybe I needed to take a plate of cookies to his office and persuade him the best way I knew how —through his stomach. But then again, Juke was getting healthy, doing yoga and meditation (almost a little too well), so maybe some healthy snacks instead of cookies? "Well, let me check on that."

"Why ask a man to do what a woman can do better? I tell you, Cricket, in my day, it was the women who knew how to get things done. Men don't do the detailed work. They don't want to knock on doors or comb through witness statements. Half of them don't even talk to the witnesses. I overturned a lot of cases because of laziness. And, little missy, you aren't lazy. You're going to be good at this. Look at you already. You've interviewed all the neighbors and talked to the gate guard."

"But Mr. Laney won't give me the gate entries from last night or this morning. Something about me not being authorized." I had taken Mr. Laney, our gate guard, some cookies that morning when Eileen had called me. I tried to inquire about suspicious characters coming and going. Mr. Laney had munched happily on the snickerdoodles while giving up exactly nothing. I had expected some resistance, so I had worn my push-up bra, which I knew was no way to conduct a professional investigation, but I had to be pragmatic. Cookies and boobs were terrific distractors. But I went zero for two on that venture. Then again, it was rumored that Mr. Laney needed cataract surgery, and the sun was very glaring that morning. That was most likely the reason I came away with no good information and an empty plate. "Don't worry though. You have people looking."

I had left Mrs. Ava's and gone home, pondering my next move.

Use what you know.

So I called my friend who was on the HOA board. I told her that the house a few doors down had a lawn service that drove a red Ford truck that had dropped a bag of straw into the street. I told her I needed to return it. Bit of waffling and lots of explaining on how I couldn't possibly keep the bag of straw as a "finders-keepers" netted me the license plate number I needed. Then I paid one of those expensive sites that somehow circumnavigates the Department of Motor Vehicles laws about records and ended up with a VIN number and a name—Peter Dahmer.

Yes, the last name gave me pause too.

Then I accessed the yellow pages, online of course, because who had a phone book anymore? Okay, some people kept that brick chunk of advertisements and teeny-tiny printed phone numbers.

Anyway, I got the Dahmer address and decided to do a stakeout and get proof that they'd taken the dog. I'd done stakeouts before, so I knew what to bring—binoculars, protein bars, and some bottled water. I tossed in a Mary Kay Andrews book because she'd written a few about antiquing sleuths and an extra battery pack in case my phone ran out of juice. I had learned two things from my last stakeout, primarily that I didn't need an expensive camera because my iPhone with the fancy lens could zoom and take detailed pictures in the dark and that the van was a better choice of vehicle. My grandmother's red Alfa Romeo Spider Veloce drew too much attention and was more fragile than I'd thought.

I made sure Julia Kate had a ride home from school, a salad from Cush's in the fridge (she was eating "clean" this week), and a printed copy of the certificate that said I had passed the private investigator's exam. Just in case. I planned to call the police if I saw any sign of Louie. Specifically, I planned to call the very dishy Wesley McNally. But then things had gotten out of hand, and right after I called Detective Cutie Pie, Louie dug out from under the fence, and the dognapper was heading off his porch and toward my van.

Diversionary driving hadn't been taught in private investigations class, so I wasn't prepared for having to hit the gas and hightail it out of Creighton Bluff. The streets were slick, and my tires were probably much the same. Let's face it, I was still getting used to having to do things like car maintenance and changing out air filters in the house. Usually, Scott did those things. If I had thought about checking my tread or things like cleaning fuel injectors, maybe I would have made it out. As it was, I fishtailed and ended up high center on an embankment two doors down from the Dahmer house.

I looked at Louie drooling on my leather seats and in the rearview mirror at a man who had to be Peter Dahmer himself and dialed the only person who I knew would come running to help me.

Thank God Ruby answered the phone.

7

Ruby

I SAT BESIDE GRIFF, trying to rationalize why Cricket would be in a neighborhood like Creighton Bluff, but I could come up with exactly nothing. The area consisted of crackerjack box houses, abandoned warehouses, and a salvage yard where my male relatives sometimes went to get parts for their collection of autos that were in varying states of disrepair. The occupied dwellings probably housed those with criminal records or those who were married to someone with a criminal record. The neighborhood darn sure didn't have a National Night Out or a homeowner's association. Here they tin-foiled their windows and minded their own business... and expected you to do the same.

Griff looked over at me as we turned down Fossil Road, the uninspiring entrance to the working-class neighborhood. "Does this have something to do with her harebrained idea that she's a private detective?"

"Investigator," I said.

"Huh?"

"I believe that's the official term."

"I don't give a rat's ass what it's called. It's stupid. And dangerous."

Aggravation rose in me. "At least she's trying something new, trying to help other people. Nothing wrong with that."

"Except she's going to get herself killed."

I waved a hand. "It's still light outside, and she has pepper spray."

"And that stops a bullet?" He might have rolled his eyes before squinting at the weed-strangled yard of a house with two less-than-savory-looking gentlemen sitting on the porch in wifebeaters—um, undershirts—and saggy cargo shorts. They also wore what looked to be steel-toed boots and so many tats it was hard to tell that they were white guys. But they were, and they looked like they'd missed the meeting about being a welcoming committee for visitors. A quarter of a mile down the road Cricket's van sat half in the road, half in someone's yard/ditch.

I pointed but didn't need to—a small collection of neighborhood people had gathered around, including one man who looked to be banging on the passenger door.

"What the..." Griff gunned the tow truck and raced down the street. I grabbed the handle above me as he skidded to a halt. His door flew open, and he stood up. "Hey, what the hell are you doing?"

Everyone turned around because, well, Griff had probably scared the holy hell out of them. I know he had scared it out of me. The overweight man banging on the door stopped and turned around.

Griff jumped down, as intimidating as any of the people gathered.

"This lady done run off in this yard and won't open her car door," one woman said unhelpfully.

Griff strode to the front of the crowd, glared at the fellow near the door, who was now backing away, and went to the driver's side. I slid out of the truck into the street, worried for Cricket.

The driver's door opened, and Cricket climbed out, looking relieved. And not nearly as concerned as she should be. She gestured to the van. "Hey, y'all. Guess I got a little stuck."

"She gotta lot stuck," an older man with an eye patch said.

He wasn't wrong. The van's front right tire was a good foot off the ground.

Cricket tried to smile. "I guess in hindsight, I might need new tires."

"And some driving lessons," the one-eyed guy drawled.

"This lady stole my dog," the man who'd been banging on the door said.

"I did not!" Cricket spun toward him. "That's Ava Easley's dog."

The man narrowed his eyes. "Prove it."

Sirens sounded in the distance, and an unmarked police car turned down the street. People scattered back toward their houses, obviously not interested in being, you know, arrested. I won't lie. I felt a bit panicky myself. Like, maybe I should wait in the tow truck. But I looked at Cricket, who had called me for help, and stood my ground. I wasn't violating my parole. I had nothing to hide except the zit on my chin which had cropped up from the stress of all I had going on.

The dark Crown Vic rolled to a halt and a good-looking man in a shirt and tie climbed out. He wore sunglasses and looked like a movie star. Like that guy who wore the rumpled white blazers back in the 80s. Yeah, that good.

Cricket looked at the newcomer. "Just so you know, I did

what you said. I sat tight. Louie came under the fence on his own."

The good-looking guy—who I guess was a detective, being that he wasn't wearing a police uniform—made a face. "I'm pretty sure you did not sit tight—"

"I decided to put him in the car and, you know, leave."

The guy looked at the van and then back at Cricket. He lifted a sexy eyebrow.

Cricket's face fell as she glanced back at her high-centered van. "My tires sorta slipped around. The pavement's very wet."

"She definitely needs new tires. Bald as a baby's backside," One Eye said.

Griff had been watching these proceedings with his normal expression—flatliner—but I could see something in his eyes at this new (and pretty damn hot) guy's arrival. Griff wasn't pleased at all. Next, he eyeballed the overweight guy making the claim on the dog and prepared to say something, but that's when Louie or whatever its name was started barking.

"See? He wants to stay with me. He's my dog," the overweight guy said.

Cricket scooped up Louie, and I winced because the dog was smearing mud onto her white shirt. "This is Louie. Says so on his collar." She tapped the plate on the sparkling color of aquamarine.

And that gave me an idea for the jewelry on the low-cut ivory chiffon blouse. A thick collar with a bold color that the fabric looped through would look good with the navy fitted trousers with the flared ankles. I filed that away as a problem solved.

"I'm Detective Wesley McNally." The hot cop pulled out a badge before repocketing it. "I need to speak to you"—he jabbed a finger at the overweight guy—"Mr....?"

"Dahmer," the overweight guy said.

"Really?" McNally made a face.

The Dahmer guy shrugged like "Whatcha gonna do?"

"And you," McNally pointed to Cricket. "The rest of you can leave."

"Except my friends," Cricket said, patting the dog and pointing to me and Griff. "They came to help pull the van out. That's Griff and Ruby. And that's Griff's truck."

Detective McNally didn't look impressed but didn't tell us to vamoose either. So Griff walked over and leaned against his truck, crossing arms and elevating the biceps he'd been working on since he went through puberty. The rest of the neighborhood people returned to their stoops, keeping an eye on the goings-on because that's what you did when the police showed up in your neighborhood.

"Okay, so you're saying this is your dog?" McNally looked at Dahmer and arched his brow. They were nice eyebrows, and I wondered if he waxed them. I glanced over at Griff, knowing that the only thing he waxed was his Harley.

"Well, sorta. I found him a few days ago." Dahmer glanced at the dog.

"*Found* him?" McNally echoed.

"Well, yeah. See, I was working a job out in Trace. I straw beds and stuff for folks. This dog was just standing by my truck like it wanted to get inside the cab. Might have been that sack of McDonald's or the way Eddie was carrying on, but anyway, I let him sit inside with Eddie while I finished the beds for this one lady. Then I called the number right there on the collar 'cept no one answered, and there wasn't no way to leave a message."

"So you just took the dog?"

"That's what I'm telling y'all. I wasn't going to leave it there. It's hot and coulda got runned over. I called the number again, and no answer or nothin', so I just been keepin' him. Eddie likes him."

"Who's Eddie?"

"That's my boy. He's what they call special needs. Brain injury in an accident."

At that moment, perfectly on cue, the screen door on the flaky house opened, and a dark-haired teen emerged. He squinted at the tow truck and people standing nearby, and then his gaze found a wriggling Louie in my arms. "Da!"

"That's my boy right there," Dahmer said, pointing toward the boy, who had sat in a rocking chair and started rocking back and forth. The boy's outstretched arms weren't toward his father. They were toward Louie.

"Da! Da!" Eddie said, growing agitated and rocking harder.

"He just wants to hold that puppy a little," Dahmer said.

And you know I could see on Cricket's face exactly what I felt inside my chest—a welling up and acknowledgment that maybe Mr. Dahmer hadn't done the right thing, but he hadn't done the wrong thing either. Louie wiggled and thrashed, causing Cricket to drop him. The dog landed on his feet and took off toward the porch.

"Louie!" Cricket yelled, chasing after the dog.

Louie didn't slow; he trotted up the sagging porch steps and danced around Eddie's rocking chair. Eddie had erupted into crowing pleasure, his excited laughter unspooling the tightest lock on the stingiest of hearts. The disabled boy clapped, his hands slapping together in a jerking motion, and the smile on his face was absolutely, well, something I couldn't find words for. I'll settle on beautiful.

Cricket walked over and stopped on the bottom step. "You like Louie, don't you?"

The boy jerked his head back and forth in the affirmative. "Da. Da!"

"Yes, he's a dog. You know, he belongs to a friend of mine who misses him so very much. I need to take him back to her, but I'm going to talk to your daddy. I think you need a puppy of your own. Would you like that?"

I'm not sure Eddie understood what Cricket told him, but his father did. I could feel that change in Mr. Dahmer, a sort of realization that Louie wasn't staying with them, but Cricket meant them no harm.

Detective McNally cleared his throat. "She's right. You took that dog and didn't make a true effort to take him back or look for the owners. I could charge you with theft, and as expensive as that pup is, that could be a felony."

"I didn't steal the dog. I saved it. It was in the middle of the street. The danged thing hopped up and wanted to play with Eddie. I did a good thing. Wasn't even gonna keep it. Just let it stay a little while." Mr. Dahmer looked back toward the porch where Cricket now sat beside Eddie, helping him to stroke the fur on the dog that had gone totally still at the boy's touch. Like he knew that Eddie was special and needed the silky smoothness of his coat. I glanced over at Griff, and his face was soft as I've ever seen it. Yeah, everyone in North Shreveport knew that Griff was a tough son-of-a-cracker, but a few of us also knew he rescued cats, bought something from every kid who came selling school crap at his door, and never took the shot when he was hunting. Under his brawn and beauty beat the tenderest of hearts. And that tamed beast watched Cricket with something I'd never seen before on his face.

"Well, that's true, so I'm not going to arrest you, Mr. Dahmer. I will, however, be taking Louie back to his owner." Detective McNally gestured toward Cricket. "Come on now, Mrs. Crosby. Bring the dog."

Cricket rose and scooped up Louie. I saw her bend down and place a hand on Eddie's shoulder and say something to him before tucking Louie under her arm and coming back to where we stood. She had mud smearing a cheek and tears glittering in her eyes. "Mr. Dahmer, your son needs a service dog who can be his companion and help him communicate better with the world."

"Cain't afford no service dog. They're sky-high, and I don't have time to train some stray neither." Mr. Dahmer scratched the back of his neck and shook his head. "Not like I wouldn't do what I could for my boy. Just some things cain't be done."

Cricket had that look in her eye—the one that said "horse hockey"—and I knew Mr. Dahmer was about to find out that Cricket was a force to be reckoned with. "I beg to differ with you. There are grants and people who are willing to help."

"Don't know about all that," Mr. Dahmer said.

"Oh, I do. And I'm on the case now. We're going to find your Eddie a service pup."

Detective McNally snorted. I wasn't sure how he knew Cricket, but he seemed to be amused by her much the same way Griff had been the first time—no, make that the second time—he'd met her. All I knew was that Mr. Dahmer better go ahead and stock up on kibble because he'd likely have a dog by week's end.

"Welp, I don't see how, but you go on ahead and try. Maybe a rich lady like you can do what a poor fella like me cain't." Dahmer shifted his gaze to the porch. "If I ain't gonna end up in cuffs, mind if I go check on my boy? This will be upsetting to him. He liked that dog."

Detective McNally nodded. "Go on."

We stood there and watched him trudge up the steps. Eddie made keening noises, which made me feel pretty bad for the kid.

"I'm going to call Karla Monzingo. She trains service dogs. If anyone needs a sweet canine companion, it's that poor child." We all watched as Mr. Dahmer tried to console his son.

Sadness welled up inside me, and that age-old question of why life was so hard for some and easy for others buzzed around my brain. I knew what Mr. Dahmer felt because I'd dug myself the same kind of hole before and had been unable to find a way out. I too had felt utterly powerless to do much about it.

Or maybe I hadn't wanted to do much about the hole I had dug. I had stewed in my juices for a long time, as my gran would say. Life had happened to me. But I wasn't letting anything happen anymore. I had strong muscles from digging and knew my way out. To an extent, Cricket also understood how it was to feel like a victim, which is why she'd worked so hard to uncover what her ex-husband and his skeevy business-partner friend had done.

But it isn't easy to find the gumption to pick up the shovel. Sometimes the hardest thing is even finding a damn shovel.

Griff unfolded his arms. "Guess we better get your van out."

Cricket nodded. "I'm making rather a habit of getting into fixes."

"I like repeat customers." Griff's vague response was either a flirtation or a true business philosophy. Cricket's face told the same tale. She didn't know where she stood with my cousin.

"Mrs. Crosby, I need to take a statement. I'm going to close the investigation but need a few things from you. While the tow driver is rescuing your van, perhaps you can step over to my car. Won't take long."

"What about Louie?" Cricket asked, as the dog wriggled in her arms.

"I'll take him," I said, not really wanting to because he was filthy. "Do you have a leash?"

Cricket shook her head. "Sorry. I wasn't planning on taking the dog back. It was merely surveillance."

I almost smiled. Cricket was serious about her private investigator's gig, and I wasn't going to pee in her Cheerios.

"I may have something." The detective strode over to his car.

"Yum," I said to Cricket under my breath.

"I know," she said, watching Wesley McNally, Detective Fine Ass, open his trunk and root around.

"Not that I'm into law enforcement. Usually give me the heebie-jeebies, but the view is nice on this one."

"He looks like Sonny Crocket," Cricket said.

"Who?"

"The character in Miami Vice."

"Oh, I didn't know the name of the actor." I felt relieved when I saw Detective McNally pull out a rope.

"Don Johnson's the actor. Oh, never mind." Cricket looked down at Louie. "At least I found Louie. Ms. Ava has been beside herself. Any disruption in her routine, you know."

McNally handed Cricket the rope, which on closer inspection was a temporary leash. "We have to be prepared for anything."

"Do you now?" Cricket gave him a smile that made me widen my eyes.

Well then.

"We're like Boy Scouts—always prepared," McNally said with an answering smile.

I made a chuffing noise and took the leash. I wanted to say "Boy Scouts, my ass," but I still had the same self-preservation mindset and didn't want any trouble. Head down. Be invisible. I took the dog from Cricket, set him on the ground, and then tugged him over to where Griff was maneuvering his truck for the best angle to pull the van out. Cricket followed McNally to his unmarked sedan, which still had a light flashing, making me, and no doubt the neighborhood, itchy.

"Need help?" I asked my cousin.

"Nope. Just mind that stupid dog."

I looked down at Louie who panted next to me. "I'm sure he doesn't mean it."

Griff didn't answer, but he cast a glance over as Cricket

laughed at something the good detective said. I could tell my cousin was annoyed.

"Her divorce was final today," I said as Griff walked around the tow truck and pressed the button that released the tow hook.

"Yeah, so," he said, refusing to look at me.

"Are you going to ask her out?"

"No."

"I thought—"

"None of your business."

"But she's into you," I said, though Griff was right. It *was* none of my business, but I knew that Cricket had a thing for Griff, and he'd done zero about it because she'd been legally married. Maybe she'd told him what she'd told everyone else—that she wasn't dating until she was officially single, if then. But her marriage had been technically over for half a year, and now she was legally free to pursue romance.

Another flirty laugh came from behind us.

Griff gritted his teeth and walked over the van, searching for the right place to connect the cables.

"Griff." I followed him. Thank goodness, Louie was good on a leash and came willingly. "Just ask her."

My cousin turned and gave me a look that could have curdled milk. "Leave it."

"Why are men so stubborn?" I presented this question to Louie. His answer was to drool on my shoe.

I decided to cut my losses and went and stood in the shade of some scrubby tree that the utility company had trimmed down to ugly. I watched as Cricket conversed with the handsome detective and Griff stomped around like a sore-tailed rooster. Fifteen minutes later, Cricket's van was on the back of the truck, Detective Hottie McHotster was doing whatever detectives do, and we were climbing into the cab with a sullen Griff.

"I can't believe my axle's messed up." Cricket slid in beside me, jostling Louie so he wouldn't drool on Griff's pristine seats. She'd rubbed much of the mud off with some Wet Wipes she'd found in her purse. Louie panted but looked cheerful about a car ride. The Dahmers had returned into the recesses of their sad house. "Wonder how much that'll run me?"

"I can suggest some mechanics... if you'll take my advice." Griff shifted the truck into drive and headed out of Creighton Bluff.

"What does that mean?" Cricket asked leaving forward and shooting Griff a perplexed look.

"You know what it means. You don't listen to the advice anyone gives you. If you did, you wouldn't have a bad axle, you wouldn't be sitting out in a dangerous neighborhood, and you wouldn't be flirting with a cop."

"I wasn't flirting."

Griff made a fake high-pitched laugh.

I felt extremely uncomfortable.

"That's not how I laugh. And he was amusing. Men can sometimes be amusing, charming even."

She said it like Griff wasn't those things. Which was true. Griff had never been the guy with the jokes or stories. Charm was poison ivy to the man. Nope, Griff was a grumpy, sexy dude with slightly Neanderthal tendencies that were overshadowed by his integrity, work ethic, and his kindness. He was the opposite of her now ex-husband Scott who had wielded charm like a sword and always had a pocketful of dad jokes. Griff wouldn't screw the tennis coach and half his client base.

My cousin said nothing. Just turned onto the highway that would take them back to his tow yard and my car.

Louie yawned and settled down into Cricket's lap, obviously bored with the conversation. Cricket looked at me, her eyes accusing, and it was then I knew she was perturbed that I had brought Griff.

But she'd been stuck, and he had a tow truck.

"So I guess you solved your first case," I said, trying to deflect.

Cricket's shoulders straightened, and she looked plenty pleased with herself. "I did. Ms. Ava will be so happy to see this knothead again. I hadn't really expected to bring him home. When I got there and saw the dog through the cracks of the backyard fence, I called Detective McNally. I know how a private investigator should handle certain things. I made an A in the class, after all." At that she glanced at Griff to make sure he took that in.

He didn't respond.

Her mouth turned down. "Well, I wanted to make sure it was indeed Louie, and I didn't see anyone around. So I rolled down the window and called his name. Sure enough, he popped his head up and came right to the fence. Could be he knew my voice. Or it was just hearing his name. He'd obviously found a spot where he could see out, and I could see clearly that it was Louie. Before I knew it, he was wriggling under the fence where there was a gap. So I jumped out—"

Griff made a dismissive sound in the back of his throat but kept his eyes on the road.

"—and helped pull the fence so he could fit underneath. And that's when this guy yelled at me from across the street. Like I was the one stealing the dog! So then I jerked Louie out, plopped him in my van, and tried to speed away. The street really was wet. Lots of potholes too. Which meant I fishtailed and skidded right into that yard. Got good and stuck. But, yeah, I solved the case."

I smiled at her. "One down."

"And more to go... if Juke calls me back. I don't want to apply to any other agencies, but I have a nice success rate, so I think I'm a good candidate."

Griff made another noise.

"And I have my first date. Detective McNally asked me out for a drink. He's going to talk to me about my investigative work. Or something like that." Cricket smiled. And it was the smile of a woman who knew what she was doing—playing with fire.

Griff growled.

"What was that, Griffin?" Cricket asked.

"Nothing." Griff floored the tow truck, and it jumped forward as if it too wanted to get away from the uncomfortable situation.

I wanted to tell my cousin he was being ridiculous, but men often are when it comes to things of the heart. Perhaps Cricket knew exactly what she was doing. She would either use McNally to bring Griff to heel, or she would cut Griff loose and let him dig out of her fence into the wide world.

Wasn't my circus, wasn't my monkeys.

So why did I always have to juggle their bananas?

8

Cricket

Ten days later...

I climbed the steps to Juke's office wearing my best pair of black pants and a white blouse that I'd had for years that had a no-nonsense business vibe. My hair was in a low knot and my makeup discreet. I looked tasteful.

Or like a server at a restaurant.

Juke didn't bother standing when I entered the office, but I didn't let this bother me. I noticed only because I was a detective, and that's what detectives do—keep our eyes open and our mouths closed. Which is why I waited a full twelve seconds before clearing my throat to remind Juke I was there.

He looked up from his phone. "Oh hey. Sorry. I was finishing Wordle. Only one more try until I'm skunked."

"I got it in three," I said, wanting him to know what a gem I was.

"Really? Guess it depends on the word you use as your first guess."

"Or one's superior intelligence," I said with a teasing smile.

Juke tossed his phone onto a stack of papers. "Yeah, yeah. Sit down."

Always an uncomfortable command because the furniture was likely unsold pieces from a garage sale circa 1984. I didn't want to offend, so I perched on a faux-leather office chair in front of his desk, ignoring the duct tape over the split seat. If he hired me, I would gently suggest sprucing up the office. I could likely find some nice leather armchairs and some updated lamps. I had no clue how to handle the carpet. Maybe Dak would help on that front. Since Juke was paying his rent on time and everything.

"So I talked to Rayanne over at LSUS, and she said you were one of the top students in the class. You scored the highest on the test and asked a lot of questions."

I tried not to preen. "Well, I was interested in the subject, and she was a good instructor."

"Yeah, so I ain't really been looking for a partner or employee. I'm kinda a one-man show... but I have this case that may require a special set of skills."

I leaned forward, excited that he realized I had a set of skills. "A disguise, maybe? Because I do a great job of impersonating a woman who frequents bars and has an occasional smoke when no one is looking. I have two wigs and some fake eyelashes and tattoos. I can borrow a leather—"

"No, what I have in mind requires you to be, well, you."

I stopped in the middle of my list of ways I could change my appearance. "Wait, you want me to be myself? Why?"

"Well, it's why I need you. I need someone who moves in certain circles."

I blinked. "What circles?"

"The fancy kind. The kind who do debutante stuff and play tennis at the club." He folded his fingers into a tent. "Seems there's a thief among you highfalutin ladies."

"I wouldn't say I'm highfalutin, whatever that is. And what do you mean, that someone is a thief?" I had heard nothing about anyone having something stolen. But then again, I had been keeping a lower profile ever since the divorce. The sensationalism around the Ponzi scheme and the takedown at the University Club had had Shreveport tongues wagging for a good month or two. Mother and I had taken Julia Kate to the Caribbean to escape the gossip and spend much-needed time healing and bonding. My mother was my mother, but every now and again, she could leave her trappings behind in order to be a real live human. We'd had two and a half weeks of a Marguerite who snorkeled, took a salsa dance class, and flirted outrageously with our waiter Conrad. She also laughed seven times, which was a record for the woman.

When school started up, I volunteered for some low-key committees and ignored the volunteer summons which I normally answered. Julia Kate had seemed relieved to have me less involved, which sort of hurt but was also understandable. She needed her own life, and I needed mine. I also skipped some board meetings and basically checked out of my normal life.

That's when my flirtation with being a private investigator had become a true desire. The past seven months had taught me a lot about myself. I had begun to think about who I'd been —a wife, mother, and eternal volunteer squiring about town on committees, hosting bridal showers, and living a somewhat shallow, palatable life that allowed my husband to step out on me because he figured I was too weak to do anything about it. And I had thought about who I wanted to be—a woman who knew her mind, who took action, and who didn't worry about whether she'd get selected to chair the spring garden study club showcase. I was done with that woman... though I had been asked to sit on the event committee for the garden study club.

I wanted to make a difference in people's lives more than just finding the perfect chandelier for their closet.

"I have a client who is missing several pieces of"—he shuffled through some papers and pulled one out—"David Yurman jewelry and one crossover purse by, um, Chanel?"

"A cross*body*. That's the type of handbag." I tilted my head. "Who's the client?"

"A Mindy Woodward who lives—"

"On Swallowtail Circle," I finished for him. "We did Junior Service League together, and she helped me chair the First Baptist Classical School's fall festival about five years ago."

"That's the one."

"But you implied that there was more than one incident."

He nodded. "Another person, Bo Dixie something, had a Louis Vuitton bag taken from her closet. She's not a client, but Mrs. Woodward told me she and one of her friends were missing several objects. Whoever is doing this knows what to take and knows to take only one or two things as to not draw suspicion. Mrs. Woodward said she wasn't certain when her belongings went missing because she wears them only for certain occasions. Same for the person missing the bag. Neither are sure about the timing of the theft. I'm purporting these items were taken on a visit or when there was a function in the home. My first thought was a caterer or a cleaning service, but I did that legwork and it's a dead end."

"Hmm." I pursed my lips and stared at the faded picture on the wall that looked like a duck that Scott liked to hunt. He'd had one mounted for his office. "Sounds like an opportunist. A criminal one. But the question is—what's this person doing with the objects they're stealing? If they wore them, people would know."

"Probably fencing them," Juke said.

"How?"

"Pawnshops. That's the usual way."

I made a face. "No one who buys Chanel or Louis Vuitton is getting them at a pawnshop. No way." I had never been in a pawnshop in my life and likely never would. Well, I take that back—detectives had to go to all sorts of places.

"So where do ladies buy this sort of thing?" he asked.

"Well, ideally, you purchase from a retail store that is a certified dealer in the brand. For high-end items, you usually go to Dallas or another large city. Here in Shreveport, there's some resale of legit designer goods at Dillard's and at places like my store where we deal in vintage items. Many of the highly desirable brands like Hermès or Fendi are timeless. Kind of like a Rolex. The classic pieces never go out of style."

"Ah," Juke said, nodding and jotting down a few notes. "You definitely know more about this sort of thing than me."

"Well, I dabble in vintage clothing, and because I have a mother who is desirous of quality and heirloom pieces and an aunt who wears high-end designers, I know my couture. I have several of these designers' bags, clothes, and shoes. David Yurman was Scott's go-to gift for birthdays and anniversaries. So I know that if someone were going to buy used pieces of that quality, they're likely going online."

"Online?"

"High-end resale shops exist online. Places where people can list goods like purses, shoes, dresses, et cetera, and get a decent profit from selling them. There are all kinds of sites for designer clothing and jewelry."

"Interesting."

"Let me show you." I pulled my cell phone from my bag, a

classic Fendi Baguette that I had inherited from Coraline. I typed in the name of my bag in the search function along with the exact year and style. The search populated all the high-end retail sites. I handed the phone to Juke.

"This can't be right." His eyes grew wide. "Seventeen hundred dollars for a purse?"

"Actually, that's a decent price. Remember, it's resale, so you can't ask the full amount... unless it's never been used and still has tags. And who would buy a delicious Fendi Baguette or Peekaboo bag and sit on it?"

Juke's mouth hung open. He looked at me like I was an alien. I probably was to him.

"What?" I asked.

"You're telling me that ugly purse you're carrying is more than my mortgage payment?"

"It's not ugly. It's a classic. Looks terrific with my herringbone jacket and Rafe Lasso knee-high boots. Very *Town and Country*, which is a great look for fall."

Juke snapped back into his chair. "And these bracelets? I'm guessing they're a pretty penny too?"

"Undoubtedly. David Yurman is superpopular, but it's a moderate tag compared to some pieces. Most of what is desirable to carry or wear by the general public are iconic brands with notable branding. You know, so people know its value when they wear it." I shrugged because this was obvious to many women who were exacting and, okay, a little vain about the fashion statements they made. I knew the whole designer game was shallow, but that didn't stop me from yearning for the new Brunello Cucinelli suede hobo bag which was ridiculously expensive... but so fine. "But more obscure, crazy-expensive pieces are harder to sell because they are way more expensive. Like a Birkin. If that were stolen, it would be easier to find because there are fewer of them. So this person is taking things that are easy to sell but worthwhile because they fetch a good price."

"That's crazy."

"Good thing you have me," I said with a Cheshire smile. "So what we need to do is find out who else is missing a few items here and there. Then we need to make a list. Maybe a spreadsheet depending how many things are missing. Then we start looking online to see if these things match up. Our thief may have several accounts."

Juke nodded. "That sounds good. Do you know how to do spreadsheets?"

"Do I know how to do spreadsheets...," I drawled with a light laugh. Spreadsheet could have been my middle name. I hadn't been the PTA secretary for five years for nothing.

"Great. And that's just part of it. I can't get into these social engagements—not my thing—so I knew you would be perfect for this. I need someone to do some snooping and gather some gossip. We need to find out what highbrow lady—or her kid, I guess—needs extra cash, and we need to figure out if this person might have attended events at the homes of ladies who have items missing."

Guess that meant no more lying low for me. If I was going to do this whole moonlighting thing right, I needed to polish up my Tory Burch ballet flats (even if they hurt my feet) and get back out there on the PTA/Junior League/ philanthropic committee merry-go-round. I planned to call a few friends on the way home and do the most hated thing of hated things —gossip.

But I would do it to help Juke and prove that I was worth my weight. I wanted to work as a private investigator, not because I was down on my luck and needed a job or needed the money—though as a single mom, I wouldn't turn cash down—but because I believed that I would be good at the job.

And, fine, I wanted that euphoric high of taking someone down.

"By the way, what am I getting paid?" I asked.

Juke snapped his head up. "Not enough to buy one of those fancy purses. That's for dang sure. Look, this is a contract-labor thing at present. Case-by-case basis. So let's start with a flat fee for the next two weeks. If we can't figure out the thief by then, we'll renegotiate."

"Deal." I reached across the desk to shake his hand. "And I have some papers for you. Since I haven't received my individual license yet, I need you to fill out this sponsorship form. I need hours."

He took the papers I pulled from my purse, squinting at them.

"I have to hand deliver my individual application in Baton Rouge." I nodded toward the paperwork. "But that will allow me to work for you as an apprentice while I wait on getting approval."

"Okay then." He rubbed his chin. He'd cut his jaw that morning with a razor, but that was a good thing because it meant he was using a razor. The man who I had hired last year to catch Scott cheating with the tennis coach was night and day compared to this man. Juke's eyes were clear, his shirt clean, and his disposition way less vague. He had a new purpose, and he'd admitted that his turnaround had happened on my case. I felt a tinge of pride that Ruby and I—and, okay, Griff—had a little to do with Juke making a comeback.

Thirty minutes later I was back home, dumping my absolutely-cute-and-not-at-all-ugly Fendi on the mud bench. I hadn't indulged in gossip, only because my mother had called, and I had to hear about the horrid color her neighbor was painting her door. As I entered the open kitchen, I caught sight of my daughter on the hearth-room couch feeding Pippa potato chips.

"She's going to vomit or get diarrhea." I sank into one of the French bergère armchairs I had upholstered in a robin's-egg-blue velvet. Beside me was the canvas basket that held all the tools of a soccer mom's trade—backdated issues of area school directories, exec committee notebooks, Junior League and other charitable committee clipboards, a set of highlighters, and a tube of undereye firming cream. The latter wasn't so much a tool. I had just forgotten where I had put it and now recalled a long night of silent auction emailing that had necessitated it. I picked up the Junior League directory. Everyone was online now, but still a good old-fashioned phone call never went out of style. I flexed my fingers, preparing for the task I was about to tackle.

"But she loves Cheetos," Julia Kate said, shoving an orange curd chip at the dog. Pippa took it very ladylike... and swallowed it in one gulp.

"I like them too, but Pippa has a sensitive stomach. Do you want to clean up explosive dog poop? 'Cause let me tell ya, it's loads of stinky fun."

Julia Kate made a face. "That's all, Pip."

She rolled up the bag, and I eyed my only child. Julia Kate looked restored after a summer of hardship. Or at least I hoped she was restored. She missed her father. That was to be expected. Still, she also knew that what Scott had done was wrong. Her hair had been cut shorter—a cute swing bob that framed her face. Julia Kate didn't like it, but the Sun-In she'd put on her light brown hair all summer long had turned the ends a horrific bronze. She'd agreed to lop it off. I liked the way it looked, especially when she used the curling iron. It made her look like me. Well, me with her father's eyes and nose.

"How was school today?" I asked.

"Good."

"What about that physical science test?"

"Made an A."

"Awesome. And—"

"Can we not do this?" She shoved off the couch. "I have good grades, Mom. And I'm taking my medicine, washing my face, going to therapy, and limiting my screen time. That cover it?"

"I wasn't grilling you. Just trying to make conversation." I said, trying to cover up how much it bothered me when she was so... teenagery.

"*Conversation* isn't about school or my grades. It's stuff like... like..."

I lifted an eyebrow.

"Just not about all my have-to-dos." She quirked her mouth. "Did you pay the electric bill? Toss out those mini Snickers I found hidden in the bag of rice cakes? Pluck your eyebrows?"

Okay, point made. "You found my Snickers?"

Julia Kate grinned like a true smart-ass. My heart tripped a little at the rare smile. "You don't have to hide your guilty pleasures, Mom. I'm not Dad. I don't care if you get fat. I will still love you."

"Well, that's a relief." I smiled and shook my head. "You're doing great, JK. I'm proud of you. I wasn't trying to pry or nag."

Julia Kate looked pleased. "Thanks. Now I have a little bit of news. But I don't want you to freak, okay?"

My stomach got a little fluttery. "I won't."

"You sure?"

Was this one of those moments that would be forever imprinted on her memory and psyche? What would my words be? I had to be careful to say the right thing. To be supportive. To give her a soft place to land. Whatever issue Julia Kate had, I would think about my words before I said them. "I'm certain. I no longer freak out about things. Promise."

So I was a liar...

"Okay, so Dad is getting married next weekend."

I blinked three times. "What?"

"To Natalie."

"Who?"

"Natalie. She works in his new office. She's an administrative assistant. They're getting married at her family's lake house."

"What?"

I was trying to grasp the fact that Scott had been dating someone. Good gravy, the man had been out of prison for less than a month. And our divorce had been final just last week. I had signed the papers, shedding a few tears as I scrawled my name on the line, my mind tripping back to all Scott and I had shared. Falling photographs of memories. There was the first dance at our wedding. The day I had found out I was pregnant with Julia Kate. The Disney World trip where he'd gotten us daylong fast passes and we tried to set the record for most Space Mountain rides. Crooked Christmas grins with wrapping paper balled in the background. Burying our cat Boudreaux under the willow at the lake. Buying the ski boat. The living we'd done, planning for a future that would never happen. We'd had dreams—and all those intentions had been wiped away by a pair of boobs attached to a twentysomething-year-old tennis coach.

"I knew you would freak," Julia Kate said.

"I'm not freaking," I said, struggling to comprehend what I was hearing.

Much.

"Well, you look like you swallowed a goldfish or something."

"I'm surprised. That's all. Just surprised." My voice sounded squeaky. I inhaled and then exhaled, scrabbling to *not* freak out. Stay calm. Stay calm. "So when did this happen?"

Julia Kate shrugged. She looked like the time she'd been competing on the balance beam—frightened but determined not to fall. And really wishing she'd chosen dance over gymnastics. "I don't know. But Natalie's nice for the most part."

I bet. "How old is she?"

"Twenty-six, I think."

"You're joking. Tell me you're joking." What in the ever-loving hell was Scott doing to attract these young girls? I knew that he was decent-looking for a guy in his forties, but he'd taken a huge cut to his pay and ego when he'd become an insurance agent after being the VP of a regional bank, and now he had a criminal record. Sure, he had some family money, but he'd had to liquidate some of his assets to pay restitution. Maybe it was the bedroom stuff that had them flocking. Back in the spring, I had found some sex toys and anal lube in a box in the back of the closet, cementing my suspicions that Scott was cheating. Experimentation in the bedroom wasn't my forte. I had told the man long ago that after all the thermometers my mother had shoved up my backside to take my temperature nothing else was going in the back door. Nor was I going to be spanked or handcuffed. I drew the line at kinky. Still, I just didn't get his appeal. Maybe it was because I had picked up his underwear, bought his hemorrhoid cream, and stepped on his toenail clippings that the thrill of Scott Crosby had faded for me.

"You're freaking," Julia Kate said in a singsong voice.

"I'm not. I'm so not." But my clipped tone betrayed my words. "Okay, maybe a little. I mean, how long has he known her? Have you met her? What's she like? Does she have kids? Oh my God!"

Julia Kate huffed, fast walked to the kitchen, and came back seconds later. I sat and tried to not hyperventilate over the fact that Scott and I had divorced last week and next weekend he was remarrying.

Clunk.

Julia Kate thunked down a bottle of Grey Goose and tossed the bag of Snickers into my lap. "You really shouldn't use alcohol or sugar as a coping mechanism, but in this instance, you might legit need a crutch. Natalie's twenty-six years old, Dad has known her for three weeks, I met her last weekend, and she has one kid—a six-year-old boy. This is happening, and there's nothing either one of us can do about it. Now I'm going to finish my homework."

I opened my mouth but closed it when she shook her head.

Julia Kate wasn't happy about what her father was doing. She was resigned. She accepted it. She was over it.

I opened the bottle of vodka and took a swig. Then another.

Then I ate the whole bag of Snickers and watched a rerun of *Bachelor in Paradise*.

9

Ruby

NEW YORK CITY is not something a person can prepare for. You can watch every movie ever set in the Big Apple, but it's not the same as climbing out of a cab and being *in* the largeness of the city. Oh, and that death-by-cab-ride thing in all the movies? Not exaggerated. I had to pry my fingers from the back seat after nearly hyperventilating a few times. Marguerite looked unruffled by the fact we'd nearly hit two other cabs and our driver had lowered the window to shout what I'm certain was obscenities in an unfamiliar language. Suffice it to say as I stepped out of the checkered cab onto the pavement in front of a towering apartment building right off Central Park, I knew I wasn't in Kansas anymore.

Not that I'd ever been to Kansas.

"Set those bags here," Marguerite instructed the driver who'd stepped from his running vehicle to help us with the luggage in the trunk. My bright bag looked out of place beside Marguerite's hard-case Louis Vuitton, like it didn't belong in the posh setting. She pulled out a twenty-dollar bill and handed it to the cab driver. I had had to help her use the credit card in the cab self-service system to get us from LaGuardia to the Upper East Side, which had necessitated a lecture from Marguerite on the evils of this newfangled world. I noted the driver took the cash tip.

Along the commute into the city, I had pressed my nose to the window, marveling at the architecture, the river, and the urban sprawl that was like nothing I'd seen before. And then when we'd crossed into Manhattan, I'd felt marvel and maybe a little trepidation. Like the pumpkinseed bream I had jerked out of Caddo Lake onto the pier, I was wide-eyed and struggling against a world I didn't know. Part of me yelled "put me back!" Part of me bubbled with excitement over this new adventure.

Marguerite summoned the doorman, who wore a burgundy uniform with the little cap and everything. "Hello, Tom. It's me. Coraline's sister. Can you see to our luggage?"

"Right away, ma'am," the older man said in a thick New York accent. And let me tell you I loved the brogue. A wave of expectation swept over me. I was here. I had made it. And now it was up to me to mold and shape my future.

Or not.

I didn't have to pressure myself to make something happen. I just had to live where my feet were.

Ten minutes later, we sat inside the sumptuous penthouse, sipping a delicious bubbly cava as I struggled to peel Coraline's scruffy teacup terrier from my leg. Seems he liked me. A lot.

"Howard Stern, stop humping Ruby," Coraline said for the ninth time as she sipped her bubbly wine.

I shook my leg to aid in the process of detaching the pup from the tight ripped leggings I'd chosen to wear with the Doc

Martens boots I'd rescued from the back of my closet. I had scoured magazines and Pinterest boards to figure out my look for arriving in New York City. I had settled on a Vivienne Westwood punk-couture vibe with a ripped T-shirt a la Richard Hell. I had strategically ripped revealing holes on the shoulders, leaving the T-shirt neck fully intact. I had paired it with a black jacket and layered silver chain. I had dyed a hot-pink streak in my hair that was somewhat tasteful but also edgy enough to suit the style. Coraline had studied me upon entry but said very little. I might have tried too hard.

"It's okay." I ignored the drool on my leg. The little guy was really going for it.

"It's not okay! Myrna, come get Howard Stern and put him in his kennel. He's behaving badly with our guest."

A diminutive woman wearing a black work dress bustled in, pried the humping pup from my leg, and left without so much as a how-ya-do.

"Now I want to hear about your protégé, Marg," Coraline said, looking at me with sharp dark eyes that almost made Marguerite's shark eyes seem friendly. "Tell me about this enterprise of yours and why it should matter to me."

"Don't call me Marg," Marguerite said with a sniff and a disdainful glance at her sister. "And Ruby can do her own talking."

They both looked at me.

I couldn't help it. I gulped. "Well, uh, it's something I stumbled onto—"

"No." A displeased quirk twisted Coraline's mouth. "That will never do."

Marguerite's younger sister wore an abrupt bob, her dark hair streaked with platinum. It fell to just below her sharp chin. Her makeup was impeccable—dark red lips, pale unlined skin, and slashing obsidian eyebrows. She wore a caftan of gold and bronze that floated around her and made her look, well, absolutely filthy rich and somewhat... bored by all the money. A pair of bright red readers hung around her neck on a chain that looked outlandish. Nothing blasé about this woman. She exuded the kind of confidence a twelve-year-old boy did—oblivious to anything or anyone who didn't rotate around him—and she made me twitchy with her dissecting perusal.

Yeah, I had been doing daily vocabulary so I wouldn't sound like I had fallen off a turnip truck.

Though I had, in fact, fallen off a truck when I was nine years old, helping my cousin deliver turnip greens to my Aunt Jean. The tumble I took off the tailgate was a standing joke in the family. Roo fell off a turnip truck.

"What do you mean?" I squirmed a little on the white velvet couch. Outside I could see rooftop gardens and the sun setting over whichever river was to the east. Surreal.

"That word. Bumble." She sipped her cava and stared at me.

"I didn't say bumble. I said stumble." I put my glass down so my trembling hands didn't give away my nervousness.

"They are nearly the same thing," Coraline said.

Marguerite cleared her throat. "Now Cora, a person must be their authentic self. Ruby did sort of happen upon her new design business. Nothing wrong with happenstance."

"Indeed, there isn't. Still, it's better to be confident around this crowd. They smell fear from a mile away. So no stumbling or bumbling. It's better that Ruby arrived at exactly what she'd been searching for. Let's say Ruby was looking for the right branding—a sort of Southern classic meets modern—and because she adores pieces from the past, she decided to marry her love of vintage couture with fresh design. See? That sounds 'intentional,' don't you think?"

I didn't adore vintage. Not really. Older clothes had been

cheaper, but still good, fabric. It made sense to repurpose it. After all, Gran rinsed out her plastic storage bags for reuse. Still, I understood what selling oneself entailed. Spin. Best foot forward. A little white lie even. "Yes, that does. My first design involved a cream Givenchy cocktail dress and some good raspberry satin. I have photos."

"But you brought some of your designs, yes?"

I nodded.

"Very good. Choose a nice one for the Rafe Lasso cocktail party in his flagship store. Take a peek at what he did in his last collection so you know what to talk about. The car is coming at six forty-five to take us to the event. Then we have a late dinner with Hadley Fern of Mare Oscuro. She wants one of her pieces on the cover and needs me for that. But she's always looking to discover the next hot designer."

My nerves sang. Rafe Lasso? Mare Oscuro?

Now it was real. Really real.

"Great," I managed to squeak since my mouth had gone dry. I picked up the cava, sipped, then cleared my throat. "So what's the dress code?"

Coraline laughed. "Something fabulous."

GOING to a cocktail reception at a NYC fashion house should be daunting. And it was. But it was also the same as the cocktail parties I'd been to in Shreveport. Okay, on a more basic level. At both there were suck-ups and people who pretended to be something they weren't. There were girls trying too hard and men drinking too much. And there were small-town ex-cons pretending that they belonged.

That last one was me of course.

But who really knew who any of these people truly were? I

figured that was sort of the point. Everyone wore a mask... and fabulous clothes.

"So dear person," the guy next to me drawled. At least I think it was a guy. Gender was blurred here. His silk pants ballooned, and his black jacket nipped tight at his waist. "What's your story, morning glory?"

"Story?"

"Yeah, like are you a model or assistant or what?" He dangled a glass of something bubbly and fruity from his long fingers. His nails were painted silver.

"I'm a designer."

"Oooh, do tell," he said with a hungry grin. Not because he was into me, more like he might pull out a bib and sharpen his cutlery at any minute. "What do you design? Did you do what you're wearing?"

I quelled the need to look down at my outfit. I had decided to go with the fitted double-breasted sleeveless dress I had reclaimed from a Calvin Klein men's overcoat in camel cashmere. I had sewn a beautiful silk lining along the bottom to, well, essentially cover my ass. And matched it at the neck. I had used shoulder pads to give an angular profile, and the effect was what I hoped was chic, understated, and well-made. "Yep. I made it all by myself."

"It's interesting. So you do menswear?" His look was dissecting. This dude was measuring me, weighing his opinion, deciding if I was worthy. I felt pressure on my shoulder pads.

"No."

"Oh." He made a moue with his mouth which was covered with purple lipstick. "I see someone I know. Nice chatting. Ta-ta."

And that was that. I never even got his name.

Coraline stood across the open balcony next to Marguerite, who looked smashing in a fitted black suit. She wore a punch of color with a magenta ruffled blouse that fell in delicious blossoms around her neck. Her hair was an ever-present helmet and her shoes those buckled monstrosities, but she looked more glamorous. Maybe it was the glittering skyline behind her. Coraline wore a ruched dress of persimmon that gathered between her breasts and then fell from her hips to swish midcalf. It was a Proenza and looked amazing against her pale skin and deep red lips. Her gladiator crisscross heels were a muted silver, her earrings geometric and jeweled. She carried a pink Balenciaga bag. The woman wore the creative director of *Vogue* coat very well.

A server came by with a plate of weird-looking hors d'oeuvres, and I waved her away. My stomach couldn't handle whatever the hell that was. I sucked down a big gulp of the champagne I held like a security blanket and moved toward Coraline and Marguerite, who were in conversation with a small woman draped in black. She wore an odd little Asian hat and no makeup whatsoever.

"Ah, here's Ruby now," Coraline said to the woman.

The odd woman turned gray eyes on me, pursing her mouth. "So you're the one who's ripping off other designers to make your own stuff?"

"Ah..." I looked at Coraline, who looked amused. Marguerite looked ready to defend me.

The little woman raised her eyebrows in expectation.

"Uh, not exactly. I repurpose vintage fabrics for my looks and often keep elements of design as an homage to the original designer. But the design is all mine."

The woman tilted her head. "Well, that's a reason, I suppose."

Coraline waved her martini glass toward the woman. "This is Cecile Smart."

She said it like I should know her. I didn't. In fact, I knew very little about any of the people in the room. I assumed the lithe women with their hair pulled back so tight they looked squinty were models, the chatty gay men were assistants or budding designers, and the other people were editors, journalists, or bigwig buyers. But names of the movers and shakers in fashion? Beyond the ones that everyone knew, I knew very few names. "It's nice to meet you."

"Huh," she said with a cackle. "Now how many people have ever said such a thing, Coraline?"

Coraline shrugged. "Guess you just got one."

I felt confused but didn't want to let on, so I just drank more champagne. A server took the empty one from my hand and replaced it with a full one. I felt a bit light-headed, so I didn't take a gulp right away.

"Cecile is the kingmaker," Coraline explained with a wave of her hand. "If she likes your collection, you're deemed a success. If she doesn't, good luck selling it to Sears."

"But Sears closed."

Coraline's lips twitched. "Exactly."

"So what is your background?" Cecile said, looking slightly disinterested in the conversation. And me.

"I learned to sew at my grandmother's knee by making dresses for neighborhood toddlers and throw pillows for their mothers. I graduated to sewing things like a prom dress that I never wore."

"Formal training?" Cecile asked, looking over my shoulder.

"Does prison count? I made a shit ton of quilts."

Now her gaze was on me. And she was interested. She narrowed her eyes. Looked at my dress in such a way that if she had been a man, I might have expected her to buy me a drink. Then she looked up. "Quilting isn't something we see much of, though Chloe did a beautifully quilted jacket for last fall."

"Did they?"

Cecile gave me a rusty smile. Her teeth were small, like a rabbit, yet somehow brutal. "I like you. You're interesting. And there is hardly anyone interesting these days."

I didn't say anything because what does one say to that without surrendering what makes them interesting? Cricket would have said "thank you" and maybe sent her a "happy," which was an unsolicited over-the-top gift for no good reason. I wasn't Cricket.

"Bring her around," Cecile said to Coraline before wandering away.

"Well." Coraline set her half-filled glass on the edge of the balcony. "That was unexpected. But now you've a story to tell me. I'm calling for the car."

"But we just got here fifteen minutes ago," I said.

"It's enough." Coraline drifted toward the inner sanctum where models in tartan plaid stewardess uniforms struck poses on a dais. A DJ worked in the corner, electronic mixed with rap that he scratched, and everyone seemed to enjoy. The head of the house, Rafe Lasso, stood in the center of the room, chatting with the well-dressed and ridiculous alike. He extended his head to Coraline, and she wafted over. Marguerite and I followed like two streamers tied to her wagon.

"My darling Coraline." Rafe lifted her hand to his lips. "I'm honored."

"You should be. I turned Jacques's invite down to come by." She brushed a kiss upon his weathered cheek. He had a tidy coif of dyed auburn hair and wore a tuxedo with satin slippers.

"And you brought company." He looked over at Marguerite and me. "Your sister, I think. Same bone structure and penchant for large diamonds."

Marguerite made a face. "Coraline wears diamonds? She told me they were overdone when she was fourteen years old, and I've never seen her wear them since."

Coraline rolled her eyes. "I've learned to tolerate overdone."

"And who is with her, wearing a very daring frock?" Rafe asked, lifting my hand to the side and stepping back to look me over. I felt sweat break out on my forehead. Rafe Lasso had spent decades curating styles that were worn by the wealthy and the "wish they were wealthy." The little anchor on his golf shirts were synonymous with privilege, and his suede riding boots, houndstooth jackets, and nautical blazers never went out of style. He had been the king of ready to wear for as long as I had been taking breaths.

"I'm Ruby." I wished I could think of something clever. I couldn't. I was a bit starstruck.

"And who made this?" he asked.

"Me."

He lifted a waxed eyebrow. "Well then."

I smiled gamely. "I'm here to learn and maybe conquer."

Sounded bold. Though, at the moment, I was a bit weak in the knees and trying to not pant.

"The confidence is endearing. So is this your own line or has someone already snapped you up? I'm not the brightest man in the room, but you're with this dashing woman, so I can only surmise you're an up-and-comer. Cecile wouldn't deign to talk to anyone who wasn't going to be somebody someday."

Oh dear God, I am a fraud. Walking around, acting like I had an actual fashion line and had done shows when I'd done nothing more than design dresses for Cricket's Grits and Glitz gala. I hadn't even *had* a show, and there I stood on the roof of Rafe Lasso being romanced by the main man himself when I was a total pretender. I felt panic latch its teeth in me, and I must have looked a bit wild-eyed, because Coraline intervened.

"Darling, get in line. Now we must run. Good luck tomorrow."

"I don't need luck. I have the best of the best working for me." When he said this, he looked at me.

My heart leaped and then tap danced on my stomach.

Now I knew that Rafe Lasso wasn't going to offer me a job, not based on my showing up at his cocktail party in a dress he was mildly interested in, but it was mind-blowing that Coraline was treating me like I was worthy of the support. I felt tears prick at my eyes. But I couldn't, wouldn't, shouldn't let any of that out. Not here.

Coraline smiled a cat smile, wrinkled her nose at him, and gave him a bye wave.

Other people were moving toward him, but he held a hand up and looked at me. "Let's set up a moment to chat. Come to the show tomorrow. I'll save you a seat next to your champion there."

I managed a nod and became very Cricket-like when I said, "Thank you. I would love that."

He turned from me, and I followed Coraline and Marguerite, who were doing a little bickering about the late hour for dinner, to the sweeping staircase. Minutes later we were in a cab, and not long thereafter we were sitting at a table, sipping some sort of artisanal gin and eating cheese that smelled like it had been left in the Louisiana sun for ten days. I tried not to gag the first time I tasted it.

Dinner with Hadley Fern of Mare Oscuro was surreal but the food a little lacking. The plates were small and the food even smaller. I came away buzzed and hungry for McDonald's. Not that I would admit that. And Marguerite came away with a number from a silver-haired fox at the bar. No kidding. She went to the restroom, stopped for a club soda, and spent fifteen minutes talking to a guy. I hadn't realized because I was so engaged with Coraline and Hadley, but Marguerite arrived back at the table with a pleased glow and the guy's digits.

Coraline teased her all the way home, and I enjoyed a Marguerite who wasn't suggesting I hold my shoulders back or blot my lipstick. She'd "suggested" those things in the elevator hours earlier when we first left the apartment. This Marguerite intrigued me. She wasn't her normally poker-up-the-ass self in NYC.

As we rode that same elevator back up to the penthouse, I leaned over and whispered in her ear, "I brought Twix in my luggage. Up for a little *Bachelor* and a snack?"

"But it's nearly midnight," she muttered.

"I have access to streaming. And four candy bars."

Marguerite looked at her sister, who was tapping on her phone. "Okay. Let me take my face off, put on my moisturizer, and take my medicine."

"You really shouldn't have chocolate and drivel the night before you must be up early." Coraline slid her phone into that delicious bag and gave us a disgusted look. When Marguerite looked surprised that she'd overheard, Coraline said, "I'm an excellent multitasker. It's a talent."

Marguerite sniffed. "You are just full of them, aren't you?"

"Yes." As the elevator opened, Coraline put her hand on the door to hold it back. We stepped into the foyer that was very much a reflection of the owner—the space had been painted a deep twilight with gilded feathered wallpaper on the right wall, a gold-leaf chandelier that looked out of a 1920s movie hung above, and some weird art that probably cost more than my car flanked the left side. Let's be honest—it cost more than anything I've ever owned. "But a Twix? Like the candy bar? I don't think I've had one of those since I left Louisiana."

"They don't sell them here?" I asked, confused.

"Of course they do. But I don't put that in my body. Still, I'm nostalgic for home. This morning I was thinking about homemade buttermilk biscuits and sausage gravy. Guess I will settle for a Twix and maybe fifteen minutes of that smut you're watching."

"I'm not sure a candy bar and bad television counts as something from home," Marguerite said.

Coraline smiled. "It's close enough."

10

Cricket

Two days later...

Esme Henrick's living room looked like someone had taken a magic eraser and scrubbed every bit of color from the space. I think her only "splash of color" was the ecru throw pillows.

"Now that you've received your notebooks, Lisa is going to call the meeting to order. We have a lot to go over since we last met. So ladies, let's get started," Esme said with a smile. She stood at the front of the room in front of the marble fireplace and artwork that was a modernist blob of varying shades of—you guessed it—white.

Those gathered around the large living room were the usual suspects, so to speak. I knew them all and had served on one committee or another with each at some point. No surprises. No newcomers. Same ol' soccer moms.

But was the thief among them?

And how was I going to casually bring up the topic of missing items?

Unfortunately, I had arrived too late for the "meet and greet" coffee time because I hadn't seen the email from Jo Beth about my being accepted as the Teacher Appreciation chair. Between juggling more time at the store and Julia Kate's fall indoor soccer league—not to mention a meeting with a Realtor to put the house on the market—I had been a bit remiss on the housekeeping stuff. And something about my mother and Ruby hobnobbing with the rich and famous in NYC while I was dusting china cabinets and reorganizing the back half of the store had me a bit sulky. Still, I had to prove to Juke that I could catch this thief, so I had hurriedly pulled on some navy pants and a decent-looking top and ran out the door to Esme's South Highlands home, arriving just as everyone was gathering around the hearth in her formal living room to start the meeting.

Esme rambled on because she liked to hear herself talk. Lisa passed out agendas. I perused those gathered, recalling what I knew about each of them—who they were married to, what businesses they owned, what cracks I could root around in to uncover any rot. It felt a little icky to be honest. I had spent so much time not looking hard at people so I could like them that to really examine them, who they were, what they had in their lives felt small. Like I was judging them.

And we had spent decades hearing how we cannot categorize, judge, or separate, and here I sat dissecting everything about how much money they had, what their morality was, and what rumors I'd heard about them.

Guess that was my job now. Not that I was telling any of them about my new gig. I reasoned that if I told my social circle I was moonlighting as a private investigator, they would draw up tighter than a pair of cheap panties, and I would get very little cheerful, vindictive gossip out of them. And some of them would dismiss my new venture as amusing, a silly hobby.

But it wasn't.

"Cricket?"

I was halfway through my dissection of those gathered, currently on Lela Knox, whose husband had lost his shirt in a lawsuit over a land title just last year. They'd sold their house in a swanky area and downsized to a more budget-friendly neighborhood. Lela still spent lots of money on auction items and wore expensive clothes. She'd not traded in her Range Rover for a Ford, that was for sure. So maybe she was working her own side gig?

"Cricket?"

"Hmm?" I murmured.

Lisa tapped the agenda. "We're waiting for your report on Teacher Appreciation."

"Oh sorry. As y'all know, I'm replacing Traci G as the chair. She's on bedrest. I haven't been able to talk to her much about the original plan, but the theme this year is Reach for the Stars. Not super original, but I'm considering playing with a Hollywood theme. Like maybe a James Dean car as a prop, tossing in some Marilyn Monroe glitz. It's a work in progress, of course. And I'm open to suggestions. My committee will meet around the first of November, and I'll have a sign-up ready online by February."

I wasn't really open to all suggestions, mostly because the last chair had some lame space theme prepped to go. Boring.

"Thank you, Cricket. And thank you for stepping in to help when needed."

I shrugged. "I'm sorry I hadn't volunteered before now. Just a lot going on, you know."

Lots of sympathetic looks and a few nodding heads, and then Lisa moved on and left me alone to contemplate the rest of the women on my mental list. A handful were worth looking at a little harder. Others I just couldn't reconcile to the idea they'd steal anything. As we moved into old business, which started a heated debate about the fall fashion show, I noticed Lela lifting her Tory Burch tote off the floor and sliding off the dining room chair Esme had moved into the room for extra seating. She slipped out of the room and disappeared into the depths of the back, toward the master bedroom.

Everyone knew that Esme's guest powder room was off the foyer. That's where she kept all those monogrammed linen towels no one used because they were too darn perfect to muss. Sure, Lela would have had to cross in front of a few people to reach the official powder room, but it was expected if you needed to use the facilities.

Now my suspicions were aroused.

And no one seemed to notice Lela slipping out.

I sighed and whispered to Cammie Rio, who'd plopped down next to me, having run even later than I had, "I gotta use the little girl's room."

I handed her my notebook and skirted the back of the room, almost stepping on Penny Jones's Golden Goose sneakers. I didn't really understand those things, but Julia Kate had sure loved hers. The hallway was dark, and the drone of the debate over using glitter on the props faded into the background. I was almost certain Esme's bedroom was to the left. The guest bathroom that her mother used when she visited was to the right. The door was closed, light peeking from beneath. Lela could legit be in the restroom, and I would have to wait in the hall until she emerged.

But then I heard a noise from the left.

I glanced around to make sure no one was watching and slipped down the hall toward Esme's bedroom. Which was also very white.

Maybe Esme wanted to see dirt so she knew what to clean. I myself chose carpets and sofas based on the ability to hide stains. After all, Pippa had a delicate stomach. But I had to admit that the bedroom was beautiful with the layered white linen bedding and European shams in a gorgeous matelassé. The carpets were plush white pieces of heaven, and the mirrored nightstands less modern than one would think. Very European and clean. Maybe once Pippa passed, I could go for the same look. The thought of Pippa passing made my heart ache, so I just focused on the sounds coming from Esme's closet.

Before I caught the thief red-handed, I wanted to take a moment to revel in the fact that I had gone to one—ONE!—meeting and closed the case.

I was good at this. Or lucky.

Probably both.

Juke was going to be so psyched and probably a little shocked because I had done it so quickly. He'd thought I wouldn't be valuable. I could tell by the way he hemmed and hawed when talking about my future at North Star Investigations. Easier to humor me, and after the whole Louie thing where I got the van stuck, I thought he might rescind our agreement for this case. I knew Griff had probably told him about the whole thing.

Fine. I shouldn't have tried to peel out and take the dog without backup. But the look on Mrs. Ava's face when I brought back a dirty and exhausted Louie was the reason I knew I had to prove myself to Juke. Helping others get justice was important to me. I had been lucky to have the help I'd had when I realized Scott was betraying me with Stephanie the Tennis Slut. Yes, I knew it was wrong to think of the woman that way, but she had encouraged my husband with her tight bottom and coveting eyes, so I would call her whatever I wanted to in my head.

More noises from the closet kicked me into gear. I pulled my cell phone from my back pocket just in case I needed visual proof. I had practiced this maneuver in my mirror this morning because when I had tried to take a picture of Scott and Steph the Whore (my other name for her) when they were canoodling on her back stoop, I had had it in selfie mode and ended up with my determined, outraged, slightly turkey-necked image instead. Technology wasn't my strong suit. Upside? I had changed my overnight moisturizer.

Carefully, I inched across the carpet, which had good padding because I made no sound. The closet door was slightly ajar, probably so it would stay lit. I spied one of those buttons that had automatic turnoff. Another thump and then something fell and hit the floor.

How to play this?

No dramatic aha was needed. Better to try to observe so that I caught Lela with Esme's new Celine bag red-handed. Or whatever she was planning on fitting into her tote. The Mini 16 bag Esme had shown off at the beginning of school was just small enough to be enveloped inside a tote, but only just. Still, thieves knew how to obscure their goods, so I had no doubt that Lela had planned well. After all, she'd done an excellent job fitting all those tables in the small room at the soccer banquet last year. And she'd had really nice table decorations too.

I eased to the side, shifting my weight so I could peer inside the closet. But the only thing I could see was the puffy ostrich sleeves of a ball gown, no doubt Esme's gown for the birds-of-a-feather-themed cotillion from five years back.

Damn it.

With no other way to spy, I just decided to fling open the door.

"So you thought you...," I started.

But then I stopped because an enormous Persian cat was taking a colossal poop on the white shag rug.

"Uh-uh." I backed out, noting the fallen shoe boxes and a pretty pair of strappy sandals dangerously close to the hunched-over cat. I started to close the door because it was disgusting, and also part of me wanted to give the cat the privacy it deserved for what was going down on that rug.

"Cricket?" someone said over my shoulder.

I jumped and fell against the closet, slamming it closed. I spun around, sort of plastering myself to the wall.

"What are you doing?" Esme asked, looking confused.

"Uh, I heard a sound in here. I thought I would check it out?" I sounded uncertain, but truth was that cat poop had unnerved me.

"In my closet?" Esme asked, her eyes growing suspicious.

That's when I realized that I likely looked a bit suspect myself. "I was going to the bathroom and heard a sound."

Lela walked past Esme and opened the closet. "Oh."

She paused for a good three seconds.

"Uh, Esme, you have a situation here," Lela said.

Esme made a face, her feathery blond bob a bit askew and her thin lips making a line. "What do you mean?"

"Your cat has... well, a bowel issue it looks like."

"What?" Esme asked, throwing open the door. "Oh my God, Van Winkle! You little bastard! That's my new rug!"

The cat didn't seem to care. It just sauntered out, sat its butt on the other rug, and licked its back haunch.

"I hate that cat." Esme slammed the closet door, leaving the cat doodle inside with her really nice clothes and shoes. I would never do that. I would have to remove the rug. Maybe burn it? I was fairly certain she would regret the decision to go white in this situation.

"But don't you want..." I gestured to the closet.

"I'll have Verdie come clean it up just as soon as she's cleared the luncheon. Y'all come on and tell everyone goodbye." Esme sort of kicked the cat when she walked by it, which wasn't very fair to the cat. I mean, the fluffiness of the rug with all those little fibers might have been too hard to resist for Mr. Van Winkle. It seemed a decent place to go, especially if the litter box required that he wade through a sea of helicopter moms.

I looked at Lela, who then shrugged at me. I could tell she wanted to laugh, but we knew it would set Esme off, so we both bit our lower lips and followed her from the bedroom. We crowded into the living room behind her, wincing at the cacophony of twenty-some-odd women all chatting about the plans for our precious pumpkins for the upcoming year.

"Oh my stars," Lela whispered to me. "What does she feed that cat?"

I glanced at Esme and saw that she was fielding a question, and so I released the laughter. "Looked like a can of chili."

Lela started laughing too. "And I thought I might be the one on her shit list. I mean, I just started my stupid period, and everything is so *white* in here. Got to the bathroom and didn't have a tampon so I had to dig under her sink to find something. All she had was one of those incontinence pads for when her mama stays with her. So now I look like I have an enormous hoo-ha. I gotta get home to change before I take Cooper to practice."

So that was why she went to the larger bathroom and why she took her purse.

A swing and a miss.

Poop.

Like literally.

Cammie waved at me, gesturing at the notebook I had dumped in her lap. Cammie was Nancy Parrington's youngest daughter, and thanks to my mother, she'd also taken an interest in Ruby. If anything, my mother had done a good job on getting everyone to grab on to Ruby's rising star. So off I went to do work for Ruby.

'Cause I hadn't managed to do any for myself.

FIVE HOURS later I found myself slipping onto the alligator-print stool of a high top in the bar of Suttons Steakhouse wearing a tight pair of pants with a top that Ruby had made to go with one of her skirts. It was very chic with small shoulder pads, a high collar that sort of popped up, and a bold geometrical print that looked nice with the black pants. I had gone bold with an electric-blue strappy sandal because I wanted one last wear before going to booties. Had to show off my pedicure and greige-painted toenails.

"Hello, Detective," I said to Wesley McNally, who had already ordered a drink. Old-fashioned. He looked like a bourbon guy, so that computed.

"Evening, Mrs. Crosby," he said with a pleased smile, setting aside the bar menu. "I told them to bring you a water. The waitress said she'll come back to take your drink order."

I took a steadying sip of water, telling myself this was not a date. It was a meetup with a colleague. Well, not quite a colleague but someone whose brain I could pick to learn more about investigative work and ease myself back into the dating scene. But I knew that Detective McNally thought it was a date.

Maybe it was.

Maybe it was good that it was.

I needed to embrace being a single woman. I was officially divorced, so I could date if I wanted to. To say that I was ready to start swiping right or left or whatever people were doing these days would be a falsehood, but I wasn't opposed to some company in my life. My girlfriends were one thing—they could take me shopping, meet for drinks, even go on girls' trips—but they went home to their husbands. There was something about having a guy take you out to dinner (or in this case, meet me for drinks) that made me feel less alone, less abandoned by my former life. Scott used to make it a point to take me out on dates, but that had faded away when we had Julia Kate. Though I couldn't even think about taking off my bra for another man yet, I didn't mind the thought of a bit of romance. Some wine, flowers, maybe a sweet good-night kiss.

Oh God, I hope I had breath mints in my purse.

"Please call me Cricket," I said, brightening when the waitress approached. "Hi, there. I'll have a vodka martini with Grey Goose, slightly dirty. Oh, and those blue cheese olives. Thanks."

Wes arched an eyebrow. "I was right. I almost ordered you a martini."

"Think you have me pegged, do you?"

"Maybe." His eyes were a nice shade of green, and when he wasn't wearing his detective facade, he seemed quite charming. I'd seen a few ladies clustered around the bar tossing looks his way. He merited the extra glances. Clad in a pair of khaki pants that weren't tailored but were well-made, Wes wore his white shirt open two buttons down to reveal a strong throat and the slight curl of chest hair. His fingernails were clean and clipped, his shave fresh, and his haircut decent. A slight whiff of a lemony fragrance hit as he leaned forward to adjust his position on the high barstool. Not bad at all.

"I bet you think you do, Detective," I said with a flirty little smile.

Detective McNally gave a throaty laugh that made me want to lean in and draw a deep breath. "Yeah, so Wes works for me."

"Okay then. Wes." I sipped my water again because he was doing little things to my insides. Not as much as Griff had done. Griff was a different beast for sure. His nails weren't dirty, but his hands were calloused and nicked from the work he did on his trucks. Griff had shaggy hair and tattoos that whirled and dipped into his tight T-shirts and jeans. He wore scuffed boots and grunted a lot. But the man could kiss. Just the thought of Griff's lips on mine did sparky things in my belly.

But Griffin Moon had never asked me to get drinks with him.

He hadn't asked me to do anything with him.

So I gave my full attention to the little flint strikes happening with Detective McNally.

The waitress was Johnny-on-the-spot with my martini, even setting the small silver shaker on the white tablecloth next to the cold glass. I took a deep draw of the briny beverage and sighed. I loved an icy vodka martini. My mother had taught me well.

"I like the way you do that," he said with a smile.

"What? Appreciate good alcohol?" I grinned, taking another sip.

He studied me. "Why did you accept my invitation?"

"Whoa, you're direct," I said, taken aback that he would come right out and ask my intentions like that. "You must be effective in an interview room. That had me back on my heels."

Wes shrugged. "I just want to know if this is strictly professional or something else. I don't like to waste time. I prefer knowing where the line is. Before I decide if I'm going to cross it."

"Can it be both?"

"Both professional and personal?"

"Well, I do value your professional wisdom and relationship. I mean, I solved your case for you," I said a bit cheekily.

He chuckled. "If you can call that a case. We don't usually classify missing dogs as one. That was a favor the captain did for Eileen."

"Yeah, well, you should have seen how happy Mrs. Ava was when I rang the doorbell with Louie in my arms. She actually cried. It was so rewarding." I had had to bathe Louie in her kitchen sink because I knew the older woman didn't have the wherewithal to do it herself. She sat at the breakfast table and chattered like a little chickadee, all the while praising the wriggling dog whose mess had me getting the mop to clean the floor. Mrs. Ava had sat on the couch and snuggled the towel-wrapped taco of a French bulldog while I cleaned up. It had all felt so very gratifying, adding to my conviction about pursuing this new part-time career.

"That's an anomaly, you know. Many cases never get closed, and often closing a case isn't a happy occasion. Usually, crime leads to ruined lives." Wes looked a bit serious. I really didn't want this meetup to be serious. Or for him to think of the sad, hard things he dealt with. I wanted to feel a bit flirty and "single."

"That's fairly pessimistic even for a cop."

"But true. And this is a pessimistic profession. You learn quickly that people are often horrible. When I close a case, I try to remember that justice is its own reward."

"That's your mission. And I guess mine now. Well, part of the time. The other time my mission is to make sure people buy pretty things that bring value to their lives the way it did for the previous owners."

Wes tilted his head. "I nearly forgot that you own an antiques store. How's that?"

"Awesome. You should come by the store sometime. I have some beautiful pieces and sell to a lot of gentlemen for their offices and such." By the look on his face, I knew that he wasn't in the market for a rolltop desk or bookcase. I cleared my throat. "I really love the store. It was my grandmother's, and we have a stellar reputation as a dealer of fine antiques. We get interior decorators and designers from all over the South. We also furnish movie sets when studios are in town. That's lots of fun, and I make good side change delivering furniture. I even got to meet Kevin Costner and Morgan Freeman a few years back."

And that launched us into a standard date conversation centering around what famous people we'd met. I finished the martini and moved to an iced tea. I normally would have gone with wine to sip, but since he was an officer of the law, it wouldn't look good to slip into the Spider after two drinks. Besides, I wanted to seem like a woman who made good decisions. Especially coming off a divorce and a broken axle from trying to recover a stolen dog. I also needed to keep my head clear so I could get to the other part of the reason I had accepted his invite for drinks—getting the lowdown on thefts in the area. I needed to know if the police had connected the recent rash of missing property in some of Shreveport's most affluent neighborhoods.

"So I have a question about how you handle certain reports. I realize that detectives mostly handle serious crimes, right?"

He set his empty highball glass on the table and motioned for the waitress. He ordered a Heineken and then turned his attention back to me. "Usually. But we're doing some zone policing, which is a new initiative. It's something we're trying in order to build needed community trust. Basically, a team of officers and detectives are assigned an area where they catch all the cases from homicides to petty theft and everything in between. This allows the community to know their officers, and it allows us to connect crimes. Often a homicide like a drive-by is associated with something like a car theft. That sort of thing. We have five major zones, and those captains share notes every forty-eight hours. Like there might be a rash of thefts in North Highlands with the same MO as ones in Southern Hills. It's just a different way to police the community, and so far, we're seeing good results. Our officers are getting to know the people in their areas and are forming relationships."

"That's great. So like, say, if there is a theft in one neighborhood in one zone and the same kind in the other, you both keep track of it?" Sounded like a good idea. Why had it taken so long to go back to probably how it was back in the day?

He looked pleased I had caught on. "Exactly. Lots of metropolitan areas are trying this sort of policing strategy. We have to try something, right? Crime seems to be growing every day."

Tell me about it.

I realized that the Shreveport Police Department had its hands full. Our city was overflowing with poverty that in turn led to more crime. Just down the street was an area known for gang violence where innocent children got caught in the crossfire too often. I was glad to hear that the SPD was trying new tactics, and I felt guilty worrying about white-collar thefts of Louis Vuittons and sparkly bracelets. But crime was crime, even if the items were luxury items. Thieves had to be brought to justice, even if the stolen goods seemed superfluous. After all, Lady Justice wore a blindfold not just for the accused but for the victims. Even if they were people like Mindy Woodward and Bo Dixie Ferris.

"So um, what about if someone takes something from your house? Like at a party? Is that theft or robbery?"

"Depends on if they came with intent to rob the person. For example, did they take a job as a server so they have opportunity? Or are they someone invited who saw a watch and took advantage of the situation?" He shrugged a shoulder.

I knew all this—I was fresh off my course for private investigations. "So intent, right?"

"Eh, pretty much."

"So say my friend Mindy Woodward had a David Yurman bracelet stolen during her husband's fiftieth birthday party, and then another friend over by, say, River Road had a purse stolen during a... Tupperware party, would you try to connect those things?"

He made a face. "Maybe. Depends on a lot of factors. Why are you asking these questions?"

"Is there a place where I can see what sort of crimes are committed in an area? Like a listing?"

"Sure, the city has an interactive map of crime." He made a face. "But you should know all this, Madam PI."

I did. But I needed more in depth than what the police told the general public. They always had suspicions and inside information. Well, according to *Law and Order*. "So do you have some interesting cases going on? I'm asking because one of my friends—Mindy—had a piece of jewelry go missing. How much theft and burglary goes on in, say, the south part of town?"

We launched into a discussion of property theft and robberies gone wrong, but I really didn't get much information out of him. Juke told me that Mindy had filed a report for the theft and that she'd talked Bo Dixie into doing the same. Bo Dixie had told a few friends, and someone else had some things missing from her home. I had texted Bo Dixie to see if we could meet up for a quick coffee at Maxine's Market before her children's elementary fall festival on Monday. Since Bo Dixie did write-ups for the social pages of the *Shreveport Gazette*, she'd been after me about commentary on the article she was doing for Ruby on the spotlight for the iSpy Festival. Two birds. One stone. Hopefully, I could glean some information about when she thought her purse was taken and what events she'd hosted at her house.

After another forty-five minutes of chatting, I slipped off the stool. "I've had such a nice time, Wes, but my daughter's probably home by now. She has a project due, and I have to do the mama thing."

"Let me walk you to your car," he said, leaving enough cash to cover the bill plus a nice tip.

"Thanks for the drinks. I really enjoyed them." I meant it too. He was easy to talk to, considering he was a police detective. And being easy on the eyes was the icing on the cake that was the delicious Detective McNally.

When we reached my car, he remarked on how cool it was, gave me a hug that got me a little nervous, and then suggested we meet for dinner next time.

"That would be nice," I said.

"I'll text you and you check your calendar. And if you need anything as you're working on the jewelry theft case, give me a shout."

I realized what he thought—that I had been using him. "I wasn't meeting you just for that."

"Oh?" His lips curved up. "I was hoping as much."

"I'll text you. About dinner."

"Do that," he said, holding the door open as I slipped into the driver's seat. "Be safe."

I backed out, my headlights catching him. He raised a hand, and I sighed. My first semiofficial date was in the books, and I had survived. No, I had thrived. I wasn't ready for much more than a brief hug, but time would tell. I sure as hell wasn't ready to marry him the way my ex was doing. I still boggled at the thought Scott was retying the knot in three days.

Just as I had that thought, my phone rang.

Speak of the devil, and he shows up.

"Hello, Scott." I sounded like I had just sucked on a lemon. His betrayal, even though I was so over him, still stung a little. I wasn't being nice to him, that was for sure.

"Hi, Cricket, how you doin' this evening?"

"I'm well. What can I do for you?" I started to toss in that I had just been on a date, but I wasn't petty. Okay, I was a little, but

I felt like keeping Wes and our little meetup on the down low. For everyone.

"So I'm sure JK told you about Natalie and our wedding this weekend?" He sounded uncertain. Maybe a little apologetic. He should be.

"Uh, yeah. She mentioned it. Congrats, by the way. Divorced on Monday and married on Sunday. That's... something. Like the title of a country song."

A long pause. "I know. But she's good for me, Cricket. After throwing away our marriage, making poor decisions, and having to shower with twenty other men at the same time, I need something to go my way."

Typical Scott. All about him. How had I not realized this when we were married? I had to have been a zombie walking through life, numb to all the crap I put up with. "Scott, I'm sure you feel that way, but I would, for Natalie's sake, say this—you can't rely on a person to make you feel good. That's what got you into this whole mess in the first place. You don't marry someone so they can make you feel okay about yourself. Marriage is work. So remember that when you make promises to this woman in a few days."

Silence on the phone.

"So is there anything else? Or were you just calling to remind me about your wedding?" I asked. With a little salt on my lemon.

"No, I'd called to ask your help in encouraging Julia Kate to come to the wedding. It would mean a lot to me."

Again, all about what he felt, what he needed. "It's natural you want her to share in that with you but understand this is Julia Kate's decision. Her feelings are valid, and your past choices have hurt our daughter. *My* past decisions have hurt our daughter. So if JK doesn't want to come to your wedding, respect her decision and try to understand how she feels."

I felt the energy shift over the airwaves or whatever allowed us to talk into a piece of plastic and be understood by a person many miles away.

"Don't start this shit again, Cricket. Your 'holier than thou' routine gets old fast. That's your problem—you think you're better than everyone else. You're the perfect mother, perfect daughter, perfect business owner, but frankly, my dear Cricket, you're perfect at being boring as fuck."

By now I had grown accustomed to his caustic, defensive words, but that didn't mean they didn't hurt. I wanted to rail at him, to tell him at least I wasn't a sucky person who cheated on the people I supposedly loved and tried to swindle them out of their retirement. But my recriminations would fall on deaf ears. Some people didn't want to know their flaws, and Scott was the prince of obliviousness. "I need to go, Scott. Remember what the therapist suggested for our daughter, whom we both *love* and both want the best for."

With those last words, I hung up and tossed the cell phone into the passenger seat.

It rang immediately.

I sighed and clicked it on. "What? I told you—"

"Oh, thank God. Cricket?" Ruby asked, sounding very distraught.

"Ruby? What's wrong?" I asked.

"I can't get in touch with your mother or your aunt. And I can't call Dak. He would try to come up here."

"What's going on?" I felt my stomach drop.

"I got arrested, and I need an attorney."

"What?" I slammed on the brakes when I realized the light was red. I skidded through and a car honked at me. "Arrested? In New York? Why?"

Ruby paused and then said, "I punched Rafe Lasso in the throat when he tried to roofie me."

11

Ruby

THE NEXT MORNING...

All jail cells look alike.

Well, at least the one in Manhattan looked very similar to the one in Shreveport where I had been cuffed and booked for possession with intent to distribute three years ago. This time, I had been handcuffed and booked for aggravated battery. Rafe had screamed that he was pressing charges. That he wanted me dragged out, humiliated, and never allowed to work in this town ever.

Ever!

That was not how I had hoped the evening would go.

But I wasn't sorry I had throat punched him. Because Rafe Lasso had deserved that and more. The man was slimy as a sick alligator. Just ask me how I know that sick gators regurgitate slimy things.

"Ruby Balthazar?" a uniformed officer called from the other side of the holding cell.

I stood, feeling sort of ridiculous in my platform shoes and peplumed jacket. When I had pulled my ensemble on last evening, I had such high hopes. The past few days of Fashion Week had been more than I had ever hoped for—I had been interviewed by someone doing a piece on designers who use vintage inspiration for *Marie Claire* magazine, I had shared my design book with Cecile and gotten very enthusiastic feedback, and I had attended several other cocktail parties, shows, and even some behind-the-scenes action at Bryant Park. I'd chatted with models, learned how buyers acquired for department stores, and met some cool bloggers and influencers, many who wanted me to send them photos of my pieces to share with their followers. Coraline and her wife—who was charming if not absolutely shy—had hosted a few people from *Vogue* on their gorgeous skyline patio. Basically, I felt like someone I had only read about or watched on shows like *Sex and the City* or *Gossip Girl*.

And I hadn't felt out of place. In fact, I had convinced myself that I belonged. These were my people.

Rafe Lasso had invited me to an exclusive party at his mansion yesterday afternoon. He signaled that he had something he wanted to discuss regarding my future as a designer. Immediately, hope had soared inside me. Maybe he was going to offer me a job or an internship? Perhaps I would soon be doing something more than sewing scraps of couture in the dusty top floor of Printemps in a town where "fashion" was a cute crop top from Walmart.

The sight of his huge house awed me. I thought everyone lived in apartments or brownstones in NYC, but I guess Rafe Lasso was different because the entire five-story structure was all his. As the Uber driver pulled into the courtyard drive, I tried to act as if I went to parties at mansions all the time. I had felt confident in satin cigarette pants and the centerpiece jacket for my collection that would debut at iSpy in a few weeks.

Well, if I got out of jail.

Jesus.

"Ruby Balthazar," the guard called again.

"I'm her," I called as I stepped over a drunk woman moaning about "Timmy" and moved to the barred opening.

The gate clanged as it slid open. "Turn around."

I did, folding my arms behind me.

She procured the cuffs, not too tight which was kind of her. "Follow me."

I did as the guard asked. I knew how this worked, so I kept my mouth shut and my head down. A few people in neighboring holding cells yelled ugly things at the uniformed officer. She kept her eyes straight ahead and showed no reaction. Just like all guards did for the most part. Didn't make sense to form relationships or share niceties with people who dreamed about killing you. Not that everyone here in the holding cells wished to do harm. But those who were doing life or long stints weren't beyond such "wishful" thinking as Big Sal had called it when she told me in splendid detail how she would kill the guard in charge of our section back at Long Pines. Let's just put it this way, I was always nice to Big Sal.

Always.

Marguerite and Coraline both waved at me when I emerged, looking relieved that I wasn't worse for wear. The guard led me to a desk where she uncuffed me and left without another word. I blinked at the dude behind the desk, waiting on him to say something.

Finally, he looked up. "Miss Balthazar, you're free to go. The victim has declined to press charges. I have a few papers for you to sign." The officer was very nonplussed, as if he was accustomed to charges not sticking. Maybe people in Manhattan were more wishy-washy than those in my neck of the woods.

"I can go?" I couldn't fathom that Rafe wasn't going to charge me with everything from trespassing to assault to whatever else he could toss my way. He'd been mad as a wet hen... if not a little hoarse from me punching him in the throat.

"That's what I'm told," the officer said.

I glanced at Marguerite before being led to an area where desks were shoved too close together and uniformed police looked overworked and harried. Ten minutes later, I walked toward Cricket's mama and her sister.

"Oh, thank goodness." Marguerite enclosed me in a brief hug before drawing back to look me in the eye. "Are you okay?"

"That son of a bitch," Coraline said, grasping my chin and angling my face so she could peruse me. "I knew he was a complete asshole. I mean, I've heard rumors, but I could have never guessed he would pull this BS with you. I'm sorry I let you go. This is my fault."

I jerked my chin away. "This is not your fault. This is on Rafe Lasso. He's the... the..."

"Predator? Pervert? Pedophile?" Coraline huffed.

"I'm not a minor, so that last one isn't true," I said, a slight smile twitching at my lips at her utter outrage.

"Well, he might as well be. You're young enough to be his daughter, for heaven's sake." Coraline took my arm. "Dear girl, I'm so sorry I allowed you to become mixed up in that sort of business. Please don't think that we are all degenerates in the fashion world. Sure, fashion is ridiculous and over the top, but we are not criminals. Or at least most of us aren't."

I felt such relief at her words because I had spent the past few hours beating myself up over thinking that I belonged here. Various voices in my head shouted I wasn't ready for all this. Thing was, after a few days of observing and attending shows, I knew I was good enough as a designer. What I wasn't prepared for was the fawning, pretending, and posturing that was needed to secure the opinions of the "right" people. Another revelation—just like beauty, talent is in the eye of the beholder. So much of what is "brilliant" to one buyer or blogger is befuddling to others. Sure, the fashion world has always had some undeniable greats. But for the most part, design is like every other art—intangible and colored by perception.

I didn't have to move to New York City to build my career in fashion, but I knew I could make it in this fashion mecca, climbing over sycophants and creatives until I reached the top of the heap. But now everything I had been so certain about the day before had fissures of doubt threatening it.

We walked out of the station and toward a black town car waiting on the curb.

"Eduardo, can we stop for coffee? I told Maggie I would bring her a latte, and Ruby here needs a big cup of something strong and perhaps an aspirin or two," Coraline said, patting my leg as I clicked myself into the seat.

The driver smiled, a bit gap-toothed, and saluted Coraline. "Yes, ma'am."

"Now before we get to the office and I show you off to all my underlings—and I say that with affection, mind you—I want to know exactly what Rafe did to cause a ruckus."

"It's over. Can we move on?" I asked.

She arched a perfect eyebrow, and I knew that it was not over.

"Fine. So I got to his ginormous house, and there were a few other people there. Same kind of scene—people dressed outlandishly, making small talk, doing drugs and stuff. Rafe had a nice bar setup, and I had something called a Kir Royal that some French woman said I would love. Rafe took me on the balcony where we chatted about fabrics and past designers. You know, like who we loved and that sort of thing."

Rafe had been charming and almost fatherly. "Here, Ruby. Sit. Let's watch the sun set. I find this sort of respite exactly what is needed in a week like this. Fashion Week is such a chore—all that rushing around, booking models, creating perfect venues, and praying the right people say the right things."

"I can imagine," I said.

"My yogi master prescribed simple timed breathing exercises that I use. I also like to focus on a simple moment in time such as this. It seems to lower my heart rate and restore my perspective."

I sank onto the navy-striped ticking of the outdoor patio furniture. The rooftop balcony looked like a photo spread for a high-end magazine with architectural urns overflowing flowering plants I'd never seen before. Well, except the asparagus fern. That I had on my own back porch. "There is something about living within a moment that sets us right."

He laughed, the faux auburn in his hair flashing in the setting sun that gilded the surrounding buildings and busy street below. Rafe sank down beside me, a little too close, his cologne a bit oppressive. I shifted away from him to give him space, but he angled toward me despite my efforts. "'Sets us right.' That's adorable. I love the way you talk. So… you."

Suddenly I felt silly. And ashamed of my upbringing. I knew who I was and from where I hailed, and at that moment I was acutely aware that I didn't belong where I was. "Well, Mr. Lasso, I'm just a simple girl from the country."

"With a dream," he finished for me.

"Yes. We all have them. Aren't you a product of a dream?"

He shrugged. "I fell into what I do. My mother was an in-demand seamstress, an overworked one, and she recruited me to help her. To be truthful, I always wanted to be an astronaut. I can still remember the thrill of watching Neil Armstrong plant the flag on the moon. I was in high school then, and everything felt so possible. I certainly didn't think I would be sewing my way into a future. But here I am."

I looked around at the splendor encasing me. "It's not so bad."

He gave a bark of laughter. "I guess many would think so. I have money, position, a sort of power, I suppose, but all that is relative."

"It's not relative. It's what everyone wants. If you're going to be ridiculous and tell me you're missing something or you don't think money matters, I might punch you." I couldn't stand when people of means made their lives sound the same as those of us who struggled paycheck to paycheck. Sure, everyone has problems, but to sit in a mansion in the middle of Manhattan surrounded by champagne and caviar and molly grub over life shortchanging you was a little much. Like, cry me a freaking river.

Rafe Lasso perused me from the top of my fuchsia streak to the tips of the platform sandals I'd found at the Goodwill off Barksdale Boulevard in Bossier City and snorted. "Somehow I think you would."

"You read people well."

"So what do you want, Ruby?" he asked.

"Everything. Nothing. Something for myself." This was what I had been thinking about all day long as I traversed the alien world of New York City fashion. What did I want? I thought I wanted to be there. The energy of Manhattan infused a person, made them feel as if anything is possible. I could grab a cat by the tail, swing it around, and hit the mark. But still the other part of me felt so small, so insignificant. If I went there, I would be alone. No coffee at Gran's, no Saturday-morning snuggles with Dak, no Cricket, no safety net. I would make friends—or according to one of the bloggers, lots of enemies who pretended to be my friends. I would become a city girl who no longer baited her own hook, unless we were talking a figurative sense. Could Ruby Balthazar, ex-con, take Manhattan by storm? Or would I be more like a small wind, blowing gently only to fade as the sunset? I couldn't know unless I tried, but I wasn't sure that people should try everything in life. Some paths you take lead to nowhere.

"That's not the answer I expected, but it says a lot about you." Rafe eased back, staring out at pigeons darting from building to building in the fading day.

I bit my lip. "I won't pretend I don't want a career in this business, but nothing here is what I expected. There is a lot of posturing, a lot of preening, a lot of bullshit. I don't know if that's something I can wade into and be happy."

"When is happy ever the goal?" He asked it lightly. The words didn't fall on me that way.

I valued happy. I didn't mind sacrifice, but no one wants to endure utter misery when life is just too damn short. Or maybe it's just too unpredictable. I had already wasted two years sewing quilts in the slammer. I wasn't slicing off any more years. Mostly because Saturday mornings in bed with Dak induced happiness comas. "I think happy should always be a goal."

At those words, Rafe waved at a gentleman hovering nearby. "Another drink?"

I looked down at the dregs left in my glass. I knew I shouldn't. But I was in the Big Apple on a rooftop mansion with one of the biggest names in fashion. Maybe a few more bubbles to celebrate living in this moment. "Sure."

The waiter dude swept away the nearly empty one and set the filled one in front of me. "Kir Royal, I believe?"

I nodded and lifted the drink. I sipped. Saltier. Not the same. I set the drink down.

Rafe looked at the glass. "Don't want it? It's Krug Clos d'Ambonnay 1995."

Now I had been in prison, so I was good at reading people. Pretty much had to be. At this point, I knew a few things: Rafe wanted me to drink up, and that d'Ambonnay—whatever the year—wasn't the same as I'd had earlier. "No, thanks."

"But we're celebrating, my dear."

"What exactly?" I asked. My tone was suspicious, and he caught on.

"You being here. With me. Tonight."

I looked at the champagne cocktail. "Did you put something in my drink?"

"Of course not. I've been here with you the entire time." He faked affronted well.

"So did *he* put something in my drink?" I glanced over my shoulder at the dude who had brought the drink.

Rafe shook his head. "You're imagining things."

I picked up the drink, and I saw a flash of triumph in Rafe's eyes. But then I swung it toward him. "You drink it."

"I don't want it."

"I bet." I set it down hard. The champagne sloshed. "I need to get back. Thank you for the invitation."

Rafe caught my arm. "Why? The evening is just beginning."

"Not for me." I wrenched away.

"Now you're being dramatic. Stay." He tugged my arm.

"Are you really going to do this?" I asked, glancing back at the champagne and then him.

"I wanted to talk about your future. The drink was just to relax you, get you comfortable. I know how daunting it is to talk to someone like me, someone who could make or break you." His words were laced with intimidation. The drink with something to "relax" me. This guy might be the head of a fashion dynasty, wearing the finest fabrics, and commanding servants to do his bidding, but he was a stereotypical creep. No different than any of the Neanderthal bubbas or the trashy troublemakers out in the trailer park where I grew up. And even they wouldn't resort to drugging anyone. Well, not intentionally.

"I'm not daunted. I'm leaving," I said, rising.

Again, he put his hand on my forearm. And that's when I punched him in the throat.

He let go then, doubling over, gasping.

I walked past him, scooping up the purse that Coraline had lent me for the duration of Fashion Week since mine was too large for evening wear. The guy who had served me the roofied cocktail scrambled toward his owner, squeaking like a dog toy.

I kept going.

"Stop her!" Rafe choked out. "And call the police!"

I hurried my steps. He might deserve to be punched, but I knew how this would play out. Wealthy designer versus ex-con? Yeah, this was going to be a problem.

"Miss?" someone said, falling in beside me. "Please stop."

I looked at the guy. This one was in a suit, like a normal suit —navy-blue, well tailored, nice haircut, nothing creative about him. He looked like a lawyer or a politician. "Rafe Lasso drugged me. And he put his hands on me without my permission."

"Let's just calm down. I'm David Morales, Mr. Lasso's attorney, and—"

"I want her arrested," Rafe whisper-shouted, his voice breaking through on the "arrested" part. He careened into the well-appointed living area open to the balcony, his hand clasping his neck. Those who had been chatting and guzzling the free booze paused. One woman stopped mid line of coke on the glass coffee table and blinked at the scene unfolding.

"I already called the police," the roofie guy said, coming in behind Rafe.

"Now Rafe," David started, clasping a large hand on my shoulder. "Let's see reason."

I wriggled away. I was done with these dudes touching me.

Several people passed me, heading toward the sweeping staircase that led to the bottom floor. I heard the elevator ding, and the cokehead in towering stilettos hotfooted it toward the sliding doors. I glanced at the coffee table where only residue remained. Waste not, want not.

Rafe was incensed, red as a hothouse tomato, and pointing his finger at me. "She's going down! She fucking punched me. For no reason. I was trying to help the little bitch."

"Into your bed, you creep!" I shouted, anger finally kicking in. I couldn't believe that he was making me out to be the bad guy when he was the criminal. "You drugged my drink!"

"Prove it," Rafe shouted, moving toward me as if he was going to fasten his hands around my neck. The attorney stepped between us, holding up his hands as if to stop Rafe.

That's when the downstairs buzzer sounded, and the flash of police lights shimmied off the silk curtains framing the balcony.

"Crap, it's the po-po," some weird dude wearing Elton John glasses and KISS boots shouted unhelpfully. Several more people hoofed it toward the staircase.

And from there, it went south for me. Police, handcuffs, being paraded from Rafe Lasso's mansion into the streets where everyone stared. Some filmed. Others took selfies.

As I told Coraline and Marguerite the story, I twisted my fingers into my bangs, knotting my hair painfully. Marguerite reached over and stilled my hands with a "You don't want to go bald, dear." She kept her hand on mine, a well-moisturized, only slightly age-spotted clasp of comfort.

Coraline shook her head. "I can't believe that bastard. I never would have encouraged you to go to his house if I had known. I mean, I had heard a few rumors back in the day that he was a bit grabby, but nothing like this."

Hollowness enveloped me, reminiscent of another time, one where I slept on a narrow cot and was merely a number. I stared out at the street churning by as we sped toward the office of *Vogue*, a world that felt so foreign. "You didn't know he would try to drug me. It's not your fault."

"Still." She looked so contrite that my heart went out to her.

"I'm okay. But I wonder why he dropped the charges? He was pissed last night."

"Because I called Dave Morales and told him that I would do an expose on designers who took advantage of subordinates. There are several in this business who think they are untouchable, and there have been wide reports of verbal and physical abuse. I'm not above pulling up the rock that is the fashion world and revealing the yuck that lurks beneath. Dave isn't a fool, and neither is Rafe."

"So you bribed him?"

Coraline shrugged a shoulder. "I may have implied that, but rest assured I will make sure this gets out. I've already called a friend in the NYPD, and there will be an investigation. You may have to testify down the line."

My stomach turned over at that thought. I didn't want to have this hanging over me. "I would just rather forget it."

"Until he tries it again with a girl who isn't as clever as you?" Coraline asked.

I wasn't good at being a crusader. People who felt powerless most of their lives rarely were good at storming the castle. Yet Coraline had a point. "If it comes to it. Maybe they won't need me. I don't live here."

"Well, I'm sorry it happened. You're a talented designer, Ruby, and this weekend was about showing you the possibilities that are out there for someone like you."

"I am grateful." I glanced at Marguerite, including her in my thanks. "This visit has been eye-opening. I've learned a lot, I've made some nice contacts, and Cecile has offered to mentor me and make recommendations when the time comes for me to work for someone else or sign contracts with a retailer. But that's my future. Right now, I have to get ready for my first show."

Coraline pressed her lips together and sucked in a breath. Her eyes crackled intensely as she thought about what to say. Finally, she gave a smile of acceptance. "I agree. First things first. But I don't want this incident to dissuade you. You have a future in fashion. This is something I know. But only you decide your path."

She understood me. I needed to explore my own art, study past designers, and learn about the business of fashion. Talent-wise, I was up to par, but understanding the world of fashion, well, there were holes. And then there was the happiness factor and the Dak situation.

Dak.

I probably should have called him instead of Cricket, but I knew what his reaction would be. He wanted to protect me from everything, even as he understood that he couldn't. When he learned that Rafe Lasso had put something in my drink so he could take advantage, Dak would be furious, and his support for me could diminish. I didn't want to color his perception of my pursuing my dreams in a big city.

Because eventually I would have to make that decision.

But not today. "Right now I'm ready to go home."

Marguerite gave a sniff. "And after last night, I'm ready to go home too."

Coraline's mouth twitched, and her normally sharky eyes danced in delight.

I lifted my eyebrows, ignoring the headache that pressed against the back of my eyes. "What happened last night?"

"My sister's date was a pay for play." Coraline's voice was laced with amusement.

"It's not funny." Marguerite shot her sister a dirty look. "I had no idea."

I blinked a few times as the numbers lined up in my head. "Wait, the silver-headed fox was an *escort*?"

Coraline craned her head to see if the driver was listening. Then she pulled something from her gorgeous Goyard bag. "Oh yeah, he was. And here's the menu he gave her when he handed her his Square so she could pay."

"Oh my stars, you kept that thing?" Marguerite made a grab for the cardstock.

Coraline nimbly pulled it away. "I was thinking Marguerite might want number five—or if she's feeling frisky, number nine."

I took the menu, my eyes going wide as I looked at the buffet of services the silver-haired fox offered. "Oh my. Number eight is illegal in Louisiana. You should have definitely gone for that one."

Marguerite jerked the nicely printed list from my hand. "I'm not even up for number one. No one is spanking me. Ever. Or doing any of those vile things to my body."

"Then you're missing out, sis," Coraline said, covering her mouth with her hand.

I started giggling. "Well, I wouldn't mind a copy of the list. I like a little number three and four when I've had a bikini wax."

"Oh, good heavens. You two are perverted."

"So you've always said." Coraline laughed, poking Marguerite, who then slapped her hand away. "Come on. Lattes are on me this morning. I'm the only one who wasn't doing illegal things last night."

Marguerite's eyes popped. "I was *not* doing illegal things."

"You bought a Fendi from the backroom of a store in Chinatown." Coraline wiggled her eyebrows. "And nearly did number two with a male prostitute."

Marguerite didn't wait for Eduardo to open the door before she climbed out of the car.

Coraline laughed all the way to the coffee shop.

12

Cricket

Two days later...

I was ready for Ruby to get back to Shreveport. For one thing, Resa was no Ruby and had accidentally broken an expensive set of bookends when she was rearranging the bookshelves in the backroom. I could forgive her for that because everyone makes mistakes, but she wasn't the least bit interested in learning anything about antiques. She kept called everything "old junk," which wasn't doing me any favors with customers. I mostly sent her upstairs to work on the piecework she was doing for Ruby which suited Resa fine because then she could listen to rap music while she sewed. Jade and I held down the store, which had been surprisingly busy. I chalked that up to Ruby's new website and the pieces we'd worn throughout the summer. The dress I had worn to Grits and Glitz had four solid offers but wasn't for sale at present. Just display.

"I'm off to pick up your Gigi and Ruby from the airport," I called to Jade and Resa as I lifted my bag and dropped a kiss on Julia Kate's head. My daughter was taking an emotional health day after attending her father's wedding. Seems he tried to get her to be the flower girl. She refused. Scott got his feelings hurt. I swear, it was like parenting two children. I had already delivered strong words to him over the guilt trip he'd given her, but Julia Kate's tears that morning paired with monthly cramps had been enough to take her to work with me.

"You want to come with me to get them?" I asked, eyeing the TikToks she was scrolling through. "Wait, have you finished your schoolwork? I let you stay home to get over whatever it is you're getting over, but you still must keep up with your work."

"God, Mom, I've already done it. I should have just gone to school."

She probably should have. I had been more lax than I should with the kid, overcompensating in order to apologize for her father and me failing her so greatly. Now she was another statistic—the child of divorced parents. And not just that. She was the child of a criminal. I still felt so horrible for my role in bringing her father down the way I had. No, I wasn't guilty about Scott getting busted. But I was sorry that I had done it in such a way that people had talked about his arrest for months. I hadn't considered my daughter when I'd done that piece of grandstanding, so I might have let her get away with more than I should these past months.

"I can drop you off on my way." I lifted an eyebrow as I scooped up my purse. "Or you can come with me. We'll grab a bite for lunch, and you can be educated on the business of fashion by someone who is building her dream."

"That's blackmail." She closed her browser and stood up. Julia Kate had slimmed down over the summer and now looked more like a woman than a girl. It hurt my heart a little to know that she had tipped over from childhood toward the gaping maw that was adulthood. But she wasn't there yet. Not yet.

I smoothed her hair and pulled her in tight. She struggled, of course, but I got a quick snuggle. "Hey, I'm not making you be my flower girl."

"It's not funny. First, I'm too old for that. And I can't believe he thought I would want to, like, show that I approve of what he's doing." Julia Kate closed her eyes and gave a deep sigh.

"He shouldn't have put you in that situation. You handled it well though. You told him no, didn't yell or scream, and stood your ground. I'm proud of you."

"Thanks," she said, lifting a shoulder. "I guess I wouldn't mind seeing Gigi. She's the one who told me that I can be far more deadly by not shouting or getting emotional."

I started. "She taught you that?"

"She teaches me all kinds of things."

"I bet. Has she taught you how to make a perfect martini and run everybody else's life too?" I asked with a chuckle. Hey, I had to give my mother credit—Marguerite had modeled how to survive as a single woman. Even if it was a sometimes overbearing one. "Let's go. She'll be happy to see you, and I bet Ruby has lots of good news. Mama indicated that she made quite an impression on a few well-known designers."

Julia Kate stared longingly at my laptop.

"Or I can drop you off at school."

"Lunch with Gigi for the win!" Julia Kate jerked her gaze from the computer and grabbed her cell phone.

Fifteen minutes later, we were dodging construction at the Shreveport Regional Airport and searching for my mother and favorite assistant. Finally they emerged—Ruby looking hot and urban and Mother looking like a British monarch. Two unlikely traveling companions. Seeing them made me smile.

"JK, help your Gigi," I commanded, switching on my hazard

lights for safety. Julia Kate jumped out, vacating the spot up front for my mother. Marguerite slid in, and I caught sight of her new bag. "You bought a Fendi?"

My mother had long ago declared the expense of a Fendi these days "highway robbery," and she could remember the days where even designer bags were reasonable. So this was unexpected. She looked down at the bag. "Do you like it?"

"I love it. Where's mine?"

"Ha."

Ruby slammed the back of the van and climbed in the back with Julia Kate. "Man, it's so hot here."

"It's the same temperature as when you left. Thin-skinned Northerner already, I guess." I wondered if being in New York City had struck a chord inside her. Did she want to move there, make a new life among budding designers, bust her hump for some other antiques shop in Greenwich Village?

Ruby smiled. "Well, it's a jungle up there."

"So they say." I pulled away from the curb, heading toward Alfredo's which had fresh gulf shrimp on Mondays. So many restaurants didn't open on Mondays any longer. The pickings were getting slim, but a nice remoulade salad would hit the spot and help me get into the dress I wanted to wear to the Friday night open house at the iSpy Fashion Festival at the end of the month. Ruby had found the slinky Halston number at a thrift shop in Marshall, Texas, when we'd gone garage sale shopping for rare finds. It was a gorgeous nude with small spangles, reminiscent of the dress Marilyn Monroe wore to sing "Happy Birthday" to President Kennedy. Or as my daughter would recognize, the one the Kardashian woman wore to the Met Gala. But it was more of a slip dress and not so formal. Of course I still needed my bumps smoothed and my girls taped high with the shaping stuff I had found online. And a few pounds dropped would make me feel more confident. So yeah, salad.

On the way, Ruby and Marguerite regaled us with tales from the fashion shows and the famous people they'd seen. Ruby had even managed to rub elbows with Lorde, some electropop singer I was unfamiliar with, signifying that I was older than dirt. But I totally recognized the name of a *Sex and the City* actress who had gone to the Dior show.

When we were seated by a window that highlighted the brilliant red maples dancing outside the large picture window, Marguerite launched into a picture slideshow with Julia Kate, a reward for the child who had taught her how to use the camera and pick cool filters. I wasn't sure where my mother was posting these photos since her Facebook profile was anemic and she wasn't on Insta. Marguerite thought TikTok was a rapper.

I looked over at Ruby. "Well?"

"Well, what?"

"I know my mother got you out of jail, but you never told me what happened," I whispered, eying my daughter who didn't know I had gotten a crazy "one call" from a Manhattan holding cell a few nights ago.

"Your aunt fixed it. With threats." Ruby ran her finger down the menu, avoiding my gaze. "She reminds me of you. Well, the new you who doesn't take crap from anyone."

"You really think I'm like that?" I asked, pleased to have a bit of badassery in my arsenal.

Ruby looked up with a smile. "Well, you did have Scott trying to choke you down at the University Club luncheon."

"Yeah," I said with a smile, casting another glance at my daughter, who was engrossed in my mother's phone. New filters. Posting on Snapchat.

Snapchat?

"Lasso withdrew the charges. It's all good." Ruby didn't look up.

"But Rafe Lasso," I mused, sucking in a deep breath. "That's so disappointing. I'm going to get rid of anything I have by him. He's disgusting."

Ruby shook her head. "He's just one of many who use their authority and power to run over others. Or rape them."

"Oh my God." I grabbed her hand. Usually she pulled away, but this time she let my hand curve around hers. "When I think about what could have happened to you, it makes me sick."

"I can take care of myself. I got them street smarts." She pulled her hand away.

"So are you going to move to Manhattan? Mom said Coraline wants you to come. She thinks you'd be brilliant at Parsons, learning whatever it is that they can teach you. I have to say you might be able to teach them a thing or two. You're already so talented."

Ruby glanced out the window, her pretty face vulnerable. Then she blinked and looked back at me. She jerked her chin forward. "For now, I'm sticking to my plan. I appreciate everything your aunt did for me. I made connections and had experiences I never would have had. But presently, I plan to win iSpy and then launch my line online. Once I get that under my belt, we'll see about the next step. I may apply for Parsons or accept a position with a house. My mentor is going to help me figure out the next step."

My mother overheard. "Not just any mentor, but Cecile Smart."

"Get out." I looked over at Ruby. "Is she serious? Cecile?"

"Why are you freaking out?" Julia Kate asked.

"Because I watched her show *Style Season* every Saturday morning on CNN. She was the editor-in-chief of *Couture Magazine* and wrote three books on fashion and culture that hit the New York Times bestseller list. She's the get at every fashion house show, and her nod launches careers." I shoved my menu into the holder as Stephen, my normal waiter, approached with a glass of Kim Crawford sauvignon blanc, my go-to on Mondays. I envisioned the seams of that slinky number squeezing me. I should send the wine back, but its pale deliciousness was as seductive as that dress I probably wouldn't be wearing.

"Dope." Julia Kate's face erupted into a smile.

Gosh, my baby was beautiful when she smiled.

"Thanks. And now I would like a club sandwich with fries." Ruby shoved her menu beside mine.

"Salad for you?" Stephen asked with no judgment. Or at least I liked to think with no judgment.

"Yes," Mother and I said at the same time.

"Dressing on the side," he said, not waiting for an answer. "And JK, I'm assuming you want the tenders?"

"Nope," Julia Kate said. "I'll have the salad too."

"Aye, aye, ladies," he said, trotting off toward the kitchen.

"Really? You love their tenders," I said.

"I'm not a kid anymore, Mom," Julia Kate said before picking up her cell phone and tuning the world out. My heart did a little squeeze thing. Already eating salads? I wasn't ready for salads, shaving legs, and push-up bras. I darn sure wasn't ready for boyfriends or driving lessons. But they were coming. I could see this.

My mother opened her mouth, likely to disagree with my daughter, but I gave her the look. She frowned but closed her mouth.

"Ruby, I was hoping you'd come with me tonight. I need your help," I said.

"Dun, dun, duh," Julia Kate intoned while not looking up.

"What? It's just a Posh Pantry party over at Carol Sue Lambert's house. It'll be fun. Besides it's raising money for Carol Sue's nanny whose mother has lung cancer. A lot of people are going to lend their support." I smiled gamely at Ruby, like she should want to come to this party where I would no doubt buy a cilantro stripper and a silicone spatula that I would never use. "Carol Sue always serves good wine."

Expensive wine was Ruby's weakness. I wasn't above using it to get her to come with me to do some reconnaissance and information gathering. If the thief made a move on Carol Sue's Louis Vuitton obsession, I could nip this whole case in the bud. After all, Carol Sue didn't have any pets.

"Posh Pantry?" Ruby said, physically recoiling, her chair making a scraping sound. "You could promise Cakebread wine, and I would still choose dime-store Moscato and my pj's. Who wants to watch women fawn over egg cookers? No, thanks."

"Please. I'm working a case, and I need someone who can be my wingman. I almost got caught snooping at Esme's house. Luckily, what I thought was the thief was only her cat taking a poo in her closet. But Esme caught me in her room."

My mother made a face. "Thief? Whatever are you talking about?"

"Wait." Ruby inched back into her normal posture. "I want to go back to the cat."

I ignored Ruby. "I'm working a case—a potential theft ring operating among some of our friends. But you can't tell anyone, Mother. Not a soul. Or you'll blow my cover."

"What in the world?" my mother asked.

I wasn't sure if her response was in regard to my working the case or the thefts.

"Yeah, I know. Expensive bags and jewelry have been disappearing over the past month or so. I bet a lot of people don't even realize they have things missing. A few days ago, I had coffee with Bo Dixie, and she verified that she has some things missing and knows of several other ladies also missing expensive items. Juke's client was an early victim, and the police aren't doing much about it." As I said those words, my mind flitted to the image of Wesley McNally and the way he'd given me that hug a few nights back. And now we had our first official date on Friday night which made me feel quivery.

"Juke took that case?" Ruby asked and then she twisted her lips. "So now I see why he's letting you work for him. He needs you."

"And he doesn't even realize how much. If I can help him find the thief and recover the stolen items, I think he'll let me work for him officially. Right now, it's a contract job. I have two weeks."

"Why do you need *me*?" Ruby asked.

"I told you. I need someone to cover my butt while I'm snooping. Like last time, you could have waylaid Esme before she got to her bedroom. You can also help gather information. Two spies are better than one, right?" It had sounded good in my head. Truth was, I liked when Ruby accompanied me on my first stakeout. Having someone else who knew what you were about was... comforting. "I mentioned to Bo Dixie that I was going to bring you with me. She writes the fashion and social column for the newspaper. She's planning a piece on you for an iSpy feature. Plus you realize there is a voting component. A lot of those women really like the lady that smocks all the bubbles for their kids. You gotta win them over."

Boom. If wine didn't get her, winning voters would.

Ruby sucked in a deep breath. "Fine. But I'm tired from traveling, so I don't want to stay long."

"We won't. Just long enough to gather some intel." I picked up my wine and took a sip. Cold and delicious.

"Intel?"

"That's what they call gossip in the business," my mother said. "I can't believe someone is stealing things from others' houses. What is this world coming to? I mean, people we *trust*. Jesus has to be coming soon. This world is doomed. Just doomed."

"Gigi," my daughter said, looking exasperated.

My mother sighed. "Well, it *is* a shame. Ever since—"

I needed to head off the standard "what is this world coming to" lecture before she got to the political climate. "Coraline texted me something about a menu you were bringing back? Something that you brought home from a date with a gentleman. Mother, I can't believe you went on a date."

My mother choked on her iced water. Ruby started laughing. Julia Kate looked relieved that her grandmother had stopped railing about the shape our world was in and started tapping away on her phone.

Ruby patted my mother on the back and pulled out her phone. She clicked something and then handed it over. "I took a picture of it."

In the selfie, Ruby held up a piece of cardstock, her mouth forming an *O*. I pinched and magnified the image. The fancy script was incongruous with the listings. "Dear Lord, Mother. What exactly did you *do* in New York City?"

My mother snatched up the phone and handed it back to Ruby. "Nothing under those numbers, I'll tell you that."

Ruby looked absolutely gleeful. "I may have"—she lowered her voice—"gotten arrested, but your mama was the real bad girl."

"I was not," my mother said, elbowing Ruby.

Julia Kate looked up, surprised at my mother getting physical. "What are y'all talking about?"

"Nothing," I chirped, trying not to laugh. "I just think your grandmother should go on more trips with Ruby. Ruby helps your Gigi loosen up."

Ruby grinned. "Which I believe is a result of doing number six."

Carol Sue held the Posh Pantry party on the large patio that she'd just had remodeled. The open area had a gorgeous built-in kitchen with a white granite top, beautiful patio furniture, a rustic fireplace, and seating for a small army. Ruby sat beside me, looking uncomfortable as the Posh Pantry rep explained how to create a fruit basket with a must-have serrated knife and a melon scooper. I had to admit that the watermelon fruit basket was a humdinger.

That was the rep's favorite word—humdinger.

Piper Montgomery moved her chair back after glancing at Carol Sue. Seeing that her friend was caught up in scooping the perfect melon ball, Piper looked... something I couldn't put my finger on.

My private eye antennae stood at attention.

"I'm going to get another water," I whispered to Ruby who had been smart enough to procure a seat next to Bo Dixie Ferris. Bo had marveled at Ruby's ensemble which was a pared-down version of a look in her upcoming show. Perfect segue into the article for the newspaper. And Bo wanted to know all about Fashion Week and my aunt's role at *Vogue*. I enjoyed hearing Ruby chat about all her adventures—minus the Rafe Lasso incident—as I examined the women around me, trying to figure out how to bring up missing purses and bangles without sounding *too* interested.

The downside to being out on Carol Sue's patio was not being able to widely mix and mingle. The large farm table accommodated sixteen people, and the small bistros scattered around the outside held three people each. Which meant I wasn't getting much accomplished in the way of learning if any other people had had things stolen. Maybe once we finished the presentation and went inside for light snacks, I could gather intel. Okay, gossip.

"You're going to be peeing all night," Ruby whispered back.

"I just saw Piper Montgomery go into the kitchen. Her husband got laid off last year. Hasn't found a new position." I rose, holding a hand up to indicate I had to be excused to the woman chattering about a set of paring knives that would change your life.

Hated to break it to her, but most of these heifers didn't cook.

Piper jumped a little when she heard the door open, and I noted the house smelled of Festive—a new candle everyone was buying—and old wood. Kinda like my house.

See? I was a good detective.

"Oh hey, Cricket," Piper said, pausing behind Carol Sue's chesterfield sofa when I closed the door. She looked nervous.

Interesting.

"Oh hey, just getting a water. I'm parched." I jabbed a finger toward the kitchen table where several monogrammed buckets sat, one holding bottled waters, the other chilled wines.

"Oh yeah, it's warm for fall." She glanced toward the recesses of Carol Sue's house. "Excuse me. Need to use the bathroom."

Huh, this felt familiar.

I didn't say anything, just moseyed toward the kitchen, wondering how I was going to handle this. Same way I had at Esme's? Just follow her? Pretend I had to go potty too?

Last night I had started making a spreadsheet of the items missing and the parties/events where they'd most likely been stolen. Juke had procured the party lists for both known thefts. So far there were twenty-seven potential suspects, including many of my close friends. I'd given him the name of two other women Bo Dixie had mentioned, one of them who was in my mother's Bible study. Juke said he would pay both women with missing items a visit over the next few days. Bo Dixie thought Laura Cummings had had her Mikimoto pearl bracelet go missing during a mixer for the Demoiselle Club, and Tory Bowen had a Goyard Saigon bag missing. I adored those bags, so

I felt so bad for Tory. I had done some canvasing of resale sites, but there were so many luxury item resale shops with so many of those items for sale. We needed something more distinctive to search for. David Yurman and Louis Vuitton were a dime a dozen on most the sites.

I had tried to talk Juke into inviting every person who'd had something missing into his office and jointly interviewing them, risking blowing my cover so I could set the victims at ease. He'd mulled it over but ultimately decided—after I mentioned the office would need sprucing up first—to keep me in an undercover capacity while he popped into the worlds of the women to gather more official information. He liked to catch people unprepared and seemed to think that my social circle avoided reality and dodged the truth.

Lip fillers and boob jobs aside, I wasn't so certain that everyone was hiding something or making themselves sound better than what they were, but then again, I hadn't worked as a detective for very long. I deferred to his judgment.

I grabbed a water, looked longingly at the tub of wine, and moved back into the living room. No drinking on the job, though I don't think a glass of pinot grigio would have mattered. Pretending to look at Carol Sue's collection of photography, which mainly featured her children, I moved toward the back of her home. I glanced out the window and saw that everyone was still watching the Posh Pantry rep scoop melon. I set the water on her piano, making sure it was on a coaster, and sort of rolled into the hallway, happy I'd worn my Sorel rubber-soled boots. Carol Sue had hardwood floors and an antique runner (that I had sold her).

I hadn't been in the personal spaces of Carol Sue's home, so I used my instinct and went left. I had spotted french doors that likely opened to the patio and pool, but I soon saw that area was a sitting room that she'd converted to a game room for her kids. I backtracked and crossed over into the backside of the house, looking to my right at a bathroom before hooking a left. Ahead were double doors that presumably led to a master suite. Carol Sue was no slave to changing style. She liked rich colors and wood, so her home was the opposite of Esme's House of White, and I had to say I preferred it. The rugs were oriental, jade jars were filled with live plants, and the paintings collected from their many trips to Italy. Traditional, classic, and tasteful. One of the doors was opened about eight or nine inches, just enough for me to peek inside.

I won't lie. My heart raced in my chest, and I felt that cold-sweat thing you got when you knew you could fail spectacularly. If Piper came out while I was there peeking through the door, she'd know I was spying on her. I could play dumb, but she'd be way more suspicious than Esme. There was no cat to blame this go-around. Carol Sue was allergic.

Easing to the side, I pressed my face closer.

In the large mirror behind Carol Sue's bed, I could see Piper. She stood at the heavy cherry dresser that I had not sold Carol Sue but I knew was an expensive French antique. On that dresser sat a large French marquetry box with a tufted capitonné interior of blue silk. Or at least it looked tufted. The burl-wood box was perfectly square, a lovely piece. From the depths, Piper withdrew a gold necklace. It looked very similar to Kendra Scott, but I knew it was an Ippolita mother-of-pearl bezel set into 24-karat gold. Carol Sue's husband had given it to her for her birthday last year, and I had complimented her on it when I ran into her at Sutton's back when I was still serving as Scott's hostess for his holiday bank party.

Piper pulled the necklace over her head and turned her head this way and that.

Damn, she had nerve.

It looked good on her though. She had smooth tanned skin

and striking dark hair that curved to her collarbones. That she was the thief made me sad. I had always liked Piper and the way she made everyone comfortable when they were around her. This is what a man had brought her to—stealing other women's things to pay their bills.

I pulled my cell phone from my back pocket, glad that I had it with me. Normally, it would have been in my purse. Or somewhere I couldn't find, which had become my MO over the past week or so. I'd felt a little cotton-headed with Scott getting married, the drinks with Wes, and Ruby being gone. She was an expert at keeping the store running. I hadn't realized how much I had come to rely on her.

I made sure the phone was on silent and angled it so that I could get a good shot of Piper in the mirror, pinching and widening so that the necklace was easily identified. I snapped a few of Piper wearing the Ippolita necklace. She pulled it off, slid open the top drawer, and pulled out a soft bag.

Double damn. She was even taking storage for the necklace she was stealing.

I snapped a few pictures of her stowing the necklace in the bag. Then as she cinched the drawstring together and slid it into her front pocket.

Click. Click. Got you, Piper.

Quickly, I moved away, hooking into the hallway and sliding into the living area, glad there was a large frond plant of some sort to soften my entry in case someone outside happened to glance in through the large bank of windows. Stepping swiftly back to the wall of Carol Sue's kids, I grabbed my water, crossed my arms, and pretended to be perusing the photographs.

Piper eeped when she nearly ran into me rounding the corner.

"Oh my goodness. I didn't see you." She clasped my upper arm and stepped back before she crashed into me.

"Sorry. I was trying to figure out who did these portraits." I crooked my head and played it so damn cool. God, I was good.

Piper inched closer, squinting at the embossed stamp. "This one is Terry Gatlin. He did my kids' first-year portraits. They were so cute. We did a picnic blanket in the park. Oh, and that one in the top left is a Melanie Lyles. She's hard to book because everyone wants her for graduation pictures and weddings. She can milk the emotion, can't she?"

"I need to get some taken of Julia Kate. It's been a minute."

Piper sighed. "I know. We take so many when they are babies and toddlers, and then *pfff*. I guess it's because they run from cameras once they reach a certain age. I'm heading back out. Carol Sue said there would be raffle prizes."

I wanted to look at the pocket where she'd slipped the necklace, but I wouldn't. "Yeah, I guess I should too. I'm not a huge fan of kitchen parties where I feel obligated to buy something."

"So don't. I just dropped a donation in Carol Sue's Venmo for the nanny's mom. I just cleaned out my kitchen and sold stuff on Facebook Marketplace. No way I buy anything to replace what I got rid of." Piper smiled and slipped out.

I followed, feeling jubilant and a little sad.

This time I had not been foiled by a pooping cat, and I had absolute proof that Piper had stolen Carol Sue's necklace. Juke had thought that I would be merely amassing information and turning things over to him. Nope. I had caught the thief just by being at the right place at the right time... and following my gut instincts. Piper had looked off when she got up from the table. I followed my intuition.

And, hot damn, she was the thief.

Case closed.

13

Ruby

THREE DAYS LATER...

"If you drop the stitch right here, it will allow for the proper drape," I said, pointing to the swath of velvet that would round out the final piece in my twelve-piece collection. I had exactly a week to fit the pieces to the models and then three days more to have all the pieces perfect for the fashion competition. I was particularly proud that my models were all shapes, sizes, and ages. I had even fitted Julia Kate in the A-line dress I had worn to New York. After I had seen so many collections presented at Fashion Week, I had gone back to my drawing board. I realized my look was all over the place, so I worked on streamlining it to create something more cohesive. The functionality wasn't as much an issue as the style and the creativity. My colors were muted with pops of chartreuse, cerulean, and violet, but the fabric very textured. The twelve pieces would all stick to the same color palate, overall shape, but with a little punch or kick of the unexpected.

Resa did as I instructed, and we pinned the skirt on the dressmaker's dummy. She closed one eye and then the other. "Looks uneven."

I stood back. "Yeah, I see what you're saying. Let's take it down and resew that seam. I have some leeway since this is the piece Marguerite's friend Nancy is wearing. She's an elegant ol' bird who probably lives exclusively on vitamins and air. We'll probably have to take it in several inches anyway."

"And this is the lady Cricket said is letting you borrow some accessories for the show?" Resa asked.

"Might. Seems Nancy had an aunt who lived in Europe back in the day and was friends with some East Texas woman who lived in the south of France and married some rich guy, but anyway, Nancy's aunt was a bit of a sensation herself, so she collected all these clothes and accessories from famous designers. She even lived with Coco Chanel for a few months. When she finally married and settled down, she had a huge collection that she gave away to her family. Nancy loved couture, so she took a good bit of it. Some of the shoes and bags are priceless. She stores it all in a cedar-lined, climate-controlled closet, but Cricket said she is willing to loan some of it to me to use for the show, thanks to Marguerite."

"These people sure are nice to you," Resa said, not looking up.

I wondered how things were going with Resa. Ever since I'd returned, she'd been subdued, not her usual wisecracking self. She'd been late this morning and a bit secretive when I'd asked how she'd been doing. I didn't think she was using again or falling into her old ways, but Resa had one giant piece of kryptonite, and his name was Garrett Jones, aka Groot to his friends, a bunch of troublemakers and criminals. I had heard stories about her ex that made me wonder if Resa had cracked her head being with him in the first place. But if anyone knew the irrationality of one's thoughts, it was me. So many women went back to exactly what ailed them because it was familiar. The unknown is scary, so instead, they embrace what hurt them in the first place. After I got out, I felt hard and bitter but also determined. First thing I did was smash my old way of thinking and scatter the pieces behind me. With the help of Gran and friends like Cricket, I had grabbed hold of exactly what Resa was talking about—friendships with people who believed in me.

"They *are* nice to me. It's sort of wonderful when you stop expecting people to crap on you. You begin to make room for something better in your life. That's what I'm trying to do here," I said, using the seam ripper very carefully. Velvet held marks easily. Thank goodness I was taking in and not letting out.

"But you're smart. I'm not." Resa said this with no irony. Just something she believed.

"That's not true."

"Do you remember how long it took me to get my GED? And that's with you helping me."

I set the seam ripper down. "But you got your GED."

Resa snorted and looked up at me. "Barely."

"But barely counts. Look, you're moving forward, Res. You're doing what you need to do to correct your past and make a new, better place for yourself. And it's hard. Changing yourself is not easy. It's easier to go back to what you know. Every person who gets out of prison has that moment where they choose—the easy way or the hard way."

"I guess I'm right there."

"Well, choose the hard way because in the end, it's the only way to save yourself."

Resa's brown eyes filled with tears. "I'm trying."

"I know you are. And I'm here to help you. That's what

friends do. They show up. And you mentioned people helping me. Yeah, that was hard for me too. You know how it is where we come from. We don't take help. We're prideful. Stubborn to a fault. But sometimes you need help. You need someone to pick you up, hold your hand, kick your ass. That's what real friends do. I learned to let people help me, and in turn, I try to show up for them."

"But they're so different. Cricket talks funny and buys me lunch. It makes me think she wants something." Resa made a face.

I laughed. "She's just Cricket. That's what she does. It's called being thoughtful. That's a notion we're sorta unfamiliar with, right?"

"Well, you're thoughtful. You bought me dinner. Gave me a job," Resa said.

"Sometimes I can be. I'm learning what friendship is. I never had it with anyone outside of you. Not real friendship anyway. I had people I hung with, people who were quick to get me in trouble. Those friendships weren't good for me. I need women who can hold me accountable, who can see what is good for me even when I don't, and who show up. Showing up is such a thing, you know? So I'm embracing that. I'm letting that happen because it's making me a better person."

Resa set the needle she'd been threading down on the makeshift workstation and looked around the former nursery of the old mansion Cricket had turned into her antiques store. Completed pieces awaiting fittings hung on a clothes rack near the mullioned windows, and a few dressmaker dummies and repurposed mannequins kept vigil at the card tables containing various stages of ongoing finish work. The upper floor of Printemps provided a makeshift work area, but when I could gather enough money together, I would rent a place that could be better fashioned into a proper design studio. Cricket's plan was for more retail and to create an event location for bridal showers and meetings. She'd been more than generous to allow me to use the space while she waited to make her own moves.

"It's happening for you, right? I mean, designers are sending you things from New York City. You're becoming somebody." Resa smiled, her little crooked tooth winking, her eyes no longer sad.

"Thing is, Res, we're already somebody. We just let the world convince us we weren't good enough for happiness. But we are. You are. So move forward. Take a few classes. Spring! will help you pay for some of them through community grants and partnerships. The step up you need is there, but you gotta lift your foot, babe."

Resa sucked in a deep breath. "You're right. I guess things feel harder than I want them to. Groot came by yesterday, and I know I said I wasn't going to even see his face, but I let him in. I wish I wasn't so weak, but he gives me all those warm fuzzies. Girl, I just wanted to climb him like a tree. You know?"

I knew it. Groot. The root of all Resa's evil. And that wasn't a *Guardians of the Galaxy* pun.

"I get it. You're lonely. He's got two arms, but trust me, what comes with those two arms will land you back where you don't want to be. I'm not saying men are a dime a dozen, but men are a dime a dozen. If you're looking for someone to quench your thirst, you don't have to go backward. Res, there are good guys who will treat you the way you should be treated. And I'm here to tell you that decent guys can be good in bed. Shocking, I know. Because all we hear about are the bad boys and how they hit the mark. Bad boys may get you off, but they'll also land you back in jail. I'm not sure an orgasm is worth eating Mickie's slop every morning."

Resa made a face. "Yeah, you're right. But, girl, I already took a drink."

"Well, dump it out. Tell Groot it was a mistake. And get the hell away from him because he treated you like crap. He hit you. He bought you smack. He got you hooked. And he led you right to where you were when they put cuffs on you."

"I know."

"So do better." My body flooded with anger because I wanted to help Resa, but I couldn't control her. And I wasn't going to let her involvement with criminals pull me down. My new business presented an opportunity I wasn't going to risk on even a friendship. The days of stupid decisions were behind me. Too much was on the line to let my guard down.

Resa grew quiet because she knew I was upset with her.

I did my own deep inhale. "Look, it's your life. You make your own decisions about who you spend time with and how you occupy yourself. I'm just trying to be a good friend."

"And you are such a good friend." Cricket came into the room, carrying lattes from the coffeehouse down the street. She looked happy these days. Okay, well, two days. Ever since we attended the Posh Pantry party where I came home with a melon scoop. It was the cheapest thing on the order form, and it went to help Lucy's mother's treatment. How could I not buy a melon scoop? I had informed Gran that I would be making a fruit basket for our Thanksgiving dinner this year. She told me she would try not to faint when I showed up with it.

"Oh hey. Things okay downstairs?" I asked.

"Not too busy. Francis McElwain is coming by to look at that armoire again. I should charge her admission. She's trotted everyone from her daughter-in-law to her housekeeper up here to look at it and decide whether it's the right style for their new house." Cricket set the drinks on the table near me. "I got your regular, Ruby. Resa, I hope you're okay with cinnamon dolce. You seem like that kind of a gal."

Resa stared at the offering like it was the heroin Groot probably offered her. "I don't know what that is."

"It's delish. I love them, but I can't have one because I'm trying to fit into that dress Ruby fixed for me to wear to iSpy opening night. Besides, I have a date on Friday."

I jerked my gaze to her. "The yummy detective, right?"

Resa watched us, carefully sipping the latte. She must have had no complaints because she sucked it down pretty good.

"Yep. We had drinks while you were in Manhattan. Just a little toe in the water. It was nice. He's nice." Cricket said.

I tried not to feel offended for my cousin. Griff and Cricket didn't make sense together—not that I could see Cricket with a detective either. Of course those could be my own weird feelings about law enforcement. Still, Cricket and Griff had sent off more sparks than a busted axle hitting asphalt at eighty miles per hour, but my grumpy cousin still hadn't done anything about those sparks. Maybe he knew more about what made sense than I did. "Well, congrats. First date as a newly single woman. Wow."

Cricket smiled. "You know, it feels good. I had been feeling a little down because, you know, Scott married a child this past weekend right after the divorce. I don't care really, but it still felt... something. Made me sad and also a little spiteful. Still, it's been a while since I focused on myself, and I like having a guy who's into me. I had thought..." She trailed off, looking irritated at herself for bumbling into what I knew was a pining for Griff.

"No, it's good," Resa said, a little foam on her upper lip. "My mama always told me that you got over a guy by—"

"Getting under a new one," I said at the same time Cricket did.

We all laughed.

"I'm not planning on getting under anyone yet. I don't think I'm ready for that level of commitment. Or excitement. But it's sort of cool to be asked out, you know?" Cricket pushed off the stool. "Well, I have to get back to the day job."

"You have a night one?" Resa asked.

"Indeed, I do. I'm a detective." Cricket looked so pleased with herself. "And as soon as Juke officially hires me, I'll print up my business cards. I have the best idea. I'm going to play on the fact I'm moonlighting as a private investigator and working for North Star. So I was thinking a nice heavy cream vellum with navy engraving and then this really cool logo with two stars and a moon. Won't that be cute?"

"What did Juke say about everything?" I asked, taking my coffee and going back to the skirt. I really needed to get this piece completed today. Time tick, tick, ticked. But Cricket's perpetual enthusiasm when it came to snooping, spying, and annoying Juke with wanting a job was amusing enough for me to take a break.

"He was pumped. I mean, I got pictures of her *taking* the necklace. He said he was going to put in a call to his contact at SPD and get the photos to them. After all, it's an open investigation for the police department. Juke talked to two more women missing things, bringing the total to five, and I bet more will come forward once the news breaks and people start searching through their stuff." Cricket paused as she moved to the door. "You know, I feel sort of bad though. I'm building my career on the downfall of a friend. Can you imagine how desperate you have to be to steal from your friends?"

"I resemble that statement," Resa said, looking suddenly shamed. "I mean, I sort of did that. I guess my excuse is that I was strung out and not myself. But I think when things are bad, people will do most anything... even to those they love. Pretty sad, but true."

Cricket shifted her attention to Resa, her expression shifting to concern. "I'm sorry that happened to you, Resa, but I'm so glad you're doing better. I can't imagine being driven to stealing or hurting people I love. But as you said, sometimes the things that happen to us drive us to places we've never been. Like I never thought I would wear a wig, trick my husband into signing bank forms, or bust him for a Ponzi scheme at the Man of the Year banquet, uh, when *he* was the Man of the Year, but I totally went there. Anger drove me to that place. But now I'm using the momentum from all that emotion to help others. And you're using your regret to make a new start. I'm proud of you for being that brave."

Resa swallowed hard. "Thank you. And thanks for, you know, hiring me. Uh, helping me start over like you did Ruby."

Resa glanced over at me, and I saw that Cricket's words had hit the bullseye I had tacked onto her conscience.

"You're welcome. I'm happy to help. But I'm a little sad that my first real successful case is taking down Piper," my boss said, her words tinged with true regret. "But Piper made the decision to steal, and she'll have to pay the consequences. The same way you two did."

"Everyone pays for the decisions they make. Or if they don't, they at least live with them." As soon as I said those words, I knew they applied to me too. Marguerite and Coraline had presented me with an opportunity in New York City. Maybe I was taking the safe route if I stayed content. I didn't want to make a decision based on the way I'd felt lying in that holding cell in New York City. If I passed up making the move to Manhattan, I would pay the consequences and live with my decision. But the opposite was also true—if I moved to New York and tried to make a go of it there, I could be throwing away all I had built here. And that included Dak because he'd settled here in Shreveport. The man liked shooting the bull at the bar, fishing Saturday morning, and Sunday lunch at his mama's house. He'd lived his dream, catching for Cy Young award winners and having a beer in every major US city while seeing his name on the scoreboards of Fenway and Candlestick. Dak craved home. And home was all I had ever known, really. What if it was my turn to find out what the world had for me?

I needed time to think, and that was something I didn't have. *First things first.*

Once I completed the pieces for the show and got to the other side of the competition, I could reason out what made the best sense for me and my career, which meant talking to Gran... and talking to Dak.

Which made my nerves jangle.

I loved him and didn't want to lose him again.

But if I stayed here for him, would I regret it? Would I begin to resent him? Would I be choosing his comfort over my opportunity?

I truly didn't know, but if I sifted under all the what-ifs, I knew what I really needed to do, and that was a bold thing.

Cricket had just walked out of the open doorway when the rat-a-tat of heels sounded on the staircase.

"Yoo-hoo?" Marguerite called in between clacks. "Jade said y'all were up here."

"I'm in here, Mama," Cricket said.

I set our work aside, and Resa followed suit. Marguerite didn't climb stairs unless she had to. Which meant something was up.

I saw the top of her head as she ascended, and Cricket moved back into the workroom. "You climbed stairs."

Marguerite appeared in the doorway, thrusting out a hand to move Cricket out of her way. Then she bent over and took a few breaths. "Why don't you have an elevator already? I'm dying."

"If you would only come with me to yoga, you wouldn't be out of breath. You'd learn about the importance of breathing through your movements," Cricket said.

Marguerite puffed a few more times, straightened like a drill sergeant, and delivered a trademark sniff of dismissal. "Bah, I'm too old for yoga."

"No one is too old for yoga. The practice is wonderful for women your age. Helps build stronger bones to combat calcium deficiency, strengthen balance and coordination to prevent falls, and promotes an overall general feeling of well-being. You really should come to the YMCA with me." Cricket tried to take her mother's elbow while hooking a stool with her foot. "You better sit down."

Marguerite jerked her arm away. "I'm not an invalid. And really, just stop with the yoga sales pitch, for heaven's sake. You sound like an infomercial."

Cricket made a face and rolled her eyes. Behind her mother's back of course.

"Who's this?" Marguerite asked, catching site of Resa.

"That's Resa. Remember I told you that I had hired her to help me with the finish work," I said.

"That's right. An ex-con. My mother will not be rolling in her grave because you are just the sort of person she took an interest in." Her words implied that Marguerite hadn't drawn her mother's interest. Suddenly I understood a piece of the relationship between her and Cricket.

"Sort of person?" Resa echoed.

"Someone who needs a second chance." Marguerite sat down on the stool Cricket had dragged over for her despite protesting the need for it. "Or third or fourth for some of them. But that's not why I'm here."

"Why are you here?" Cricket asked a bit too dryly.

"Piper Montgomery was arrested this afternoon. Hauled out of her house in handcuffs. The rumor is that it's for stealing something at someone's house." Marguerite pulled her cell phone from the side pocket of her black purse which was a designer I couldn't remember and strong enough to brain someone. "Debbie Morehead sent me the video. A neighbor filmed the whole thing."

Cricket had gone a little white. Or maybe it was green. "This afternoon?"

"Yes, I have the video right here." Marguerite wagged her phone.

We all moved toward her like metal shavings to a magnet, unable to resist the image of Piper being taken down.

Marguerite pushed the button. Then stopped it to widen the screen. Then pushed it again.

The video showed a woman whose dark hair was in a lopsided ponytail being led from a home in handcuffs. She was crying, casting glances back at her husband who held one of her toddlers and looked dumbfounded. The police officers were very matter-of-fact. The husband called out, "Don't worry, honey. I'm calling Mark. I'll be there as soon as Mom gets here to watch the kids."

Piper's only response was to cry harder. The officer put his hand on her head as she lowered herself into the back of the police car. She shook her head, her face absolutely horrified, and her mouth moved though we couldn't hear the words, but it looked like, "I don't understand."

I remember how that felt. In fact, I had said the same exact thing.

"Oh my God." Cricket pressed her hand across her mouth. "I had no clue it would be so horrible."

Marguerite looked up, a hawk sensing movement in the grasses. "Do you know something about this? Is this your case? The theft one?"

Cricket bit her lip. "I... uh, maybe?"

"Oh my stars. That's why I told you to drop this silly private investigation stuff. I've been friends with Merle Montgomery for over fifty years. How in the world will I be able to face her at church knowing my daughter helped put hers in jail?"

"Well, Mother, I don't have a clue. But Piper stole a necklace from Carol Sue. Just took it in broad daylight. Instead of being upset with me for bringing criminals to justice, maybe you should direct your disgust toward someone who takes other people's things."

"I don't believe Piper is the person taking things from people. I've known her all her life, and she's about as bold as a snail. She wet her pants when I fussed at her in Girl Scouts. And her mother has all sorts of money from all those men she married. I'll never know how she knew to choose the richest ones with the weakest hearts. Such a talent." Marguerite clicked off the video and put her phone into her purse.

"Well, I saw her take the necklace with my own eyes. In fact, I have her on video on my phone pocketing Carol's Ippolita necklace. So you're wrong, Mother."

I trotted away from Marguerite, and Cricket and Resa must have had the same sense of self-preservation. It was like running from a bomb seconds away from detonation.

Get out! Get down! Take cover!

But Marguerite didn't do anything other than rise, sniff (again!), and walk out.

The woman knew how to shut someone down, that was for damn sure.

Cricket's eyes narrowed, and she set her hands on her hips. "Ugh, that woman. I swear she can't ever support me. I do something good—I bring someone to justice—and I'm the villain here? Ridiculous."

Wisely, I remained quiet. Resa put her head down, threading a needle that didn't need to be threaded.

"I can't deal with her. With this. I didn't know it would be like this." Cricket sounded miserable.

"What? Being a private investigator? You knew that it was likely going to be someone you knew if it was someone in your social circle who was stealing things. Being someone who busts others isn't all fun and games." I sounded like her mother. Lord. I didn't want to be anyone's mother.

Cricket swallowed. Then she did as her mother did and walked out, leaving behind the coffee she'd brought.

And I felt like crap.

Who was I to lecture Cricket on anything? Technically, Cricket was correct—she'd done a good thing even if it was sort of icky.

Resa cleared her throat. "Guess this is the downside of that community you're building. Sometimes it ain't so fun either. All emotional and stuff."

14

Cricket

Two days later...

My stomach quivered as I thrust the earring post through my ear and secured the back. The gold-beaded dangles looked fine against the smooth line of my neck, which I slathered with alpha hydroxy moisturizer nightly. I'd swept my hair up into a twist, allowing wisps to fall around my face, painted my lips a perfect plum, and slipped into one of my favorite little black dresses that my mother would have deemed too short but was so flattering I took the risk. To complete the look, I pulled on a pair of high-heeled booties with a wood wedge. Not too dressy, but nice enough that it looked like the date mattered.

Date.

Like a legit date.

I rubbed my lips together and blew myself a kiss in the mirror. "You're ready for this."

"Who are you talking to?" Julia Kate said from the open doorway.

"My inner chicken. I'm trying to bolster myself."

"Why?" She plopped onto the velvet-tufted bench that sat between the two vanities. "You said it was just dinner with a friend."

"It is." I said, doing a hard back scrabble on my words.

"But you're acting like it's a date. Like, you look all nice. Like it's a *date*." Julia Kate sounded a bit petulant. As if she had caught me in telling a lie. Which could be true because dinner with Wes was a date. But after the disastrous oversight months ago when I worked with law enforcement to take Scott down in spectacular fashion, I now tried to think about the feelings of my daughter before taking action. So I might have downplayed this dinner too much.

Lying to someone wasn't protecting their feelings.

"I'm having dinner with someone who has been helping me on a case I'm working for Juke. Detective McNally also happens to be an attractive man who asked me to dinner. So that's what this is. I mean, I wasn't going to wear sweats and sneakers."

Julia Kate didn't say anything. Just studied me.

"What?" I asked.

"So it's a date?"

"Maybe. I don't know. Yes. I think so." I straightened my neckline and sucked in a breath.

"Well, you look nice." She kicked her bare feet onto the upholstered top and studied her toes. We'd done mani-pedis a few weeks ago, and Julia Kate's Hail to the Chief navy blue was already chipped. Soccer was rough on her toes. "Don't you think it's weird? Dad is married, and you're going out on a date. Like, this time last year we were all happy and still a family."

Ouch.

"Yeah, it *is* weird. Really weird. Not what I would have picked, for sure. Guess life is like that though. You just never know when someone's going to jerk the rug out from under the feet of your reality. Or the reality of where you stand. You know." I wasn't great at metaphors—or grammar for that matter.

"Yeah. I guess."

Damn. She sounded so sad that my heart flinched. "But we're doing okay, right? Dad is making things right or trying to. He told you he was sorry for the whole wedding thing. And you're doing great in school. And I'm, well, I'm trying to find my own place in this world. If you want to know the truth, baby, I'm scared to start dating. I feel too old for this." I stopped because maybe this was too real to share with someone too young to understand. "I guess what I'm saying is that... yeah, it's weird."

Julia Kate looked up and gave me a smile. "But still, you look pretty."

I rubbed her head and glanced at the clock. "I left you some money to order pizza. Is Reagan coming over?"

Julia Kate slid off the ottoman just as Pippa erupted into a round of "someone just pulled into the driveway" barking. "Yeah, and Hannah too. We're going to watch some old BTK videos and then binge something on Hulu. Regular ol' Friday night."

The doorbell rang.

I lifted my shoulders and looked at myself in the mirror. "You're ready for this."

Julia Kate rolled her eyes. "Adults are so weird."

I went downstairs, shushing Pippa, and opened the door, hoping that I was indeed ready for this. But the fine Detective Wesley McNally was not standing on my doorstep as expected.

Nope. It was the deadly sexy Griff. Looking fierce and holding a brown paper bag.

"Oh." I stepped back, unable to keep the surprise off my face. "Griff."

He took me in from the top of my wispy updo to the tips of my cute booties. "Cricket."

"What are you doing here?" I asked, spying his bike in the driveway. Evening crept in, fallen leaves scudded across the loop drive, and the filtering breeze held a chill. My neighbor Mr. Shively stood at his mailbox, gaping at the tough-looking guy standing on my porch.

Griff wore a black leather motorcycle jacket with decals I didn't recognize, scuffed dark boots, and jeans that hugged his thighs. His dark hair was plastered against his head, likely from the helmet that sat on the bike seat, and his overall demeanor was one that made a man step backward and a woman step forward. Amid the land of golf balls and tennis skirts, Griff was a sight to behold. Mr. Shively began creeping across the street. Maybe the older man planned to write down the license plate on back of the Harley. Maybe redeeming himself for not getting the plates off the red Ford that took Mrs. Ava's Frenchie.

"Uh, come on in," I said, asking as a politeness and to keep Mr. Shively from staring at us like a science experiment. As I closed the door behind Griff, I glanced at the grandfather clock that Scott's mother had insisted we take from her house. 5:48. Wesley said he'd pick me up at six o'clock on the dot. Cripes.

Griff moved into the foyer, and I might have shrunk against the wall a little. The man filled a room. Or a foyer rather.

"I picked up the seals for you." Griff jiggled the bag.

"The what?"

He pointed at the bag. "For your sink. I was in the hardware store today and remembered that you needed a new seal for the spray nozzle on your sink at your store."

"Oh," I said, taking the proffered bag. "That was kind of you."

He grunted but said nothing. Just looked around my living room, which was a little fussy, but hey, I was an antiques store owner and liked fussy things.

"What do I owe you?" I asked, peeking into the bag because I wasn't exactly sure what he was talking about. It was a flat rubber ring.

"Nothing. It was cheap."

"Okay then."

He sorta stood there. "You going out?"

"Uh—"

"Because I thought you might wanna grab a beer or a burger or something."

My stomach flopped over. Griff wanted to take me for a burger? And a beer? Even though I truly didn't like beer—just pretended so I didn't look like a snob who always ordered the sauvignon blanc. I had been waiting for months for Griff to show some sort of interest (other than beating me at Words with Friends), and he made a weak-ass move on the same night as my first official date as a newly divorced woman?

I mean, of course, this would happen.

"Uh, well, that would have been nice any other night, but—"

Ding. Dong.

I looked at the door, knowing that Wes would be standing behind it. Griff shoved his hands in his pockets and glared at the door as if he too understood that another dude was behind the eight ball.

I held up a finger and moved back to the front door. Opening it, I tried to still my nerves. I couldn't believe this was happening. Griff stood on this side, and on the other—

Mr. Shively.

My across-the-street neighbor stood on my porch, holding my mail and looking concerned. "Hello, Cricket, I was out at my box and thought I would do you the favor of walking your mail over. Your box looked full."

I hadn't checked it in a few days, so it was quite a stack with circulars sticking out and the package from Amazon containing Pippa's new collar. I hoped my business card samples were in there somewhere too. But I knew that Mr. Shively was looking out for me. He'd told me at the mailbox last week that now I was divorced, he'd keep an eye on me. Which was nice but not necessary. The man was eighty-four and likely unable to give chase or karate chop any intruders. Though I wasn't going to count him out because I had been around enough elderly people to be surprised at what they could do.

"So nice of you, Mr. Shively." I took the giant stack of mail, trying not to let anything fall to the porch. Mr. Shively took that time to peer around me at Griff standing in the foyer. The small package from Amazon slid off the top, and as I bent over to grab it, I saw Wes pull in.

Oh, fun and games.

"Everything okay here?" Mr. Shively asked.

"Oh, just peachy." I stood as Wes climbed out of his car, gave Griff's bike a curious glance, and started up the walkway.

"All right then." Mr. Shively gave a wave and stepped back as Wes reached the porch. Behind me, I felt Griff appear like the shadow of death over my shoulder.

Three men at my entry.

I couldn't have dreamed this up. Of course, Mr. Shively wasn't one I wanted to kiss. Maybe a small side hug. The other two, well, I'd had visions of my lips on theirs.

"Hey," Wes said, looking very nice in a pair of jeans, gingham button-down, and ostrich boots. His hair was combed, cologne wafted, and he held a small bouquet of flowers in one hand. Total date material. Unlike windblown and grumpy behind me.

"Hey, Wes. My nice neighbor just rescued my mail from

overflowing into the street." I nodded toward Mr. Shively, who seemed to realize that I was fine and there were too many men here. Maybe he heard the faint sound of that weird *High Noon* showdown song on the fall breeze and was getting the hell out of Dodge. Mr. Shively lifted his hand in farewell and started the trek to his own house. I didn't blame him at all.

"Need some help?" Wes asked, looking at my toppling stack of junk mail.

"Nah, I got it. Come on in." I turned to the doorway. Griff filled the entire space, reminding me of a rottweiler waiting to rip out a jugular.

"Wes, this is my friend Griff. You met him when I got the van stuck. He brought by some supplies for my sink at the store." I did my best to sound like this was run of the mill. Just a friend popping by.

"Hey," Wes said, climbing the two steps to the door.

Griff didn't move.

I made a frowny face behind Wes, sending Griff a message with my eyes. Griff glanced at me, hesitated, and then stepped back, allowing Wes entry. Then Griff stepped down onto the porch, brushing against me, making me nearly drop all the stupid mail. "I see y'all are busy. Got things to do. Catch you later, Cricket."

My heart sort of sank because something in his words said he would not catch me later. That he was done. That Wes could have me. And though I had no clue if I were reading the situation correctly, my heart hurt at that thought. Part of me wanted to dump the mail, run after Griff, and dramatically kiss him. But the rational part of me... or maybe some deep down biological inkling... said I needed to put my mail on the foyer table and go on the date I had planned. Maybe that inkling knew more than my brain did. Maybe that inkling understood that men liked to give chase and only valued what they thought they couldn't have.

Maybe Griff needed to step up his game if he wanted to have a shot with me.

"Thanks for the seal things, Griff," I called.

He lifted a hand and kept trucking.

I closed the door. "Sorry about that. When it rains, it pours."

Something my mama always said.

"Does it?" Wes asked with a bemused smile. "You know, I don't think that guy likes me."

"Don't worry. He doesn't seem to like anyone," I said with a smile, eyeing the flowers. "And *I* like you. That's what matters here."

Wes's eyes sparked, and he held out the bouquet. "These are for you, to honor your first date since the divorce. Or at least I think it is."

"It is, and that was very thoughtful." I took the flowers and gestured to the kitchen, appreciative of his manners and sense of humor. Not every guy would be pleased to be greeted by a nosy neighbor and a surly grump ass.

Fifteen minutes later, after a brief introduction to Julia Kate, whose friends arrived and hastened our departure, we walked into Bella Fresca's, one of my favorite restaurants. The table was a corner one, suitably intimate, and the music played softly enough for good conversation. Happy chatter and delicious cocktails were the perfect ending to the workweek, though I would have to go to the store the next day to do some inventory. The next week would conclude with the iSpy fashion show, and there was much to do in between. Even if Ruby hurt my feelings with the whole Piper thing.

"How was your week?" I asked. Boy, I was a sparkling conversationalist.

"Not too bad. Yours?"

So he wasn't great at it either.

"Pretty good. I'm helping my friend Juke on a case. Remember when we had drinks and I told you about some of my friends missing jewelry and stuff?"

He perked up. "That's right. I had forgotten about that conversation."

"Well, I solved it." Maybe it was too braggy, but the truth was without me at Carol Sue's snapping the incriminating evidence, Juke would still be interviewing people and wishing upon a star. Was there anything wrong with being proud of oneself?

"You solved it?" He looked a little amused and somewhat confused.

"I mean, yeah. Pretty much. I knew the lady who was stealing. I actually took pictures of her stealing a necklace at a Posh Pantry party last week."

"*You* took the pictures?"

Something weird prickled on the back of my neck, like he knew about this case, like he was... "Was that your case?"

"Actually, yeah, it is my case."

"What a coincidence." I sipped my lemon drop martini, which was cold and slightly sweet, the way I liked them. I was about to say you're welcome but had a mouthful of Grey Goose and fresh lemon.

"You know that Piper Montgomery was released, right?" he said.

"What? She was released?" My body sort of zinged, like when I touched my tongue to a battery. Not that I did that often. Only once.

Okay, twice.

"Mrs. Montgomery had permission to take the necklace. The homeowner is a friend, and there was something about Mrs. Montgomery going to a cousin's wedding in Belize and borrowing the necklace to wear with her dress. No charges were filed." Wes no longer looked amused. He looked interested. More like a detective than a charming date. "In fact, the department is looking into how the photographs were procured. I guess now I know."

"Are you serious? Piper wasn't the thief?" My body felt all floaty and warm. Unfortunately, it wasn't from the alcohol. More like the shock and ensuing shame.

I hadn't solved the case. In fact, I had gotten everything spectacularly wrong.

And my friend had been hauled into jail in front of her husband and children.

Oh God.

"Looks like it. And our captain's pissed because we made a bad arrest, mostly based off information from a private investigator," he continued.

"But someone came by my house and asked questions. I mean, I saw her take a necklace. It wasn't bad information. It was what I saw." I took a gulp of my drink, embracing the fire of the vodka dropping into my stomach.

"You didn't know she had permission. We've had Carol Sue Lambert down at the station raising all kinds of hell. Her brother is a city councilman, and her husband is a big donor to the Back the Blue campaign. Even though Mrs. Montgomery wasn't charged, we got egg on our face."

I blinked at my suddenly empty glass. "I feel terrible. I thought I had busted the person stealing things. Instead, I traumatized my whole community." I pressed a hand to my forehead, wishing I were anywhere but where I was. When Piper found out that I was responsible, she would hate me. All my friends would. I would be persona non grata, never invited anywhere.

They couldn't find out it was me.

I picked up my phone. "Will you excuse me? I need to call Juke."

Wes's lip quirked. "Look, I get that you're feeling shitty right now, but it's okay. It's not like anything was done intentionally. We can't prosecute your firm because it wasn't false information. I mean, it was, but it wasn't done out of mischief or anything. Besides, the most interesting thing is that something *was* stolen that same night. An expensive handbag was taken without permission."

Pausing in my attempt to slide from the booth, I turned toward him. "You're joking. Someone stole something, but it wasn't Piper? How in the world?"

"Come on back." He patted the booth seat. "It's not that bad."

"Yeah, it is. Because if Carol Sue or Piper find out, they will hate me."

"How will they find out? Unless you tell them, or unless you told someone else?"

That was the rub. I had told Ruby, of course, because she'd been at Carol Sue's. But I had also blurted it out in front of my mother and Resa. Now my mother would be too embarrassed to leak such a thing to anyone in her circle of friends. She hated that I was working as a private investigator. Sleuthing was probably on her list of "common" things. Resa? I wasn't sure. She wouldn't tell anyone who would know Piper or Carol Sue. But she might tell someone who knew someone who knew someone who knew one of the two women. Shreveport had maybe four degrees of separation. We didn't need Kevin Bacon for any degrees. "No one knows outside of my mother and assistant."

"See? And don't worry—the whole world is angry at the police these days. We can bear it."

I sank down, still feeling dejected.

Wes signaled the waiter. "Let me get you another cocktail and remind you that this is how it goes with investigative work.

We run into walls and false leads every single day. Your work will be no different. You're going to fail. It's part of it."

I felt so stupid. I had thought it would be so simple to nab the thief, and of course breaking cases wasn't so simple. If it were, we'd be without crime. My success in catching Donner Walker and his dastardly Ponzi scheme through spying on my husband had given me a false sense of ease.

My own hubris had been my downfall here. I thought I was better than I was at investigation.

You have much to learn, grasshopper.

"You're right. I got carried away and didn't think about any other possibility. I saw Piper take the necklace and made an assumption. One that was wrong."

"It happens," Wes said, clasping my hand and giving it a squeeze. And he didn't let go. I didn't mind because it felt nice. He had soft hands. Not effeminate or anything. Not that there was anything wrong with girlish hands. Wes's felt strong, capable, and clean. He'd used hand sanitizer when we'd sat down, another bonus.

The waiter delivered another martini, and I reminded myself to go slow with this one. I didn't mind a buzz that allowed me to feel less awkward, but no need to get sloppy and lose inhibitions. After all, it had been a good nine months since I'd had any kind of sex, and there was a piece of me that craved the feel of a man against my body. Or maybe I needed a crumb of affection. So yeah. *Careful, sister.*

"Thank you," I said to the waiter. I turned my hand over and clasped his. "So what got stolen? Carol Sue has a thing for Louis Vuitton."

"Yeah, I think that was the name of the purse taken. She explained that it was a special edition. Something about a lock and key. Distinctive, at any rate." He perused the menu, sounding like he didn't want to talk about work anymore.

But I needed to.

"That might help track down the thief. If it's distinctive, the purse may be easier to find on online resale sites. That could be a big break." I needed to call Carol Sue and see if I could get the deets. I already had the resale boutiques bookmarked on my computer. Nothing would be suspicious to my friend if I, say, wondered about her bag because my mother was thinking about getting one. I could bring up Mom's new Fendi. Or something that was a fib but believable.

I was determined to fix the mistake I had made with Piper by finding the real thief. It was the least I could do.

Wes made a "maybe" face. "We already have a lead. My partner got a call, and there's someone involved who bears some further scrutiny."

"Really?" My mind jumped to all my friends. Who required scrutiny? People hid all kinds of things. A few of my friends had been a little wild in college. Maybe a drug addiction? Or maybe… "Is it someone I know?"

Wes looked at me. "I don't know who you know. Do you want an appetizer?"

So he was done with this conversation. I got it. We were on a date. Still, swirling around inside me was frustration, shame, and the need to do something to rectify getting poor Piper arrested. But, yeah, I needed to be fair to Wes, who had given me a heads-up about a new theft. "Um, sure. What about a charcuterie board?"

"That's the fancy word for a bunch of cheese, right?"

I chuckled. "Pretty much."

The waiter arrived on cue, appetizer was ordered, and Wes redirected the conversation to his nephew whose high school football game he was missing for this date. Which made me feel both bad and good. Bad that Wes was missing it. Good because he considered me worth missing the game for.

One hour faded into two hours, and before I knew it, we were pulling into my driveway, full of good food and spirits because as far as dates went, this one had been a solid eight or nine. Wes and I had mutual friends, a mutual appreciation of national parks, and no awkward silences or moments where we remembered that we hadn't known each other our entire lives. He'd made me feel flirty and attractive, which are the two things every woman should feel on a date.

"Would you like to come inside?" I asked, not sure if I wanted him to say yes or no. "My daughter is likely still up and watching videos or playing Xbox with her friends, but we could have a last drink in the hearth room. Or on the patio?"

Wes killed the engine and turned to me. "I would like that, but I need to get home to let my dog out. Which sounds like I'm not interested, I know, but it's the truth. Vader's old and a bit incontinent, which embarrasses him. But know I'm interested. Very interested."

My initial disappointment faded as he leaned over.

He was going to kiss me.

I was ready for it. Totally ready for it.

Then the driveway lights went on. The garage door lifted.

Foiled by my daughter.

Julia Kate and her two best friends tumbled out holding a soccer ball, their laughter piercing the peacefulness of the inky darkness. I would have been annoyed to have my date-night kiss interrupted if it hadn't been so good to see my daughter enjoying herself with her friends. It had been too long since I'd seen her so happy.

"Guess I better get inside. Tonight was lovely, Wes. I really had a nice time with you." I reached for the handle.

"Yeah, I had a great time too." He leaned over and brushed a kiss on my cheek. His warmth and scent tilted me toward him, but I caught myself before I snuggled into his neck like some drunken loon.

I squeezed his hand and climbed from the car. "See you soon, I hope."

"Count on it."

I straightened just as the girls froze, catching sight of me. "Hey, girls. Late night penalty kick practice?"

"We'll be quiet, Mom. We promise," Julia Kate called out as she rounded the corner toward the net Scott had set up in the side yard.

Wes pulled away, tires crunching on the drive. I stood for a few minutes, watching his headlights retract and then the red brake lights disappearing down the street. A man who cared about his incontinent dog? Wow. That was pretty damn sweet, and I couldn't be upset with someone who saw his dog in that light. Even if I had wanted to see how his lips felt on mine.

Oh well.

I sighed just as someone touched my shoulder.

"Agh!" I spun around, cranking back my fist, ready to punch whoever was lurking in my driveway.

"Hey, hey, hey, it's me," Griff said, holding his hands up.

"Griff?" I screeched, my heart galloping a million beats a minute. "Oh my God. What in the hell are you doing here?"

He just looked at me.

"Were you spying on me? I mean, seriously?" I took a step back, the adrenaline still flooding my body, my legs a little shaky. Griff stood there, wearing what he'd had on earlier when he stopped by. He hadn't gone home. "What are you doing here? This is... sorta weird. And a little off-putting."

"I don't know." He sounded as if he truly didn't know.

I blinked. "You don't *know*?"

"No." He walked toward me. "I don't know why I'm here. I left but then, I don't know..."

"Well..." I raised my hands, still feeling incredulous. "I mean, I don't know either because I have spent months waiting for you to—"

Then I couldn't talk because suddenly I was in his arms, and he was kissing me. And not the soft good night sort of kiss I'd been anticipating.

No, Griff was inhaling me.

And, oh my stars, it was good.

15

Ruby

Friday night was normally a date night for me and Dak, but I had so much to catch up on I told him to go to his cousin's football game and then come by my place when the game was over. Resa and I stayed at Printemps until after nine p.m. doing as much finish work as we could manage so that we could fit the models on Monday. I had a good idea of how much material to leave on each piece, and I figured we'd make the deadline by a thread. Pun intended.

"Welp, I think that's all we can do until Monday. Tomorrow I will work on updating my website and doing some social media stuff. Cricket reminded me that voting is important too, so I need everything updated." I switched off the sewing machine and surveyed the room. We'd knocked a nice dent in it, and I was relieved. My stomach had been in knots ever since I had gotten back from New York, and then with Cricket getting bent out of shape over my reminding her about jumping to conclusions, I'd been popping antacids like Tic Tacs.

Resa shoved the wrappers from our earlier sandwiches into the paper bag and nodded. "Dude, your stuff is so dope. People'll be crazy not to vote for you."

"But still, I have to run in my wheel."

"What?"

"You know, like a hamster," I said, mimicking a furry rodent by holding up my paws and wriggling my nose.

Resa snorted. "All I know is that you are doing this, Miss Thang. Even I can see what you're building here. Oh, not to mention, that fine man you go home to. I want me some of that. I can be a hamster."

I laughed. "You're doing good too. You really are. Mr. Mac over at Spring! said you're the prize pupil. Believe in yourself, Resa."

Resa dumped the bag into the trash can by the door. "I am. Like I said to you and Cricket a few days ago, it ain't easy, but I'm trying my best to make a change in my life. I told Groot to lose my number, and then I blocked him."

"Good." I moved toward the door, digging in my bag for the keys to Printemps. Cricket had arranged for her security company come out and update her alarm system. While I was doing the finish work on the collection, Nancy Parrington, who was Marguerite's BFF, was going through her prized collection of vintage bags, shoes, and jewelry to pair up with my pieces. Monday she would come and look at the collection, and then we could start pairing the accessories with the designs. Cricket was so excited that Marguerite had talked Nancy into loaning the pieces, and she'd been working with Nancy's daughter Cammie to write descriptions that would be in the program for the iSpy Fashion Festival. She'd also recruited some of her friends to be my sponsors, so I was able to pay for hair and makeup for all the models.

As irritated as I sometimes was with Cricket, I was also very grateful to her.

"Oh, another sample arrived today." Resa jogged over to the miscellaneous table where we stored supplies and a box of Girl Scout cookies Cricket had brought out from her freezer. "This one is a kick-ass purse. I looked it up, and it's, like, a three-thousand-dollar one."

"Who in the world would send me that?" I couldn't fathom someone sending something that expensive. Maybe it was a gift from Cecile. Most of the samples I'd received were from vendors who got my name and address and thought I was an influencer. Ha. Little did they know. But I had been faithfully showcasing their products with a thank-you on my growing Instagram and FB page. My reach wasn't great yet, but it was the least I could do. One of the necklaces sent would be perfect with the pantsuit in my collection. Unless Nancy had something better.

"There wasn't a return address or a note. Just the bag wrapped in Bubble Wrap. The box was addressed to you care of Printemps though. Just like all the others."

"Well, that's odd." I turned out the lights.

Resa handed me the box, and I tucked it under my arm and went down the steps. I had to pull out my phone for the new alarm process which I had put in my notes, but I managed to get it set without the alarm going off. Resa and I walked to the gravel parking lot behind the store, aware of our surroundings because someone had broken into several cars a few nights ago.

"Thanks for staying and helping me," I said to Resa. She was driving her aunt's old Chevy Tahoe after having renewed her license and paying her aunt insurance money so she could be on the policy. Her aunt was allowing her to pay a little each month toward buying the car. Another feather in Resa's banged-up cap.

"You got it. And you're paying me, so it's not like I'm going to pass up money." Resa paused and then smiled. "And it's not like I got any other plans. But you do. Tell Dak I said what's up, and if he gets tired of your ass, my calendar can open up real quick-like."

I laughed, tossing the box into the passenger's seat and starting the engine.

Fifteen minutes later, I was stepping into a hot shower. Two minutes after that, Dak joined me under the warm spray, scaring me enough that he earned a shriek but not enough to stop the water from growing cold while he showed me just how much he missed me these last two days. We dried off and, in between sweet kisses, dressed in comfy clothes for a Friday-night movie marathon in which I would fall asleep on the couch and Dak would turn the channel to *SportsCenter*.

Some might have found this predictability boring. And some were nuts because nothing beat popcorn on the couch with Dak rubbing my feet. Except maybe what had just gone down in my shower.

"How was your day?" Dak asked, passing me the bowl of popcorn.

I rubbed my cozy socks against the cushions of the couch and snuggled even deeper into the worn quilt Gran had made me for my twelfth birthday, very cognizant of just how terrific this moment was. "Good. I'm nearly caught up on everything I set aside when I went to New York City. It's going to be close though. I only pray that all the models show on Monday afternoon. I hear that can be like herding cats."

"What? Wrangling models?" He settled in across from me, lifting my feet into his lap and cracking a beer.

"That's what they say," I said, groaning as he rubbed the ball of my foot.

"But this ain't New York City, and the models here are part of your support network. They'll show." He picked up the clicker and went to the streaming services menu. "Oh, that reminds me. I have something for you."

Dak picked up my feet and slid off the couch, going to the jacket he'd hung on the back of a dining room chair. I watched intrigued because Dak brought flowers and food, but rarely anything else.

What he pulled out, made my stomach sink and my heart speed up.

A jeweler's box.

"What's that?" I asked, no doubt with apprehension because Dak's face flashed with amusement.

"What do you think it is?" he asked.

"I don't know," I said, my gaze never leaving the red box with the shiny gold letters of a local jeweler.

He eased himself down onto a knee, holding the box in front of him.

"Seriously?" I squeaked, swinging my legs around and setting my feet on the floor. "What is this? You're not—"

He pressed a finger against my lips as I grappled with what was about to go down. I wasn't ready for this. Why was he doing this? Good Lord.

"I've been thinking about things lately. You know, how happy you make me. I never knew what I was missing in my life... until you came back into it. I can't believe how great things have been. How whole I feel now."

"Oh God," I whispered, my heart beating in my ears. He was going to propose to me. And I didn't want to be proposed to. I thought he knew this. That I wasn't ready for that sort of commitment.

"And then I thought about you, about how you're being so brave, taking chances, and going for your dreams. So I wanted to give you this." He opened the box.

And I nearly died.

Lying on the red velvet was a lovely little golden thimble charm.

"A thimble," I said, a smile automatically curving my lips.

"It's a kiss," he said, rising with a little gleam in his eyes.

"From *Peter Pan*." I plucked up the pretty charm attached to a thin gold chain. "The first movie we watched together."

"And exchanged thimbles at." He unclasped the chain and slid it around my neck. The tiny thimble fell between my breasts, almost warm on my skin though I knew that was impossible.

Years ago, our first "date" entailed Dak coming to Gran's house for burgers. After we'd eaten with the whole clan, enduring teasing that turned our ears red and had me regretting inviting him over, we'd snuck off to the den (with Gran's blessing and the door open, of course) and selected a movie to watch. Dak had never seen *Peter Pan*, and so I put that one into the player, heart thumping as Dak slid his hand into mine. In the movie, Wendy wants to kiss Peter, and he misunderstands what a kiss is. She gives him a thimble in place. Then she gives him a kiss that she calls a thimble. It became a little code word for us after Dak gave me my first kiss. Or thimble as we joked. Since that time, I'd always had a fondness for the adorable little protector of tender fingers as I sewed.

"It's perfect." I cupped the little thimble and gave him a kiss. A real kiss. "Thank you."

"I figured you're going to be nervous the next few days, and maybe when you wear it, you'll remember that I love you and I believe in you." He kissed me again.

"You love me?" I whispered against his lips.

"I do. And I'm so proud of you." He leaned back and looked at me.

"I love you too. I wanted to say it but was afraid. Like things have been so good that I felt like the other shoe was about to drop." My heart felt like it was going to explode. Tears fell, trailing down my cheeks. "Things just feel too good for someone like me."

"Come on, Ruby. Why do you say that? You preach all these things to Resa that you don't believe yourself. You don't think you deserve to have good things happen? To be loved by me?" Dak brushed my tears away.

So I got busted on that.

"I do. I mean, maybe you can't understand. You haven't done anything shameful the way I have. You haven't lived inside a prison and then gotten out with nothing to show for your life. I do believe that I deserve good things. It's just that I have had to work hard to overcome the voice inside me that keeps whispering that I *don't* deserve all this." I looked around at my cozy apartment and then cupped his face. "That I don't deserve you."

"Ah, Ruby, you are such a tough nut sometimes, but worth the effort." He pulled me into his arms and tucked my head beneath his chin. "You just returned from New York where you have plenty of offers for a job, and you are about to enter, and win, a contest that will give you money, prestige, and exposure."

"I don't know that I will win, and I haven't picked up anything anyone is dropping down in New York City, though I may." I pulled away, looking up at him. At his hard jaw, broad cheekbones, warm eyes, and hair that flopped over his slashing brows. Such a strong face, such a tender dude. "Would you be okay with that?"

"You're asking me if I want you to move to New York City? You know that answer." He shrugged a shoulder. "I want you here. I want to build a life with you."

"But what if I can't?" As soon as I asked that question, I knew I had tilted us into a place I didn't want to go.

"Can't commit? Or can't stay?" His voice had gotten serious. Yep. We were going there.

"Can't stay here."

Dak shifted, and so I moved so I could better see him. He pressed his lips together, pausing as if he were weighing his words. "I know you want me to be okay with the possibility of you moving away, and I want to be okay with it. I do. But after that whole thing that happened up there, you're still determined to go live in that world?"

"Don't throw that back on me. I handled it."

"And ended up in cuffs."

I pressed my lips together and tried not to get angry. The date rape drug incident was a deflection, a reason to keep me here. "I am not living scared, Dak."

He sucked in a breath. "I trust you to know what's what. Look, I don't want to hold you back, Ruby. You deserve a chance to fly and spread those wings. I just don't know that I can fly with you."

"Why not?" My stomach hurt. I had taken a beautiful moment and thrown rotten eggs at it like a moron. Why had I gone here with him?

"Because everything that I have built is here. Listen, I spent four years in a crap apartment in Baton Rouge, and then eight years on the road with no real place to call my own. I was miserable. I'm thirty years old, and I want to put my head on the pillow in *my* house, the house we'd dreamed about long ago. If you have to go, if you have to live in New York City or Milan or Paris, or Timbuktu, you will have to do that... but probably not with me." He sounded so sorry. And so adamant.

Which made me crazy because why would he give up me and not a freaking house? I wasn't worth more than a bar, a lake house, his mama's fried chicken? He was giving me an ultimatum. Stay here or be done with him.

And that was fucking unfair.

"I can't believe you're throwing us away," I said, scooting back on the couch. "Like, why do you get to decide our relationship like that?"

Dak shook his head. "I'm not. I'm not throwing anything away. You know I want you in my life. And you know I want you to grab hold of your dream. I'm just being honest. I don't want to live in New York City. Like at all. Ever. Not even if you paid me ten million dollars."

Anger roared inside me. He was putting conditions on his love. He was saying "I will love you if you stay where I want you to stay." *His* rules for a relationship. "That's not fair."

"Life isn't fair."

"Oh, so profound, Dak. Thanks for that. Now things are so much clearer for me. I get two choices: be in a relationship with you or pursue the dream of designing my own line."

"You already did that. You have a line." He was getting angry now.

"But I'm not successful yet. I'm just starting out, and I don't know where this could take me. Guess now I'll pray that I can have success here. That my dream is here in Shreveport. Because obviously that's my limit. If anything else comes up, some fantastic opportunity, then I can't take it because I would lose you. That's just, you know, effing awesome."

"Stop being so dramatic, Ruby."

Light exploded behind my eyes. And not the good kind. "What? You're accusing me of being *dramatic*? Are you insane?"

Dak stood, one hand slicing the air. "You know, I think we both need a little time to think, so we don't say something we don't mean. It's obvious you're stressed and have a lot going on, so it's not the right time for this conversation."

"Oh, so you're gaslighting me. My emotions are so big because I'm nervous about iSpy. Not about the fact that you just dropped an ultimatum, whether you want to call it that or not. Because that's what you mean—this or that? Me or a career?" I stood too, so agitated that I wanted to punch something.

Okay, fine. I *was* nervous and stressed. I could admit that. And this probably wasn't the best time to talk about our future. But stress wasn't the reason I was upset, and to cast my concerns as due to the upcoming show was a dick move. Damned surprising for Dak who never pulled out the macho bull crap or treated me like an irrational female. He might as well have tossed out the ol' PMS comment while he was at it.

"That's not what I meant. I'm not gaslighting you either. Or I don't intend to. I just think it's not a great time for this." He pushed a hand through his still damp hair. "I think I should go and give you your space."

He might as well have reached over and pulled the plug from my soul. I felt myself deflate with utter loss. Not only was he being such a dude, but he was not even staying to finish the conversation. "Fine. That's probably for the best. One thing you are correct on—now is not the time. I need to concentrate on the task before me, and that means putting my energy into getting everything right for this competition."

"Fine." He grabbed his jacket, knocking the red jewelry box to the floor. We both looked at the tumbled box. My heart broke apart. The beauty of his giving me the thimble necklace had faded into something nightmarish. The thimble charm felt like two pounds of regret around my neck. Why had this happened?

"I'll talk with you later," Dak said as he moved to the door.

"Dak," I said, an apology in my voice.

"No, look, we knew this was coming. Let's just take some time to really think about what we want. But don't accuse me of being deceitful or that gaslighting crap. From the get-go, I have been up front about what I wanted in my life. I have never misled you."

"But I'm not worth it to you?"

Dak shook his head. "Don't do that, Ruby. Don't make this about choosing you over my bar and home."

"Why not?" I stomped toward the door. "That's what you're doing to me."

Dak opened the door. Moths flitted around the porch light, stars sparked against the velvet sky, and insects did a churring that reminded people that life went on even when hearts were breaking. Dak looked back at me. "Like I said, let's just take a moment to figure out for ourselves what we want."

I knew what I wanted. Fashion, fame, and Dak beside me. But that was impossible. Deep down I had known that all along. "Okay. Good night."

He closed the door, the thank-you for my necklace still on my lips. Probably better left unsaid.

I thumped my forehead against the door and let the tears go. This time they weren't tender. No, these were the bitter tears of rejection, regret, and what couldn't be.

One would think I would be used to them by now.

I twisted the lock, clicked off the television, and trudged to my lonely bed where I would release my emotions because God forbid someone see me cry. I knew I wouldn't be able to sleep. My tissue paper heart had been ripped into jagged parts.

Yet after crying for a good twenty minutes, I fell into a deep, exhausted sleep.

And awoke, foggy-headed, to the police at my door.

16

Cricket

GRAY MORNING LIGHT sliced through the heavy drapes I had failed to fully close exposing the reality of what I had done last night. And early this morning.

I lay naked beneath the sheets my mother had bought me—claiming they were more than her car payment—praying that Griff had parked his motorcycle out of sight. I had forgotten to ask. Mostly because I had been busy having orgasms.

Yeah. Plural.

And though I should be burning with the shame of my transgressions (also plural), I couldn't help but bask in the delicious weightlessness of my body and the presence of the solid, warm, very talented Griff beside me.

He snored only lightly, which I found adorable.

Damn, I hope I hadn't chainsawed my way through sleep last night. Not that I got much in the way of z's.

"Morning," he rumbled, his big hand clasping my hip.

"Morning." I rolled over toward him.

"That was fun." He cracked one intense gray eye.

"Some would call it fun."

He hooked an eyebrow. "What would you call it?"

"Very pleasing." I couldn't stop the blush that bloomed in my cheeks.

Griff issued a little laugh and dragged me to him. His beard brushed the tenderness of my neck, making me shiver. Surely he was too tired. Too exhausted. Too worn out.

His lower part aligned with my lower part.

Ah, no, not worn out at all.

I hadn't planned to spend last night having toe-tingling sex with Griffin Moon, but when the man had been so confused about wanting me and then delivered that earth-shattering kiss, well, things just sort of happened. In other words, I lost my mind. Then my body. To him.

Simple as that.

What was not so simple was the fact my daughter and her buddies had shrieked outside my bedroom window, disavowing that they would be quiet while I got superbusy with Griff.

And that getting busy had been wonderful. Selfishly wonderful. And although I felt like Worst Mother of the Year, I'd give no take-backs on what had gone down several times over the course of the night. After the first round, I had texted my daughter an out-and-out lie—I had a headache and was going to bed. Lock up. Have fun with friends.

And then I moved on to round two.

There was also a round three after we'd fallen asleep for a few hours.

And now round four was commencing. Who was I even?

But just as Griff did something wonderful with his mouth, my phone jittered on the nightstand. With Griff's mouth—uh, yes—right there—I wouldn't have dared reach for it, but some little niggle in the back of my head told me to answer it.

"Griff," I groaned, stretching for the phone.

"Mmm?" he asked against my tender skin before using his tongue.

"Oh Lord," I murmured, my fingers grasping the edge of the nightstand.

"Nope. Just Griff," he said with a lazy smile in his voice.

My hand found the phone, and I brought it to my ear, trying to ignore what was building inside me. Damn, the man was good. So good. So— "Hello?"

"Cricket? It's Ruby. I'm at the police station. I need a lawyer. They think I'm the thief!"

I pushed against Griff's shoulders, as I slid up in the bed. "What?"

"I don't know! They found Carol Sue's purse at my apartment, and they think I'm the one who's been stealing all the stuff."

"What?" I squawked.

"I just told you! They brought me in, and I told them I want an attorney. I need you to call a lawyer please and not that idiot who defended me last time."

"Is that Ruby?" Griff sat up.

"Wait... is that *Griff*?" Ruby asked.

The sheet fell away from me, and even though Griff looked concerned, he didn't miss my torso being exposed.

"Uh, yes?" I said, not sure of who I was answering.

"Jeez. I gotta—" The phone went dead.

"What did she want?" Griff grasped my thighs and pulled so that I slid beneath him. Which was a place I really wanted to be... but couldn't be. Because Ruby needed help.

I struggled against his hands and my desire. "Griff, I gotta go. Ruby's in trouble."

He stilled. "What do you mean she's in trouble?"

"They took her to the police station because they think she's the thief," I said, digging my feet into the mattress so I could shimmy out from under the magnetic pull of Griff. Then I slid out of bed, hoping that my bottom didn't jiggle too much in the brightening morning light. I grabbed a T-shirt and yanked it over my tangled curls, thrusting my arms through the holes, before looking for my panties. They were on the ground by the door, which I remembered Griff had pressed me against once I had managed to lock it. He'd done fantastic things to me against that door.

I was going to hell for sure.

"What do you mean? For what?" Griff lay back on my pillows, watching me struggle into the inside-out panties. And I do mean struggle. Balance wasn't my forte.

"For all those missing purses and jewelry." I kicked the black date dress toward the toile-covered footstool, a flashbulb of guilt at the thought of my date last night, before rushing to my closet and pulling out some velour sweatpants. I didn't match at all. On the way out, I grabbed a scrunchie from the accessory bin on the shelf under the belts I never wore but still held on to. I located a pair of backless sneakers that I shoved my feet into, and I then I trucked toward the locked bedroom door.

At the foot of my bed Griff stood like an Olympic god in his boxer briefs—good heavenly days, what a sight!—my bra dangling from one finger. "Give me five minutes and I'll take you."

"Do you think you should?" I took the bra and expertly hooked it around my waist, pulling my arms through the T-shirt and pulling the straps into place.

"I do, and that was a cool trick."

"My mother expected a foundation beneath my garments

ever since I got these puppies. I'm a pro at taking off and putting on beneath my clothes. It's a bit harder with a girdle."

"Why would you need that? I prefer every part of you accessible."

My stomach grew gooey, and I looked at the rumpled bed. Maybe we had time for... No. I had to call an attorney. "Uh, yeah, about that. Maybe we shouldn't have, you know..."

"Oh, I think we should have. No doubt about that." He reached for the jeans that he'd slid off last night. His jacket lay sprawled in the chair. But... whoops. I had on his T-shirt.

"Oh," I chirped, lifting the hem and tugging it over my head.

Griff ogled me like a woman liked to be ogled by a man she wanted to wrap her legs around. "Looked better on you. But since I can't go shirtless to the police station..."

I grabbed a sweatshirt from my closet and found my phone, which had only a twenty-five percent charge. One minute later I was on the phone with Jackie Morrisette's call service. Jackie had been my divorce attorney and was a known local legal shark. If anyone could get Ruby out of lockup lickety-split, it was Jackie. I left a message with her assistant, Julie, and opened the bedroom door, sticking my head out like a naughty coed who planned to sneak her one-night stand out of the dorm room. 'Cause that's what I was doing. I shut the door, turned, and whispered, "My daughter cannot know this happened. Cannot. I already lied to her about the headache, and I'm going to roast in hell for being a horrible role model. So please be quiet."

We tiptoed out of the room. Okay, I did. He just walked.

And I nearly died when I found Julia Kate and her friends sprawled all over the living room, popcorn bags on the coffee table and a Korean boy band looped on the television. Pippa raised her head and yawned.

"Shh!" I whispered to the dog while gesturing for Griff to

hurry by the teens who could wake at any moment. Someone probably had an early soccer game.

Thankfully, he seemed to sense that I was freaked out about what I had done, so he scooted into the kitchen without much fuss. I grabbed my bag and keys and gestured to the kitchen door.

A gorgeous fall morning greeted us, just cool enough to remind me summer was over and warm enough to not need a jacket. I hurried over to my van just as the phone rang. Jackie. Thank God. "Hey! Thank you so much! I know it's early."

Twenty minutes later I was at the city lockup, Griff tailing me on his Harley that probably woke the dead when he cranked it in my driveway and left little doubt for my neighbors that I had gotten laid last night. Jackie had put in some calls trying to get Ruby released. However, after waking up an irritated Judge Polk, Jackie learned that the police hadn't officially charged Ruby with anything—she was merely being held for questioning, and that could take up to forty-eight hours. Her release was up to the detectives on the case. I hoped that I could work some magic because I happened to know one of the detectives was Wes.

Wes.

My heart stutter-stepped when I thought about the handsome detective who'd taken me out to dinner last night. And then how I had slept with Griff only minutes after Wes had pulled out of the driveway. Shame burned inside my stomach.

I was a terrible person.

What kind of woman did something so horrible after a lovely first date with a gentleman who liked her? Who respected her? Who took care of his senior dog?

A terrible one, that's who.

But Ruby's career and freedom were at stake, so I summoned up the nerve to dial Wes's number as I shifted into park and turned off the van. Griff pulled in beside me, bike yammering to remind me of my whore ways.

The call went to voice mail.

"Uh, Wes, this is Cricket. I'm calling because you have the wrong person. Ruby isn't the thief. I promise you that she isn't. Uh, anyway, could you call me back please?" I pressed the End Call button and sighed. How was I going to convince Wes that he had the wrong person? What proof did they have on Ruby? Sure, she was an ex-con, but that didn't mean she stole something from Carol Sue. As far as I could remember, Ruby never even left the patio during the party.

No, wait. She did.

She went to the restroom right before the party concluded for the evening. Everyone had made a mad dash to use the facilities before they went home because the wine and water had flowed, well, like wine and water after everyone had bought their cantaloupe scoops and avocado smashers. The powder room off the foyer had proven occupied when Ruby tried the door, so Carol Sue had sent her to the toilet in the back of the house. Ruby had passed Cammie on her way back into the living room, knocking Cammie's drink out of her hand. I remember only because I had fetched the club soda for the expensive rug.

Griff appeared at my side. "They probably aren't going to let her out until Monday."

"Jackie called a judge. They haven't officially arrested her. They're only holding her for questioning." I opened the glass door of the downtown police station and eyed the glass window where a member of SPD sat. "I called Wes so maybe I can talk him into releasing her and clearing up most of this misunderstanding. We might be able to get them to release her based on the simple fact that she didn't steal those things. And Jackie is on standby if they charge her."

The gentleman behind the glass arched a brow. "Help ya?"

"Yes, you can. You are holding my friend Ruby Balthazar. And I need to get her released. Now." I said this with all the confidence in the world.

"Okay, sure. I'll just jog back there and get her for you." He went back to his crossword puzzle. Sarcasm was even more unbecoming on old desk sergeants.

I looked at him with the deadpan look my camp roommate Ruth taught me when people weren't doing what you wanted them to do. It worked fifty percent of the time.

He stared back, not moving.

We were locked in a battle of staring. I could feel Griff's confusion wafting from beside me, but I refused to give in first.

Fortunately for Officer O'Connell, my phone chirped a text message. Wes.

Got your message. Will call you later.

I tapped into the phone. I'm out front trying to get past Barney Fife.

A few seconds later the door swung open, and Wes stood there in a pair of slacks and white shirt. His hair was mussed. Maybe Ruby was giving him hell.

"What are you doing here?" He looked irritated.

"You've got the wrong person," I said.

"Like we haven't heard that before," he said, amusement suddenly shadowing his face. He waved me toward the open door. "Come on back."

I looked at Griff. He stood there, looking, well, uncomfortable, which rarely happened. Never was Griffin Moon ruffled or bothered. Except maybe last night when I tried out reverse cowgirl. Inner fist pump.

I looked over at Griff. "You want to come too? She's your cousin."

"Think I'll wait out here." Griff moved toward the plastic

visitor chairs lining a wall. I wasn't sure he would fit into the bucket chair, but I didn't stick around to find out.

"My desk is occupied, so we'll have to use an empty conference room." Wes moved toward a bank of steel doors with scratched paint. The place looked like a stereotypical police station on television, all scuffed and depressing. Wanted posters were on a bulletin board, and there were dry-erase boards with crime-scene photos that I refused to decipher. I didn't want to throw up.

The door he opened led to a small interview room holding a table and two chairs. No two-way mirror like on *Law and Order*, but I caught sight of a video camera mounted in the corner of the room. Despite the fact I was innocent—well, of crimes at least—my stomach jangled and my knees grew warm. I sank into one of the chairs, wondering if the legs were shorter. I had once read about intimidation techniques.

"So what's this about my suspect?" Wes's knees cracked when he sat in his chair—one that didn't seem to be taller than mine after all. At least I wouldn't feel any more uncomfortable than I already was.

"Ruby can't be a suspect. She hardly knows Carol Sue." I folded my trembling hands and tried to focus on what was important. Ruby.

"And you know this how? Because you've been investigating the case?" He still sounded amused. That annoyed me.

"Because Ruby works for me. She's my friend."

"Ah." He took out a tape recorder and set it on the table. "You know, just because you think you know someone doesn't mean they're innocent. Bet you thought you knew your husband too."

Touché. Wasn't wrong there.

"Mind if I record our conversation?" He gestured to the tape recorder.

"Are you serious?" I asked, alarm creeping up my spine.

Knees were full-on jelly. Glad I wasn't standing. "And aren't those cameras recording us?"

"Should they be?"

"No."

"It's only for my notes. After all, you obviously know the suspect well and might be instrumental in helping us wrap this up."

I pushed the tape recorder back toward him. "No. I'm not helping you."

"You aren't?" He tilted his head. "But you just said you know Ruby Balthazar didn't steal Carol Sue's purse, an item which we actually found in her apartment."

"What?" I choked out.

"Yeah, so the stolen item was recovered in your friend's apartment."

My mind tripped over itself. That couldn't be true. No way. "I can't believe that. Ruby isn't a thief."

"But she hangs out with them. Theresa Miller is a known associate of the suspect. Theresa was busted for assault and a B and E back in 2018. Theresa's boyfriend is a known drug dealer. Lots of 'knowns' here. And your friend Ruby did two years at Long Pines Correctional. Did you know about that?" Wes looked concerned for me. Like I had hit my head hard and couldn't remember where I was.

"Of course I know Ruby did time, along with Resa. She works for me too. Both women are in a program called Spring! that helps keep them out of trouble. Ruby has no reason to steal anything. She's an up-and-coming fashion designer. In fact, she just got back from New York City only last week and has an important show on Friday. Why would she steal purses and jewelry and jeopardize all she's worked so hard for?"

"Why does anyone steal? They need money. Miss Balthazar has student loans and rent due. She's not swimming in money.

The item we recovered is worth thousands of dollars. Reselling that purse would be a nice windfall for anyone."

"Wait, was Carol Sue's purse a Twist?" I thought back to the conversation I had had with Carol Sue and Twyla Simmons on the cute twist lock. "That's a really nice bag."

"Yeah. It is." Wes studied me. "So when was Miss Balthazar in New York City?"

I gave him the dates then asked, "Wasn't one of the bracelets taken then?"

"Hmm." He leaned back and latched his fingers. "Ruby isn't talking. I get it. She's learned that from her fellow criminals, but if you could get her to talk to us, we might be able to let her go. As long as she can clear herself, that is."

Hope bloomed inside me. "Really?"

He nodded and stood. "Come on."

I scooted back, the sound of the chair on the floor making me wince. We walked out of that room and directly into the next room, where a weary Ruby sat with a cup of coffee in front of her. She wasn't cuffed, thank God.

"Cricket," she said, standing. "What in the hell are you doing here? I said an attorney."

"You don't need an attorney, Miss Balthazar," Wes said, hooking his foot on the door and dragging in a spare chair. "I told you. We're just asking some questions."

"Yeah, I remember how that works." Ruby sank back into her chair. "I'm not saying anything until you get me the lawyer I'm entitled to. I know my rights."

I pulled the spare chair up to the table. "Ruby, they aren't charging you. They just brought you in for questioning. You didn't take anything. I know you. I was at Carol Sue's party, and you didn't even bring a bag with you, remember? Only your credit card shoved into your phone sleeve. Where were you supposed to hide the Louis Twist? In your hoo-ha? You're as slim as a reed and were wearing those tight leather pants."

Ruby frowned at me because some of that wasn't necessary, but she said nothing.

"And why would you need it? Nancy is letting you use some of the most delicious vintage pieces that are worth twice as much as that purse." I looked at Wes. "Why would anyone jeopardize their new career and new life for a few piddly purses? She doesn't have a motive."

"But the purse was *in* her apartment." Wes arched an eyebrow.

Ruby bristled. "Because someone sent it to me. I told the officer who cuffed me. The FedEx box is in the trash bin. No return address." She turned to me. "I thought maybe Cecile sent it. She's been sending me a few things here and there. And some of those vendors sent me pieces, you know, because I'm one of the iSpy designers. I had no clue the purse was stolen. It came to Printemps addressed to me. Resa opened it and said there was no note. Just the bag."

"See?" I looked at Wes. "I knew there was a perfectly good explanation for this. Where did you find the bag at Ruby's place?"

Wes made a face. "It was on her kitchen table."

"Aha!" I snapped my fingers. "No thief worth their weight would leave stolen property out in plain sight. It's obvious someone is framing her to throw off suspicion. Which means we're getting close. The heat is on."

Wes narrowed his pretty eyes. "This isn't a movie, Cricket. We found stolen property at this woman's house, and she was present at the event where the item was taken."

"So? That doesn't mean she took the purse. It means that whoever the real thief is knows enough about Ruby to frame her. Lots of people know about her past and her redemption story because they've been playing it up for the iSpy Festival. Everyone loves an underdog. Ruby's the most likely person to frame, right? How am I seeing this, but you're not?"

He deadpanned and said nothing.

"Besides, you said you would release her if she talked to you. She talked." I folded my arms like this was over.

"To you. Not me." Wes knocked a knuckle on the table.

Ruby rolled her eyes. "I don't want to talk to you because I know how this sort of thing goes. Your department is lazy, and I'm an easy person to pin this on so y'all can go back to eating donuts and harassing people. So you arrest me, close the book, and tie a bow. Case solved. But it's not. Because I have no reason to steal all that crap. People are friggin' mailing me stuff to put on my site. If I were going to sell some shit, I'd just use those freebies. Besides, why would I risk everything to sell things on resale sites? Too easy to prove the theft—you give out your email, bank info, and all that junk. If I wanted to make a dime on high-end stuff, I'd just get one of my dumbass cousins to hawk it at a pawnshop for me. Harder to trace."

"But no one would go to a pawnshop for a Louis Vuitton. Well, maybe for a Neverfull, but not a Twist. Too specific and expensive," I said.

Both Ruby and Wes looked at me like I'd dropped my loose screw.

"Truly," I said.

Wes set his hands on his hips, looking at Ruby. "I get you feel like we just want to close the case. We do. But that doesn't mean I'm going to make a bad arrest and have the case fall apart. Give me a few minutes, let me write down some info, examine what you've told me, and I'll send you home."

Ruby narrowed her eyes. "How did you know to come to my house? How did you get a search warrant?"

"We got a tip that indicated someone saw you take something at a party. We looked you up and..." Wes shrugged.

"Who gave you the tip?" I asked.

"Anonymous."

"Huh," I said, my wheels spinning because now I knew that Ruby had been framed, and the thief could feel us breathing down her neck. Desperate people did desperate things. They were more likely to make missteps. Which meant the suspect pool was narrowing because the thief had to have been at Carol Sue's Posh Pantry party. Or at least know who attended. "Well, that should make you suspicious. I mean, why not give her name when she called?"

"Who said it was a her?" Wes asked.

"It wasn't a her?" I tapped my chin, thinking... thinking... thinking... "And I guess there was no number associated with the call?"

"I never said it was a call." Wes gestured toward the door. "Now if you don't mind, Ruby and I have some things to discuss. You can go back to the desk sergeant, and he'll let you back into the waiting area."

I rose, sending Ruby a look that I hope portrayed that the Blue Moon Sting Posse stuck together... even though I had thoroughly enjoyed my date with Wes last night. #TeamRuby. #BlueMoonStingPosse #AboutToCatchTheRealThief #HangToughSister.

Griff rose when I reentered the waiting area, lifting a questioning brow.

"She's going to answer his questions without an attorney. They have nothing on her except some planted evidence. I don't know if they can arrest her because the evidence they have was mailed to her. And then someone called in a tip about her stealing the purse."

"Fuck," Griff said, and I realized that was the first time I had ever heard him use that word. It should have rolled off his lips like unspooled satin, but it didn't. Sounded odd. "They're going to pin this on her."

I pressed my hands into the air. "I don't think so. Let's just wait and see. Wes is a man of his word."

"Wes is a cop." Griff spat those words.

I decided not to engage him in that. Instead, I sank down next to him and started counting off the minutes. Which ended up being fifty-seven minutes of Griff sending pointed looks at the desk sergeant and me playing word games on my phone so I wouldn't go insane.

Finally the door opened, and Ruby walked out, looking pissed. Wes followed behind her looking, well, sort of pissed. Must have been an interesting "talk."

Griff immediately stood and moved to stand beside Ruby. "You okay, kiddo?"

Ruby jerked a nod but remained stone-faced.

Wes angled his gaze to Ruby. "Remember, this isn't cleared up. Stay in town."

"I'm not going anywhere. I have no reason to." Ruby spun on her heel toward the door. Griff and I followed like a gaggle of ducklings. Or whatever a group of ducklings is called.

Before I slipped outside, I turned back to Wes. "Thanks for listening to reason."

He shook his head. "I'm following the law. Something's not right here. Just pay attention, Cricket, so you don't get hurt."

As if I weren't paying attention. I was a professional. Well, almost. Hadn't he understood as much from my analysis of the situation in the interrogation room an hour earlier? I understood perfectly what was going on—someone felt the noose closing in and had diverted attention to an easy mark. Plain as the nose on my face. Also, why would I get hurt? Ruby was my friend, practically my family.

Being in such a hurry earlier, I had forgotten my sunglasses, so the Saturday-morning sunlight assaulted me when I stepped outside. Blinking, I noted Ruby had beelined for Griff's bike which sat beside my van.

"Don't you want me to take you home? It's on my way." I hurried my steps to catch up.

Ruby never turned around. "Griff can take me."

"I don't have an extra helmet with me," Griff said.

"I'll take my chances," Ruby said, not looking at me.

Wait. She was mad at me?

"What's wrong?" I stopped beside my van, thankful for the shade of the oak above.

"Nothing's wrong. I'm peachy," she said, still not looking at me.

Griff stood there, seemingly sensing that movement one way or the other could result in a loss of limb.

"Wait, are you upset with *me*?" I asked trying to move into her sight line.

"Why would I be?" Ruby shrugged a shoulder and stared at her cousin. "Come on. I need to get home."

"No, wait. You're definitely mad at me." I looked at Griff whose eyes shifted back and forth between me and Ruby. Still hadn't moved. "What's the deal?"

"Just drop it, Cricket," Ruby huffed and gave Griff "the look."

"No. Why are you mad? I came down here. I talked Wes into letting you go."

Ruby whirled. "You *should* have done all that. I wouldn't be here if you hadn't dragged me into your stupid shenanigans. I was the 'easy mark' because you offered me up as one. I might as well have had an apple in my mouth."

I stepped back, confused. "You're blaming me for this?"

"Yeah. Because if I hadn't gone to Carol Sue's, none of this would have happened. Whoever the person is that's taking the stuff saw me there or found out I was there. And because you're a bored housewife, playing detective games, I got framed."

Bored housewife? Playing detective? I grappled with the words that sliced me into two halves. "I... I... can't believe you're saying this."

Ruby's face had twisted into rage. "Really? 'Cause maybe someone *should* say it to you. I know you think you're good at this stuff, but these are people's lives, Cricket. Not some game to amuse yourself so you can dress up and play Nancy Drew. I got led out of my apartment this morning by two uniformed cops. I got accused of stealing your friends' shit. You know that I'm trying to make something of myself, trying to undo my past. So how does this look for me? The competition is days away, and this happens. I just can't deal with this right now. I need to go." Ruby turned to Griff. "Take me home. Now."

"You're not being fair," I cried, stepping toward her. "And I'm not playing. I'm helping your cousin. I have a certificate."

"Yeah, well, tell that to Piper Montgomery. I'm sure the fact you possess a worthless piece of paper makes her feel better about the colossal mess-up you made that had her in cuffs in front of her children. Wait. Oh jeez, this feels familiar... another person falsely arrested. All thanks to you."

If she'd taken out a knife and stabbed me between the shoulder blades, I wouldn't have been more stunned than I was at that moment. Ruby blamed me. Wanted to get away from me. Maybe even hated me.

Oh God. My heart crumbled into itty-bitty pieces.

Griff held up a hand. "Hey, come on. Let's not blame Cricket for what happened here. She's right—she's only trying to help Juke."

"So you fuck her and now you're on her side? Is that what this is?" Ruby threw out her hands, her voice venomous.

I didn't recognize this Ruby. This Ruby was a stranger.

Griff must have recognized her fine because he narrowed his eyes. "That's enough, Roo."

"No, I don't think it is, cousin." Ruby stomped around us both, heading back into the police station. "Know what? I'll get my own ride."

"Ruby!" I called, spinning toward her retreating form. "Please don't do this. You weren't even arrested officially, and they know you didn't do anything."

"They don't know shit, and neither do you." Ruby yanked open the door to the waiting area and disappeared.

Griff ran a hand through his hair. "Let her go. She needs space to cool down."

Swallowing the lump in my throat, I turned toward my van. "I don't know why she's so mad at me. I didn't do anything but be a good friend to her. Or I tried to."

"She's scared. That's all."

"Ruby is never scared. She's the toughest person I know," I said, tears lacing my words. I felt numbed by her accusations, stunned by the turn of events, and a little nauseated because I had plunged out of the fantasy of sexy times with Griff into the reality of Ruby's ire.

"People who have no power use what they have at hand. Ruby has ugly words to throw at you because she has nothing else in her arsenal. She doesn't mean it. She's just terrified of losing everything she's been working for. In the past two weeks she's been arrested twice, and she spent two years in prison for something she knew nothing about. Ruby's rattled. She doesn't trust the police, and she's probably angry that she trusted you. But she's wrong. Well, about you. The police? Eh." He made a see-saw motion with a flat hand.

"How do I fix it? I don't know what to do..." I pressed my hands against my face, fingers digging into my eye sockets as if that could stop the tears pooling in my lower lashes.

"Give her space. She'll realize she was wrong. Way wrong."

I dropped my hands and noted that Griff had picked up his helmet and cupped it beneath his arm. "You're leaving?"

"Yeah, I need to get to the yard. Listen, last night was..."

"Irresponsible," I finished for him because that was the thing I was absolutely certain about at this moment. I'd lost my mind. Now whether being irresponsible, selfish, and horny was the biggest mistake of my life, well, only time would tell. "I know you don't do complicated relationships. Ruby has told me that a million times. And I'm a newly single mother, so things are *definitely* complicated."

Griff didn't say anything. He just looked at me.

"Look, you don't owe me anything. I'm a big girl."

Griff shook his head. "You jump to a lot of conclusions, don't you?"

"Oh, not you too." I groaned, making a face. "I'm just trying to be a modern woman who doesn't take the fact you made me... um, you know, and we had... uh, you know... as an indicator of anything more than... what it was."

Griff walked over to me and dropped a hard kiss on my forehead. "Okay, modern woman. I'll talk to you later, 'kay?"

I blinked up at him. "Okay."

He sauntered back to his bike. I watched as he climbed onto the Harley and cranked it. And despite the fact my heart was broken by Ruby, I had to appreciate the way the man straddled a bike, jeans taut across his thighs, shoulders somehow broader in that bomber jacket.

Damn.

As he pulled away, I turned back to the police station and found Wes standing outside, hands on hips, looking at me.

Oh well. Let us name all the ways I've effed up this morning.

And it wasn't even nine o'clock.

17

Ruby

THE SWING CREAKED as I pushed it into motion with my big toe. A decent breeze wafted through the trees, cooling my sweaty face and damp hair. Like always, a bit of yard work gave me space to clear my head and a place to apply the emotions threatening to swamp me. Those dandelions hadn't stood a chance.

I had screwed everything up in my life, but I had managed to weed the entire front bed and mow the yard. There was that.

"Want some lemonade?" Gran asked, pushing the screen door open to echo the creak of the old wooden swing. She surveyed the freshly mowed grass with pleasure.

"Nah," I said.

"I can put vodka in it."

I arched an eyebrow. "Well, in that case…"

"Be right back then," she said, doing a one-eighty and reentering the house. Her departure gave me about five minutes to figure out my defense because I was certain a lecture was forthcoming, and Gran didn't believe in wearing gloves. Nope, serious bare-knuckle smackdown on the way.

The front yard of the old homeplace was pretty, even in the dying grasp of fall. Sweet gum leaves spun down to join the sticker balls beneath the branches, ones that Ed Earl or Jimbo would complain about because even though the women in the family loved the fiery fall beauty of the sweet gum, the men hated the pointy seeds with a passion. Red spider lilies from bygone days popped up like bad pennies around the pine trunks, and the sagging porch across the street held assorted lawn chairs and wooden boxes that would have had those picker guys on television salivating. Gran's place was an old country house on a patch of Saint Augustine that had earned Pawpaw yard of the month three times out of every year he'd lived there. Gran was still religious about the upkeep of her precious grass, even though her husband had been dead for too many years to name.

"I gave you a double 'cause after the morning you had, even prissy Lois Fisher would overlook the strong spirits. Lois swears she ain't never had a drop cross her lips, but someone told me that back in the day, she had her own stool up there at the Channel Marker. But whatever, if she wants to pretend like she ain't never been a sinner, that's between her and our Savior." Gran waggled a glass at me.

"You didn't use a jelly jar," I said with a slight smile, taking the offering.

"Oh hush," Gran said, settling herself into her favorite rocker. "Now spill the tea."

I nearly choked on my first sip. Not because of the double shot though. "Spill the tea? Who are you? A nineteen-year-old blogger?"

"I know things."

"That you do." I said, leaning back and tucking my feet so that I sat cross-legged on the swing and could set my icy vodka lemonade on the flat slats in the nook of my thighs. "Well, I said some really ugly things to Cricket."

Gran lifted her eyebrows—ones she drew on each morning. "Oh?"

"Yeah, and I'm sorry for it, though I do think I have a point. Her playing at being a detective has caused a lot of problems. She got me and one of her friends arrested."

"But not on purpose."

"No, not on purpose, but she has this notion that she missed her calling as a detective. It's like the high she was on when she busted her husband put a bad notion in her head. At first her wanting to do the private investigator thing was amusing—but now it doesn't seem so funny."

"Mmm" was all Gran said.

"I just don't think she should be doing this silly snooping around stuff. She's not street smart, and she thinks she knows what she doesn't. She's like a Southern female Inspector Clouseau but without the cool accent." Despite my reflective mood, my mouth twitched. Until that moment I had forgotten about how much I loved the Pink Panther films as a child.

"Some would say that she does have a cool accent. Very Southern upper crust, which I have always adored, sug-ah." Gran affected a haughty accent which made me smile. She clucked her tongue and continued, "You know, I understand how you feel, especially since it came back on you. It does seem as if this go-around Cricket's gotten some things wrong."

Gran paused, looking out at the yard. Old Man Fussell had come out clad only in his coveralls to yell at two dogs rooting near his fall garden. Gran waved at him. He waved back and continued shooing the dogs. Such was life in tiny Mooringsport, which clung to the edge of Caddo Lake. Daily living here was simple—the sound of the train, heads bowed at the supper table, day lilies exchanged in the gas station parking lot. People still wore aprons and borrowed books from the small library across from the elementary school. A slice of the old ways.

"But...," I prodded.

"You're still young. Not even thirty years old so you don't know yet how it is to be a mama, or a woman left behind. Cricket has a kid going to high school. You remember when you went to high school? How much you loved hanging out with me?" She laughed.

"Yeah, but I was fourteen and trying to grow up too fast." I sipped the lemonade, feeling the vodka doing its job by warming my tummy.

"Just where that child of Cricket's is. She's trying not to need her mama, which is always harder on the mama than the child. And then there is the husband—"

"Ex-husband," I clarified.

"Yeah, and he cheated on her. That does something to a woman's confidence. Cricket needs purpose right now, and doing what she's doing feels like something to her. She couldn't fix herself and all the things that happened to her, so she's trying to fix things for other people."

I mulled over those words. Cricket *was* at loose ends—a marriage over, a child moving on, her mother investing in me, and her life shifting from the country club to whatever it was she was doing. Maybe she was at an emotional crossroads, a place where she didn't know who she was anymore. I knew the thrill of being a detective made her feel useful, excited. Gran was right. Cricket believed she could right a few wrongs. "I guess so."

"I know so." Gran closed her eyes and drew in a breath. "Cricket found out that the garden she worked hard to plant yielded not much in the way of sustenance. She'd created something that on the outside looked mighty fine, but on the inside had a worm. You know, like my squash plants, all big yellow blooms and tiny green squash one day, and the next shriveled like an old man's pecker."

"Gran." I nearly choked on my lemonade.

"Sorry. I still feel mighty resentful about my squash plants this year," she said, her lips twitching a little. "But even I had to start over, ripping those suckers up. Cricket's doing that too."

I sucked in a breath. "But that doesn't mean she should continue to pursue this path. Investigating a theft ring is something for the police to do. Juke knows the score. He's done this for years. Cricket's investigative experience comes from gossiping with other PTA moms or finding out who sent the cookies with peanuts to the bake sale."

"But she caught her husband and his criminal partner and put them in jail. And maybe she is making progress with this theft thing. After all, whoever is stealing those things obviously felt the need to throw out those tack things that blow tires."

I blinked a few times, trying to grasp that wise analogy. "What?"

"I was watching a movie, and that's what the police do in a chase. They throw out these strip things that blow the tires out and slows the bad guy down. In this case the bad guy is trying to slow the good guys down. They mailed that purse to you and tried to set you up so that the police would be forced to slow down their investigation and look at you."

"But it was a dumb plan. What if I hadn't opened the box? What if—"

"Who doesn't open a box sent to them? Lord, Jimbo runs for the Amazon boxes on the front porch like it's Christmas morning. Whoever mailed that box knew you'd open it. And they called the tip in or whatever right after it was mailed so that you didn't have time to figure out why you got it in the first place. So Juke or the police are making this thief twitchy."

"Maybe. I still think that mailing the purse thing wasn't well thought out. I could have left it at Printemps. I could have given it to Resa or Cricket."

"But the police would have come to you or to your place of work to search the premises based on the tip. You're still on parole, so it was probably easy to get a search warrant for your home and work."

"Who are you even?"

"The mother and grandmother of people who make bad decisions." Gran flattened her mouth and looked irritated that she even had to mention how many times she'd bailed people out of jail. Poor Gran.

I put my foot down and kicked the swing into motion again, my fingers sliding up to the thimble nestled between my breasts. "Maybe you're right. But it's not just Cricket and the theft ring. I think I screwed things up with Dak."

Gran's sharp eyes studied me. "How'd ya do that?"

"I don't know. I seem destined to push everyone away. Self-sabotage is my way of life it seems." I sounded sad. I *was* sad.

"Okay, here's the thing, Roo. I feel like it's second verse same as the first with you. You're worth loving, sweetheart. You're deserving of good things. So if you're standing in your own way, you need to figure out why. If you're pushing people away, why? And baby, I can't answer all that for you, though I know you want me to. I'm your grandmother who knows you like I know the freckles on the back of my hand—I refuse to call them age spots—and even I can't tell you what you need to do."

"Yes, you can."

"Yeah, I could, but figuring your life out is your job. I did the hard work long ago. I've watched you fall down, and I've learned that while I can bring the Band-Aids and the boo-boo kisses, I can't stop you from yourself."

Tears pricked at my eyes because I had come here looking for Gran to tell me what to do to fix things with Cricket. And patch me up from the injuries sustained when I waded into unknown territory with Dak, very much aware of the huge mines buried beneath the surface but going in anyway. I had survived the blast but didn't know how to move forward.

Basically, I knew nothing.

"And while you figure things out, focus on what you can control. You have words, so use them. You have time. Let the seconds fill the space. And you have hands to get those designs just right. It's Saturday evening. Come Monday morning, you have a mission. Use your brain, but don't forget that the heart sometimes has to take over. Delicate thing, that balance."

"I suppose." I sighed and stared out at an afternoon that inspired art and poetry. Wedgewood skies, golden leaves, woodsmoke, scampering squirrels, pumpkins on porches, and school-weary kids shrieking as they tossed the pigskin. Fall in Louisiana could be a gift or a betrayal. "Can I just have more vodka?"

"No, but you can help me make the gumbo. LSU plays tonight, and I promised your uncles something good to help the Tigers achieve victory." Gran rose and gave me a smile that relayed just how much she understood where I was.

The in-between.

"I'm not sure gumbo is going to help LSU beat Florida."

"Well, it ain't gonna hurt, now is it?" Gran toddled toward the screen door that needed some WD-40.

I dutifully rose, prepared to debone a chicken and make a roux. A million things needed to be done to prepare for iSpy

Fashion Festival, and just as many things needed to be said to the people I loved—but at that moment I needed the respite gumbo would offer and the soft hymns Gran would hum under her breath as she stirred the pot.

Everyone needs careworn hands, soft places, and full bellies sometimes so they can figure out their lives.

18

Cricket

Monday mornings were rarely much fun. This one was no exception.

I had spent the rest of Saturday washing my sheets and telling myself that Ruby was an asshole and Griff was nothing more than a booty call. Single women had booty calls all the time. Or at least they did on television. And Ruby was overreacting on the whole questioning thing.

So I wasn't going to hell. Or bad-friend purgatory.

And I probably wasn't going on any more dates with the hunky and irritated Detective McNally. He'd walked away after catching Griff kissing me with a look of irritation. Understandable since he'd picked up the check last night, and I'd leaned in for that almost kiss. He'd probably thought we were on the right track. Until he caught me with my big mistake the morning after. I wasn't proud of myself for my behavior after Wes pulled away from the driveway even if my body was still giving my bad decision a standing ovation.

Sunday, I'd gone to church, surprised the roof didn't collapse upon my entry, and prayed about my situation and the sin I had committed that felt wrong but also so right. Then I had moped around, missing Julia Kate, who'd gone to spend the afternoon with her father and his new bride, both recently returned from the Grand Hotel in Alabama where they'd spent their honeymoon. After Scott and I had gotten married, we'd spent a week in Caneel Bay in Saint John's, swimming with sea turtles and making love in our fancy suite. I won the honeymoon battle, but I guess Natalie had won the war. Then again, it wasn't a war I was interested in winning anymore. I had refocused my life.

Or I thought I had. Now I was certain of nothing.

When I had signed up for PI class, my intentions were clear. Working for Juke would be rewarding and would bring some thrill into my life. Sure, many would say it was a silly pastime, but I had many friends who worked a full-time job and still taught yoga, painting classes, or violin. My friend Regina even played bass in an all-girl band called Ladyfinger. So why not private investigation as a side hustle?

Yet after Ruby's harsh words about my meddling in people's lives paired with the misdirection and false starts, I was doubting if being a private eye was a good idea.

Maybe I wasn't truly talented at tracking down cheaters and thieves the way I thought I was. For the most part, working for Juke had felt like it would be a harmless way to ply my skills—wasn't like I was working dangerous murder cases. Just the occasional inappropriate slap and tickle or disability fraud. Handling those sorts of transgressions didn't require me to carry a handgun or learn kung fu. More like spreadsheets and eavesdropping. Those I could handle. Or I thought I could.

Still, Ruby's recriminations echoed in my head. Her words had been harsh. Ugly. Surprising.

Never would have guessed Ruby thought I was silly. Okay, so yes, I was, well, me. I sometimes stumbled or had lettuce between my teeth, so no James Bond here. But Ruby had always seemed supportive of me learning the trade. Hell, she went with me on stakeouts, helped me disguise myself, and loaned me her cousin for protection. So why did she say those things?

Griff's words joined in on the fun, tangoing around in my brain.

She's just scared.

Understandable. Being detained by the police so quickly after the arrest in New York City had to be alarming, but they'd released her—it was nothing more than questioning her about the purse and how she got it. The police questioned people all the time, either at the station or at places of businesses or homes. No different than what a private eye would do to uncover the truth.

Maybe that's what I needed to do—just let it be known I was working for North Star. Perhaps if I had been more upfront about my investigation, Piper would have told me that she was borrowing the necklace and the real thief would have been too scared to take anything. And Ruby wouldn't have been framed. No more covert, undercover Cricket.

Or maybe I was being ridiculous chasing this career and should toss my newly embossed private investigator cards into the trash can. Even if they were so adorable with the stars and in the most delicious sapphire ink. Ruby was probably right—I had no business pursuing a second career. My miscalculations had caused trouble for two people I cared about.

If I hadn't already known she'd tell me to forget about being Cricket Crosby, Private Investigator, I would have talked this over with my mother. Marguerite had never wanted me to take the course in the first place. Griff seemed to think it was too dangerous. None of my friends knew. And the one person I thought I could count on to fix my tiara when it was crooked had just declared the opposite, so I was certain that no one would be unbiased when it came to deciding whether I should give up on my new career or stick it out.

As I climbed the rusted and peeling stairs to Juke's office, I decided to stop thinking and just get through this meeting. Juke had called last night with a terse request to get together to see where we were since my two weeks' contracted time had been up on Thursday.

I knocked.

He opened the door.

Shocking.

"Good morning, Juke." I stepped inside, my eyes going straight to the new couch. "Oh, a new couch. And in camouflage."

"It was on sale."

"I see why. There's a certain irony in a private investigator having a camouflaged couch, I guess," I said, smiling even though I didn't feel much like it.

Juke looked clean. He wore an unwrinkled shirt, new jeans, and a pair of running shoes that were tied. Hair was combed, face shaved, and he smelled like a fresh shower. Such a different man, which made me pleased each time I saw the positive changes in him.

He looked at the couch and made a puzzled face. "Huh?"

"Are you doing well?" I asked, perching on the camo couch, noting it was very soft and comfortable. Also I was unlikely to catch a disease from this one.

"Yeah, so let's cut to the chase. It's been two weeks, and we got nothing. Except Ruby arrested and some chick that is raising so much of a ruckus with the chief of police that my contact at the SPD has closed up tighter than a nun's thighs, so I gotta think-"

"Ruby was taken in for questioning. Not arrested." I wanted to be clear on that point.

"Right. Yeah, but she's their prime suspect at present. I got that much out of my source before he essentially told me to eff off."

"Well, the police are wrong. Whoever has been taking all that stuff is just feeling the heat. Lots of people know about Ruby's past—she wanted to be transparent about her record going into this competition. The real thief just wanted to trip the police up. Luckily for our client, the real thief doesn't know we're working the case, so we don't have to waste time chasing the wrong person like the police do."

Juke shrugged a shoulder. "So what do you have for me?"

My stomach sank because what I had wasn't much. I pulled a folder from my bag which Juke probably thought was ugly. But he wasn't a man of great taste. I glanced down at the sofa. Obviously. "So I went through the top resale sites and looked for matches to the exact bags and jewelry that were stolen. I looked for the same seller. I cross-checked every site and have a list of users who might be leads. But none of them have the same username. That makes sense because our thief doesn't seem to be lazy or stupid. She probably has several usernames attached to separate Gmail accounts. Some sites don't even list the seller. I took the top ones—Vestiaire, the RealReal, Poshmark, thredUp, Fashionphile, and so on—and listed the numbers of each stolen item they have available. Some have been for sale since before the thefts, so I crossed those out."

"What's your conclusion?"

"That there is a huge resale market for luxury goods. Our thief mostly stole popular designs by the most coveted designers. For example, one of our victims has a hot-pink shearling

Chanel No. 19 flap bag that wasn't touched. That's because it would have been easy to find on the resale shops because it's not basic. So the thief took the Bottega Eve in black." At Juke's confused look, I tried to clarify. "It's like no one is going to steal a Himalayan Birkin in Nilo crocodile. It's rare. Not that anyone in Shreveport has one of those."

"Why not?"

"Because they cost over three hundred thousand dollars." I shoved the spreadsheets toward him.

"You're joking."

"No. Birkin is Hermès highest-selling line. But because they are so expensive—"

"There aren't as many of them," Juke concluded.

I pointed my finger at him. "Bingo. So our thief is smart and likely sells 'used,' which evades suspicion and keeps her under the radar. After the riots a few years back, resale boutiques took steps to keep track of bag numbers and receipts so that stolen goods weren't moved through their sites. That involved tracking a lot of 'new' items. I've found a few listings by the same seller, but it could be totally random. Those two sellers have a lot of other items for sale. We really need to have access to the resale stores' databases. Don't think that's going to happen."

"So we're at a stalemate?"

"Looks like it. I can keep up the snooping at events, but as you pointed out, that didn't do much of anything other than get some friends of mine, well, embarrassed. Ruby's really ticked at me for dragging her to that party to help me." I flopped back onto the couch. It was truly comfortable. The thing was growing on me.

"I've been working some cheating spouses while you poked around this theft thing. Guess I need to redirect my attention toward this. I think you're right that the thief is feeling nervous. So she may slow down or stop altogether. We need to come at this from a financial angle. As in, who needs extra cash? Or who might be a klepto?"

"You're talking about being a kleptomaniac?" I asked.

He nodded.

"Sufferers of that disorder don't usually take high-end items. It's more like things people won't miss. Like a knickknack or shot glass. I knew a girl who knew a girl who suffered from it. That isn't this. Selling purses for three grand and bracelets for a few thousand more can add up, so I think this is someone who needs money, not someone who is suffering from a disorder. Maybe I should look at the prices on these sites? I would think a thief wants to move them quickly and so may take less than what she might if she were the real owner. So maybe luxury bargains?" I liked that idea because if I were desperate for funds, I would likely make sure my similar items were priced less. I should also look to see how long the persons selling had been on the sites. Opening accounts all at once would be fairly suspicious. It was worth a shot.

"Good idea. I will lean on my guy at the precinct to see what he knows. Maybe he'll throw me a bone, but this Detective McNally is a by-the-book sort. He doesn't seem to want to reveal much about what he's thinking."

Boy, did I know that.

"So you want me to stay on the case?" I asked, itching to show him the cards I had in my purse, hoping he would want me to stay working for him and thus dash my doubts.

Juke shrugged. "To be honest, I had planned to take you off, but you just made some good points. Still, your gut instincts—I think that's what you called them—aren't great. And gut feelings are not what we go on in the investigative world. You need to ignore hunches and weird vibes and stick to facts."

"My mistake wasn't a hunch. I had photographic evidence of Piper taking the necklace."

He looked at me. "A few weeks ago, you gave me a list of women mostly likely to steal based on their"—he rifled through his desk and withdrew my monogrammed stationery—"overall morality scale including how much they drink and gossip. This isn't something that stands up in court. And Piper wasn't even on this list."

I sighed and tried not to roll my eyes. "Okay, so it wasn't a list based on anything other than my observations over the years. I also gave you a list of people who have been having financial issues and someone who didn't pay taxes for several years. I know people. Just like Donner. I knew he was too slick for his own good. And that son of his was just as bad. He poured honey on all his words."

Juke looked at me like I was a few sandwiches shy of a picnic. "But having a feeling is not evidence. It's not even circumstantial evidence. It's conjecture, and not even good conjecture at that. You need to follow the facts. You must look at cold, hard evidence to make a play."

"I'm doing that. That list was preliminary stuff. It's not like I was naming the perp based on her lack of participation in Junior League or the fact she got busy with another dad in the dugout at Little League. That happened, by the way. I just thought if we wanted to make one of those murder boards like they do on police shows and having lists like that might jar something loose." So now it seemed a little ridiculous, but at the time I was reaching for anything to move us toward a suspect.

Juke sighed and leaned back in his chair. I winced because it looked like the chair could break under his weight. "For now just focus on Ruby and the show."

"You don't want me to actively investigate?" My voice wavered despite my attempt to play it cool.

Juke thought I sucked at this even after all I had just given him on the online resale boutiques.

"Just for now. Let's regather after the event this weekend. Ruby has worked hard and needs all the support she can get, especially after all that went on Saturday."

A little reminder of my part in Ruby's being taken in for questioning. Was there an admonishment in his words? Did he too blame me for Ruby getting framed?

"Fine," I said, rising and reaching for the folder. "I'll take these and add to them when I have time. There are still some minor resale boutiques I didn't get to, and I want to look at the dates that items were added."

He set a hand on the folder. "Or I can file this with my notes so they are all together."

I jerked the folder loose. "Nope. I have more to add."

I wasn't leaving him with my work. He hadn't even paid me yet. Should I mention that to him? Nah, just probably get out of his office before I did something even more embarrassing, like cry.

Juke said nothing as I crossed the room and shut the door. I felt demoralized, defeated, and a little mad.

Everyone thought I wasn't capable of being a good private investigator. Even those people who I thought were my friends, my cheerleaders, my posse had bailed on supporting me. People had humored me my whole life—cute little Cricket with her sunny smile and tasteful... everything. My mother had demanded good taste, handwritten thank-you notes, and smiling even when you wanted to throw a tantrum. Which meant I had never thrown a tantrum.

I stomped down the stairs, working myself up.

Shoulders back, Cricket.
Say thank you, Cricket.
Don't forget your manners, Cricket.
Listen to authority—

I picked up a rock and hurled it. It hit the side of a dumpster and ricocheted, thumping against Juke's van.

My eyes widened, but then they narrowed. So what? Maybe it left a mark. I didn't care. I continued my stampede toward the Spider Veloce, the car I had chosen over the practical minivan this morning because I could. I stalked toward the car, feeling like Godzilla trampling through downtown Tokyo. Except Tokyo was a parking lot with weeds and bottle caps. Just for good measure, I picked up a loose piece of concrete right before I got into my car and heaved it toward the chain-link fence. It hit hard, vibrating the metal, and that made me feel a little better. If not absolutely juvenile.

I fired up the car and drove to Printemps.

When I walked in, juggling a box of items that needed to be returned to my office, I heard Ruby upstairs working with Resa and Jade laughing with Chris at the front counter. Normally, I loved when Chris popped in on my day off, but I wasn't in the mood for his droll observations and witty banter.

"There she is!" Chris crowed, using his Jack-from-*Will-and-Grace* voice. He really was over the top, embracing the stereotype of every gay interior decorator. I had asked him about that once, and he had made a face and said that he would be exactly who he wanted to be, and if that was a middle-aged queen with diva-ish tendencies, then he would damn well talk and walk the way he wanted. In his words, "I don't owe anyone anything, including the gay community. If I want to drawl 'fab-u-lous' every five seconds, I'll do it. I spent too many years playing Tonka trucks and spitting to pretend who I am any longer."

"Morning, Christopher." I set my bag down on the counter, noting that Jade was pricing the ornamental broaches I'd picked up at an estate sale. She was using the guidebook my grandmother had created along with the internet to look for going rates. The woman was a gem. "What brings you to my humble store?"

He sniffed. "Humble, my ass. Since when has Printemps, the star in the crown of all Southern antiques stores, ever taken a back seat to anyone? Speaking of back seat, I heard that Ling's husband has been climbing into the back on the regular with Ashley Albritton. Thank goodness BMWs have good suspension."

Idle gossip wasn't something I wanted to indulge in. Ben & Jerry's to drown my sorrows and alleviate my doubts? Maybe. But learning my friend Ling's husband Darren was doing the horizontal mambo with someone else made me sick. "I hope that's not true."

"Book it," Chris said, sobering and looking contrite. "Or not. I shouldn't have brought that up. I forget that your heart was broken by that dick Scott. Men are such horrible creatures. I may renounce my manliness."

Jade snorted.

"What? I'm manly." Chris grinned at me.

I managed a small smile. "So what's been going on with you?"

"I'm redesigning Katie Clare Reardon's living room and foyer. It's been stuck in the 1990s so long that I swear I hear echoes of NSYNC in the halls. I'm looking for something fabulous for the entry, a table that can hold a pair of lamps I found in the attic that would make you drool."

"The Reardons have been in that house over a century. I would kill to look at all the stuff they have in storage. Old Tency Reardon had a good eye and too much money." I nodded my approval at Jade, who noticed and preened a little even though she would deny it. "Let me set these things down, and I'll show you a few pieces that might work. You have pictures of the lamps?"

"Does a woodchuck chuck?" Chris quipped, sliding off the stool in front of Jade. He wore bright blue trousers and a corduroy jacket with paisley patches at the elbows that just matched the lavender dress shirt beneath. Beau Brummel had nothing on Chris Winnfield.

I took his phone and whistled at the pair. "Danish pottery?"

"Ja."

"Maybe Søholm?" I asked, noting the blue and gray swirling. Now this was what I was good at—recognizing quality antiques. For the past seven months I had abandoned my zeal for working with clients to find the perfect armoire or drop-leaf table. Another reason to set aside my insane plan to become a private investigator.

Maybe.

"Yoo-hoo!" someone called out, the front doorbells jingling merrily.

Nancy Parrington. I glanced at my watch. Eleven thirty on the dot. I had forgotten that I told her to stop by to sign the insurance paperwork at this time. "Back here."

The tap of shoes indicated that at least two people were heading our way as we stood in front of the first piece that might work with the lamps.

"Hello, Cricket," Nancy said, her coral lips turning up into a familiar smile. Nancy and my mother had been close friends for as long as I could remember. When my father had run off with Crystalle years ago, Nancy had stood in our kitchen and made soup and poured my mother vodka. She'd thrown me a wedding shower, a baby shower, and a grand-opening party when we first moved the store. When I introduced vintage fashions as a new feature, Nancy bought the first dress and wore it to the Dallas Symphony opener. Her daughter Cammie was younger than I was, but we'd grown up together, tolerating being dragged to ballet, piano, and the country-club pool. Cammie had moved away to Plano a few years back, but she and her husband had moved home six or so years ago and opened several new restaurants. We ate at the romantic Zhivago's a few times a month and Chee Whiz even more often because Julia Kate loved the grilled cheese sandwiches.

"Well, the whole gang is here," I said with a smile as Cammie and my mother peeked over Nancy's shoulder.

"I wanted to see some of Ruby's pieces. Mother couldn't decide on some of the accessories. She seems to think I have good taste," Cammie said, running a finger over a Herend bunny figurine.

"You have impeccable taste, my dear." Nancy moved the bunny figurine away from her daughter as if it were an ingrained habit.

"And I wanted to check on Ruby," my mother said, giving Chris's outfit a once-over. "Chris, you look like spring and fall vomited on you."

"So you're saying I should pick a season? Can't. I love them both," Chris said with a grin. "And you, my sweet Mrs. Quinney, obviously couldn't decide between Mrs. Doubtfire or Cruella this morning."

My mother didn't look amused. She sniffed. I, however, giggled.

"Don't giggle, Cricket. It isn't ladylike," Mama said.

"Who said I was a lady?" I joked, immediately thinking about how I had ridden Griffin on Friday night. Nothing ladylike about that.

"Rrrrr," Chris cooed with a naughty smile.

"I called Scott and tossed him this bone, only because he could get the paperwork done quickly," I said, gesturing to my broom closet, aka, office. "Jade said he dropped the papers by Friday afternoon. Let me grab them."

"I'll check in on Ruby. Horrible thing the poor child

endured," my mother said, straightening her blazer jacket that was, in hindsight, a bit frumpy. Her concern for Ruby ignited a flare of jealousy inside me. My mother had taken more of an interest in Ruby's work than she ever had mine. Why was that?

I stomped out the stupid feelings that shouldn't be there, mostly because I was so happy that Ruby had support and that I wouldn't have to go face her at present. I turned to Chris. "I'll be right back. Until then, look around. I can give you twenty percent off. Maybe twenty-five if you behave."

"So twenty percent?"

Nancy and Cammie smiled and followed me back to my office. I grabbed the folder which lay exactly where Jade said she'd put it. Nancy had insisted on an insurance policy for the items she would loan Ruby to be used in the iSpy event, and since Scott was drumming up business and owed me favors for the rest of my life, I got him to put together a personal articles floater policy for the borrowing of the prized items. "Here we go. All I need is an itemized list with the estimated values. Once we have that, Scott will enact the policy to cover the loan through the weekend. Shouldn't have an issue because I know Ruby will be careful with everything. She says a prayer before she even makes a cut on any ruined garment she buys. And I will make sure everything is transported to the event. Oh, and I have a new security system. Scott had been after me for months to do that anyway."

Nancy took the insurance papers. "We aren't sure what she's using yet. Guess we need to take a peek at the collection. I have a list of what I think are the most desirable pieces. One is a fur stole."

Cammie shook her head. "I know they were popular back in the day, but not these days."

I pointed to the paper. "Whatever you bring, even if it doesn't get used, still needs to be listed. I doubt we'll have to worry about protestors and red paint, but better safe than sorry."

"True." Nancy looked at Cammie. "Want to go up and see the designs? I would love to see if the velvet Chanel cape works with that pantsuit. It's the prettiest piece in the collection."

I gestured toward the stairs, wanting so much to be part of matching Nancy's aunt's collection to Ruby's but dreading how Ruby would react to my being there after our exchange this weekend. The morning had already been rough with Juke firing/not firing me—I wasn't sure which one—and I couldn't bear her frosty silence. "Y'all go on ahead. Don't forget the papers. You need to drop them with Scott before you bring the items to Printemps so he has the record."

"Will Thursday work?" Nancy took the folder. "Because I have a meeting on Friday and a hair appointment on Friday afternoon. I feel like Ruby needs to have everything done by Friday morning."

"Yeah, that's perfect. She has to speak on a few panels on Friday, and then the show is Saturday so..." I shrugged, answering for her when I shouldn't. "But you should ask and confirm it with her."

"Thanks, Cricket." Cammie gave me a smile. "This is so much fun! I hope Ruby wins! And I bet Mom's stuff will be a nice conversation piece. Bo Dixie is doing a whole layout on the collection after the show, so she'll have the *Journal*'s photographer pay special attention to Ruby's designs. People have been begging Mama for years to loan her items to the Louisiana Museum for an exhibit, and I think I have convinced her to do it. Talk later."

Off they went, clunking up the stairs, and Chris appeared to bargain over an Enrique Garcel waterfall desk that would look danged spectacular with the Søholm pottery lamps but had a pricey ticket because of the excellent condition. We agreed on five thousand dollars with a promise to mention the sale in my quarterly newsletter so that Katie Clare could get some bragging rights. I convinced him with that last bargaining chip especially since he hadn't had to buy the lamps. Chris could drive a hard deal, but I was even better at it.

Again, a reminder that I was good at what I did.

Wasn't that enough?

Did I really need the thrill of sneaking around and spying on folks? Had I really missed my calling as a detective or was I just looking to fill an empty space in my life that had appeared when I found out Scott was cheating? I was certain that everyone had something they were missing out on, but that they learned to accept the path they chose. I had made a lot of decisions in my lifetime, some good, some not, but overall, I was proud of what I had accomplished. I owned a premier antiques store that dealers and designers from all over the nation visited on the regular, I had a darling daughter who was growing into a smart beauty, and I had friends and a community I had never found fault with before the divorce.

So why push for something that wasn't right for me?

I reached over for my purse and pulled out the business cards I had tucked into my purse to give to people.

And I tossed them into the trash can.

19

Ruby

THURSDAY MORNING...

I still hadn't made up with Cricket.

Or Dak.

Things had been awkward AF too. But I just didn't seem to have the words, and I wasn't sure I was ready to discuss my future with Dak or was over being mad at Cricket. Dak had sent me a text that essentially put everything we had on pause until after the iSpy fashion show. He said he needed time to think about our relationship, and he knew I needed time too. I hadn't seen him since Friday night, which made me achy and heavy. When I told him I missed him, he'd promised that he'd be at the show, that he loved me, that he was proud of me, and that we would be okay.

I hoped so, but I wasn't certain that our relationship could weather me leaving town and doing a long-distance relationship. But I knew if the right opportunity came along, I would have to roll the dice on myself. But that was a big "if." Winning the iSpy Fashion Festival could only help me climb the next step in my career no matter where that ladder led. So for the moment I needed to focus on the show and my collection. I would think about the "what next" after I got through the next few days.

As for Cricket, I realized that she'd meant me no harm when she asked if I would go to that kitchen gadget party with her, but damage had been done. Not only had I endured the horror of being led off my property by the police, nosy neighbors watching as I schlepped to the cruiser in an old T-shirt, hair sticking up in eight different directions, but one of the other competitors had gotten some footage of me being cuffed in New York City and released it to the media here. Didn't matter the charges had been dropped. Whoever it was had posted it with a fake account or one that was protected, according to Juke, and had made me look jealous and half-cocked. Pair that with the questioning in the theft-ring case, and I was now the talk of Shreveport.

Nothing I had designed could overcome the dents and dings in my reputation. It was one thing to be redeemed from my old ways—a poster child for turning around one's life—but the support stopped when I was cast into repeat-offender light. People assumed I was showing my roots, so to speak. All the comments on the Instagram posts implied once trash, always trash.

Thing was, I wasn't so sure they weren't right. A person can only run from who they are for so long. I had convinced myself over the past year or so that I had changed, but still my past clung to me like bad cologne. Just couldn't shower it off.

Resa and I had put the finishing touches on the last of the outfits. All the models had dropped in for final fittings throughout the week except for Cricket, who still had to try on her navy crepe gown.

Cricket's gown was the showpiece of the collection and would be the final piece to go down the runway. I had found a vintage 1940s dress, likely handmade by a decent seamstress, and used the skirt, tearing away the weird pink chiffon that lined the fabric. Instead, I used a gathering of ivory lace to create a waterfall spilling out of the wrap skirt. For the bodice, I found a cream 1950s Milton Saunders linen party dress online. The neckline had crystal beads and light turquoise silk fabric leaves around the neckline. I lopped off the sleeves to create a strapless bodice with a sweetheart dip between the breasts. The light turquoise embroidery complemented the severe navy of the skirt, and I salvaged enough of the embellishment to sew a bit down the open edge of the skirt. I thought it truly stunning, something that would elevate Cricket into Grace Kelly. I had requested soft makeup and a simple chignon for her styling. Nancy had a pair of navy shoes from the 1960s that might work, but if not, a simple neutral sandal with a heel would be fine.

Cammie and Nancy had come by on Monday and taken pictures of my collection. Throughout the week, Cammie would text me the accessories they thought would complement each look, waiting for me to agree before setting them aside to come to Printemps on Thursday. We'd settled on the Chanel cape, several Dior wraps, a few pairs of gorgeous Cornelia James gloves, and of course some fabulous bags, including an early Birkin that Jean-Louis Dumas had given Nancy's aunt right before she passed away in 1986. Aunt Felicia had not liked the purse much, but the valuable bag had stayed in her collection because of the personal nature of the gift. There were also a few hats and fascinators, jeweled combs, and some exquisite jewelry. I was so excited to be able to pair such interesting pieces with my reimagined creations. It felt perfect to blend the old with the modern collection I'd worked so hard on. Overall, I was very pleased.

The sun was already setting, and I was thankful that Cricket had given me time throughout the workday to creep up the stairs and fiddle around with whatever last details I needed to fiddle with. I stood looking at my collection hanging on the rack, covered, with a bag containing the accessories attached to each piece. The only one not ready to roll out tomorrow morning was Cricket's dress.

Just as I cast an eye on the gown still attached to the dress form, I heard footsteps on the staircase.

"Ruby?" Cricket called up.

"I'm still here." I steeled myself for the conversation I needed to have but didn't want to endure.

Cricket appeared in the doorway. Her ponytail was crooked, and she had bags under her eyes. A flash of guilt hit me, but I pretended it away. Such a habit now.

"I figured you needed me to try on the gown so you can have it ready," she said, eying the collection which hung in the garment bags, hidden from sight.

"I do." I gestured toward the dressmaker dummy. "Let me unpin it. All I need to do is fit it on you and then put the zipper in. Won't take long since I already had your measurements from last time."

Cricket nodded, shucking out of her shirt, revealing a camisole. She kicked off her jeggings and walked toward the dress in her underwear. She'd lost weight, so that could be an issue but not enough to make it too painful to take in. "Looks like you have everything ready to go."

"I do. Nancy and Cammie just brought all the pieces for each look earlier today. It's crazy they're letting me borrow them, especially after what happened this week."

Cricket looked like a dog that had been kicked. "I'm sorry about that, Ruby."

"I know you are." I unpinned the gown. "Look, I said some things I shouldn't have said to you. I was—"

"No, you were right." Cricket held up a hand, waving off my apology. "I have been thinking a lot about this second career I've been chasing. I think you're right. I don't have any business playing around with investigations. It was a pipe dream or some moment of insanity. Just forget about it."

I hadn't expected that. "What? I thought you were determined to do this."

Cricket sank down on a stool. "Yeah, but I've been thinking. When all that stuff went down with Scott last spring, I felt powerless. Just down on myself. I mean, my husband was cheating, but it wasn't just the actual betrayal of the vows we took. It was the dismissive way he did it. Like I wouldn't find out, like I was too stupid to know. Remember what he said? That I never rocked the boat. Those words did something to me. I didn't want to be that woman. I wanted to take control of my life."

"You weren't that woman," I said, the flicker of guilt becoming a tsunami of shame for making her think she couldn't do what she set out to do. I was lower than a dog. No, lower than the flies that swarmed around dog poop. Maybe I was just the dog poop.

"No, I wasn't. But everyone *thought* that. I know what people think of me. I'm harmless, fluffy, and silly. But I'm no airhead. People trust me to follow through and make sure their office has the perfect credenza or they've chosen the perfect font for their wedding invitations. That sort of thing. But no one takes me seriously. And last spring, it felt good to do something. I surprised myself."

"I understand. You took action. You didn't let it happen *to* you." I unwrapped the gown and laid it over the table—careful to make sure the table was completely clean.

"Exactly. Silly as it was, those disguises and working with you, Griff, and Juke to do something big like bringing down Scott and Donner made me feel like a different person. I liked that power. I liked meting out justice."

"I did too."

"I don't know. I guess I thought I could continue it. Like maybe I was good at righting wrongs. For some reason, I needed that more than I needed to be good at finding the perfect light fixture for Sarah Tatum's dining room. I liked the danger, the carefully orchestrated sting, and the feeling of nailing that jackass to the wall." Cricket looked at her hands, avoiding my gaze. "But I think after getting Piper arrested with my assumptions and then thoughtlessly putting you into a position where you could get framed by the thief, well, that got me to backtracking on my plan. Thing is, I'm not sure I'm good at it. I just *want* to be good at it."

"Cricket, I shouldn't have said what I said. I was upset and scared." I rose and rubbed at my face. I hadn't been sleeping well, so I was certain my eyes looked as tired as Cricket's. We could both use some spa services, not that I had ever gone to a spa. Case in point on the apple not falling far from the tree. Ruby Balthazar wasn't a chick who got seaweed wraps and wound Chanel wraps around her shoulders. She shouldn't be swilling champagne on the roof of Manhattan penthouses. She shouldn't be featured in the *Shreveport Gazette's* Living section.

Cricket had been playing detective while I had been parading around as a fashion designer. Maybe we were both reaching for something that wasn't meant to be.

"I know you were being somewhat reactive. Anyone would have been, but there was some truth to what you said. I fear I'm projecting my desire to be a badass onto something that might not be right for me. Thing is, sometimes a person needs to accept they have a certain lane that they're supposed to stay in. I think I need to stay in my lane." She sounded sad about it, and that hurt. I didn't want Cricket to be so easily defeated. Even if the words that had broken her intentions had been my own.

"Would you say that to me?" I asked.

"What do you mean?" She jerked her gaze up.

"Well, I'm just a nobody who's ripping up dresses and pretending to be a designer."

Cricket's mouth fell open. "You aren't pretending anything. You *are* a designer. Talent doesn't lie. Your designing ability is irrefutable, so we're not going to play games here. What I'm talking about isn't anything like what you're doing. You have the support of everyone who meets you. You went to New York, and all the big names wanted to hire you. Cecile Smart is your mentor. Cecile Smart! Ruby, we're talking about different things here. You can't be stopped. And I probably should be."

I didn't say anything. Just stared at her. At how passionately she defended me to myself. It was what friendship looks like. I hadn't really known, but over the past seven months, Cricket had been teaching me. She'd knitted together a community of support, starting with her own formidable mother. Then she'd steadily added to the bunch. Now I had Coraline, Celine, Nancy, Cammie, and even Julia Kate, all cheering me on. Jade had joined in too, recruiting her friends to model for me and giving me suggestions for avant-garde looks. Even the family I had sworn off after doing jail time for Ed Earl had rallied around me. Ed Earl had given me eighty thousand dollars as blood money and my gran had pitched in with help on cutting patterns and fixing fabric issues. Jimbo had—well, he'd not done much of anything, but I knew he was in my corner. For a girl who'd thought she was totally alone in the world this time last year, I had a big, boisterous Team Ruby standing behind me.

All this because of Cricket.

"You believe in me," I said quietly.

"Of course I do. You're incredible, Ruby, and I'm so proud of you. You had every reason to hide from a world that betrayed you, but you didn't. Instead, you stuck out your chin and put one foot in front of the other. The girl who crept in and filled out that application and the one standing in front of me now are night and day. You're ready to rock this world, Ruby, and I won't let you play tit for tat with me over my private eye thing just to make me feel better about myself."

"I'm not." I picked up the dress and walked over to her. "But you just told me how proud you were of me for not running. Well, you showed me how to do that last year. You could have curled into a ball and let what Scott did to you define you. But instead, you set up a sting, tricked Scott into giving you what you wanted, and then made him play the fool in front of all the world. You weren't afraid to fail then, so why are you now?"

Cricket made a face. "Well, back then I was fueled by the need for revenge. And don't forget my reckless pursuit of getting even led to Julia Kate needing a lot of therapy. I chose humiliating her father over her thoughts and feelings. I'm still trying to fix that mistake."

"Step in," I said, holding the dress open so she could ease into the gown. Cricket stepped in, and I slid the gown up her body, settling the waist and then pinching together the top. She stroked the side of the dress and tried to peer into the mirror.

I went over to the work desk and grabbed a box of pins. "Don't move."

"I won't."

"I'll pin it, and then we will try the accessories to see what works best. I'm thinking the dangling sapphire earrings that Nancy brought."

"Real ones?"

"Yep. I'm nervous as a pet coon having those suckers here, but I think they are going to make this dress look even better than it already does on you." I started the process of pinning her into the gown. "But going back to what I said before, I don't think my words were well thought out or fair to you. Those words were about me and how I felt, not about you and what you're trying to accomplish. You've given me support. You've gathered people around me to help me on my way. I haven't done that for you. The only time you asked for my help, I had to be convinced to go with you."

"Well, now it's understandable why you didn't want to go. The thief used you to her advantage. You being at the party became a sure-fire way to misdirect the theft investigation. It's like we tossed her an escape pod."

"Maybe so, but that's not what I'm talking about. You're trying to do something hard—take on a new career at a point in your life when it's hard to pivot and change. But you haven't let that stop you. And, well, no one has really given you much support, especially me. And Cricket, I really should have. That's on me."

Cricket sighed. "It's okay, Ruby. I think there are times in life when you need to stop pushing so hard. I've been shoving a square peg into a round hole. I'm not a private investigator, and it was silly to think that I could be some supersleuth. I've been watching too much *CSI*, and my one venture into investigation gave me false confidence. I've made peace with the fact I... well, must drive in my own lane."

I shoved the last pin in and stood, looking at her critically. Needed to be taken in by a good half inch at the waist. The hem was perfect, thank the good Lord, and she filled it out, creating the perfect silhouette for the dress. "I have other things to say about that conclusion, but all I can say right now is 'wow.'"

"Let me see," Cricket said, pulling away.

She walked to the mirror, and her eyes widened. "Ruby! Oh my! This dress is like a final crescendo in a sonata. Do they have those in sonatas? I'm not sure."

Not to brag, but the dress warranted her response. The dark skirt fell straight, the ivory lace at the split wasn't too showy, and the bodice with the beadwork and satin leaf embroidery created an elegant bit of pizzazz. I shoved Nancy's shoes her way, which could be a bit blocky, but when Cricket put them on, they allowed the hem to barely brush the floor.

"What do you think about the shoes?" I asked, eyeing them critically.

"They're vintage and I think they suit the style. If you went with a strappy sandal, it might look too modern. Well, you may want more modern. This is, after all, your collection. I think the design is vintage enough on its own." Cricket lifted the dress, turning this way and that to get a better look at the shoes.

I nodded. "Yeah, I think I prefer a strappy sandal. You have something nude?"

"If anything, you can rely on me to have the right shoe. And if I don't, then it's an excuse to buy the right shoe," Cricket said, with a wry smile. "Are there any other pieces of Nancy's that we're not using? If so, I think we need to keep everything together so maybe we take it with us tomorrow morning?"

"Good idea." I unpinned the gown so she could step out of it. I would need only about half an hour or so more to sew in the zipper and make the slight adjustments. Then I would slide a plastic cover over the gown, bag up the accessories, and hope Cricket remembered to bring her own sandals. Worst-case scenario, she could wear the vintage satin Chanel shoes. "I have a bit more to do here, and then I'm letting it go. Whatever will be will be with this collection."

"It's a great collection, Ruby. You're going to win," Cricket said, setting her hands on my shoulders and giving me a slight jostle. "Believe in yourself."

"Pot. Kettle." I shook my head. "You know, Cricket, life is hard enough without us making it harder. We have to support each other. You're good at that. But I suck at it. If you want to be a private investigator, then do it. I will support you, and I'm very sorry I made you feel bad about something outside your control. I'm still learning how to be a friend. Don't give up on me, and don't give up on your second career just because I acted like an ass."

Cricket gave me a half smile. "I still have some thinking to do, but it's nice to have your support. Now let's do this. Let's win iSpy and show everyone why Ruby Balthazar is the next fashion star."

I shrugged. "Hell, yes. Let's do that. Who cares that I've been arrested a few times in the past few weeks? You gotta take a few punches on the chin... and throw your own fist sometimes. Can't let the bad things stand in your way, not if you want something badly enough."

Cricket tugged on her clothes and readjusted her ponytail. "And you gotta know when to duck and weave."

"Dang, life is tough." I grinned and headed toward the sewing machine.

"But it's better when you have someone watching your back," Cricket said, giving me a knowing look. "See ya tomorrow morning. Don't forget to set the code and double-check the locks. All we need is to have Nancy's collection go missing."

20

Cricket

It's weird that when you finally come to a decision on something, like giving up on being a private eye, the world conspires to make you doubt everything you thought you knew. That's what I pondered as I drove the long way home, listening to Carole King (my go-to artist for making life's decisions) and turning over Ruby's words. They were guilty ones. It was obvious that my younger friend felt crappy about the things she'd said to me last Saturday. And, yeah, she should feel bad. Because her accusations were harsh. But the question was—were they wrong?

I wasn't sure.

Maybe the conclusions I had leaped to were reactionary. Perhaps I was giving up on my new dream too easily. But there was a better chance I had jumped the gun on this whole new career, glamorizing playing detective to such a degree that I could almost envision who played me in the made-for-TV movie. Reese Witherspoon, by the way. Or maybe pretty Isla Fischer who was so good at being loveable. See? Prone to fantasizing and creating stories in my head, I had spent much my life imagining what wasn't there or making silk purses from sow's ears, which is a really disgusting euphemism if one really thought about it.

As I rolled into my driveway with the crisscross thyme that was the envy of many a Master Gardener even though I did nothing to make it grow other than ensure the sprinklers hit it, I grimaced at the sight of my mother sitting on the porch with Julia Kate, sipping a martini.

I glanced at the clock.

Past her normal cocktail hour. During daylight saving time, Marguerite started earlier.

"Hello, Mama," I called climbing from the car, glad I had redone my ponytail.

"Cricket, you look a mess. I suppose a new shipment arrived today and you've been working in the back?" Marguerite sipped her martini, the two olives wedged onto the rim clinging for dear life.

I hadn't been in the back unloading anything. Telling myself lipstick and pinching my cheeks was enough to detract from the purply smudges beneath my baby blues, I had sallied forth and sold an old trunk, two ginger jars (Chris had returned them, sigh) and a dining room set that had seen too many months at the front of the store. That last one was a real coup considering my shirt was rumpled and I couldn't remember if I had even worn deodorant. "Of course. I would never go out in public like this."

Relief flashed in my mother's eyes, and I nearly ruined everything by smiling. Lord have mercy, the woman was a piece of work.

I said that phrase often. Only because it was true.

"You have dinner yet?" I asked Julia Kate.

"I ate the leftover penne and marinara Daddy got me on Sunday. You think it's still okay to eat, huh?" Julia Kate held her phone in her hand and tapped, focusing on the screen not me.

"Guess we'll know soon enough." I climbed the stairs, realigning my focus on my mother. "You have one of those for me?"

Mama looked at her drink and then at me. "Vodka is in the freezer. Olives in the fridge."

"Well, I knew that much," I muttered.

The house smelled like parmesan cheese and garlic, not the best smell to greet you unless you liked the slight odor of vomit. Pippa came skidding in from the kitchen, her mouth noticeably red. "Oh no."

I stuck my head back out the door. "JK, did you leave your food out?"

"Oh shit." She hopped up, pocketing her phone.

"Watch your language, young lady," Marguerite said, totally affronted but not enough to miss another sip of her cocktail.

"Sorry," Julia Kate said, bypassing me and sliding into the kitchen via the dining room in her socks.

I looked down at Pippa, who looked full of Italian food and happy I was home. "You're a naughty dog, but I get it. Some things are hard to resist when they're just lying there."

An image of Griff popped into my head, and I remembered fondly how good he had looked lying there on the expensive sheets Marguerite gave me, never imagining they would host such delicious activities.

Pippa followed me into the kitchen where Julia Kate mopped up red sauce from the travertine pavers. I grabbed a paper towel and relieved Pippa of her inelegant mustache and then grabbed a martini glass from the fridge along with the vodka and vermouth. Olives were for good days. I padded back out to where my mother sat enjoying the dusk as it settled through the oaks and magnolias that dotted my yard. Mr. Shively swept leaves from his walkway, and Mrs. Ava walked Louie on a leash in her front yard. Louie hunching over, doing his business, was the only wart on the landscape of a perfect autumn evening.

"What are you doing here?" I asked my mother, not that she needed a reason to come by and say hello to her favorite girls. She often popped in unannounced these days, and I cherished that she desired our company.

"We need to talk." My mother looked down at her nearly empty drink.

"We do?"

"I got a call from Georgina Baird this afternoon."

"Really? How is she? I haven't seen her lately, but I saw Jenny at church on Sunday. She looked great. I think she and Marcus just got back from France. They renewed their vows in an old French monastery. Or maybe it was a nunnery. Is that what they call it? A nunnery?"

"Cricket, I have no idea, nor do I care." Marguerite sniffed and drained the last of her drink, setting the empty glass down on the garden stool that served as a table a bit too forcefully. "You've been found out."

"What?"

"Someone told Piper that you were the person who took the photographs. That you were spying on her and framed her." My mother arched her eyebrows in an "I told you this would happen" manner.

The vodka I had just consumed burned a trail down my throat, sinking into a stomach that had dropped a few inches with my mother's revelation. "Piper knows?"

"I told you this would happen."

And there it was. The words that matched the disapproving arc of her brow.

Marguerite continued. "Everyone knows that you're a snoop and a sneak."

"I'm not a snoop or a sneak." I straightened my spine in spite of the dread pooling in my gut. "I'm a private investigator who was contracted to work on the theft-ring case. I have a license to spy."

"You used your friendships and our position in the community to get dirt on our friends. On the daughter of my friend. Now I'm involved in this fiasco. How do you think this looks? It's a betrayal, that's what it is. Poor Piper. Poor Merle. She's the one who called Georgina. She was aghast, I tell you."

"Not aghast," I muttered, trying not to roll my eyes at my mother's theatrics. "Look, I understand it's not ideal, but I wasn't trying to hurt Piper—or anyone for that matter. The fact remains that someone is stealing items from people's houses at parties and get-togethers, and though Piper didn't steal anything that night, someone else did. Shouldn't we keep in the forefront that a crime was committed... and it wasn't by me?"

"No, we should leave investigating crimes to the police." My mother folded her hands, leveling her gaze at me as if I should have already understood this long ago.

"The Shreveport police force is understaffed and focused on violent crimes. A bunch of rich women missing a bracelet or a purse isn't keeping them up at night. That's why Juke was hired. And why I was put on the case. I wasn't doing anything wrong, and if Piper had turned out to be the thief, Georgina would be calling to thank you for raising a daughter smart enough to catch the perpetrator."

"But you haven't caught anyone," my mother said, her words like bullets ripping through my flesh. "That person is still at large. The only thing you've managed to do is isolate us from our friends because you're having a midlife crisis after Scott left you."

My mouth fell open. "He didn't leave me."

But that wasn't true. Even though I had had the last laugh in the end, Scott had gathered his things and moved out before I could tell him to hit the road. He'd left me. That hurt. A lot.

And midlife crisis?

Was that what this was for me? Getting the private investigator license, drinking beer from bottles, sleeping with tow truck drivers—was this my version of a Corvette and hair plugs?

My mother's words carved through my earlier what-ifs after my conversation with Ruby, and suddenly I felt like an utter fool. I shrank back into my rocker, unable to defend myself. "I'm sorry you feel that way."

Marguerite must have sensed that she'd gone too far. "I'm sorry, Cricket. I wasn't trying to hurt you. Only make you see that your actions affect others. Me. Julia Kate. Even Ruby, who has been trying to build a platform to win iSpy. This morning I went to yoga with some friends who were talking about her, speculating if she had gone back to her old ways. I assured them it wasn't true, but her being taken in for questioning this past weekend and that whole Rafe Lasso thing in Manhattan getting out hasn't helped her in this contest."

"And you're more concerned about her, of course." I wished my feelings weren't so hurt, but I was unable to stop the petty words from spilling from my lips.

"What do you mean by that?" My mother leaned forward and looked at me as I stared out at the darkness, trying not to cry. "I thought you wanted me to support Ruby?"

"I did. I do." That much was true, but the chip in the dam of my ego had become a dislodged chunk. Deep, sinful jealousy had shot through, widening the breach, crumbling the wall of defense I had added to for decades. "But you never support me.

On anything I do. From the time I was little and wanted to be a cheerleader to my taking over Grandmother's store. No matter what I do, it isn't good enough or worthy enough of the great Marguerite Quinney's blessing."

"Well, that's just not true," my mother said, sounding offended. "And cheerleading is so noisy and obvious."

"No, it isn't, and you not supporting me is a fact. Tell me a time when you were proud of me? A time when you were there, cheering me on? A time when you didn't tell me to brush my hair, hold my shoulders back, or write a damn thank-you note? When have you given me a crumb of your approval?" All the week's frustration had clumped together into a big ball of anger and hurt. I was tired of taking everyone's crap. Tired of people telling me that I was doing it wrong. That I was at fault. That I screwed things up.

"Cricket, don't use that sort of language with me. It's—"

"What? Offensive? Unladylike? Well, I don't care. I'm tired of trying to please everyone, tired of walking on my tiptoes so I don't annoy anyone with the click of my heels. I want to make noise. I want to cause a ruckus. I want to be unladylike. I like it. It's freeing, something you should try sometimes. I mean if you want to screw John, then do it in Shreveport. No one cares, Mother. You don't have to go to a Bossier City hotel to get it on. If you want to eat a Snickers, watch *The Bachelor*, or dance naked by the light of the moon, do it. Life is too short to worry about what Georgina, Merle, and every other stuck-up, repressed, snobby old bitch in Shreveport thinks about you."

"Cricket!" It was Marguerite's turn to shrink back in her rocker. She was shocked by my words.

Good.

"I mean, for heaven's sake, Marguerite, grow a pair. Tell Georgina to mind her own damn business. That your daughter is a private investigator and nearly fully licensed by the State of

Louisiana. Tell her that I am the catcher of cheaters. The righter of wrongs. The shadow in their yard. And tell them I'm going to figure out who is taking all that shit from people's houses." I rose, grabbed my glass, and chugged the rest of my martini which caused the vodka to shoot up my nose, but I didn't even cough or sneeze. Nope. I stalked off right past my shocked mother and opened the front door. "I think you can see yourself off. I have work to do."

Then I stomped as hard as I could into my house, wishing that I had worn high heels even though they would have looked ridiculous with my jeggings and wrinkled Oxford shirt. It would have had the desired effect.

I shut the door.

Convicted.

That's what I felt. The same way I had months ago when I learned that Scott didn't think I could rock the boat. Gone were my doubts. Gone was the flipping and flopping. My mother would be aghast—ha!—to know that she had moved me exactly where she hadn't wanted me to go.

I had a case to solve.

I fast walked into the kitchen and picked up my tote with the folders I had refused to let Juke keep. Overcome with doubt about my role, I had ignored the spreadsheets over the past few nights. No more stalling. Time to sit down and do the hard work of cross-examining the items for sale, dates they were listed, and the date the seller joined the resale site. If I couldn't catch the thief in the act, I would catch them in the cold hard data the way Juke had suggested. Wasn't as much fun, but catching a thief didn't have to be fun. Just done.

I dumped the bag on my bed, started the shower, and shucked out of my clothes. Ten minutes later, clad in my favorite satin pajama, nursing a cup of tea because the vodka had zipped right to my head, I sank onto the pillows piled against my headboard. In the background I could hear Julia Kate watching television. I hadn't even checked to see if she'd done her homework or let Pippa out to potty.

Well, no one would die over it.

Two hours later, I turned off my lamp and lay in the darkness. I had found nothing worthwhile. None of the dates matched up. No similar usernames on the sites that listed the seller's name. On one site three bracelets like the one stolen were uploaded for sale around the same time period. Same for the other items. Resale sites were popular, and our thief had been smart enough to take pieces that had duplicate offerings. Most sellers didn't offer up their location, but on the ones that did, I found too many in North Louisiana. And a good chunk of that was in Shreveport. I needed an algorithm. Like all those ones they used to pop ads onto your Facebook page or Insta feeds. I needed to find a computer nerd to figure out math stuff to cross run the data and populate results that might matter.

I released a sigh into the darkness, glancing at my phone to note that Griff hadn't taken his turn on Words with Friends. It had been three days since we'd spoken. Three days since we'd played the silly game. What did that mean? What did our night mean to him? Had he even thought about me at all?

My phone dinged, but it was just Carla Monzingo letting me know she'd found a dog for Eddie, the special needs child. One little victory in this exhausting roller coaster of a day. I texted back my thanks, hit the white noise sound on my clock, and turned over, inviting sleep to take me. Information weaved in and out, intentions and to-dos fading into weird, dreamlike images.

Daisy Duck Lover. Chanel. What word should I play next? Depended on...

Poconos Cowgirl.

Wait.

I sat up and reached for the laptop I had abandoned. I knew that last nickname, and it had been a username on one of the resale sites. I clicked, scrolled, clicked.

And there it was.

Poconos_Cowgirl_825.

"Holy shit." I looked up at my face which glowed in the dresser mirror across my room. I knew that name. I knew those numbers. "I know who the thief is."

21

Cricket

I SPRANG OUT OF BED, knocking the spreadsheets on the nightstand to the floor.

Didn't matter. I didn't need them any longer.

Because when the epiphany came, everything fell into place, and I saw exactly the game that was afoot.

And I was going to stop it.

Tonight.

I shucked off my pajama pants, hopping on one foot toward the bathroom en suite. I knocked my knee on the door-frame, yelped a really bad word that would have shocked my mother, and then stripped off my pajama top. No time for a bra, I pulled on the sweatshirt I had tossed onto my tufted bench Sunday night telling myself I would put it away later. That had never happened. Fortuitous. I found a pair of jeans draped over the cabinet in my closet and tugged on my running shoes without socks, which was sort of *ew* but not enough to stop me.

I ran out of my bathroom, through my room, and down the stairs. Julia Kate had left the television on, but not even that waste of electricity could stop me. Grabbing my keys, I opened the garage before doubling back for my phone.

One point two minutes later I was backing down the drive while simultaneously calling Juke.

"Pick up, pick up, pick up," I chanted, nothing that it was ten forty-five and probably plenty early enough to get the jump on the thief.

"You've reached North Star Investigations. We are unable to take your call at the moment...," Juke intoned.

"Crap." I pushed the End button. Better try again. Yeah, it was late, but not ridiculously late, and Juke had been tailing cheating spouses. He should be up.

The beeps of his phone number sounded on the Bluetooth microphone of my car as I took a corner too fast and nearly ran over a jogger. I waved an apology, and the dude might have flipped me off. Well, he shouldn't have been so close to the middle of the street and wearing dark clothes. The HOA had asked time and again for joggers and walkers to wear reflective clothing when it was dark. *Read your newsletter, for heaven's sake.*

I made it to the back of the neighborhood, drumming my fingers as I waited for the gate to open at the speed of a slug while also waiting for Juke to cycle through all his instructions for leaving a message.

"Juke, this is Cricket. I know who it is. I'm heading out to stop her. Call me when you get this message. I may need backup."

I clicked my phone off and thought about calling Ruby. She would probably be awake, unable to sleep because of her nerves. But what could she do? I didn't want her rattled. She had to be on her game tomorrow. This was something I could handle now that I knew what game was being played.

Juke would get my message.

Unless he didn't.

Shit. Just a month ago, he disappeared, and no one had been able to find him. Three or four days of nothing. Would the man have gone on another meditation retreat? Or maybe he meditated at night or didn't answer the phone after a certain time. He had no children, so he wasn't like every mother I knew—phone never on silent at night.

A ding sounded on my phone as I finally pulled through the gate. Griff making his move on Words with Friends.

I picked up the phone and dialed his number. It rang over my Bluetooth.

"'lo?"

"Griff, it's Cricket," I said.

"Hey, I just put in my word. Sorry for—"

"Never mind about that. Do you know where Juke is? He's not answering his phone."

"Dude, I'm not his keeper. If he's not answering, he's probably asleep or on a date."

A date? I didn't realize Juke had started dating again. Good for him. "Okay, well, um, I think I figured out who is stealing all the stuff and why. Or maybe stealing all that stuff was the initial plan that didn't work, but anyway, I'm on my way to my store to stop the steal. So if you happen to talk to Juke—"

"You're not going by yourself, are you?" He sounded alarmed.

"I have to."

"No. Call that dipshit you've been dating."

"He's not a dipshit, and that's probably a good idea. But I don't know. I mean, I could be wrong, and if I am, I'll feel really stupid. I've already messed up two or three times already. And thing is, if it's who I think it is, I have to catch her in the act.

Otherwise, I'm not sure I can prove it." My mind raced as I thought about the police investigating the databases of the resale sites. They could probably get the information to trace back to the thief, but it would take a long time. They would need warrants. Before they could get a warrant to get into those systems, they would need enough evidence to justify it.

Fact was I needed to catch this person in the act. Once I saw that I was right about the thief, I could call 911 and have them come and catch her stealing the Parrington collection. "I'll call the police. I promise."

Then I hung up because I didn't want to deal with Griff or hear about how I wasn't capable of preventing someone from stealing priceless coats, gloves, and jewelry. It's not that I was being stubborn. Okay, maybe a little stubborn. I wanted to catch the thief. I needed this in my life. To be good at something more than spotting diamonds under coats of dust. Still, I wasn't so stubborn that I wouldn't be careful. As I hit the on-ramp that would take me into the heart of Shreveport and Printemps, I opened my glove box and rooted around for the pepper spray Scott had bought me the time I'd gone to New Orleans. I found it and set it on the seat next to me. Then I grabbed a dark scrunchie and pulled my hair up so that it was tight and out of the way.

Fifteen minutes later, I turned off Line Avenue onto the street beside Printemps. The front of the store was dark as always, but there was a light on upstairs.

Bingo.

I drove past the parking area because it was gravel and would make noise when I pulled in. And there was the little issue of headlights. As I drove past, I noticed Ruby's car in the parking lot.

"What in the hell?" I whispered to myself, ignoring the ringing of my phone. It was Griff. Not Juke. I didn't have time for his fussing or warnings. I wasn't an idiot. All I needed was to put eyes on the perp, and then I would call the police.

But Ruby was a complication.

Wait. Dak could have picked her up. Just because her car was in the parking lot didn't mean that Ruby was upstairs. But if she were still working, then the thief wouldn't show up until she left. So that meant I was in time to set up surveillance and record everything. If I were a betting woman, I would say the thief would appear right when Ruby left.

I pulled into a driveway in the neighborhood behind the store, turned around, and then pulled to the curb where I would have a clear view of the back door and Ruby's car. I killed my engine and looked at the clock. Just now eleven o'clock.

Picking up my phone, ignoring the little green boxes with Griff's *Pick up, damn it,* I dialed Ruby's number.

It went to voice mail.

Not a big deal. Ruby was of the generation who rarely answered. I texted instead.

You up?

No response. Which, again, not a big deal. If Ruby were upstairs, she'd be working. Might take her a few minutes, but she always responded quickly. Generationally speaking, people Ruby's age were never far from their phones, unlike Juke whose generation rarely texted. Juke always called.

I tried again.

Where are you? Need to talk.

No bubbles. No response.

Huh.

I sat there a few minutes more, and then I got this weird feeling. Like something was wrong.

Now I had just had a conversation with Juke on Monday about gut feelings and not chasing wild hairs. He was right. Facts were facts. But every mother knows that there are these feelings you get when someone is sneaking gin from the butler's pantry or someone is watching porn on the family iPad. It's the feeling you have when you know friends were just talking about you right before you walked up. Or the feeling you get when you go a different route home only to find out that someone was carjacked at the intersection where you normally stop. That last one probably only happens in Shreveport, but anyway, I had that exact feeling. Like Ruby was in trouble, and I didn't need to wait any longer.

I sucked in a deep breath, grabbed the pepper spray, and flicked the little button that stopped the interior lights from coming on when the door opened. I had learned that little trick from a book I read and knew it would come in handy one day. Thankfully, I wore dark clothing though my tennis shoes had fluorescent swooshes. Cool air rushed around me, and I shivered as I tried to close the van door as quietly as possible. I slid the keys into one pocket, my phone already switched to silent in the other. I kept the pepper spray canister in my hand as I strolled up the sidewalk, careful to stay in the shadows and away from the streetlights. The motion sensor light in the parking lot would come on, and the security camera should have alerted me to anyone who had entered the building. But as I approached the back of the old house that served as my antiques store, I noted the security camera's little red light wasn't on—which meant the security system wasn't on. The motion sensor light didn't come on either. I glanced up at it and noted something coating the sensor. The only light was from the streetlight.

I darted toward the stairs, knowing I looked suspicious. If anyone in the neighborhood saw me, they would call the police.

Which might be a good thing.

I patted my pocket with the phone and then shifted to the pocket holding my keys as I slowly and stealthy walked up the steps. Pulling the keys from my pocket, I held them tight so they wouldn't jangle. Of course I had too many on my leather loop keyring. Scott used to make fun of me keeping all the keys I ever owned on one key chain. Now for once, I wished I had listened to him and cleaned them off. But as I stretched to insert the key into the lock, I noted the door wasn't closed all the way.

Whoa.

My thief was here.

And probably Ruby too. Which meant my friend was in big trouble. Or not. I mean, Ruby had been to prison. I might find her sewing away, the thief tied up in a corner awaiting her finishing a hem. Surviving two years of a correctional institution tended to make a person very aware of being sneaked up on. If Ruby was even here.

Which I wasn't sure.

What I did know is that someone was in my antiques store.

And she was up to no good.

22

Ruby

I KICKED against the double doors of the closet one more time, yelling against the duct tape over my mouth. My hands were firmly bound behind me with that clingy mover's wrap we used on carpets because that bitch obviously knew how to truss up a person.

Who would have guessed it of that woman?

Doors in these old houses weren't cheaply made and held up well. The doorknobs were made of heavy steel or iron and didn't budge. I suspected that a chair was wedged beneath the old glass knobs for good measure. The skeleton key that locked the large linen closet had been removed as well, so even though I had managed to inchworm my way forward, I wasn't going to be able to bust out.

I suppose I should be glad that I was still alive.

Because someone had a plan in place, and I was pretty sure that part of her plan was now for me to cease to breathe.

I reared my feet back and kicked again.

Nothing.

I lay back and wished for the fifteenth time in the past half hour that I hadn't stayed at Printemps as long as I had.

After Cricket left, I had set about getting that gown just right. As the hallmark of the collection, I wanted it to be perfect. No uneven hems, no crooked seams, no wonky darts. Perfection. Ensuring all this took longer than I thought it would. And I might have gotten distracted by social media. Going to the iSpy Fashion page on Facebook was a time suck, and then I'd fallen down the rabbit hole looking up old Insta and YouTube posts about my competition. The hours sped by, I texted Resa some crap about my competitors, and then tried to downplay the nerves performing *Rent* in my gut. I snooped on their profiles then sewed. Read comments then sewed. Ate some M&M's and put in the zipper for the gown.

As I worked (and wasted time on social media) I kept turning over Cricket's words about her pursuing the private investigation thing and then my own situation. Cecile Smart had called twice, and I knew I couldn't run from her much longer. She wanted more for me, had already set up tentative interviews and meets. But she was adamant—eventually I would need to go to New York City. Or Paris. Or Milan. Or London. Some place where fashion was more than a cute sundress from the mall. I could go all in and leave Shreveport to pursue a career in the Big Apple, or reside on the fringes of fashion, designing on a smaller scale, building myself year after year on my own timeline. Essentially, it boiled down to did I want to stay in my lane or take the off-ramp? Drive the Volvo or climb into the Maserati?

Fact was, I really didn't know. My lane was taking me somewhere. I wasn't off to the side changing a flat tire or anything.

And Volvos were nice. You could buckle infant seats in the back, haul bikes to the mountains, pull a trailer with wood for the gazebo I wanted at the lake.

I glanced at the clock—ten o'clock on Thursday night. Then I sighed and plugged the steamer in. The dress would need to be steamed before the runway event, but I needed to make sure one seam was even, and that meant taking some of the memory out of the fabric. While the steamer heated, I went downstairs to grab a sparkling water and see if Jade had left any of the cookies Chris had brought by. I didn't bother with the kitchen light, just opened the snack tin and spied one cookie left. Poor thing was beat up and crumbling, but I wasn't choosy when it came to tea cakes, so I grabbed it and started back up the stairs. And that's when I heard the kitchen door open.

Weird.

I started to double back down, thinking that Cricket or Jade might have left something, when I got a strange feeling.

I reversed and scampered as quietly and quickly as I could up the stairs. My phone was in the studio, and I felt like I was going to need it, so I darted back into the room, scanning for where I had laid it. But I didn't see it. When had I had it last?

Sounds below told me that whoever was in the store was starting up the stairs.

"Shit," I whispered, panicking because I was all alone, and my stupid phone wasn't in sight. I recalled Dak teasing me about always leaving it somewhere, and I berated myself for being so forgetful.

Footsteps on the stairs. And an odd banging sound. Like someone was dragging something.

I had to hide.

What was this person doing? Why would they come upstairs? The register was downstairs, along with the safe, though I knew very well that Cricket didn't leave money in the register anyway. But whoever it was hadn't messed with the office or anything in the antiques store. They had headed for the stairs which meant...

Oh shit. They were going to steal my designs.

Was this sabotage?

I had started moving toward the covered racks of clothes that would go to the Municipal Auditorium where the competition was being held, but if they were here to steal my clothing or destroy it, I would be found. Darting my gaze back and forth over the room, I lunged to the nearest closet where Cricket kept boxes of magazines and books. She constantly claimed she needed to clean it out, so it was a tight fit. I sucked in and shut the door, leaving it open just a crack.

I tried to slow my breathing. My pulse galloped, and I could hear the beat of my heart in my ears. Closing my eyes, I concentrated on slowing down my body's fight-or-flight response. Breathe in. Slowly. One, two, three. Then out through the mouth. Quietly. One, two, three.

Whoever was there to destroy my collection thumped into the room. Sounded like a rolling suitcase. Slowly I shifted, trying to see who it was, but couldn't see anything through the narrow slit in the door.

But someone was definitely there. No figment of my imagination.

The suitcase or whatever it was started up again, along with the slight squeak of footsteps. Tennis shoes. Whoever it was wore sneakers. I felt a shadow cross me as the person moved toward the collection. Every fiber of my being screamed to stop... her.

I could just make out a woman with strawberry-blondish hair. Slight. Black ball cap. Black yoga pants and a tight dark athletic jacket. She looked like any other socialite heading to barre class. If she'd held a Starbucks iced latte in her hand, the look would have been complete. Or one of those expensive-ass water bottles with her monogrammed initials. She paused in front of my worktable, and I noted the steamer puffing away.

Crappola.

Then my phone jittered.

My stupid cell phone had been under the scrap of leftover fabric I had tested the steamer on.

Shit.

She stilled. Then turned her head to the steamer with its red light glowing and the phone beneath the fabric.

Unaware of the danger, my phone jittered a merry little dance. Then it stilled before emitting a little ding. Text message.

The woman reached out and picked up my phone. Her hands were small, nails freshly manicured. She read the text. Then set the phone down.

Her head turned as she surveyed the room.

Cammie?

What in the hell was going on? Why would Cammie Rio be here to sabotage my collection? She was one of the people helping me. She'd been the one with the idea to loan Nancy's collection to me for the competition. She'd said it would bring interest and then maybe Nancy would relent and let the Louisiana Museum display the collection. I glanced at her feet. At the rolling suitcase that seemed empty.

Then it hit me.

She wasn't here to sabotage my collection. She was here to steal her mother's things. Like cogs turning in a lock, my mind whirred. Click. Click. Click.

She wanted the insurance money.

That's why she'd insisted on Cricket taking out that big policy to cover the collection. Cammie was stealing the six-figure stoles and jewelry so she could file an insurance claim. Holy guacamole.

And now she knew I was in the store.

"Ruby?" she called.

My eyes widened. Oh crap. What should I do? I could jump out and pick up the steamer and hit her with it. The large scissors were lying right beside—

Cammie picked up those monster shears.

They were big—I cut heavy materials with those suckers. If she stabbed me with them, they would do damage. Hell, I had seen one woman at Long Pines shivved with a plastic spoon to the jugular. She'd nearly bled out before the corrections officer got to her.

I swallowed hard and waited. Better she come looking for me.

Her head swung from side to side as she sussed out my potential location. There was a double-door closet at the back of the room. Or I could be down the hall in the bathroom. Or any other room upstairs or down for that matter. Cammie released the handle of the suitcase and walked around the table holding Cricket's dress. She lifted the bodice and let it fall, and I could see her mind turning over the possibilities.

"Ruby? It's Cammie. I had forgotten to bring the Dior shrug for the gown you made. You still here?" She frowned when there was no answer. Her eyes swept the room. Landed on this closet. She narrowed her gaze, moving toward me.

Shit.

Fine. When she got close, I would fling the door open, knock her down, kick her in the head, and then run. That was a solid plan.

Except she moved so that I couldn't see what she was doing through the crack. She was on the other side now, out of my line of sight. She seemed to sense I was there and would give me no advantage. If I flung the door open, it may or may not hit her.

Suddenly, the door sprang open, and something swung toward me.

Something hard.

My head exploded, and I saw stars. Literal flashing stars. The floor rushed toward me, and I hit the hard oak, my cheek breaking my fall. Then there was an explosion of pain in my side. She'd kicked me in the ribs.

"That's right," Cammie muttered, jumping on top of me and holding me down as I began to struggle. "You aren't so smart, are you?"

I wasn't. I should have jumped out the moment she rolled into the room thinking it was empty.

Pretty dumb.

But of course I didn't have time to think about this because… pain. "What are you—"

Then I stilled because she had the open scissors at my throat.

"You're going to behave." Cammie eased off me, jamming the steel blade into my neck hard enough to probably draw blood. "Stand up. No funny business neither or I will shove this right into your throat."

This was insane.

Cammie, sweet Lily Pulitzer–wearing, gingham-tote-carrying, PTA-momming Cammie Rio was holding a blade to my throat and talking like she'd done this fairly often. Cricket often joked that society girls would cut you if you got in their way, but I didn't think she meant literally.

I held my hands up and scrabbled to my knees. "Cammie, what are you doing?"

"I'm sure you've figured it out by now. This collection is worth a lot, but it's worth even more in insurance money. And I need that money." She sounded so matter-of-fact. "Keep your hands where I can see them and sit on that stool. Right there."

She kept the scissors at my throat as I sank onto the stool. Blood dripped in my eye, and my ribs pulsated. She might have cracked one with that kick. Damn it. I could hardly breathe.

What should I do?

Once she took the blade away, I could tackle her. She had a slight frame even though she was fit. I don't know what she'd hit me with earlier, but if I could find it, I could use it to my advantage.

She withdrew the blade, and I started forward.

But then something slammed into my head.

And I didn't remember anything else.

When I came to, I was in a dark space, head pounding, ankles and wrists bound, and mouth taped. Based on the clink of glass in the boxes I brushed against, I knew I was in the back closet of the sewing studio where Cricket stored the extra Fostoria and other pieces of china and silver plate. Cammie had knocked me out with something heavy—I could still taste blood in my mouth. While I was down, she'd been efficient in incapacitating me. I remembered waking briefly when she dragged me but sank back into unconsciousness when she'd let my head fall against the closet floor. Then I had been out for a few minutes or so.

I had to do something to stop her.

Mostly because I knew she couldn't leave me as a witness. I knew everything now.

But could Cammie really kill me in cold blood?

I stomped on the closet again even though my head hurt like the devil.

The door flew open, the light from the room blinding me.

"Stop it," Cammie hissed, her face twisted into rage. "You screwed everything up, you stupid bitch. Now you're making me do things I don't want to do."

She was angry at me. Like a child. Behind her I could see

that she'd ripped the bags from the outfits they'd been paired with. The suitcase was open, now filled with the collection her mother had doted upon. I could see a swatch of the Chanel cape, the ochre satin lining face up.

"I'm leaving the door open so you can stop all that banging. Neighbors might hear you." She turned and went back to pulling items from each duster bag I had painstakingly stored the valuable gloves, jewelry, and wraps in. She wasn't careful. Just tossed them pell-mell into the case.

I struggled to sit up, trying to ignore my head which thumped as if a thousand tiny elves with pick axes were carving out my skull. My vision swam, but I persisted, catching sight of a piece of metal that stuck out from the jamb. The framework around the double-door closet was old, and the placard that held one door to the floor had a sharp edge sticking up. I scooted closer to the metal piece knowing that it would slice through the flimsy plastic wrap which was cutting off my damn circulation.

"Cammie!"

I jerked my head up at the same time Cammie did.

Cricket stood in the doorway, holding a canister of pepper spray like it was a gun. Which any other time might have been amusing, but at this moment wasn't so much. "You can stop that right now. This whole thing is over. I'm calling 911 right now."

"Cricket!" Cammie froze, shaking her head. "No, wait."

Cricket hesitated. "Why are you doing this? This is crazy. Your mother loves these things. They are her legacy from your aunt. Surely, you aren't planning to—"

"What?" Cammie asked, her hands falling into the folds of the Chanel cloak. "Destroy this? It's just a cloak. A piece of fabric."

"Yeah, but I don't understand why you would do this. Was it you? You were the person taking the things from people's houses? Why?" Cricket eased into the room, her voice conversational, like they were at a Junior League meeting and not a standoff during a serious crime.

Don't trust her, Cricket. Call the cops.

My silent messages weren't received because Cricket kept moving toward her friend like she didn't know that Cammie's cheese had slid off her cracker. Cricket hadn't seen me yet. Or maybe she had? I wasn't sure. Her present focus was on her friend. I sawed faster now that Cammie's attention was occupied.

"Why? Because the restaurants are bankrupt. We have to close both of them. And our house is about to be foreclosed on. The boys' tuition is two months late." Cammie sank onto the stool, dragging it over, looking distraught and not at all like the lunatic who'd assaulted me.

I caught sight of the old-fashioned iron that Cricket used to prop doors open. Cammie had beaten the shit out of me with that thing, and it was close at hand.

"But surely your mother—"

"Ah." Cammie smiled giving a bitter chuckle. "Mama's money is gone. Dried up. We're just a family of pretense now. Mother has been selling furniture and paintings for years. Oh, not here. Dallas. She would never let anyone in Shreveport know our family was essentially destitute. We're Parringtons, don't you know. We have a wing at the art gallery. Bought the steeple for the church. Streets are named after my grandfather and his brothers. The restaurants were supposed to give us breathing room. Then came COVID, inflation, recession. All the fun stuff that shutters businesses."

Cricket fell silent. "I didn't know."

"You wouldn't. That's the way we wanted it. And this stuff," Cammie picked up a glove and examined it. "It's just old stuff. Yeah, the queen may have worn these, but it's just a glove. You can buy them at Walmart. The insurance money would have held off the creditors until we could rebound in some way. It's just stupid stuff, Cricket."

"But it's a crime. Just like all those purses and jewelry you stole. From our friends." Cricket sounded so sad. I could feel the plastic shredding. I had slipped and cut my wrist, but I knew what Cricket hadn't figured out—Cammie wasn't letting us go.

I wasn't sure what she was going to do to us, but it wouldn't be good.

"Do you know how much useless stuff our friends have? Do you really think Carol Sue will miss that Louis Twist? Her husband has enough money to buy her five more and never miss it. And all the other girls, same thing. Hell, Bo Dixie didn't even realize her bracelet was missing for two months. But it didn't matter. I couldn't sell that stuff fast enough to make a difference. Poor David is at his wits' end. I keep worrying that one day I'll find him dead. I mean, it's that bad. And my boys are already starting in on going to Vail with their friends for the holidays. I had to do something. It was all on me. You know how that is, Cricket. It's always on the women to pick up the pieces and make do. I sold a few of my things on resale sites and made good money. I was able to pay the tuition. I even made a payment on the note at the bank. I just needed a little more money and a little more time. And our friends had all that stuff."

Cricket looked solemn. Maybe sympathetic. "I get it. Life is tough for a lot of people right now. Just close the suitcase and we'll go downstairs. I can fix us some tea. We can chat and figure things out together. Like we used to when we were little and messed up. Remember when we broke the pool pump?"

My wrist restraints gave away, and I was free.

Victory.

But with my feet bound, I couldn't do much. I needed to undo the plastic on my ankles. Carefully, I twisted my knees, praying Cricket didn't look my way. At this point, Cammie had forgotten about me. I slid them to the side and searched for the end that was stuck to the plastic, ripping it with my nails, praying that I could unwind the stupid stuff in time.

"I wish I could, Cricket, but it's too late for that." Cammie seemed sad about that. Maybe she was.

"It's not. You can return the things. Or just face the consequences. Sometimes we have to, you know," Cricket said, holding up her phone and starting to dial.

And that's when I saw movement behind Cricket.

A gun.

Pointed at the back of her head.

"Put the phone down, dear."

23

Cricket

THE PRESSURE of a gun pressed to the back of your head is enough to make you pee a little.

I totally did.

Ruby had managed to free herself and seemed to be doing a good job of looking like she hadn't. Out of my periphery, I could see her against the doorjamb of the double closet, a bit banged up, blood tickling down her forehead. I didn't look fully at her because I didn't want to draw Cammie's attention to Ruby being partially free from her restraints.

"Christ, Mama, I told you to stay in the car," Cammie said.

I won't lie. I felt shocked to my very core learning that the person holding a gun on me was Nancy Parrington. This was a woman who'd put Band-Aids on my knees when I'd fallen trying to skateboard down her driveway. She'd taught me how to apply mascara. Baked cookies with me and Cammie. Always made sure I was buckled up in the car. My second mama. Marguerite's best friend. Stealer of her own collection. Holder of the gun.

Even with cold steel pressed to the base of my skull, my heart broke apart.

Of course it explained why things had gone missing from different houses with no commonality of invited persons. Cammie had covered her friends' houses, Nancy her own friends. A dynamic duo of society thieves.

"You should be glad I didn't stay in the car. I saw Cricket slinking around and knew you were in trouble. And I was correct. Cricket was about to call the police. But thankfully I had your father's Colt .45 under the front seat of my car. You're welcome." Nancy sounded the way she always did. Imperious and Southern, she made you feel silly for not agreeing with her, but in a Georgia highbrow way that made you forgive her automatically for being so high on her horse.

Well, I wasn't forgiving her for this.

"I have things under control, Mama," Cammie said, sounding her typical self—put out with her mother.

"Mrs. Nancy, y'all can't do this. This is crazy," I said, holding my hands aloft, my phone clutched in my hand.

"Well, sugar, I would agree. It is, indeed, insane, but once my daughter embarked on this fool's errand, I was forced to help. That's all there is to it. She couldn't have pulled it off by herself."

Cammie frowned. "I could have. The whole thing was my idea. And it's still going to work. Just not how I planned."

My former friend looked at me. And I saw that Cammie's plan had changed because Ruby and I knew what was going on.

"Cricket, I'm going to need you to toss your phone over toward that table please," Nancy said as if she were asking me to take some more punch to the ladies in her Bible study. "We can't have the police coming. Not yet."

I did as she asked, pleased with myself for having already texted Detective Wes McNally before entering the room in the first place. I had filmed Cammie stuffing the suitcase with the collection for good measure, even though I didn't have context as Juke suggested I should have in every investigation. But I knew the context. I wasn't born yesterday. When I had seen that username, I had remembered Cammie's love for horses growing up and how she'd worn stirrup pants and saved her birthday money for a fancy Western saddle. Every year their family joined her father's family at one of those old-fashioned hotels in the Poconos where Cammie would ride and enter competitions. Her father had called her his little Poconos cowgirl. She'd even worn an airbrushed T-shirt with those words on it. I had forgotten all about it until I saw one of the David Yurman bracelets listed under that seller's name.

Then I started thinking about how Cammie had pushed for a large insurance policy to cover the collection while it was on loan. She'd cited the recent string of car burglaries around Printemps as her reasoning. I had agreed because we'd had a few burglaries in the area. Which is why I had updated the security system too. Her request on her mother's behalf hadn't struck me as odd. More like responsible and sensible for our city these days with the skyrocketing crime. Thing was, when I saw that username and all the dots connected, I just sort of knew what she planned. Mostly because it's what I would have done if I were a thief. Insurance fraud was hard to prove and lucrative.

Thankfully, Wes had responded to my text and the video I sent him. He'd relayed that he was en route and was sending several units to my antiques store.

I hadn't planned on confronting Cammie. I had watched her via the full-length mirror that leaned against the wall that Ruby had placed there for fitting the collection on her models. I had stayed behind the open door and filmed without Cammie knowing I was there. It was only when I caught Ruby's movement from the peripheral and spotted the blood that I knew Cammie wasn't just a thief. She was dangerous.

I wasn't sure if Wes and the cavalry would make it before Cammie did something more to Ruby. My former friend had been nearly done in looting her mother's collection. I figured she couldn't take on two of us with no weapon. So I took the calculated risk.

I just hadn't planned on two thieves.

"What are you going to do to me?" I asked, trying to stall. I thought I heard sirens but maybe not. Wes knew that Cammie was stealing the collection. He might have told them to come quietly. I had no clue.

Cammie inhaled deeply. "Well, if your stupid friend Ruby had gone home when she was supposed to, then we would have taken the collection, staged a break in, and no one would be the wiser. Tomorrow morning, we would have been shocked, dismayed, and sad that Mother's aunt's collection had been stolen, probably to be sold on the black market."

"The black market?" I asked.

"Yes, Cricket. There are private collectors who desire these sorts of collectibles. I already checked. Plenty of people acquire priceless items via sellers who aren't as scrupulous as, say, Sotheby's. Why do you think so many paintings and sculptures are still missing from World War II? Pillagers don't like to be discovered, but they can be found if you know the right people to ask."

"You're going to get the insurance money and still sell the collection?" I asked, sensing that Nancy was getting a little tired of holding that heavy gun. I could feel her hand dropping. Maybe she wasn't being so attentive.

"I told you, Cricket. We need the money." Cammie sounded exasperated. Maybe irritated. Put out with the whole thing.

"Mother is opposed to selling, but sometimes we do what we must. Our family name is worth more."

"But we know about everything." I winced as Nancy repositioned her grip.

"Well, that's the really sad part. There's going to be an unfortunate accident. Ruby accidentally left the steamer on, and it malfunctioned or maybe fell over, igniting some fabric that was too near"—Cammie picked up a bottle of solvent that Ruby used to clean buttons and other bits she used for her reconstructions—"this flammable stuff. You and Ruby were here working late. Before I left this afternoon, I overheard her saying she needed to remake something, and you'd need to come back to the store to be fitted. By the time the firemen get here, Printemps will be a total loss, and you and Ruby... well, it's not what we wanted."

"You're going to *kill* us?" I asked, truly shocked that Cammie and Nancy were going to let us die over money. "How about I just loan you some cash?"

I tried to turn to Nancy. "Mrs. Nancy, my mama can help. You know she will."

"Young lady, you turn around before this gun accidentally goes off." Nancy jabbed my nape with the barrel. "Cammie's correct. This is not what either of us desire, but our hands have been forced."

"You can just walk away. Go ahead. Ruby and I won't say anything."

"Sugar, why didn't you just stay out of all this mess? You and this whole private eye ridiculousness, and when we found out you were helping that dead beat private detective investigate the thefts—good heavens, Cricket—your mother was just appalled."

"Mrs. Nancy, you can't do this. I'm your best friend's daughter."

"I'll help your mother through your death, Cricket. She'll be strong for Julia Kate. We all will be. But it's your fault. If you and

Ruby would have just made better choices, this wouldn't have happened." Nancy sighed the way she had when she'd made the decision to put her cat Sparkles down. Sad, but determined. Nothing more she could do.

It was at this moment that I saw something in the leaning mirror. Something big. Something moving our way. Something about to hit Mrs. Nancy like a locomotive engine.

Griff.

I met Ruby's gaze right as I braced for impact.

"Ruby! Move!" I shouted.

Suddenly the gun was gone from the back of my head. Nancy just sort of disappeared behind me as steam-engine Griff thumped into us. I went down, breaking my fall with my hands. Behind me Nancy yelped as she hit the floor hard, completely tackled by the six-foot-three tow truck driver. I heard the revolver clatter to the floor, and at the same time, Cammie screamed. Thank God. Ruby had gone for Cammie.

I rolled to the side, coming up on my knees, my gaze searching for the gun.

The Colt .45 had skittered across the floor toward the mirror. I crawled there as Griff struggled to stop the slippery Nancy from going for the gun herself. I reached the revolver right before my mother's best friend did, flipping onto my back, and holding it out like I was freaking Dirty Harry.

I swear to God, I almost said, "Go ahead. Make my day."

Which would have been so cool, and at the same time, so cringe, as Julia Kate would say.

Nancy froze at the sight of the barrel trained on her. Her normally coiffed hair was sticking out, her silk blouse ripped at the collar, and her aged hand, once outstretched toward the gun, dropped to the floor.

Ruby reached my side just as Griff hauled Nancy to her feet, clasping her to him in a bear hug that ensured she wasn't getting away. I turned my head and noted Cammie lying on the floor, moaning. Ruby had gotten her with that antique iron I used to hold open doors. Blood dripped from my former friend's strawberry blonde hair with the highlights I had just complimented her on that afternoon. Cammie didn't look like she would be getting up soon.

"Are you okay?" Ruby asked, her eyes wide, her breathing shallow. She looked like she could be going into shock.

"I'm fine, but you're hurt," I said.

"She hit me with the iron and kicked me in the ribs," Ruby said, blinking. Yeah, she could be going into shock.

I wrapped my friend in a hug, careful with her ribs. "Oh my God. Oh my God, Ruby."

Maybe I was going into shock too, because I began to tremble, and my legs felt weirdly shaky. During the confrontation I had been ice, but now I was noodle-legged and weepy.

Red and blue lights flashed in the windows, and this time I could tell the sirens were on. Thank God.

"Stop struggling, old lady, before I knock your lights out," Griff growled at Nancy who, resembled a kitten caught by a coyote. Cammie groaned and then started crying in defeat. The gig was up. She knew that their family name wasn't going to be saved. Neither was her house or her restaurants. Her two boys, bless them, were going to be thrust into a spotlight they didn't deserve. I would share Julia Kate's therapist's name with David. They were going to need a lot of sessions to get over this.

The sound of Wes and company coming up the stairs was comforting enough for me to release Ruby. But Ruby hadn't gotten that memo and was clinging to me the way Julia Kate used to when she'd had a nightmare. So I just held her.

I turned her so I could see Wes who entered with his gun drawn.

"What... what's happened?" he asked, looking at Griff who still held Nancy prisoner.

"I wish I knew," Griff said, jerking his head toward me. "I'm guessing. But I think these two women are the ones who've been stealing things. And it looks like they were going to steal something here?"

I squeezed Ruby to let her know that I had to release her and clear up some things. "It's like I texted you—they were going to steal their own collection for the insurance money."

"We were not," Nancy shrieked, struggling against Griff. "She's lying. She's crazy."

I looked at Wes and the men behind her. "I'm not crazy, which is a horrible thing to say about anyone, Nancy."

Ruby wiped her face. "Except not to these two. They're not only thieves; they were planning to kill me. And Cricket. They were going to make it look like an accident, lighting the place on fire and letting us die. That's the definition of crazy."

"She's lying," Nancy said, stomping her foot on Griff's boot. He gave her a shake.

Wes's gaze swept the room, pausing on the open suitcase with the accessories spilling out and then on Cammie who lay crying on the floor. "Is that the stuff they were stealing? The stuff in the video you sent?"

Ruby seemed to have shaken her momentary shock off. She turned to the open suitcase sitting above the prone Cammie. "This collection came from Mrs. Parrington's aunt's estate and is very valuable. They took out a large insurance policy on it when they loaned it to me for my runway show."

I joined in. "Cammie admitted to me that she's been stealing the purses and jewelry from our friends. They hatched this scheme only because she couldn't move those things quickly enough. If you take a look at the Parrington and Rio finances, I think you'll find your motive. They are overextended and essentially broke. And I have her confession on my phone—though I didn't have her permission to tape her, so it's probably inadmissible. But I think you're smart enough to find all the evidence and build the case."

"You hush your mouth, Catherine Ann," Nancy hissed, looking more unhinged than her daughter was, which was saying a lot considering Cammie was planning on roasting me and Ruby.

"You know what, Nancy?" I gave her the same look I gave my daughter when she'd done something incredibly stupid. "If you had just been honest and real about your situation, it wouldn't have come to this. I could have helped you sell your collection for a nice profit, and Mama would have been supportive. Instead, you allowed your pride to lead you to a place of crime. So don't you tell me to hush. I didn't steal from my friends, plan insurance fraud, or try to kill someone. You did."

"I did nothing wrong. Nothing. And don't act like you or your mother would have done anything to help us. We're alone in this world, and it's up to us to take care of ourselves." Nancy tried to stomp again, but Griff had learned his lesson and set her down.

"We can sort everything down at the station. Booker, cuff the older lady and send for EMS. That one looks like she needs some attention." Wes holstered his gun and reached for his cuffs, walking toward Cammie, who hadn't moved much or stopped crying. Cammie knew it was over. Pride goeth before a fall, and she was down for the count despite her mother's proclamations.

"You're wrong. Friends support one another. They show up. Even when you're at your worst," Ruby said, wincing and gingerly touching her head where she'd been hit.

I nodded, sliding my hand into Ruby's. She squeezed it. "Even when they mess up."

Wes helped Cammie sit up. "Ma'am, we've cleared the building, and we're going to have EMS take a look at you. Also, you're under arrest for criminal trespassing, attempted burglary, assault, and intent to commit murder. Anything you say can be held against you—"

I blocked out Wes and turned to Griff. He'd relinquished custody of Nancy to one of the police officers who was reading the Miranda warning to the older woman. She responded by staring stoically at the wall.

Griff walked over and wrapped us in a hug. "Jesus, I told you to wait, Cricket."

"I know. But I don't do what I'm told sometimes. I mean, I'm tired of always doing what I'm told, but I called Wes before I did anything. And I had to do something because Ruby was hurt," I mumbled into his shirt. He smelled of clean laundry and safety. I began to shake, as everything slammed into me.

Mrs. Nancy was going to let me die.

Oh my stars.

Griff's arms were tight around me, and Ruby's chin sharply jabbed me, so I struggled loose, stepping back. "Ruby needs to go to the hospital. Cammie hit her with something."

Griff grasped Ruby's chin, angling her head. "I think she's going to live."

My friend inhaled then exhaled, seemingly trying to catch hold of herself. "Well, I'm pretty hardheaded."

At that moment, the missing member of the Blue Moon Sting Posse skidded into the room. Juke wore pajama pants, hunting boots, and a long-sleeved T-shirt that said NUTS FOR SQUIRRELS which might have been true because I had once heard him talk about eating squirrel stew at his mama's house. He blinked at the situation spread before him while simultaneously shaking off one of the other officers' grasps. "What in the world?"

I really didn't have the energy to go through it all again, so I just walked over and patted his shoulder. "We solved the case."

"We did?" He scooted aside so the EMTs could steer the stretcher over to Cammie. One set a bag down by Ruby, pulling over a stool for her to sit on. "I got your message about getting here to catch a thief, but why are the police here? Isn't that your mama's friend?"

"Yep. And they're here arresting the people responsible for the theft ring." I turned and looked at Nancy being read her rights, Ruby getting checked out, Cammie being lifted onto the stretcher, and even though my insides felt like a can of root beer that had been left in the sun on a hot day, I felt a ding of pride. I had figured it all out. And though, sure, this whole situation might have gone south, and I could have been killed, I had managed to crack my first real case.

"You solved the case?" Juke still didn't seem to understand.

"Well, Juke, I work for North Star Investigations. We always get our guy. Even when the guy is my mother's best friend and daughter."

24

Ruby

THE LIGHTS LOWERED, and the music swelled.

Showtime.

I stood behind the curtain, fiddling with the gold thimble around my neck, trying not to barf. Here was my dream come to fruition on the stage in the auditorium where Elvis crooned to adoring fans and Hank Williams changed the course of country music. The sound system had switched from "Dream a Little Dream of Me," which had accompanied the smocked children's line of clothing, to a pulsing, electronic instrumental that screamed "we about to rock this bitch." Which was really needed after all the oohs and aahs of the children sucking their fingers while they toddled down the runway. There had been one crier and one who refused to walk. His mother had just about lost it, and I was suddenly very glad that I had had a mother who never showed up for any of my activities.

But only just for that one moment.

Honestly, support felt pretty amazing right now.

I peeked out as Jade cranked her head from one side to the other in classic "I'm about to kill this" posturing. Gran sat with a few of Marguerite's friends, wearing a floral dress that she'd bought at Sears for one of my cousin's weddings. Can't remember which one. She also had on the painted earrings I had given her for her birthday and the strand of pearls my Pawpaw had bought her for their thirty-fifth wedding anniversary, right before he passed away. As best I could tell, Marguerite's friends were clad in a St. Johns knit. So different, but they were all chattering away, the polished ladies smiling as my gran no doubt regaled them with suggestions for their house plants (chicken poop) or Jimbo's latest dating fiasco (accidentally taking out his second cousin).

To her right was Dak and his mother. He looked nervous for me, and that made my heart contract. He'd sent flowers, simple yellow carnations. A man who knew my heart.

I touched the tiny thimble again for good luck.

Resa flitted back and forth between the models, straightening the hems and lining up the zippers.

"Oh my goodness, it's happening," Cricket crowed beside me, interrupting my perusal of the people who loved me chatting in the audience. She was clad in the ball gown and looked about as gorgeous as I had ever seen her. Many would say it was the hair and makeup, but I knew it was the glow from within. She'd solved the case, one-upped everyone, and probably saved my life. Success agrees with most people. It really outdid itself on Cricket.

"Yeah, it's happening," I said, covering my mouth. Because, again, vomit. But that was mostly because the pain pills made me slightly nauseated.

"And we all look so dope. Even without Nancy's old crap," Julia Kate said.

Julia Kate looked so grown up that Cricket had started crying when she saw her. I'd put her daughter in the dress I had worn in New York City, pairing it with Cricket's knee-high boots and a high ponytail that gave off a sixties Mod Squad vibe. Big hoop earrings, borrowed from Jade, brushed her shoulders, and she carried Marguerite's knock-off Fendi.

The police had kept the collection Nancy had inherited from her aunt as evidence. They'd wanted to keep my collection too, but Jackie Morrisette, my new attorney, had nipped that intention in the bud. And since I didn't have anyone to wear Cammie's outfit, Jackie had volunteered to walk the runway as her stand-in. Marguerite was clad in the power suit that Nancy was supposed to model. Thankfully, Marguerite and Nancy were about the same size. Jackie's had needed a bit of adjustment, but she rocked her look.

Marguerite, of course, had been heartbroken when she'd learned of her friend's betrayal, so she was more stoic than normal. I knew she would be hurt for a long time. I couldn't imagine that sort of betrayal. The thought of Cricket doing something so vile just couldn't permeate my consciousness.

I guess that meant Cricket was officially my bestie. If your boss could be your bestie. Of course I was certain that she wouldn't be my boss for long. Thankfully, Resa had proven good at finding antiques at estate sales, and she'd promised Cricket that she would study some of the books she'd been loaned. I found it amusing that my friend who used to steal valuables was also good at spying them.

Last night, after a trip to the ER for a CAT scan, I had been released by the doctors. The bump on my head had gone down, and I had only had to have five stitches which were so near my hairline that cutting bangs had hidden it. My ribs were still tender because a few showed hairline fractures on the x-ray, but it was nothing that ibuprofen couldn't keep at bay. Cricket had picked me up from the hospital and driven me to the police station so I could give my statement about all that had transpired.

Wes McNally even apologized to me for hauling me in for questioning. I was gracious. I told him that I understood that he was trying to do his job and that as someone on parole, I knew my past transgressions made it easier to be a suspect for pretty much anything. Still, I was pleased he'd apologized.

Once we'd left the police station, Cricket had taken me to her house. Honestly, I didn't want to be alone, and I hadn't called Dak yet to tell him all that had transpired. Though when we reached Cricket's house, we found him, Griff, and Juke waiting in the driveway.

Just like old times.

When I opened the door, Dak moved to help me out of the car, and I just sort of fell apart at the sight of his face.

He wrapped his arms around me, carefully, because I guess Griff must have told him that my ribs were bruised and cracked.

"Shh," he said, kissing my temple. "You're okay now."

But I didn't feel okay. I felt so not myself. I had let Cammie get the jump on me. I had been a victim—weak, afraid, and betrayed. Someone tough like me wasn't supposed to give in to those fears, but I couldn't seem to stop trembling. My therapist at Spring! would likely call this being traumatized. "I don't feel okay."

He nodded against my head. "Nothing wrong with not being okay, Ruby. You're not an island."

Those words sent me into tears.

"Let's go inside. I'll make some coffee," Cricket said, slamming her car door. She walked toward the house, not bothering to see if anyone was following. She seemed perfectly fine. Regular ol' Cricket.

Juke and Griff moved around Dak and me as we stood together, still clasped in each other's arms. As Juke passed me, he knocked my arm. "You good, kid?"

I managed a nod though I wasn't sure if I was telling the truth.

"We'll be in in a few," Dak called as the garage door opened and my cousins disappeared into the light of Cricket's kitchen.

The night should have felt intimate, but instead I just felt exposed. "We should go in. I need to sit down."

Dak swooped me into his arms. I squeaked and clasped my arms around his neck as he stalked to the front of Cricket's house where two rockers sat in the porch light. Cricket had cute pumpkins sitting beside her door with some Indian cornstalks in an urn. First-rate autumn display of course. He set me down in front of one chair and then took the other.

I sat and drew my knees up, wrapping my arms around them and staring out into the darkness, trying to gain some composure, some rational thought, some gravity.

Dak made a noise, and I realized he was crying.

"Dak," I said, reaching out a hand. "Don't."

"I can't help it, Ruby. You scared me to death. And then when it was over, you didn't call me. I... why didn't you call me?" His tortured expression ripped my soul apart.

"I wanted to, but you said we should wait to talk, and it felt... weird. I wanted you there. I was so scared, and I can't be scared with just anyone. I needed you. But I didn't know where we stood or if we were over. I wasn't sure what to do."

"Ruby," he groaned, wiping his face. "We're not over. Why did you think we were over?"

"You implied that you needed time and that my career wasn't going to jump over what you'd drawn out for your life. I wasn't sure if... God, I don't know, Dak. I know you want to talk about this stuff, but I don't think I can right now. I feel so... scared. I feel scared, Dak." I crumpled into a ball and cried into the knees of my pants.

"Oh, baby, don't you know that it's okay to be afraid?" His arms came around me. He was kneeling in front of me. I fell into his arms, wishing I were stronger than what I was, but taking what he was offering. I needed someone to lose my shit with, and Dak was that person. So I cried. I sobbed. I held on to him.

Then I sat up and wiped my face with my shirtsleeve, which was sort of gross, but Dak didn't seem to care that much. He'd spent a lot of time with other baseball guys, and stray camera shots proved all the time that they're disgusting in the dugout.

"Thank you," I said, sniffling a little. "For letting me cry, for letting me be weak."

"It's not being weak. It's being human. And I'm your person. No matter what our future brings, Ruby. I'm your person."

My heart grew about eighteen sizes. Yeah, I beat the Grinch by a good fifteen sizes. "Oh, Dak. I do love you."

"And I love you. We can figure tomorrow out tomorrow. Or the next day. Right now, just know you're safe, I'm here, and you're about to kick some ass in this competition."

I stilled. "I don't know how I can do that. Everything I'd planned for the collection—the shoes, bags, everything—is probably being bagged and tagged as evidence. They may even take my collection." Alarm curled inside me.

"I'll talk to Cricket. She'll know what to do."

I laughed. "Maybe. I mean, she showed up with a can of pepper spray holding it like a gun. That was sort of funny. I mean, that was all that was funny, but she looked like some avenging angel swooping in with that tiny canister."

Dak smiled. "I bet. Look, you need some rest. We all do. Let's go inside and get you settled. Or I can take you to my place."

"You," I said, closing my eyes. "I want to go with you."

"Done."

We went into the house where Cricket, Griff, and Juke were gathered around the kitchen island. Griff sipped a beer and looked about as ragged as Dak had. I gathered from his earlier words that he'd told Cricket to wait on the police and had been perturbed at her. I was thankful that he'd known she wouldn't wait and had gotten his ass to the antiques store. He'd shown up in the nick of time.

"All okay?" Cricket asked, lifting her cup and eyeing my swollen face.

"I'm good," I said, looking at Dak. "I'm going home with Dak. I appreciate you letting me come here, but—"

"You need your fella," Cricket finished for me with a smile.

She didn't look shaken, even though she had been in as much danger. She looked like a duck in the water. Like she had found her pond. Spread her wings. Maybe even found a mate.

Well, that was judging by the way Griff kept looking at her rack. I'm pretty sure that Cricket had been braless for our Printemps adventure. And she hadn't bothered with one since she'd gotten home. Thus, his attention had been commanded by beer and boobs.

Juke looked at his watch. "Yeah, it's getting late. Only four more hours until the sun comes up, and I need my beauty sleep."

"Boy, do you." Griff sipped his coffee, totally deadpan.

"Okay, pretty boy, watch it," Juke said, jabbing a finger at Griff. Then he turned to Cricket. "Come by the office on Monday for your check. Also, I need to you fill out a 1099 for the IRS."

Cricket brightened. "You do?"

"Like you said, North Star Investigations cracked this case. Guess we have a new star in the agency. Might want to get some business cards printed up."

Cricket smiled. "Already have them. And I would like to talk to you about your office. I have some ideas for a filing system, and I think we need to get a new carpet. We need to talk to the landlord." She shifted her gaze over to Dak.

He stiffened. "Great. Just what I needed. Someone with standards."

That made me laugh, and God I needed that. We said good night, and the last thing I saw was Cricket pulling a box out of the small oriental trash can in her living room.

Then I went home with Dak.

And woke the next morning ready to resume being the tough-as-boot-leather Ruby who wasn't going to let someone like Nancy or Cammie Parrington destroy her shot at the fifty-thousand-dollar prize money or the title of iSpy Fashion Festival Prima Donna.

But of course intentions were one thing, reality another.

Thus I stood behind this curtain, my gut in knots as the emcee came over the mic.

"Ladies and gentlemen, the final contestant in our First Annual iSpy Fashion Festival Runway show is a local lady who learned to sew at her grandmother's knee. From simple pillows to her own prom dress, Ruby Balthazar showed early promise of being a designer who eschewed traditional patterns for her own designs. After a stumble out of high school, Ruby rebounded with the help of her friends to create her own line, Deconstructed. Taking pieces of vintage couture dresses and reimagining them into new, dynamic designs, this native Shreveporter is poised to break into the New York fashion scene under the tutelage of *Couture* Magazine's former editor and *Style Today*'s hostess of impeccable taste, Celine Smart. Prepare yourself for the talent of Ruby Balthazar's Deconstructed."

"That's right," Jade said, throwing me a wink before strutting out onto the runway like she'd been born to own every damn place she ever went.

"Oh," I breathed, tears springing to my eyes. This was happening.

One by one, my models went out, looking oddly professional, popping hips, swagging their way past the crowd in teetering heels, turning heads, hitting all their marks. I could feel the audience's response. They liked the collection. The colors, the fabrics, the absolute delicious styling of each piece. With each look, my stomach grew calmer and calmer.

A feeling of certainty came over me.

This was my destiny.

I was made for this.

Then suddenly Cricket was beside me. She reached down and squeezed my hand. "You're a marvel, Ruby. A marvel."

Then she was off, the gown parting as she exposed those legs she toned in Jazzercise. She hit the center point akimbo, both her hands on her hips like Wonder Woman. I heard gasps. I heard a smattering of applause. I might have smiled.

Then Cricket walked that runway like she was effing Heidi Klum. The skirt of the dress swished open, moving so perfectly it was like a symphony being played. The small iridescent beading shimmered under the lights while the embroidery looked delicate. I had never felt so moved by something I had made.

The moment she stopped at the end of the runway, looked out at all Shreveport, and smiled, I let the tears fall.

Because I knew I had won.

No one had to say the words.

I just knew it was true.

Ten minutes later, they made it official.

"The winner of iSpy Fashion Festival Runway is Ruby Balthazar."

All my models jumped around like kindergartners on Popsicle day. Jade pulled out the Veuve Clicquot and popped the cork. We drank that expensive champagne right from the bottle. Even Marguerite, who I saw wipe the lip before she drank. Balloons fell. Hugs abounded. And Dak stood in the middle of all those ladies and blew me a kiss.

I touched my thimble.

He smiled bigger.

And that's when I knew that everything would be okay.

No matter what came my way.

25

Cricket

Ruby won, and I felt... well, a small portion of her sense of accomplishment.

I hope my mother did too, because finding out Nancy and Cammie were responsible for stealing items from our friends' homes, plotting insurance fraud, and willing to kill her daughter to cover it up had weighed heavy on her. When I had asked if she suspected the Parrington family was broke, she said she'd seen signs but nothing that would have led her to believe her best friend could be capable of doing something so diabolical. I sent my therapist a note about my mother and then bullied Marguerite into making an appointment.

If anyone on the planet needed therapy, it was Mama Quinney.

And most especially after finding out about Nancy.

"You had a hunch about Ruby," I said to my mother who still

looked so sad.

"I did," she said, taking a glass of champagne from one of the waiters. The organizers of iSpy had been smart—they'd made the ticket an exclusive one replete with a cocktail bash after the announcement of the winner.

I glanced over at Ruby who was fielding congratulations and being dogged by Bo Dixie who was doing a piece on the winner, chronicling the celebration for an online blog connected to the paper she worked for. Dak stood beside her, looking handsome in a tailored suit while also handing Ruby her lime-infused water and hors d'oeuvres so that she didn't faint from hunger.

"She's on her way now," I said, nodding toward Ruby.

"It's gratifying to see someone come back from where she was, but I can't take credit for finding a diamond in the rough. You saw her. You gave her a job. You showed her friendship and what her world could be. That's not a little thing."

A compliment from my mother.

I looked above me to make sure the ceiling tiles weren't dropping.

"Oh, don't be impertinent," Marguerite said, handing me her champagne and tapping a waiter. "Dear boy, is there something stronger than champagne? Like vodka perhaps? 'Cause if so, I will have one straight up with a twist of lime. One lime only."

The waiter nodded. "Yes, ma'am."

"Good boy," my mama said.

"He's not a dog, Mother. And thank you for the compliment. I have a bit of my grandmother in me. I like extending a hand, but so do you, though you pretend indifference in most cases. I know where your money goes. I see you too."

My mother sniffed. "Well, the woman raised me."

"Are you still upset with me about the words we exchanged?" I asked, hoping she'd gotten over my strong performance on the porch. Surely my brush with death had brought forgiveness?

"Not really. I mean, they were hard words to hear, but I invited John, didn't I?" She gestured to a man wearing a dark suit with a bright red bow tie. He was about as opposite as my father as a man could be. A bit nerdy, slightly nervous, and very uncomfortable around my mother's friends, who seemed to be cross-examining him on some matter or the other. I hope it wasn't sex with my mother. Poor man.

"I'm glad you did. He's a nice man. I've heard he's a tiger in the sheets."

"Don't be crass, Cricket." Marguerite eyed John and gave a quirk of her lips. "More like a lion."

I giggled. But then stopped when I spied Scott and his new wife. I hadn't met her yet and wasn't planning to. I'd had a call from Scott after the police contacted him about the Parrington's insurance policy. I'd ignored it. I would continue the trend. "I need to get some air, and you need to rescue poor John."

I slipped around my mother, brushing a kiss on her cheek so she would know that I loved her and was sorry I had lost my manners Thursday night. But I meant what I said. I was going to work part-time for Juke, and I was choosing my own path in my life.

Slipping away from the throngs of people, I made my way to the hall outside the auditorium. I hadn't lied to my mother—I needed to catch my breath and take a moment for myself. Choosing to go right, I curved around toward the empty hallway.

I still wore the ball gown. Truthfully, it fit me like it was made for me—okay, it was—and it made me feel beautiful with the sassy ruffled split and gorgeous embroidery. My hair was in a bun at the nape of my neck, soft swooshes of hair escaped to frame my face. Makeup was tasteful with a plumping pink lipstick and thick lashes that would peel off later. Jade had dusted my décolleté with shimmery gold dust that made my skin glow. Mama had loaned me her dangle sapphire earrings that looked better than the vintage ones Nancy had. My feet hurt in the strappy nude sandals, so I slipped them off and slunk toward the dark recesses of the hallway that wrapped back toward the stage.

Griff stood beneath an exit sign, nursing a whiskey and looking impossibly handsome in his navy wool suit that I was almost certain had come from a local men's store known for their custom suits. His shirt was white, tie undone and draped around his neck. His collar open, of course.

"Of all the gin joints," he said.

Oh, the man knew classic cinema. Add another point to his column. "I get around, sailor."

He crooked his finger. "You were far away on that runway. Come closer so I can see if the beading on that gown is as stellar as the woman next to me declared."

"A woman seated next to you discussed beading with you?" I asked.

"Do you believe that?"

"No," I said, walking toward him because I wanted to. Not because he'd asked me to. "I think she probably tried to buy you a drink and then pretended to be fascinated by tow trucks."

He smiled. "Who doesn't want to know more about towing?"

"Is that a sexual euphemism?"

"Do you want it to be?" he asked, wrapping a hand around my waist and taking me in in the scant light of the exit sign. God, I hoped my skin still glowed.

"So?"

"What?"

"Do you think the beading is exquisite?"

Griff gave me a wolfish smile. "I don't know. I'm looking at your tits."

I simultaneously turned pink and got a little dizzy. That's what Griff did to me. Had from the beginning. Okay, so at first meet, he ruffled my feathers. But oh, those muscles and all that absence of charm. Who knew I was a sucker for complete asses who volunteered to take out my cheating spouse within an hour of being introduced to me? "Well, they are on display."

"And I thank you for that," he said, dropping a kiss right at the neckline.

My body sang, I tell ya. Like, I went from tired and overwhelmed to "do me, big daddy" in point zero five seconds. "You wanna go make out in that hospitality room over there?"

Griff had started in on my neck. I closed my eyes for a moment, my breath going all ragged, knees a little weak. He stopped. "What's that?"

"It's a place where you can get what you want."

He chuckled against my neck, his hand sliding to that part in the skirt. "Well then, the answer is yes. I would love some hospitality."

I took his hand. "You know I don't normally do this sort of thing with guys like you."

Griff picked my hand up and kissed it. "You're very good at it though. It's almost like you're a natural."

Feeling flirty and pretty dang good about life in general, I said, "Oh, I'm not a natural blond."

Griff kissed me, making my blood hum. "Oh, sunshine, I know you aren't."

And that's really all it took for him to get me into that hospitality suite and out of my Spanx.

Of course no one would ever find out that Griff and I had a little tryst in the room where Elvis drank Cokes and practiced his snarl. That's because when you know how to find evidence and catch bad guys, you also know how to get rid of evidence and bring bad boys to heel.

Just a feather in the cap for Cricket Crosby, private investigator.

ACKNOWLEDGMENTS

Writing a book is never done in a vacuum - a writer needs lots of cheerleading, questions answered, and, frankly, the occasional cocktail.

This book wouldn't be possible without the help of Captain Brad Walker of the Natchitoches Police Department who patiently answered questions about private and police investigations. Any mistakes are mine and not his. Another thank you to Kelly Stetson who was a contact for Brad and the proofreader of the manuscript. A warm thank you to Lori Whaley Stratton who loaned me huge books from her uncle's *Vogue* collection. Thank you MaryAnn Schaffer and Anne Marie Gruskowski for beta reading and making solid suggestions.

An author needs writer friends for all sorts of things. Thank you to Phylis Caskey for coming up with the idea of a theft ring long ago. Jennifer Moorhead for suggesting the thief in the book. Ashley Elston for teaching me how to make cutout dresses for my author booth. Jamie Beck for reading it first and making her normal insightful suggestions. I'm so appreciative of my support groups. I have the wisdom and cheerleading of Jamie Beck, Tracy Brogan, Sonali Dev, Virgina Kantra, Sally Kilpatrick, Priscilla Oliveras, and Barbara O'Neal every single day. I also have been blessed with the smartest of smart indie author friends - Pamela Kelley, Karen McQuestion, Tess Thompson, Grace Greene, Nicola Marsh, Christine Nolfi, and Susan Boyer -

my own personal "Author Hive." Also a huge shout out to the Your Book Escape authors who always answer questions along with my new fantastic "Badass Women Who Write" group who have already given me wings.

And, as always, I am thankful for my friends and family who overlook when I get lost in thought, answer FB messages "real quick," forget to pick up dry cleaning, and generally check out of RL to write and do this wonderful author thing I do. And if I forgot anyone, I'm doing these acknowledgments on one cup of coffee so I'm a bit foggy. But YOU are appreciated!

If you find any mistakes in the book, please send that information to liztalley@att.net rather than Amazon so that I can fix it directly.

And I would SO appreciate any reviews and recommendations you can give for the book. You have so much power to help Cricket and Ruby find new readers. Use it! LOL.

Thanks for the support!

ABOUT THE AUTHOR

A finalist in both RWA's prestigious Golden Heart and RITA contests, **Liz Talley** loves staying home in her jammies writing emotional women's fiction. Her first book starred a spinster librarian – *Vegas Two Step* – and debuted in June 2010. Since that time, Liz has published over thirty more books with Harlequin, Hallmark, and Montlake, reaching number one in kindle romance, hitting the USA Today Bestsellers list, and reaching Publisher's Weekly mass market bestseller list. Her stories are set in the South where the tea is sweet, the summers are hot, and the porches are wide. Liz lives in Louisiana with her childhood sweetheart, two handsome children, and two pups. You can visit Liz at www.liztalleybooks.com or follow her on Instagram or facebook to learn more about her upcoming books.

Made in the USA
Middletown, DE
26 October 2023